For Jack, the most dedicated of early readers who helped
immensely in bringing this book to exist

ORDER'S TRIALS

BOOK ONE

A TWIST

OF FATE

AUSTIN WINDSOR

CHAPTER 1

NORTHERN MIRADOSI TUNDRA

Richard crouched low, his breathing steady as he pulled the bowstring back to his ear. They hadn't seen him, or, more miraculously, heard him.

His arrow sliced the wintry air with a hiss and took the beast down. Its allies reacted with guttural cries and hellish roars as they searched for their assailant, but they soon joined their fallen companion in death after two further arrows pierced them through the eyes in the same fashion as the first.

Richard approached from his concealment and quickly glanced around the village, or rather its remains. The Corrupted had razed it, leaving peasants' houses torn to shreds and every last inhabitant dead.

He started a fire in the centre of the village and collected the bodies strewn around the area, meticulous as to ensure he didn't miss any. They fuelled the fire and allowed it to burn high into the sky, melting the lightly falling snow before it could reach the ground. Such was the nature of his land's curse – any bodies that weren't burned only ended up rising again in a form to be feared. And, in Richard's profession, a form which was more profitable.

He hacked the head from one of the slain creatures and strapped it to his mare, Rosie. The sun was already falling from behind the clouds, and he was determined to make it to shelter before nightfall. Luckily, he knew of an inn along the northern road.

The Old Oak Tavern on the horizon was a welcome sight – Richard had been on the road for a long time. He encouraged Rosie into a canter for the little remaining distance before the

1

both of them could finally rest. Fortunately, the tavern had a stable, so he could leave her somewhere warm as well – or, at the very least, protected.

Dark grey smoke belched from the fractured cobblestone chimney protruding from the slanted roof – the building was ancient. As he approached, he hadn't even gone inside before warmth began to circulate his body. Upon entering, the remaining snow on his hunting jacket melted immediately in the comforting heat of the fire roaring in the hearth.

"I've come to collect a bounty," he said, slamming the head of the slain Corrupted onto the bar.

"You'll 'ave to talk to the men at the garrison," the innkeeper replied, scrubbing a tankard. "They've stopped handing out bounties to inns. War means money is tight."

"Right," he grumbled. "How much for some horse feed and a place in the stables tonight?"

"Fifteen rions," the innkeeper replied, reaching for a sack of oats.

"And a mug of ale?"

"Another two."

Richard handed over the coin and took the oats from the innkeeper, heading back out to secure Rosie. He found an open space in the stables and left the oats in the feeding pouch, leaving Rosie inside. He then went to rest his own legs and dampen his senses.

He sat down at one of the empty tables inside the tavern, untying his wild pine-bark hair, allowing it to flow freely around his shoulders. He ordered a meal from the innkeeper and relaxed in the comfort and safety of a remote tavern in the height of winter.

After a few hours, the door swung open to produce a detachment of Miradosi soldiers. The captain, recognisable by his golden rose badge, marched towards the innkeeper and handed him a slip of parchment before he and his soldiers settled down at another empty table.

As Richard rose to talk to the captain about the bounty, he was disturbed by the innkeeper.

2

"You're Richard Ordowyn, right? You look like him – I've heard travellers talk about you." He handed over the parchment as Richard nodded. "I thought you might find that interesting."

"Thanks," Richard replied, mulling over the parchment. A bandit contract, apparently particularly troublesome. As the captain was still present, he decided it would be a good opportunity to scavenge more details before taking on the contract.

He walked over to the table where the soldiers sat, eating, drinking, swearing, and shouting throughout some crude game of cards.

"Mind if I interrupt?" Richard asked.

"Not at all," the captain replied. "What is it you want?"

"I'm a bounty hunter and I was interested in the contract. Can you give me any specific details about the bandits? What they've been doing, any places they've gone to and from a lot?" he questioned.

"They've been ransackin' supply carts wherever they can. You don't need to go very far north of this here inn before wreckages of their doing start showin' up. We think they've set themselves up in the forest, I'd say... three miles northwest of here. We can't use any troops while Sanskari still hack away at our border – we'd 'appily pay fifty rions if you bring us their leader's head. A blonde fellow with a scar running across his right eye."

"I've a counter-proposal," he stated. "I completed the bounty posted in another inn for the Corrupted traipsing the roads near what's left of Dyalos. Pay me the reward for that and I'll get rid of the bandits for free."

Not often would Richard take on a contract free of charge – it was his only source of income. However, when the Sanskari were involved, his morals won out over his need for money. Even when his menial efforts to assist his country's cause felt useless, as news would only reach him later that the front line continued to move further south.

The captain reached into his satchel and retrieved a jingling pouch of coins. He carefully counted out three hundred rions and pushed them towards Richard.

"Thanks, lad – at the very least, come by the garrison for some arrows."

3

"No need," Richard dismissed. "I have plenty."

Richard returned to the innkeeper and asked for a room, for which he paid and retired to for the evening – but not before refilling and emptying his tankard.

The following morning, he awoke to the sounds of a scuffle outside. He picked up his weapons from the bedside table – an elegant self-made bow, his first choice, with a quiver of sixteen arrows; a steel short sword at his waist; and a relatively small dagger tucked into a sheath in his jacket, in the event that he needed a last resort. The scuffle outside grew louder, spurring Richard to quickly finish pulling on his breeches and brown leather boots. He cautiously opened the door to his room as to avoid attracting attention. He couldn't see much from his current orientation, so he silently crept from the room and nocked an arrow, preparing for trouble. As he rounded the corner, he observed a group of four men surrounding the innkeeper, rusty swords and clubs in hand, demanding he empty his safe. One of them, the one making the demands, had long, blonde hair and a scar across his right eye.

Convenient, Richard thought.

"I think we've been bloody clear about what we want, innkeep. Give us the coin without a fuss, or we burn your tavern down findin' it. I know what I would choose if I was in your—"

He was unable to finish the sentence as the first of Richard's arrows pierced his larynx. The other three bandits were undeniably shocked by the sudden turn of events as they didn't even react before two more had been taken down in a similar fashion. The last rushed toward Richard as he drew his sword. The bandit clumsily swung his club in an arc, missing Richard entirely as Richard's sword entered his stomach. The bandit collapsed and Richard retrieved his sword, wiping it clean on the bandit's already bloodstained tunic.

"Sorry about the mess," he told the innkeeper, dragging the bodies towards the door.

"You have nothing to be sorry about, you just saved my hide! Please, take this for your travels," the innkeeper exclaimed, handing Richard a bottle of ale and a sack of oats.

He helped the innkeeper dispose of the bodies, but not before severing the head of the blonde, cauterising the neck and placing it in his satchel.

4

In all the commotion he had forgotten about Rosie. He rushed to the stables to find that luckily, the bandits hadn't decided to check for any horses they could steal. He saddled her up, stroking her sepia fur and feeding her from the sack he had just received. He then led her out of the stable and mounted her, ready to depart.

It was another cold day, snowflakes drifting through the sky and the smell of pine smoke from the tavern's fireplace still present on Richard's clothes. Richard decided it wouldn't hurt to check the area where the captain detailed, on the small chance that the bandit whose head lay in his satchel wasn't the right bounty.

He set off on the road northwest and after only a mile, he found evidence that the soldiers weren't lying. Battered carriages, ransacked wagons and frozen human remains were all examples of the gruesome sights along the stretch of road towards the border.

The forest of which the captain had spoken began to materialise on his right, so he turned into it and searched for a clearing. A fire appeared to be burning in the distance, a possible indicator that there were more bandits than the ones he had eliminated in the tavern. He dismounted his horse and tied her to a tree some distance away from the camp before sneaking closer to inspect. Upon closer investigation, it turned out he wasn't dealing with bandits at all. In the clearing, around a roaring bonfire, sat three lightly dressed Sanskari soldiers, roasting a boar on a spit. Only moments before letting the arrow fly, he decided not to make a rash decision and instead to observe the soldiers for a time. It was peculiar, to say the least, a small detachment of Sanskari soldiers taking residence in a deserted bandit camp. Perhaps they were deserters.

"How long do you think it will be until we reach Myana?" asked one of the soldiers to his comrades.

"Given the current rate that we're ploughin' through at, no more than two months would be my guess. These useless Miradosi would need a miracle to prevent it. At least when we're done capturin' this wasteland, the emperor can shift his focus to the North."

5

"We don't even need to do any fightin', 'cause the bandits are doing a good enough job. I knew the Miradosi were uncivilised, but I didn't know we could break 'em down just by payin' off a few cutpurses!"

The three erupted into laughter – cut short by the first of Richard's arrows. The second and third followed shortly after.

He sauntered into the abandoned camp and retrieved a carving knife from what looked like the sergeant and used it to shave off a piece of the roast boar. He sat down on one of the logs around the fire, allowing it to extract the cold from his veins. Upon finishing his unexpected breakfast, he sliced off a few more pieces to take for later and stored them in Rosie's saddlebags, untying her and bringing her closer to the camp. It was a strange sight, one that didn't entirely make sense – he had killed four bandits in the tavern, yet there were eight beds. He assumed the Sanskari soldiers had been staying in the camp, probably to keep an eye on the bandits. That accounted for seven of the beds, but the eighth was still a mystery – until he felt a gloved hand tap his shoulder.

In a lightning-fast motion, he stepped forward, simultaneously rotating to face the mysterious figure and drawing an arrow. Before him stood a hooded woman, dressed in an ashgrey robe to match her hood, which concealed her face.

"Who are you?" Richard asked.

"Just a lonely traveller," the woman calmly replied, with the hint of a northern accent.

"In the middle of a bandit camp?"

"That looks to be the case. Would you please lower that or at the very least point it somewhere else?"

Richard reluctantly lowered the bow, keeping the arrow nocked. The woman sauntered over to one of the logs where the boar roasted, carving a piece off for herself.

Richard followed but remained standing. "I'll ask again. Who are you?"

The woman removed her hood, revealing a jet-black head of hair, tied into a braid which reached her upper back. Her most striking feature was her piercing emerald eyes.

"Jade Synderon," she told him. "And you?"

"Richard Ordowyn. Why are you here?"

She chuckled. "My, full of questions, aren't we?" She beckoned Richard to join her in sitting. He slowly took a seat on the log opposite her, arrow still nocked.

"I can see you don't easily trust. My dear, had I been any threat to you, we wouldn't be having this conversation right now."

Richard was no fool and wouldn't be misled by idle threats. The least he allowed himself was to relax his muscles.

"So this is how we're going to go about it. Fine. As you can see, I'm apparently the last remaining survivor of this camp. But I would hope you've deduced that I'm neither a bandit nor a Sanskari soldier."

"What are you then?" Richard asked, his patience running thin.

"I was working with the Sanskari, who were in turn working with the bandits. Before you loose that arrow as rashly as you did to those three soldiers, allow me to ease your mind. Officially, I'm a Sanskari advisor, stationed at the garrison in Limara. They sent me on a supervision mission to ensure those soldiers you left over there don't get overexcited. However, I can trust you're true to the Miradosi cause, so I'll confide in you my true mission. I seek to aid in dismantling the foundations of the Empire."

"You're a spy?"

"One might put it that way, although I don't work for any Miradosi officials. It's more 'for the greater good' kind of work. Though who defines good and bad? I'm sure those soldiers you thoughtlessly slaughtered would have viewed you as the bad, believing in their own cause. They could have had children and wives who now will never see them again. But that's okay, because Richard Ordowyn, the lone bounty hunter, felt like he was doing the right thing."

Richard tensed his muscles again.

"Now, before you make any more thoughtless decisions, let me just point out that I'm still on your side. Just perhaps not as sincerely. I regard issues in life from a neutral, objective viewpoint, always have done. Knowing that every decision, every action has more than one consequence allows one to hold an enlightened view of the world's issues."

"Interesting lecture. You still fail to explain what you hoped to achieve by babysitting those three."

"It was a very educational experience. I learned of new colloquialisms used by the soldiers, I learned of their attitudes towards your people, I learned of their motives and their strategies in taking your country. Altogether it will allow me to accomplish far more in the future when I report back to the officer in Limara.

"It doesn't take much observation to work out the fragility of the Empire. It rules with a fist of glass, not of steel. All it takes is enough pressure in the right areas and it would shatter. Corruption runs deep, from the top of the hierarchy all the way down to the commanders in charge of individual garrisons. It's against the Sanskari codex to associate with bandits and is downright forbidden to work alongside them. But men are far from perfect, with greed being one of the most common traits you'll find in any of the Sanskari superiors. Those three paid off those bandits to cause havoc, yes, but they, in turn, received a share of the loot they would bring back. Loot which they kept to themselves, to put money in their own coin purse.

"I seek to learn how to utilise this corruption, as knowledge is often more powerful than a battalion of soldiers. If one learns where to destabilise the foundation, the whole system swiftly collapses. Do we see eye to eye now?"

Richard took a few moments to process the information. He was not well versed in politics, always leading a simple, routine life.

"What would your next move be?" Richard asked. "Nothing we do has slowed them. They'll reach Myana come summer."

"It's all about causing domestic conflict. The Empire is sovereignly controlled by the emperor, sure, but individual countries are still under the control of appointed princes, dukes, barons. Princes, dukes, barons all liable to corruption. I have reliable sources that express severe concerns about major corruption involving the ministers of Jakaris, Rendon, Handor and Floria. All northern Sanskari states, ones that have been under their control for the longest, some fifty years. Vast sums of money have mysteriously disappeared from the court treasuries, notorious people in power have gone missing. It

8

wouldn't take much to turn these ministers against the Empire they serve. Form an opposition force too large to quietly eliminate; enforce passive resistance among the citizens; collectively refuse to pay taxes. The citizens are more than capable of overthrowing their ministers, yet they are restricted by fear. We need someone who isn't to light the first flame. Someone like you would do splendidly."

Richard didn't know what to think about that. "I wouldn't know what to do. I've never known anything but bounty hunting."

"Yet you've known suffering and oppression. You're a skilled fighter and seemingly rather intelligent – there aren't many more traits you would need. In fact, we can experience what it would be like together. Come with me to report to the Sanskari garrison in Limara."

It was an abrupt offer, and he was nearly as abrupt in turning her down. However, after a moment of pondering the concept, he reconsidered.

"How far away is Limara?"

"In terms of war, not excessively far – a couple days' journey north. The front line is currently stagnant thanks to last week's battle, both sides are licking their wounds and calling for reinforcements. They would welcome new informants with open arms."

"And what's stopping them from putting a bolt between my eyes?"

An endearing smile appeared on her face. "You'd be accompanied by me. They know to cross me is to cross their superiors in Virilia, and they'd rather not do that. Otherwise, they find a noose around their neck."

"Alright, I'll go with you. Don't expect it to become permanent. We'd best burn the soldiers' bodies first."

Richard wandered into the forest to gather more firewood. He was unable to shake the feeling that there was something suspicious about her but couldn't tell if that was simply his observational mistake or if she was exceptionally stealthy, which would be odd for an advisor. He also noted her immaculate attention to detail.

He returned to camp with arms full of deadwood. It took a while to get the fire burning at a reasonable level but after an

hour of trying and failing, it was finally ready to burn the bodies.

Magic was outlawed across Valoria, but dark magic was woven through the soil. None in the modern world knew its
origin, but it was there, cursing the land in which crops are
sown and bodies would be buried. This curse was what produced the Corrupted and what meant Richard's profession
was exceptionally profitable. It was also what forced armies to
stop their progress post-battle to clean up both their and their
enemy's mess – otherwise, they would be slaughtered far
more efficiently than any opposing army could manage.

To the average person, they were notoriously difficult to
kill: physically resilient and unable to feel pain. Despite this,
Richard found a knack for it, drawing upon his reputable skill
with a bow and arrow. The Corrupted boasted adept resistance to damage and would not be halted by non-debilitat-
ing wounds. His arrows couldn't inflict an injury serious
enough to prevent a Corrupted from moving, but he could
strike them with dazzling accuracy. He discovered that the
Corrupted have a fatal weak spot – their brain. An arrow
piercing through their eye is more than enough to completely
disable them.

"Shall we go now?" Jade asked, when Richard was content
that the bodies would be destroyed. He also added the bandit
leader's head from his satchel to the flames.

I hope they work it out.

"Let's go," he replied.

CHAPTER 2

CAMELION, SALYRIA

The door to the throne room in the Blue Palace finally gave way. The last line of defence, the King's Guard, sprang into action and began dropping like flies as the invaders' crossbowmen showered the helmetless guards with a volley of steel bolts. Within moments of the breach of the throne room, there were no obstacles left before the King.

A muscular, young blonde man dressed in polished steel plate armour appeared from behind the crowd of invaders.

"Your Majesty, I believe we've had the pleasure," the man said, bowing. "In case it's escaped your fragile memory, allow me to reintroduce myself. Hortensio of Heathervale."

The King remained seated in his throne, unmoving and seemingly unworried. "I know who you are, Hortensio. It was a foolish oversight to let you leave with your head."

Hortensio casually strolled towards the throne. "You know why we've come. Salyria wants a new ruler – one who actually has the bollocks to fight our enemies instead of hiding away in the thick stone walls of this magnificent palace. They're sick of you. We are sick of you. So, we came to take control of our country. Salyria will once again rise as the most powerful kingdom in Temerios and will no longer be subject to the deficiencies of a weak throne. We've come to get rid of you."

He unsheathed a freshly polished steel longsword, glowing in the sun shafts blazing through the throne room's circular windows.

"A brand-new sword. What do you think of it?" He flauntingly twirled it around. "All important swords are given a name. I've inscribed my sword's name on the hilt, just here. Would you like to know its name?" he asked.

Finally, the King rose from the throne.

"Thirty years I've sat on that throne. During those thirty years, Salyria has known nothing but peace and prosperity. And you would storm my palace, slaughter your own brethren, and declare yourself king so you can waste more innocent lives in petty conflict? Sending soldiers to their deaths so their sacrifice feeds your ego? No. I refuse to die like this." He clumsily drew his own sword and struggled to hold it straight.

Hortensio gestured to his men and they receded, allowing a sizeable area for a duel. "Come on, old man. I look forward to wetting my new blade."

The two dived into combat. While the King took heavy, directional steps, Hortensio remained light on his feet, running circles around him. Every strike the King attempted was effortlessly parried, Hortensio consistently at least two steps ahead. It was like watching a cat toy with a mouse before striking the killing blow.

The King charged towards Hortensio and swung his sword wide. Hortensio gracefully ducked under it and effortlessly sliced through the King's forearm, just below his elbow. His sword clattered across the worn marble floor and he fell to his knees in defeat, grasping his new profusely bleeding stump.

Hortensio loomed over the defenceless ruler. "You never answered my question. Would you like to know my sword's name?"

The King responded only by spitting at his feet.

"Kingslayer."

In one clean motion, the King's head was removed from his shoulders and rolled across the floor, leaving a trail of blood.

Hortensio retrieved his crown, still on the King's head, and placed it on his own, before slumping onto the throne. His men fell to one knee before him.

"Long live the King."

CHAPTER 3

SANAÍD, TYEN'AEL

Sanaíd was bursting with life. Elaeínn had to push her way through tightly packed crowds of people swarming the streets. Shopkeepers were struggling to keep up with the incredible demand which would be unseen on a normal day. But it wasn't just a normal day – it was the King's birthday. As such, it was a national holiday in Tyen'Ael and the monarchy invited all to visit Sanaíd to participate in a multitude of festivities, dining on a sumptuous assortment of delicacies and generally making merry. All paid for by the King himself.

People from all across the country had travelled to the capital either by leaving the night before and travelling by carriage or through a portal, which many of the Aeli elves were able to do – either by spontaneously generating a temporary portal with a spell – a particularly physically exhausting task – or owning a portal frame in their home which could be powered with a slightly less draining spell. The other prerequisite for travelling via a portal was having knowledge of the location beforehand, meaning anyone intending to visit must have already done so beforehand and have a clear image in their mind of the target destination. Regardless of which method of teleportation was used, most high elves weren't held back by the energy toll – they were trained in magic from the moment they were able to walk. Therefore, they were taught to harness magic's power very efficiently – resulting in it being a useful everyday tool in small doses as opposed to a last resort for difficult situations.

As Elaeínn hustled through the crowds, her dirty blonde braid thumping against her back, she didn't neglect viewing the attractions – sages bending flames into dragons; your typical juggling act, the balls replaced with Tayannan sabres; a ranger picking off sky lanterns in an archery act. There was plenty to see. Mouth-watering smells from Tyen'Ael's finest chefs and bakers flooded the streets, and the best part was that the food was free – anyone could take anything they wanted, within reason. Blazing bonfires occupied the main squares, where the religious visitors would occasionally toss in a coin, praying to the prophet Kaen'Raeris for a trouble-free year. It was for this reason that the Grand Raerist Cathedral had pilgrims queueing for at least a kilometre. On this day, all anybody wanted was to feel redeemed.

Eventually, after a lot of pushing and shoving, Elaeínn reached her destination. A group of other inconspicuously dressed young elves, having chosen a variety of beige, khaki, and brown tunics, breeches, and skirts. They, as with Elaeínn, had also prepared similarly coloured cowls and masks in their satchels. They wordlessly met and exchanged instructions with nods of heads and subtle gestures. Then they made their move.

Elaeínn and the other woman, Kíra, tied their hair up into buns, before them and the two men, Allek and Delíen, donned their hoods and masks. They moved at first as a group, using the crowds for cover and keeping low. It didn't escape their attention that some people noticed them and made comments or even moved out of their way out of fear. But they weren't a problem.

They reached the Common Square, where the elected leader of Tyen'Ael, Veranamos Jaelaar, was giving a speech on the far side in front of the backdrop of the Tyen'Aíde – High Elven for High Houses. Enormous, relatively new buildings only constructed after the establishment of the Tyen'Aeli democracy under King Elgaer the Fair a few hundred years ago. At the time, the country was experiencing a social renaissance following a line of unpopular monarchs before King Elgaer the Fair claimed the throne from his brother – Daerek the Bold, who had fallen to his death from one of the palace's balconies, heavily inebriated.

Elgaer had been extremely ambitious about his plans – and he was mostly successful. Many of the country's residents

14

were fighting a fierce struggle against poverty, but elves were notoriously opposed to change. Luckily for Elgaer, he was the King, so he could do as he pleased. Including placing restrictions on his own power by establishing the first democratic system of government in the world.

He was also successful in creating a monumental hallmark of his reign, as the Tyen'Aíde's red spires and expansive glass windows were traits allowing it to be one of the most notable structures in the city, outmatched perhaps only by the majesty of the Serenna Palace, historical residence of the monarchy.

As Elaeínn, Kíra, Allek and Delíen continued weaving their way through the crowd, they had to be increasingly careful of the heavier presence of guards. They had been placed throughout the crowd specifically to catch the likes of Elaeínn, considering this wasn't the first time she and those with whom she aligned herself had been behind civil disruption.

They made their way closer and closer, only metres from the platform containing their target. More civilians pointed them out, but none acted. Until they did.

"Terrorists! It's the FTA!" an older elf shouted.

The following result was instant pandemonium.

Everyone and everything fell into disarray. People were screaming and trying to run, but the throng was just too packed to make that easy. Elaeínn and Kíra broke off from the men and swiftly made their way to the left side of the podium, while Allek and Delíen went for the right.

Heavily armoured guards were less complacent than they had hoped, immediately lining the entire perimeter of the platform and drawing their swords in defence. There was almost no way of getting through. Almost.

Kíra led Elaeínn in the direction of the panicked civilians and found a quiet alley between the Tyen'Aíde and a neighbouring shop. She traced a portal with her hands and pressed forwards, grunting with the effort. Through a shimmering window in space they could see the platform ahead of them. Elaeínn drew her flip knife, crafted by an FTA-sympathising blacksmith, and leapt through the portal.

She tackled the elven leader as she soared through the air, clearing the space between her and the window into the Common Chamber in one bound. He provided no resistance, and she placed her knife against his throat and looked to the crowd, frozen with anticipation.

"An end to corruption! An end to dictatorship! An end to the lies and deceit of the Nationals and the King! Free Tyen'Ael!"

As she moved to slit the Prime Minister's throat, she heard Kíra cry out in pain behind her and faltered. She withdrew her knife from his throat and moved quickly to her feet, where a metal-clad fist smashed into her face and sent her quickly back to the ground, an explosion of pain and alternating spots of light and darkness dominating her consciousness.

"Kíra!" she cried, searching excruciatingly for the other elf. She spotted a strand of her coal-black hair that had escaped the bounds of her cowl and found that it led to her body, collapsed to the floor. Her stomach dropped and she felt a heavy sense of dread as she was dragged to the middle of the podium and thrown to the side of Kíra's motionless body.

The guards became preoccupied with commotion on the other side of the platform, giving Elaeínn a chance to place her hand on her fallen comrade's chest. Feeling her heartbeat gave her the courage to go on.

She fought through the pain engulfing her cranium and rose to her feet, once again brandishing her knife. Unfortunately, the Prime Minister had already been escorted away via the Common Chamber. In that regard to their mission, they had failed. But they were still alive, and they could still make a scene.

Delíen and Allek were engaged in a frenzied swordfight with the heavily equipped Regal Guards, clearly outnumbered. Elaeínn cried and jumped out of range of the one guard that had spotted her and ducked between his legs, looking for a nook to place her knife. There weren't many, and even fewer which were accessible.

The guard pivoted around on the spot and didn't take his cold, yellow eyes from her. He thrust his sword forward and Elaeínn nimbly dodged the blow and feebly attempted a parry with her remarkably underpowered knife. The guard overpowered her and almost managed to knock her down with a surprise swing of his fist, but she ducked in the nick of time.

16

Allek cried out, and Elaeínn wasn't sure if it was in pain or joy or fury. One thing was clear – the detachment of guards she spotted streaming into the square from a neighbouring street indicated that they had run out of time.

"Del! Get K and get us out of here!" she cried.

"Held up at the moment, Elle!" he responded angrily, harmonising with the clanging of steel on steel.

The guard she had spent the past minutes dancing around attempted yet another swing of his sword, which she dodged again.

He isn't trying to kill me, she thought. *Otherwise he would have done so by now.*

She exploited this thought and ran straight towards the guard, catching him off-guard. She climbed him like a ladder, finding a purchase on various parts of his armour and digging her knife into a nook between his right spaulder and breastplate. He grunted in pain and thrust her away with a powerful sweep of his left arm but didn't pursue her any further, instead retreating to tend to his wound.

"Del! We need to leave, now!" she shouted with increased intensity.

Delíen and Allek, tired and incapable of passing the four soldiers barring their way, leapt backwards and merged into the crowd. Elaeínn roared with the effort of picking up Kíra and also hopped from the podium. The two men found her quickly and Delíen quickly whispered a spell to open an anonymised portal, the target destination hidden from everyone except him. They entered without a doubt and once through, Delíen uttered another spell to seal it shut. Then he collapsed with exhaustion.

"Did you not manage to get the Prime Minister, then?" a masculine voice spoke, accompanied by soft footsteps as he approached the group of weary freedom fighters.

"Fuck off, Berri," Elaeínn cursed, removing her cowl and allowing her braid down onto her back.

"We send a senior FTA fighter with a crew of her choice and... what happened?" the golden-haired elf called Berri asked.

"She had the chance to kill him," Allek revealed. "Still not sure why she didn't."

"I heard Kíra cry out behind me—"

"You heard one of your companions cry in pain while on a job they know full well involves danger? And you decided that was a valid reason not to eliminate the Prime Minister?"

"Fuck you, Berri! What's killing the Prime Minister going to do, anyways? He has dozens of other cronies that could replace him. The issue is deep-rooted within the system. It's the bureaucrats as a whole that control everything, not the Prime Minister himself. He's just a bloody mouthpiece."

"It sends a message and it makes us look strong. It shows that we aren't just measly terrorists like they portray us to be. It lets people know what we stand for and that we refuse to allow the likes of Veranamos Jaelaar and his Nationals to put us away. And above all, it makes them look weak. The majority of people couldn't care less about which group of people are in charge of the country, as long as they feel like they can have faith in them. As long as they don't disrupt their lives. As long as they appear strong and unifying. A dead leader certainly doesn't do that."

Kíra finally stirred and slowly sat up, pressing a hand against her forehead with a groan. Elaeínn quickly rushed to her side and ensured she was healthy, which Kíra assured her she was.

"Did you manage to accomplish anything, then? Anything at all?" Berri exasperatedly questioned, readjusting his cuffs.

"I stabbed a guard," Elaeínn mused.

"Anything noteworthy? Anything that will make the people think 'Wow! Perhaps we really ought to act as well!'?"

The four sheepishly failed to match Berri's gaze and said nothing.

"Fine. Get some rest, I have other jobs for you. And then perhaps you can simply enjoy the festivities as members of the public. Even if we don't align ourselves with the government, that doesn't mean we can't celebrate the King's birthday, as the two institutions are supposedly separate."

Berri walked away and Elaeínn tended once more to Kíra, while Allek and Delíen moved off towards the kitchen.

The location to which Delíen had teleported the group was the headquarters of the FTA – the Free Tyen'Ael Army. The

organisation had formed just over three years ago, with Veranamos Jaelaar's ascension to the role of Prime Minister and
the National Party's newfound control of the Tyen'Aíde.
Elaeínn and numerous other founders of the group had
fought long to prevent their election – when they were voted
in, they had to turn to other means.

One of the first courses of action was organisation. That
meant finding a suitable location from which to manage their
yet-to-be-named resistance. In the end, they combined two
stone-brick terraced houses already owned by early members
of the organisation along a backend street of the capital into
the head of operations for what would quickly become the
most renowned group of freedom fighters – or terrorists, depending on your point of view – in the country.

Since then, they had acquired more funding through a
number of perfectly legal and extremely illegal methods and
managed to expand, upgrading to a three-storey house in a
city called Garaennia, fifty kilometres to the north of the capital, so as to avoid interaction with the Regal Guard. It had
been purchased under the name of one of the city's most influential businessmen who had been miraculously impartial to
their cause. It was then renovated in its entirety, being retro-
fitted with a number of smaller bedrooms to house any travelling FTA fighters, a large kitchen and dining room, an alchemy laboratory, a meditation chamber, and a ramshackle
armoury in which to stash their limited weaponry. The doors
were always left closed, the windows removed during the ren-
ovations. They had managed to go undetected by the authorities as of yet.

Kíra stood up on her own despite Elaeínn's attempts to
help and the two women decided to follow Allek and Delíen's
lead in heading to the kitchen to recharge.

The scent of something meaty wafted from the stairway
and they almost raced to liberate some. Allek glared at the two
disgruntledly but didn't argue when they took a pork chop
each when it finished cooking.

"Berri!" Elaeínn shouted. "What do you want us to do
now?"

Berri appeared from the neighbouring armoury, clipboard
and ink-dipped quill in hand.

"Give me a moment to think, would you? And give your companions a moment to regenerate. You might not practice magic yourself, Elle, so I'll tell you now that I'm sure Del and Kíra would like a moment to rest."

Elaeínn looked expectantly at Kíra, who had just swallowed the last piece of pork from her plate and returned her gaze as if to hesitantly agree with Berri.

"Alright, I'll stay here for a bit. Then shall we go back to Sanaíd? At least the food is free."

"As long as I'm not the one that has to open the portal," Kíra said.

Both women looked at Berri who sighed and placed his clipboard on the table before tracing a circle in the air and pressing forward, opening a window to the packed streets of Sanaíd. They walked through and it closed no more than a second after Kíra placed her feet on the cobbles.

Both Elaeínn and Kíra were relatively young in terms of elven years, being twenty-two and twenty-one years old respectively. An elf was officially recognised as an adult at the age of twenty but may live on to be as old as five hundred. The oldest known high elf to ever have lived survived the reigns of seven kings, two queens and finally popped his clogs at six hundred fifty-two.

Without their cowls, they blended in with the crowds entirely. Nobody batted an eye in their direction, which they took as a good sign that their identities remained uncompromised.

As they meandered around, taking part in a variety of festive activities and exploiting the free food, they took note of the heightened security – guards were more or less swarming the streets, leaving little room for manoeuvre at their borders. But not just guards – some were dressed unconventionally in lighter armour and armed with cheaper swords. The Tyen'Ael Army.

"Why do you think they've got the army in?" Elaeínn asked Kíra as they passed a group of six soldiers.

"To scare us into submission, most likely. Come on, let's go see Saníya."

Saníya was the librarian at the University of Sanaíd and as such acted as an excellent font of information in regard to the activity of the aristocracy. She, like Elaeínn, was opposed to the National Party's government, but not to the degree of fighting to depose them. Instead, she chose just to be an informant.

They arrived at the University and were given clearance to enter on the grounds of visiting the library, which was traditionally accessible to all members of the public, while the rest of the University's facilities were limited only to students, professors and those who had been granted permission for temporary use.

Saníya was sat at her desk, writing what looked to be a report, stone-faced and expressionless. As the two young elves approached, her lack of expression morphed into one of worry, of pain.

"I heard about Common Square," she whispered. "I'm happy to take your side in the name of democracy, but not when you attempt to murder the Prime Minister."

Elaeínn pressed a finger to her lips and gazed sternly at the librarian.

"Have you gone mad? You can't say things like that out loud," she scolded.

"No, Elle. You've gone mad. I knew you stole from the state, disrupted them, whatever. But murder? I can't support that. Regardless of who it is."

"It's necessary, Saníya. They would do the same to us, hell, they would do much worse."

Saníya looked down at her report, her face contorted with guilt.

"I'm sorry, Elle. I had to do it."

The clanking of metal footsteps resounded from the entrance to the library and a group of eight Regal Guards made an appearance, swords screeching from their scabbards. Elaeínn gave the librarian a look of disgust as she stood up and walked through the door behind her desk, locking it from the other side.

Elaeínn drew her knife and slowly backed away from the advancing guards. Kíra stood behind her and looked around for an alternative exit. The library was lit by a number of high windows and an overhead skylight, none of which were accessible.

"How did Saníya know we would visit her? This is an ambush!" Kíra hissed.

"I don't know," Elaeínn whispered, continuing to steadily back away. "Climb the ladder to the higher platform. Go to the reading room. Smash the window in there, we can escape."

Kíra ran for the ladder leading up to a second platform for access to books on the higher shelves and the elevated reading room, and as a result caused the guards to charge. Elaeínn quickly followed her partner, boisterously twisting and shoving her way through other visitors, and they bounded up the ladder and made a break for the neighbouring chamber.

A white ball of magical energy nearly took Kíra's head off as she went to open the door to the reading room, but it narrowly sailed past her face and crashed into the wall.

At the sight of destructive magic, the other visitors recognised their time to panic. Those in the library streamed to the exit, causing problems for the advancing guards aiming to access the ladder and providing time for Elaeínn and Kíra to get to the window through which they hoped to escape.

The reading room was silent, interrupted only periodically by the flipping of a page or the furious scribbling of notes. That changed the moment they slammed open the door and seized the attention of every occupant inside.

Elaeínn looked around feverishly for something with which to break the window while Kíra stood behind her, muttering a spell. She held her hands together as if holding a ball, and then she finished muttering and pressed her hands forward. A rush of air roared through the room and shattered the window, with the side effect of toppling two small bookshelves in the vicinity of the blast's direction of travel as well as destroying an old researcher's notes and ripping his glasses from his face. He glared viciously at the two women, but they didn't remain in the room for long enough to hear anything he had to say.

Careful to avoid the thousands of shards of broken glass, they jumped through the window, landing in a small patch of greenery, painstakingly organised by the University's gardeners. The two sprinted across, trampling an assortment of exotically bright flowers, and leapt to the cobbles below.

Now their only obstacle to escape was the Uniguard, a set of specially trained personnel in charge of university security. It was clear by their rigid positioning around the exits that they had already spoken with the Regal Guard, so now Elaeínn and Kíra's best option was to try to act casual.

They strolled to the archway which led to the streets of Sanaíd and were stopped by two Uniguard officers.

"The University is on lockdown. Please return to your studies."

"We're just visitors," Elaeínn exclaimed. "We have no business at the University, we only came to visit a friend. What's going on? Why is there a lockdown?"

"That information is not for you," one of the officers curtly retorted. "Please return to the library."

Elaeínn glanced at Kíra, who understood at once.

They rushed forward together, taking the officers by surprise and knocking them out of the way, sprinting away before they could draw their swords.

"Stop!" one of the officers cried, feebly attempting to run after her, but it was too late. The two women merged into the throng and became impossible to detect. They had escaped.

CHAPTER 4

FREE CITY OF DANNOS, SANTEROS

"Mr Redwinter, sir, I come bearing news from the West. Hortensio of Heathervale has overthrown King Valkard and claimed the throne. Word is already circulating about his plan to raise an army and sweep through Temerios."

Elton Redwinter turned to face the messenger.

"Good," he remarked in his gravelly voice, lighting a pipe. "Carry on."

The messenger briefly bowed before rushing from the room to continue his rounds. Elton turned back towards the table he was previously observing and resumed studying the floorplan of the Dawn Bank's primary facility. He had been mulling over it for days, making seemingly insignificant marks in various places while his senior henchmen grew impatient with each passing hour.

"Regi, when is anything going to happen?" one of said henchmen, also one of his closest friends, abruptly intruded.

"Each time you interrupt, that time is pushed further back," he coolly retorted.

The henchman – a young, bald man of average stature – briskly stepped over to the table and snatched the floorplan but couldn't step away before Elton drew a dagger and placed it against his throat, its curved blade caressing his neck.

"I was looking at that. Please return it."

"I'm bloody well aware you've been looking at it. You've spent the last three days doing bugger-all except looking at this dusty piece of paper."

"And I will continue looking at that dusty piece of paper until I'm confident my next move will be the right one. Now, put the paper back."

He leisurely removed the dagger from the henchman's throat as he quickly placed the floorplan back on the table.

"Aren't you too old for this yet? I mean, how many years have you been running this place?"

"I'll never get too old to think, Paul. I might not have the spring in my step that I once boasted, but my mind has only grown in my old age. Besides, I only need to think in order to run this organisation. I think, then I tell people to do something, and it gets done. Quite a simple process."

Paul sighed. "Spring in your step, slender waist, legs capable of running... Lots of things you don't have anymore, boss. How many people will be going to the bank?"

"How many do we have in Dannos?" Elton inquired.

"Enough money to buy all the mercenaries in the city. But totally loyal to us, probably two thousand. We sent five hundred of 'em to Trader's Trail last week. We could always call for more from Santhion, they've got loads there."

"Two thousand will be more than enough. You forget that Dannos is a city of disloyalty – even if they aren't totally loyal at heart, their loyalty is as strong as their pay."

"Alright, well, I'm heading out. You stay there and think or what-bloody-ever."

Paul grabbed his newly forged steel short sword from the weapon rack on the wall and left, jogging down the stairs.

Elton sauntered down the stairs himself, to the wine cellar on the lowest floor and picked out a bottle of Knight's Relief, expensive red wine from Camelion. He supposed the news of a change in the monarchy would make it harder to come by, but the cellar beneath his house was grand, with thousands of marks' worth of wine, spirits, and other drinks to which he enjoyed treating himself on a daily basis, which often changed to an hourly basis depending on the circumstances of his current work. Now was one of those times.

The Dawn Bank was the only legally run bank in Dannos. There used to be multiple more, but their managers had mysteriously disappeared or died in one way or another, the businesses being taken over by Syndicate representatives posing

as the deceased owners' sons or nephews or whoever was closest in blood, using forged documents as proof. The banks then
subsequently closed down within the following week, reducing the competition for the wide-reaching Redwinter Bank.

Elton was the mastermind behind all criminal activity in
Dannos. Organised gangs who didn't work for Elton still paid
a weekly levy to the Redwinter Syndicate to prolong their survival. Hot-headed bandits had tried defying him in the past –
their bodies soon became rat food. Even petty thieves paid the
Syndicate a portion of their earnings if they didn't join the organisation instead.

He returned upstairs and instead of re-entering the study,
he chose to retire to his bedchambers, confident that the following day would be the day of the assault. It had grown late,
the moon casting ghostly light from above the horizon. From
his window, he had a view of the entire Silverstone Square, its
dull sandstones glowing white in the moon's rays where tall
buildings such as his own cast shadows in the opposite street.
During the day, the square was a hub of activity for merchants, herbalists, alchemists as well as pickpockets, burglars,
cutthroats and the like. Elton's men were responsible for
many of the latter. During the night, a blissful silence fell
upon it, occasionally interrupted by a harlot's scream or a beggar's sobbing.

Elton's house in Dannos was nothing short of luxurious. It
comprised four floors: the top floor, where he had his bedchambers and his study; the first floor, entirely outfitted with
a modern alchemy lab in which he spent vast quantities of
time working when not reading or organising missions for the
Syndicate; the ground floor, where he had basic necessities on
a huge scale. Like his expansive kitchen, containing an expensive stone oven, for which he always needed a fresh supply of
wood to fuel. A pantry full of exotic foods from across the
continent – mangoes from the rainforests of North Benetia,
apples from the temperate orchards in Salyria, coconuts from
the scattered isles in north-eastern Temerios. The kitchen also
led to a small outdoor area with a fireplace. In other, more
forgiving climates, the area might have been called a garden,

but Dannos's climate didn't allow for grass to grow without assistance. Finally, the cellar was used exclusively for his alcohol supply.

He undressed, leaving his crimson gambeson and chainlink shirt on a wooden rack next to his reinforced oak bed. He slipped his onyx leather boots off, placing them with the rest of his clothes before also adding his charcoal breeches and chain-link trousers to the rack. He did, however, retrieve his dagger from the gambeson and place it under the bed, as he did every night. This routine was followed by fastening several locks on the door which all required a unique key to unlock from the outside, as well as several latches scattered around the four borders of the door to go alongside them. Then, he walked over to the singular window in the room and attached a thick steel grate to its interior borders before rigging a bell above the window to chime if it was opened.

Confident the room was secure, Elton donned a silk nightgown, a deep crimson matching his gambeson. He eased in between thicker silk sheets and a wool-stuffed mattress, resting his head on a collection of feather-stuffed pillows. At his bedside, he left a candle burning on a small table. He dangled a wrinkled hand between the table and the bedframe and brushed his fingers along the dagger's hilt, caressing its pommel. He fell asleep, the handle still in his grip.

His routine upon waking up was no less thorough than when going to sleep. He returned to his normal clothes and undid all the security measures, sheathing the dagger, exiting, and wandering downstairs, seeking the kitchen.

Paul burst in as Elton retrieved a cast-iron pan from one of the kitchen's cupboards and an egg from a basket on the counter.

"Good night, Paul?"

"Absolutely bloody brilliant. There was this loony twit, drunk off his arse, pottering around the high street singing what must 'ave been a mix of every song every bard has ever made. Turns out he was sauced enough to have thought it a good idea to wear a diamond necklace into the streets. He probably borrowed it off his wife, he looked the middle-aged merchant sort. Here, proper good quality, this."

Paul produced a sizeable diamond-encrusted pendant attached to a silver chain.

"Best part is, I didn't even have to do nothing to get it. Geezer came over to me and before I even had time to raise my blade, he asked me if I wanted to buy it off him for a few marks. Just so happened that I would gladly do so. Seems he thought it were a bit of thread or somethin' else in his state."

"Are you ever going to learn to speak properly?" Elton inquired.

"You understand me, don't ya?"

"Most of the time, though there are occasions where I only pretend to understand your drivel."

"That's alright then, no need to waste my time speakin' properly when everyone understands me anyways. I almost forgot! Right after I dealt with that blithering fool and nabbed his necklace, there was this dirty whore who came up to me and you would not believe it if I told you what she could do—"

"I'd rather not hear any more. You really are a blithering fool yourself, Paul. I've told you already, half the strumpets in this city are riddled with syphilis and the other half with lice. If you fancy brain rot or itchy balls, carry on as you are."

"Heard you mention somethin' of the sort before. Whatever. Fancy fryin' me an egg? Bloody starvin' after last night."

Elton sighed and grabbed a second egg from the basket before walking outside and taking a seat on a stone bench in front of the fireplace, which he took a few moments to light with a piece of flint and iron. It was early in the morning and the day's heat was yet to descend, so the fire's warmth was a treat in the cold, refreshing morning air.

"Paul, make yourself useful and slice up a couple slices of bread," he called inside. "And bring a knob of butter with you."

"Alright, where do you keep the bread again? This cupboard, weren't it?"

Paul's question was followed by a series of metal clangs as an assortment of pots and pans fell to the floor, in harmony with his curses.

"Never mind, found it."

Elton allowed a grin to cross his face, always amused by Paul's ineptitude. After a series of more curses over the next few minutes, Paul arrived with a couple of aberrantly shaped slices of bread.

"Here you go, bossman." He tossed the bread, missing Elton's hands entirely and landing both pieces on the dusty sandstone floor, one on top of the other. Elton sighed again, putting his head in his hand.

"Right, you're having the bottom one. Brush the dust off yourself if you have an issue with it."

He reached for the top piece of bread and placed it on a grate licked by the peak of the flames, where he had already placed the pan to warm up. Paul grimaced as he picked up the sand-caked slice, quickly brushing off all that he could before placing it with Elton's. He also threw the knob of butter into the pan, this time successfully hitting his target. Finally, he was able to sit down on the stone bench on the opposite side of the fireplace to Elton.

"We will carry out the heist today," Elton stated, beginning to fry the eggs. "How would you like to take part?"

"Would I bloody ever!" Paul excitedly answered.

"Good," Elton remarked. "Once we've finished our breakfast, go find Jerry and Felix, see if they're interested. You three can lead the operation."

"They'll be well happy about it, I can tell you right now. Felix himself has been having a spot of bad luck recently, lucky bastards gettin' away from 'im when he tries to convince 'em out of their valuables. Jerry too, but he's been having more trouble with the ladies than with his work..."

"Spare me the details." He flipped the toast over, now perfectly browned on one side. "The Dawn Bank has around fifty guards in total. Take one hundred men, you should easily overpower them. And when you find the manager, a tall, slender man called Rafio Benito, don't hesitate to put a blade through his heart. You'll recognise him by his strong accent – a Benetian man, though he speaks fluent Santerosi. Should be easy enough to take over with him out of the way, as he has no living relatives, except for his 'brother' – me."

"Clever as always, Reg. How much gold you reckon they've got sealed up in their vaults?"

"More than enough to prolong our existence for years after my death, providing whoever takes my place doesn't squander it. How do you have your eggs, Paul?"

"Just cooked on the one side, please, boss."

"Bloody mental. Right, here you go." Elton snatched a slice from a tool rack nailed to the house's exterior wall and placed Paul's egg onto his toast, which he immediately began wolfing down.

"Dear God. When you're finished that, hustle over and get the word around to the men, will you? I'd like to have this done by sundown. Tell them to take positions on all the streets leading the bank. Also, creating a diversion elsewhere in the city for the City Guard to chase after would be very useful."

Paul, his mouth full, gave a thumbs-up and wandered off, slamming the heavy front door behind him.

Unwilling to waste time savouring his morning meal, Elton finished and left the house shortly after Paul. Silverstone Square was already swarming with merchants hoping to set up in the best spot to peddle their junk, hopelessly unaware of the legions of thieves and pickpockets taking advantage of the rush. The Redwinter Syndicate's main facility – dubbed the Redhouse – was found a short jaunt from Elton's house on the square, in the wealthier area of Dannos. Generally, the more honourable thieves lived and worked in the vicinity of the Syndicate's reaches, whereas the slums near the northern outskirts were congested with all manners of filth. The Syndicate's influence was widespread, but Elton never spent his time investing in the poorest areas.

The City Guard were employed by the city's governing body and were the only public line of defence. However, it was common knowledge that the City Guard were miserably underfunded, so many of the city's residents turned to the Syndicate for protection. Even a number of the City Guard were employed by the Syndicate, outlining the ease of the system's corruption – but the authorities were powerless to stop it as long as Elton Redwinter remained alive.

The Redhouse became visible upon turning the next corner. Bright white sunlight glinted off its pale, flaxen-yellow sandstone bricks. Above the grand entrance, the Syndicate's symbol was painted over the bricks – a bleeding snowflake enclosed in a red circle. Carved sandstone pillars supported the low roof leading to the main, ovular entrance, the height of two tall men, the width of a horse-drawn cart. Four sentries worked shifts day and night defending the exterior, with another six directly inside the entrance. Most of the time, these sentries were unnecessary as there was always a constant flurry of people shuffling in and out, regardless of the time of day. Though the notion that the Redhouse was defended by trained guards was good for discouraging governmental interference. There had been attempts to raid the facility in the past, during the organisation's early years. However, this coincided with the earliest days of the City Guard's re-establishment, so they lacked the numbers needed to effectively infiltrate and they also lacked the necessary combat training to fight off time-hardened thieves, some of which were war veterans, exiled knights, and retired mercenaries. All found solace in the comforting embrace of the Redwinter Syndicate.

Normally, Elton would order an escort whenever he travelled through the city, even negligible distances like what he had travelled that day – even given the fact that he had never been directly confronted before. That day, though, he was confident that nobody would confront him. Any of the members of his enterprise wouldn't be willing to dethrone him on the day of the heist, or more fittingly, the raid.

Paul awaited Elton at the entrance, joined by Felix and Jerry. Felix was younger than Paul and the newest recruit from the three, having turned to crime after his parents' murder when he was only eleven years old. This left him alone, his closest relatives living a thousand miles away in the South. He boasted flawlessly smooth skin and an impressive head of unrestricted, curly brown hair cut just above his shoulders, with matching eyes. Out of Elton's senior henchmen, Felix was certainly the prettiest. Jerry, on the other hand, was the ugliest – he was the oldest of the three, in his mid-thirties, and his face didn't betray his experience, covered in numerous scars. His anthracite hair was a dishevelled mess, dangling over his grey eyes. It failed to conceal his abnormally large nose, a significant wart protruding from its tip.

31

"Gave these two the news boss, and I told you they'd be happy," Paul said as Elton approached, turning and passing through the entryway.

"Indeed," Felix chimed in. "Didn't quite have Paul's luck last night with the rounds. My sword-arm is itching to be used."

"Don't worry, you'll get to use it today," Elton reassured. "Are all the men ready?"

"Went 'round 'em all, boss, we've got a hundred and ten or thereabouts ready to go to the bank, with fifty watchin' the streets leadin' to and from the bank. Nobody is gettin' past without us knowin'," Paul reported. "Everythin's ready to go."

"Then grab your blades. We leave immediately. The guards shouldn't give you any trouble, most of them patrolling this district are on our payroll today, so there should be no issues with getting to the bank. Don't hesitate to put down anyone who stands against you."

"You comin' with, boss? Could use your gruff face to scare off that Rafio fella."

"I'll join you in going to the bank, but I'll stay off to the side while you deal with the guards. I'm certainly too old to fight. And keep in mind, we don't want to 'scare off' Rafio, we want him taken out."

"You'll like my new playthings then, Regi." Felix opened his red jerkin to the side to reveal an array of viciously sharp throwing knives, twelve in total. Each sported a uniquely shaped blade and hilt, and some were even decorated with a gemstone – sapphires, rubies, emeralds, and amethysts, all elegantly cut, occupying the pommels of more than half of the more expensive-looking knives. "I fancied an upgrade from my rusty old ones."

"Bloody hell, those are gorgeous!" Paul said. "Where'd you get 'em?"

"The ones with the carved pine grips and the gemstones are special orders from Kina – cost me a small fortune thanks to the Santerosi offensive, and I ordered them a few months ago. Fantastic quality steel, and if this raid goes as planned, which I have no doubts about, then I'll more than make my money back. The other, plainer ones are from Thorne. Don't think there's a single blacksmith in this desert who can make

32

good quality steel, and Thorne is easy to access by the Trader's Trail."

"Might have to watch yourself, Felix," Jerry interjected. "I've never thrown a knife before but looking at those, I think I might take it up."

"You can get your own. These are my babies." Felix mockingly buttoned his jerkin back up and reached his arm across his body.

"Alright, I think that's enough. Let's move," Elton commanded.

"As you say, boss," Paul responded, before turning to the crowd packed inside the Redhouse, growing restless with impatience. "Alright, you miserable lot!" Paul shouted. "We're leavin', so grab your blades and let's go!"

A murmur of assent spread through the hall, followed by the shuffle of a hundred and ten pairs of feet mobilising to follow Paul and the others. Paul took the lead in navigating, standing just in front of Elton, Jerry, and Felix, who was twirling one of his new knives around his finger, Jerry enviously glancing from time to time.

As they took to the streets, residents of Dannos were quick to clear a path, well versed in the city's order. Merchants who had travelled from elsewhere were not so quick to move and some had to be forcefully thrown aside, which Paul or Jerry took great delight in doing. Some were clearly not very happy about it, but any idea of standing up to their assailant quickly fell from their minds when they saw the throng of armed men and even handful of women orderly marching behind them.

As predicted, every city guard they passed curtly nodded, turning a blind eye to the passing small army of outlaws. Elton was certain that some of them even smiled beneath their face covers, understanding that they would soon be receiving a bonus.

The Dawn Bank was one of the city's noteworthy points of interest, constructed from sandstone like the majority of buildings in the city, but dwarfing the surrounding area in its grandeur. The building itself was five hundred years old, constructed when slavers first founded the city, bringing thousands of slaves from the South to construct a new city in which the masters could rule. They were successful in this endeavour and the city's population exponentially grew in proportion to the masters' wealth, who decided to employ advisors to ensure the constant flow of gold from the mines into their vaults.

Peace didn't last forever – eventually, the slave population grew to such a substantial number that no amount of gold could protect the masters. The slaves revolted, seizing power and erecting the system of government still seen in modern-day Dannos. Although the new government abolished slavery, they quickly grew overly attached to their newfound power and the total equality they planned to implement was forgotten. A new social hierarchy fell into place and over time, the city's wealth was slowly drained through misuse and corruption, allowing for organisations such as the Redwinter Syndicate to arise and take total control.

The bank stood atop a base, thirty feet high with a wide set of stairs leading to the main platform, creating a pyramidal shape. Twenty guards stood on duty around the perimeter of the platform with more inside the main building. It was clear by the sudden rush that they were unsuspecting of the attack. On Paul's command, the Syndicate attackers quickened their pace, jogging towards the stairs and beginning to ascend while the bank's guards organised into a shield wall, spears occupying the gaps.

The guards were lightly armoured, each wearing a light breastplate, the left breast adorned with the bank's emblem – the silhouette of a rising sun over a uniform horizon, with a mustard-yellow background. Their helmets covered the top, sides and back of their heads, leaving their faces exposed. Between the waist and the upper thigh was also unprotected, as their legs were dressed by thin brown linen trousers, wearing flexible greaves which covered the area below the upper thigh to their steel plate boots. Each guard also wore a pair of light steel bracers which covered their forearms, allowing slight arm protection at no cost to manoeuvrability.

Their main defence was the enormous domed shield carried by each, big enough to allow complete cover when crouched. They were crafted from a thin layer of metal attached to a thicker sheet of hardwood, mostly preventing piercing projectiles from passing through. Each shield also contained a small incision on both sides, allowing for their spears to be thrust through when lined up in a shield wall. The guards' attributes were more akin to a monarch's army than an arrangement of hirelings, but they had all trained in a specific Santerosi military combat college which produced mercenaries for use by companies like the bank. But some rulers across Temerios also possessed regiments of these mercenaries in addition to their normal armies, as their proficiency in combat was noteworthy and they could often be more valuable than a battalion of knights.

To a king who collected multitudes of taxes, the mercenaries could be afforded in the hundreds. To avoid being labelled as slavers, the school which trained the mercenaries required anyone interested in purchasing to provide each mercenary with a salary as well as paying a significant commission to the college. Private companies, such as the Dawn Bank, could not afford quite as many which resulted in a well-trained but undersized defence force.

Elton, through Paul, commanded his forces to halt, and he began to ascend the steps alone.

"Halt!" called one of the guards, when Elton had climbed three quarters of the stairs. "State your business and begone."

"You know who I am?" Elton asked.

"Regi Redwinter – leader of the scum. I detest your kind."

Elton sarcastically smiled. "Please, call me Elton. I always despised that nickname."

"Elton Redwinter," the guard repeated. "State your business and begone."

Elton raised a hand and gestured to the group of Syndicate henchmen at the bottom of the stairs. "I needn't explain my business and I will not be leaving. I offer you a chance to avoid bloodshed."

"We do not negotiate with criminals."

"You're all mercenaries, no? On probably a lacklustre weekly pay under Rafio Benito, the greedy swine. Tell me, sir, how much do you get paid?"

"My salary is no business of yours. I serve with honour."

"If you and the rest of your unit lay down your arms, my men will do the same and we will take the bank without a wasteful skirmish. I have a monopoly on this city and your life is included in that monopoly. All it takes is a gesture and those impatient souls down there will stampede, which you have no chance of fending off. And to sweeten the deal, if you lay down your arms, I will hire you on double the pay you currently receive."

The guard was unmoving, but the glint in his eyes betrayed his intentions.

"Lay down your arms or we will do so for you," Elton coldly offered.

"I must consort with my companions," the guard finally responded after a period of silence. He shouted a command to the other guards defending the top of the stairs who retracted their spears, stood upright, and marched over to form a circle, where they remained for a few minutes, discussing amongst themselves. Unlike the common rabble found in the Syndicate's lowest ranks, Elton valued patience above many traits, finding it useful in avoiding wasted time.

Eventually, the guards, scowling, made their decision. One by one, they tossed their spears and shields in a pile to one side before standing to the side opposite each other, forming a path between them allowing Elton to pass freely.

"Thank you for choosing wisely, noble sirs," Elton mocked.

"Speak no more, criminal scum. You will pay us six months' wages and we will leave this wretched city."

"That can be arranged." Elton turned to his followers and ordered them to ascend the stairs. Their passage through the guards was accompanied by jeering from some of the Syndicate's ranks, but the guards' stony expressions were unchanging.

The guards from inside the bank had finally realised what was happening and rushed outside but followed in their comrades' footsteps when they saw the group of thieves walking towards them.

"Stop!" a voice boomed from above. On a balcony extending from one of the bank's upper floors, a tall, slender man had appeared, his exceptionally pale complexion, short, blonde hair and baby-blue eyes instantly labelling him a foreigner. Although a foreigner, his expensive, gem-inlaid tunic and fur collar, entirely inadequate for Dannos's hot weather, acted as a boast of wealth. This effect was intensified by the gold bands he wore on both wrists and silver gemstone rings on both ring fingers. Around his neck hung an enormous, blood-red ruby pendant on a silver chain.

"Rafio Benito," Elton began, stopping. The rest of the Syndicate forces continued inside. "I'm afraid to inform you that as of your death, the Dawn Bank is now under the ownership of your brother, one Lyrio Benito. I'm sorry for your loss."

"You're making a mistake, Redwinter. Withdraw your forces or you will regret it."

"Idle threats will achieve nothing. Your guards have made the right choice, but you, sadly, do not get a choice."

"So it goes. I warned you, Redwinter. Remember that."

Rafio clambered atop the balcony's barrier, and, glaring menacingly at Elton, leapt off.

CHAPTER 5

LIMARA, OCCUPIED MIRADOS

It had been a lengthy journey, lasting two days, as Jade had suggested. Richard knew they had nearly arrived when black banners adorned with the blazing phoenix began to sprout from every other window.

"Are the people genuinely this proud or are the banners handed to them with a sword at their throat?" Richard asked in disgust.

"What do you think?"

After spending the previous two days together, Richard had finally begun to trust Jade. A combination of time, secrets and intelligence had won him over.

"Either you willingly take the banner and hang it from your window, or the soldiers take great pleasure in battering your door down and doing it themselves."

Limara was a beautiful city, far warmer for the time of year than across the Miradosi tundra. The city had once belonged to Mirados but was conquered a few years back in the endless Sanskari expansion. As such the buildings exhibited traditional Miradosi architecture, an intricate frame constructed from oak logs from the surrounding forest with walls of whitewashed wattle and daub. They had steep slate roofs and tall stone chimneys, each house owning a fireplace. The wooden windows from which the banners hung from were able to be opened and closed using handles.

The city was built upon a river, its source found further north and running out to sea in the Nimena Bay. This was the city's main water supply, with peasants walking down to the river daily to fetch water for drinking and washing. There were also wells scattered around the outer reaches of the city for those who lived furthest from the river. It was somewhat polluted, as multiple cities and settlements used the same water upriver – when the water arrived from those populations, it had already been filled with waste.

Limara wasn't an excessively large city by any means, stretching to around two miles in radius from the central castle, where the local governing body operated. The castle, named the Old Keep, was ancient – dating back thousands of years to when men first colonised the region, travelling from Temerios by ship. It was visible from nearly everywhere in the city, as it contained a thirty-foot-tall watchtower which allowed for a view of the entire city and the surrounding landscape. The castle walls themselves stood fifteen feet tall, dwarfing any passers-by. The only way to access the Old Keep was by a drawbridge which extended over a deep moat of water. Each wall's rampart was manned by two soldiers and a scout would occasionally occupy the watchtower, surveying the area, though the threat of resistance was so low that generally, one would only ascend once every six hours. It was a formidable structure and served well as a base of operations.

Another significant landmark in Limara was the Church of the Deities of Balance, a building even older than the Old Keep. The most commonly followed religion in the city, worshippers believed that the Deities of Balance defined worldly events and would punish those who upset the balance. There were four deities, all representing a desirable trait: the Deity of Valour, honouring those who fought valiantly in battle and never committed acts of cowardice; the Deity of Honesty, seeking favour from those who never told a lie; the Deity of Altruism, whose tenets stated that worshippers must donate a portion of their income to those in need and to always act out of kindness; and the Deity of Wisdom, praising scholarship and encouraging followers to forever seek knowledge and to never act without thinking.

The Church was the first creation of the original pioneers to colonise, various historical sources citing it to have been built at least seventy years before the Old Keep, as religion's importance was placed above control and order. Ever since, it became the majority of the city's population's place of worship, a ceremony taking place every Sunday. Luckily, the religion was yet to produce extremists, unlike what is seen with other popular religions such as followers of the Holy Flame or Lanthanism.

Apart from religion, most of the city's focus revolved around the market which took place at a small scale daily and at a much larger scale on Sundays, when merchants and worshippers would travel from neighbouring villages and hamlets to participate in the church ceremony and then traverse the various market stalls, peddling wares from artisan foods to gem-encrusted gold and silver jewellery to exquisite pieces of modern art. Stalls would border the cobbled streets from just outside the church all the way to the Old Keep. Most peasants living in the city or visiting had far from enough coin to be able to afford even the cheapest of commodities, but the merchants relied on the city's nobles who would often spend large sums of money on new accoutrements or decorations.

"Let me introduce you. They're likely to be wary when I've replaced the detachment with you," Jade warned upon approach to the drawbridge.

They reached the cobbles opposite the entrance to the castle astride their horses. A Sanskari officer, dressed in black steel plate armour, decorated with the phoenix icon on his breastplate, appeared atop the ramparts.

"Lady Jade. I welcome you back to Limara. Where are the soldiers you took with you?" he inquired.

"I'm afraid the bandits they chose to pay off didn't honour the concept of honesty. They killed them in their sleep," Jade responded. "The clumsy clattering of their swords woke me, however. There was no fathomable way to save the soldiers, I barely escaped unnoticed myself."

"A shame. We shall have to call for reinforcements. Who is your companion? I don't recognise him." He gestured to Richard.

"This is Richard Ordowyn – a bounty hunter. He helped me travel the dangerous roads of Mirados, a task I'd frankly rather have not undertaken alone."

"I suspect you'll want a reward, bounty hunter. Allow me to fetch you some coin."

40

"That won't be necessary, Francis. He has other forms of reward in mind. Would you please be so kind as to lower the drawbridge? For myself and my companion."

The officer, Francis, motioned to some unseen soldiers and the drawbridge subsequently began to fall.

"He is to leave his weapons with us while he is inside."

Francis stepped down from the ramparts and reappeared at the gate as Richard and Jade approached. They dismounted their horses and Richard reluctantly handed over his bow, quiver of arrows and sword. Disgust pulsed through him at the idea of a Sanskari handling his prized possessions.

"We have a stable for horses over here, if you would follow me," Francis said, marching to an area fenced in with short stone walls and covered with a thatch roof supported by a wooden frame.

They tied up their horses before following Francis across the courtyard and into the main building of the keep. A black banner, like those flying from the city's houses' windows, hung above the entrance. The interior of the keep was infused with warmth, a fire blazing in the hearth at the centre of the first room. Francis led the two into a separate room probably designated for interrogations, judging by the positioning of the chairs and table. Francis took a seat in the solitary chair on the far side while Jade sat in one of the available other seats, Richard following suit.

"What made you choose to escort Lady Jade if not money, bounty hunter?" he questioned. "It is unlike your kind to do something like that out of the kindness of your heart."

"You don't know anything about me," Richard retorted. He felt Jade subtly hit him under the table.

"I'm sorry, Francis. From what I've gathered, he isn't much of a people person," Jade supplied.

"Forgive me, I didn't mean to sound bitter. I've never been good at first impressions," Richard added, feigning a brighter attitude. "In honesty, my travels as a bounty hunter have dried up somewhat. Ever since witnessing the order your people have implemented in Mirados, I've been interested in ways to help the cause. Jade offered me an opportunity."

"Well, well, a welcome surprise. I take it you possess a greater skillset than the average conscript?" Francis responded.

"I should imagine so. I've mainly built a reputation on my prowess in eliminating Corrupted but my abilities extend beyond accuracy with a bow and arrow. I've taken out many a bandit without their compatriots noticing." Richard struggled to find the words to speak to Francis, despite having no need yet to lie.

Perhaps it wasn't such a good idea to try my hand at espionage, he thought.

"The Sanskari always have a need for people with your capabilities. However, you would have to first prove your value by performing a task. Standard procedure and whatnot, measures to prevent any old idiot from joining up."

Richard began to feel nervous.

"We've recently run into some trouble. Residents in Limara are unhappy with our occupation, people who remember Limara as a Miradosi settlement. We would generally like to deal with issues like this personally, but we're afraid doing so would only tarnish our fragile reputation. I think you would do perfectly," Francis continued, speaking with no hint of remorse.

"You want me to do what with them, exactly?"

"Well, they're no use to us as they are. And we'd rather not use valuable prison cells for troublemakers like them."

"You want me to assassinate them," Richard concluded coldly.

"You are a bounty hunter, no? Surely you have no quarrel with this manner of work."

Richard felt frozen, fearful of his options. Then, Jade cut in, preventing him from saying anything he'd regret.

"We require additional information about the targets. Who are they? Would they be well defended?"

"No, they're just ordinary peasants. The nobles have embraced our presence while the lesser citizens feel it necessary to cause social unrest. We have detailed sketches of their appearance, their names, and the location of their houses, or rather shacks. All we need is someone to take them out."

"Would you happen to be in possession of these profiles?"

"Not at this moment. I can fetch them if you'd like."

"Please."

Francis left the room to retrieve the profiles and Jade used the precious time to lecture Richard.

"Listen – you just need to accept the job. We can find a way around it, I always do. You won't have to kill anyone. And drop the bitterness unless you'd rather be hanged," she scolded.

"How would we do it without killing anyone?" Richard asked, flustered.

"Just trust me."

Francis re-entered the room, holding the profiles. There were three in total, each detailing a different peasant.

The first, a young, brown-haired man called Edward Langham. Lived on the city outskirts and frequently created and distributed anti-Sanskari propaganda.

What a terrible offence, Richard thought.

The second was another brown-haired man called Joseph Fletcher, slightly older, who lived closer to the city centre. Charged with giving a speech one day praising the heroic efforts of the Miradosi soldiers and slandering the Sanskari conquest. Sentenced to death.

The third, and perhaps the most horrific, was a young girl – no older than ten. She had apparently been selling flowers one day and was overheard to be giving discounts to those with Miradosi affiliation. But the Sanskari wanted both her and her parents.

Stone-faced, Richard found his words.

"I can do this, just… give me a couple days."

"Fantastic. You can take however long you'd like, as long as they end up out of our hair. You may go." Francis extended his hand and Richard forced himself to shake it. His weapons were then returned before he and Jade turned and left the room, walking out of the keep and back towards their horses. He contained his rage until a safe distance away from the castle.

"They want me to kill a child!" he exclaimed, not loud enough to draw attention.

"Yes, I thought you understood their morals. Now you have even greater reason to detest them," Jade calmly responded.

"And what's your magic way of bringing them the heads of these three targets?"

"Exactly that. Magic."

He stopped, puzzled.

"What do you mean, magic?"

"Is it not clear? I can construct perfect replicas of their severed heads. Our main job will be to convince them to leave the city, permanently. Once I've studied their heads, of course."

"You're a... witch?"

"I prefer sorceress."

"I've never met a sorceress, or anyone who wields magic, in fact."

"I'm almost certain that's not the case. I'm just the first magic wielder you've met who has revealed it to you. I'm sure you're aware of laws surrounding the use of magic in Valoria."

"So the Sanskari don't know about your magic?"

"Well I haven't found myself roasting on a pyre or drowned in the rising tide yet, so, no, I assume they don't know. I sincerely hope I can trust you."

"Do you have to channel your magic from the gods like they say?"

She rolled her eyes. "It appears you're full of questions again. Believe me, I'll happily answer them all one night when joined by a bottle of wine. But to answer your question: no. I've never been religious and quite frankly, when it comes to religion, more people are ruined than granted salvation. Don't let yourself be fooled by stories about humans relying on divine support to perform magic, because we're just as capable as the elves or the dwarves. Most spells do require a great deal of energy, and that remains the case until you're a veteran and have truly mastered your craft. Even then, not many are capable of constantly casting spells over extended periods of time. There is however another method to cast spells effortlessly. The use of what's called a lirenium crystal."

"And what's that?"

"In honesty, I don't know much about it. All I know is that they're magical crystals which somehow enable magicians to channel magical energy far more efficiently.

44

"And while I was rambling, we appear to have arrived at mark number one's house. Shall we introduce ourselves?"

They strolled up to Joseph Fletcher's house – similar design to most other houses in the city centre but ever so slightly larger. They knocked on his door and waited.

The door swung open and a fat, middle-aged man appeared to greet them.

"Can I help you?"

Judging by his choice of clothing and the luxuries that could be seen inside, he must have been a merchant. His above-average waist circumference was also a giveaway.

"You need to leave the city, Mr Fletcher. The Sanskari want you dead. They sent us to collect your head," Jade explained. "Don't worry, we have no intention of doing any such thing – but it's absolutely imperative that you leave Limara by tomorrow and never return."

"The Sanskari sent you...? But that means you're working for them! Why do they want me dead?" he frantically asked.

"We have your profile right here. They aren't happy about your motivational speeches – slander, as they put it." Jade coolly responded.

"Why aren't you killing me if you're working for them?"

"Clearly we have other plans. You have one day to pack up and leave Limara, otherwise it's likely they'll send someone more dedicated to kill you. I expect to see this house abandoned by noon tomorrow. Are we clear?"

"But... where am I to go? What am I to do?"

"That's up to you, but you'd best decide whether you prefer a new life or none at all."

He stood in the door, cheeks growing red with rage. "I've lived in Limara my whole life and I won't allow some Sanskari dogs to threaten me. If they want me, they can come and kill me themselves instead of sending some lackeys. Be on your way."

"If that's what you want, so be it," Jade scathingly retorted.

As they walked away from the door, he remained there, motionless, showing no intention of moving.

"What are we going to do about him?" Richard asked.

"I will return later to have a conversation with him. I can be very persuasive, given the right setting. Who's next?"

45

Richard glanced at the remaining two profiles. "The girl and her family live near the church, so they're closer. Did you get a good enough look at Fletcher's head?"

"More than enough, it doesn't require excessive observation. The critical thing is ensuring their face is precise. Come on, let's hurry to the last two."

They briskly visited the other two targets, who were about as enthusiastic about the news as the first. Thankfully, none of them were argumentative about leaving, completely understanding the true threat staying in Limara would pose.

Evening fell and Richard and Jade returned to the Old Keep to stay overnight. Sleeping surrounded by the enemy – not Richard's first choice, but Jade was well respected among the keep's inhabitants. And Richard trusted Jade – to a certain degree.

As they approached, they were greeted again by Francis. "Lower the drawbridge," he ordered. "How goes the hunt?" he asked, turning back towards Richard and Jade.

"We were only scouting today, teaching Richard the city's layout. He plans to return tomorrow with their heads."

"Lady Jade, I've been wondering: do you always speak on behalf of Richard? Does the man lack a voice of his own?"

"As I mentioned earlier today, he isn't much of a people person. I've been meaning to ask him about it."

"Hmph. Very well."

They entered the castle walls and Francis ushered them into the keep. "We have a spare room on the floor above your room, Lady Jade. Your friend can use that for tonight." He nodded at Richard.

"Excellent. How are the wine supplies?"

"We received a shipment after you left this morning. I reserved a few bottles of Virilian Red for you. They wait outside your door."

"You consistently serve above and beyond, Francis. I shall recommend you for a promotion. Come, Richard. I'm personally famished. Francis, if you would be a dear and have two meals delivered to my chambers, I'd make sure to put in more good words about you with the Chief Advisor."

He saluted before sprinting off towards the kitchen.

"Now, I'd like to learn more about you. Let's go to my chambers."

They ascended three flights of stairs before reaching a bland stone corridor with doors on both sides. Jade led him to the first on the right and escorted him inside, but not before picking up the crate of wine waiting outside. Inside, it was a thoroughly different atmosphere to the rest of the castle. Her bed was constructed from fine, solid oak and held a luxury woollen mattress. She also boasted an opulent feather-stuffed duvet, a comfort which Richard had never experienced in his life.

Across the room was a wooden desk covered in various pieces of parchment and inkwells and quills, as well as an assortment of tomes, covering subjects ranging from alchemy to magic to history. There was also a grand wardrobe attached to a bookshelf, which held even more books along with a collection of scented candles and incenses.

"Aren't you worried they'll see all the books about magic?" Richard asked, perusing her collection.

"No one in this castle would even dare to enter my room without my direct permission. Besides, I possess the only key. Francis is supposed to have another, but I stole that and disposed of it." She sat down on the bed and produced a pair of goblets from the adjacent bedside table. "Grab the chair from my desk. And do you drink?"

"Of course. But I've never tried wine, only ever ale," he said, taking a seat.

"You're missing out," she said mockingly, pouring him a goblet. "Virilian Red. Straight from the Sanskari capital. They might be awful people, but they produce the finest wine on the continent."

He graciously accepted and tasted. It was different to anything he'd drank before, but it was indeed exquisite – infused with spices and rich with flavour.

"Explain to me then, Richard, why is it that you talk so little?"

It was a difficult question.

"I don't really know. I've always travelled alone and it's never a problem when I work, but I don't really spend much time talking with people, so perhaps I never learned to take

47

part in much casual conversation. I always prefer to be brief – it's always saved me time."

"So you've never formed a band when bounty hunting? Would that not make the job more exciting? Less lonely?"

"It's exciting enough having swarms of Corrupted lumbering towards you or fighting off a camp of bandits single-handed. But I guess it does get lonely sometimes. At least I have Rosie."

"Are there any friends you would ever visit?"

"I never was good at maintaining friendships. The last friend I had was when I was still a boy, living in Myana. I cut myself away from him when I set off one day, all my possessions able to fit in Rosie's saddlebag and my satchel."

He found the conversation to be gradually saddening.

"And I was in a band, once. But that fell apart a while ago."

He downed the remaining wine in his goblet and Jade offered him more, which he didn't hesitate to accept.

"You seem detached to me, Richard. You need new friendship. I want to be that friendship." She gazed at Richard with an inviting smile, one he returned. Upon doing so he was engulfed in warmth, completely alien emotions finding their place in his head.

Night fell over Limara, the passing of time losing its meaning as Richard and Jade soaked themselves, Richard revealing more stories of his past. About his parents and their deaths. About particularly memorable contracts. And about Linelle, the one person he had ever loved.

Jade listened attentively, her consciousness not nearly as impeded upon as Richard's. And she remembered everything.

48

CHAPTER 6

Nendar Varanus, sometimes referred to as the Vanquisher, tirelessly scribbled away at paperwork, which he received in reams. Often, he would go through multiple quills and several pots of ink a day, but this was no trouble, as servants rushed around to serve him at his beck and call through day and night.

Although he was unnaturally driven to complete such monotonous work, he still found it dreadfully boring, which is why he was overly delighted when a sealed scroll materialised on the surface of his desk where he worked.

Hardly able to contain his excitement, he opened the message, ensuring no servants were around to watch.

Your Grace,

I have successfully made contact with him. It appears he indeed has no memory of the events and believes the implanted memories. The procedure was a complete success.

I now accompany him to ensure the memory loss is permanent. The mission still remains a complete secret – even our own forces are unaware of my true identity. And he in particular believes everything I have said.

Father – if his memory is restored, I do not know if it would be possible to partially erase it again. It is a dangerous spell and we were lucky the first time, but a second time could cause irreversible damage to his brain. It would be kinder to just terminate him if his memory is restored. For now, I will continue to observe and progress him. If all goes well, he will be our powerful puppet in no time. We would be able to take control of the elven lands and they could do nothing about it.

49

If you are to send another message back, place it into my hands. As of this moment, he is asleep in my chambers, so I cannot risk him seeing it.

– Val

Nendar smiled upon reading the message's end.

"That's my girl."

CHAPTER 7

SANAÍD, TYEN'AEL

"I've had enough of the King's birthday," Elaeínn declared upon finding a relatively clear street in which they could actually hear one another.

"If you're expecting me to teleport us back to Garaennía, you're mistaken," Kíra drawled. "I'm spent."

"I'm still confused about how Saniya knew we were coming," Elaeínn prompted, changing the subject. "There must be someone else who— shit. Run."

She exasperatedly pointed to two Regal Guards across the street who were gazing intensely at the two and had started to walk towards them, fondling the handles of their sheathed swords. They quickened their pace after being noticed and broke into a sprint after Elaeínn and Kíra began to run.

"Come quietly and you will not be harmed!" one of them shouted.

"So much for the secrecy of our identities," Elaeínn muttered. "I've had quite enough of fleeing today."

It wasn't difficult to outrun the guards, who were drastically slowed by the weight of their armour.

They made the decision to seek out another sympathiser, one who ideally wasn't in league with the Regal Guard. This sympathiser was a teacher at the School for Young Magicians, an institution visited traditionally by every high elf before the age of five. Elaeínn was sent there by her parents when she was four, but she was a rare case, completely incapable of understanding anything they tried to teach her. She then revisited another magic school when she was eleven, but still found it extraordinarily difficult to carry out even the most basic

51

spells and procedures, and as such never paid much attention. Which led to her relying on others for magical aid.

Classes weren't taking place due to the national holiday, but Caeran was there, diligently organising files and going over work from the week. He was quite meticulous about organisation, and was frequently found in such a situation, staying overtime to ensure a pleasantly orderly workspace.

"Caeran!" Elaeínn called as they approached, now entirely out of energy. Judging by the expression on Kíra's face, she wasn't feeling any better.

"You look like hell, girls," the teacher said, brushing a strand of umber hair out of his face. He was also relatively young, at only forty-seven. Most of his colleagues were between one and three hundred.

"Yeah, well, we've had a shit day," she retorted. "I assume you heard about Common Square?"

"Was that you, then? I heard someone tried to kill Jaelaar. Apparently, you got rather close."

"Doesn't matter. We failed, but we escaped. Then we came back and visited Saníya. You know, the librarian at the University. She betrayed us and we had to break out of the reading room to escape once again, and then when we do escape, some guards recognise us and start chasing after us, which I've taken to mean that our identities have been compromised."

"Shit luck," Caeran said. "What do you want from me?"

"Take us back to bloody Garaennía," Kíra groaned.

"Garaennía, Garaennía... it rings a bell. Kíra, if you would, gift me knowledge of it so I can actually open a portal."

"If I absolutely must..."

She extended her hand towards Caeran's head and murmured a spell. Caeran closed his eyes for several seconds while Kíra was speaking, and then opened them again when she had finished. Then he turned around and opened a portal through which they could see the cobbles outside the FTA headquarters.

"Excellent. Thanks, Caeran," Elaeínn said, looking to the increasingly exhausted Kíra.

"Anytime," he responded as they stepped through the portal.

Something was immediately amiss. As they surveyed the surroundings and observed the FTA headquarters, they made note of one particular object out of place. The door was wide open.

"That's odd..." Kíra exclaimed.

They sauntered to the entrance and peeked inside the door, which they also found to be wide open. From the doorway, they could see nobody. Creeping inside, an eerie silence prevailed, interrupted only by the sound of their footsteps on the wooden floor panels.

They decided without words to remain silent and continued sneaking through the abandoned house. The dining room and kitchen were a mess – the dining table had been split down the middle and the chairs were in various states of disrepair. In the kitchen, cooking implements, pots, pans, and the like were strewn across the stone-tile floor.

"Shit, Elle, look," Kíra whispered, crouching down. The interior of one of the open cupboard doors had been decorated in a streak of blood.

They continued and entered the alchemy laboratory, which they found to be in an even worse condition. Glass jugs, beakers, tubes, and dishes were all smashed to varying degrees – some to the point of being unable to recognise the original item. The large cauldron in which Berri brewed substances in bulk was completely untouched, with traces of the last of Berri's concoctions on its inner surface.

"I think we can stop sneaking around now," Elaeínn announced, just a moment too soon.

A group of shadowy figures flowed into the room, dressed entirely in black, masks hiding their faces, armed with vicious steel daggers in both hands. They said nothing as they knocked the two women to the floor and bound their hands behind their backs with strong rope.

"Who the bloody hell are you?" Elaeínn cried, receiving no response.

One of the masked figures, his daggers sheathed at his waist, was holding a cloth. He stepped forward and held it against Kíra's face, causing her to collapse. Elaeínn resisted fiercely as he then moved his attention to her but could do nothing as the incense entered her lungs and forced her to sleep.

*

Elaeínn woke up in a dark cellar, listening to the periodic dripping of water and its lengthy echo. It was dark – the only source of light came from a hovering orb atop a table to her left. She tried to stand up but found that she was tied to a wooden pole behind her. Kíra wasn't there.

She shivered. Goosebumps blazed up along her arms and she called out into the vast chamber but heard no response.

"Kíra!" she cried.

Once again, she heard nothing.

She shifted her attention to the ropes binding her to the wooden pole. Whoever had tied them up had done an excellent job – it was impossible to move her hands at all. But what she could do was shift them up and down. She began to do this with the hope of wearing down the rope and was beginning to lose faith fifteen minutes later when she felt as if she had made no progress. But she kept at it.

Finally, she heard something other than the dripping of water and the scraping of rope against wood. Determined, heavy footsteps coming towards her.

A dark figure appeared in the weak illumination of the light orb. He was dressed completely in tight-fitting black, including his face, exactly like those who had captured her. A single strand of golden hair escaped the confines of his balaclava.

"Miss Tinaíd," the man spoke, with a voice as soft as silk.

"Where is Kíra?" Elaeínn demanded.

"Miss Karíos is in an alternative location. We were less interested in her as we were in you," he provided, laying a bag down on the table on which the light was situated.

"Where is she, you bastard?"

"There's no need for that, is there? She's being interrogated, much like you will be momentarily. But you can ask anything you want; I'm not going to tell you."

"So what are you, some secret service?" Elaeínn tested.

The man stayed true to his word and remained silent.

54

"Well, at least tell me your name so I won't have to call you 'bastard' every time I want to refer to you."

"You will know me only as R."

"R? What's that stand for?"

He once again chose not to answer.

"Now, let's get down to business," he said, plucking a metal instrument from the bag. "The names of your superiors. Tell me."

"Fuck off."

He brandished the scalpel and looked up and down Elaeínn's body. Then he knelt down next to her and cut through the fabric around her inner thigh, narrowly avoiding cutting into her skin. She knew better than to resist as a sharp blade was only millimetres away from contact, but the moment he drew back his hand, she extended her unbound leg and attempted to kick him. He quickly reacted and avoided the attack.

"That's how we're doing it? Fine."

He stood up and grabbed another length of rope from the bag before kneeling again and grabbing her legs. She resisted vigorously, squirming and trying to kick him again, once successfully. This only led to him uttering a spell which caused her to lose feeling below her waist while he tied her feet together and then readjusted her to a standing position, bound to the pole with her hands above her head and feet tied to the bottom. Then he uttered another similar-sounding spell, returning feeling to her bottom half.

"Now, let's try this again," he enunciated, retrieving the scalpel, tossed into the darkness on the other side of the cell in the commotion. "The names of your superiors."

Elaeínn said nothing.

R stepped forward and used the scalpel to cut away the top half of her robe, leaving her top half entirely exposed, apart from her cloth breastband. The cold intensified and her breathing became rapid as she shuddered.

He gently traced the tip of the knife along her goosebump-ridden arms.

"I wonder if Kíra will be resisting so aggressively. And I haven't even turned to pain yet. I don't suppose my allies will be so merciful, though."

"Who are you working for?" Elaeínn spat.

"May I remind you of our earlier agreement?"

He moved the scalpel to her stomach and ran it along her right side, then her left.

"I must say, I've always been fascinated by prisoners' desire to resist interrogation," R said. "You're going to tell me what I want, because eventually I will reach such a degree of discomfort so that you can't bear resisting any longer. It would be far easier and simpler if you just told me what I wanted while the only discomfort was the cold air over your bare skin."

"I'd sooner die than tell you anything."

"They all say that. Is it ever true? No. Now, I suggest you do the smart thing, because I can tell you're somewhat intelligent. The names of your superiors."

Elaeínn remained silent.

R stepped back to the table and set down the scalpel. He returned to Elaeínn and looked directly into her eyes. She felt a surge of disgust and looked away.

"Stage one," R declared.

He extended his hand and murmured a spell.

Elaeínn screamed as violent pain erupted through her head, forcing her restricted body to convulse as her cries echoed around the chamber and the magic's influence destroyed her link with consciousness. The pain lasted seemingly endlessly, and she felt stuck. Until, all of a sudden, it stopped, and it was as if it had never happened.

Her breathing was even more intense than before and R still stood before her, having retrieved the scalpel.

"The names of your superiors," he asserted.

"Never," Elaeínn wheezed.

He used the scalpel to cut away her skirt and discarded it to the other side of the room. He knelt and traced her bare legs with the knife.

Elaeínn shivered violently.

R made a show of sauntering to the table and placing the knife down detestably slowly.

"Shall we advance to stage two? Or will you tell me what I want?"

Elaeínn swore through her chattering teeth.

"So be it."

56

He extended his arm, and Elaeínn braced herself for the sudden burst of agony. But it didn't come.

Instead, she shivered unhealthily rapidly, her entire body quivering. The temperature continued to plummet as R continued to whisper. But she held out.

R stared at her as her breathing rate continued to climb and each breath produced a visible cloud of vapour. R still continued to cast the spell.

"You're stubborn," he stated, retracting his hand and almost unnoticeably shivering himself. "Very stubborn."

He stepped forward and kicked her mercilessly and forcefully in the stomach. She retched and subsequently vomited, almost showering her captor in half-digested pork.

He picked up the knife and twirled it around in his fingers before putting it down again. He then moved forward, moving his foot backwards, aiming to kick her again.

"No," she whimpered. "Please."

He relented and stepped carefully around the puddle of vomit.

"I'll... t-tell you," she stuttered through the chattering of her teeth.

"At last," R drawled.

Once again, he chanted a spell, this time to increase the temperature of the room, and to a pleasant degree. The erect hairs along Elaeínn's bare skin fell and the goosebumps disappeared, while the chattering of her teeth grinded to an eventual halt.

"The names of your superiors," he asserted.

"You didn't... didn't c-catch him, then?" she seethed. "When you raided the... raided the house, he w-wasn't there? And that's why you stayed... to capture Kíra and me?"

"An excellent deduction. One that could have been made by a child. Now tell me the names of your superiors, else you will experience pain like you have never known."

"Master!"

A voice echoed from further away and R immediately turned to look into the darkness. An unnaturally short elf appeared from the shadows, dressed in the same anonymous fashion as R.

"Master, we need to leave now! We're under attack!"

"Under attack? Ludicrous!"

"Dwarves, master! A squad of them!"

"Impossible! Are they bandits?"

"No, sir! Soldiers!"

"What? Let me see?"

"There's really no time, master! We must evacuate!"

R swore under his breath as the valiant cries of dwarven soldiers echoed down the cellar. He quickly opened an anonymised portal and stepped through, followed by his shorter subordinate. The portal sealed shut as the first of the dwarven soldiers reached the light and unsuccessfully charged to follow the elves.

"Adilik, est kazok," the dwarf said, directing more dwarves from the shadows. They nodded at whatever he had said and began shouting something down the cell. Moments later, dwarves dressed much more lightly than the first soldiers appeared and began muttering something in Dwarven, followed by the appearance of light orbs along the length of Elaeínn's prison. Its illumination revealed it to be nothing more than a long, bland corridor – excessively wide and tall, explaining the echoing. The incessant dripping of water proved to be from a crack in the ceiling near the turn from which the dwarves had arrived.

The dwarves, having arrived, numbered many – at least twenty, by a quick tally, and more were streaming in. They had taken notice of the almost completely naked prisoner but were yet to act on her presence, instead being preoccupied with what Elaeínn could only guess were the orders of the first dwarf to have arrived – though all of the dwarves were sturdily built, this one was particularly imposing, and his flaming red hair only accentuated his noticeably fiery temper.

"So whos are ye?" he finally turned to Elaeínn, concluding the last of his orders to his soldiers.

"Elae... Elaeínn T-Tinaíd," she attempted to respond politely and composedly, despite her embarrassment.

"Who were they?" he continued.

"I don't... I don't know," she claimed. "Probably... probably with the govern... government... the Nationals... After all, it... it... it isn't beyond them t-t-to abduct their own people..."

"Nationals?"

58

"The p-people in charge..." her head grew cloudy, "of Tyen'Ael. That is where we are... right?"

"Erm, no. Ye've found yerself in the dwarven Kingdom of Hamatnar. Where've ye come from?"

"I was abducted from a city... north of Sanaíd. You mean to say that I've been teleported... halfway across the continent?"

"We's near the border, so not so far. But we's certainly not in Sanaíd or anywhere northwards. Come, let's get you down from there."

He placed his comically large axe into a strap on his back and revealed a dagger, which looked more akin to a short sword in comparison to the dwarf's shorter stature. He wielded it expertly and in two quick, precise, if not somewhat dangerous, cuts, removed Elaeínn's bindings. She fell and almost crashed into the solid stone floor, but the red-haired dwarf leaned forward and caught her in the nick of time.

"Tynak Llavadi," he introduced, helping her up. "Captain of the Elite Division."

"Thank you... Tynak," Elaeínn said, gathering her damaged clothes and dressing herself in them as much as she feasibly could, though her tunic had to be tied together, leaving her midriff uncovered, and she found no possible way of wearing her skirt.

"Come back with us, lassie, we'll find yous something in no time at all," Tynak chimed. "Estirit! Petilok winitit enskezit!"

One of the lightly dressed dwarves stepped forward and carried out the very same motion as she had seen hundreds of times before practiced by her elven companions in order to open a portal. It worked very much the same, and they were able to preview the entrance to a camp surrounded by trees, the centre of which was adorned by a roaring fire with entire boars and turkeys roasting on spits above it. They stepped through and immediately she felt a rush of warmth as the atmosphere revitalised her senses and extracted the cold implanted by the cellar, while at the same time clearing her head of the lingering effects of the torture.

"You speak High Elven exceptionally well," Elaeínn commented, awkwardly trying to cover her bottom half as Tynak pointed in various directions, followed by separate soldiers marching in the given directions.

"It's a useful skill, being able to speak the language of yer neighbours," Tynak explained. "What about yous? Do you speak any Dwarven?"

She shook her head sheepishly, but Tynak chuckled.

"Ye needn't be ashamed, you only look like you've barely escaped childhood. You must be what, twenty-one? Twenty-two?"

"Twenty-two," Elaeínn confirmed. "And I want to learn Dwarven, I really do. Just... haven't had the time to get around to it."

"As I've gathered. Why you, then? What makes you so special to be kidnapped and taken across the border?"

"I really have no idea. He seemed to want information from me that I simply didn't have."

"If ye say so," Tynak chuckled. "But there's something ye aren't telling me. Here, something for yer bottom half. It, err, might need a wee bit of adjustment."

She accepted the exceptionally large dwarven men's breeches and stepped into them, knowing beforehand that they would never fit her slender figure. Some fiddling and rope later, it was just about enough, though they weren't nearly long enough, ending up more like shorts.

"Now, Elaeínn," Tynak said dramatically, leading her into a large beige tent and then to a square wooden table, at which he encouraged her to sit across from him. "As I said beforehand, ye aren't telling me the entire truth. We dwarves are happy to provide hospitality, it's in our natures. But this here is no ordinary encampment. The Hamatnarian Elites are the finest, carrying out operations across not just the country but the continent. We have an assortment of the wisest mages, the strongest warriors, and the cleverest tinkerers. And I am the captain. I report directly to the King himself. In the interest of national safety, it's me duty to interrogate yous. I won't be applying any of the horrific methods that left ye in the state we found yous, but we do need to know what ye were doing there and who ye really are."

"Have you heard of the FTA?" she asked, this time deciding not to resist.

"Tyen'Aeli terrorists."

60

"Freedom fighters," she corrected, straightening her posture. "I'm one of them. And I was abducted from our headquarters by a group of anonymous agents, their identities completely concealed. Both myself and my friend, Kíra. And who knows how many other of our allies."

"Ye mean to say ye have absolutely no confirmation as to the identities or the allegiance of your captors? None at all?"

"They must be working for the Nationals. They're the only people with reason to have us taken out of the picture and the funding to do it."

"But no solid evidence?"

"I—No. No solid evidence."

"Ye mentioned another of yous had been captured as well. Where is she?"

"I don't know."

Tynak raised an eyebrow.

"I really don't know. All I remember is waking up in that cell and being poked, prodded and my mind invaded with magic. He wanted to know the names of my superiors. And then you turned up."

"Alright, I think that's quite enough. Yer clearly not a threat to the dwarves. What I'd really like to know is why some high elves have got a little gig running in our land. Whether they're working for yer government or not. Regardless, yer job is over. Now it's me who has to get to work."

Tynak stood and began to walk away but stopped at the tent's exit and sat back down.

"Ye say yer part of the FTA?" Tynak questioned.

"I am."

"I might have some use of yous yet. Or rather, King Kagyan will. Come with me."

CHAPTER 8

FREE CITY OF DANNOS, SANTEROS

Elton approached the body, which landed face-down, and rolled it over.

The neck was incredibly disfigured, and some teeth had smashed against the ground and fallen out in the impact. His smooth, white forehead was now dented and coated in sand. Elton fished into the pockets of his tunic and found a set of keys, which he took for himself, as well as a handful of expensive gemstones, which he also took for himself.

The Syndicate forces exited the bank and Paul, Jerry and Felix sauntered over to join Elton in observing the body.

"Alright you lot, scram! Bonuses will be handed out when they're handed out, don't go asking about them!" Paul bellowed. The crowd quickly dispersed into the adjacent streets.

"Well that's miserable," Jerry said. "He looks even uglier than me now."

"Could he not have even had the courtesy of allowing us a bit of fun?" Felix grumbled.

"What happens now, boss?" Paul pressed. "Gonna bury the body? And make yourself the boss of the bank?"

"Suppose we should do something with the body," Elton answered. "Don't worry about the bank, I just have to sign a few documents and we have free reign."

"Also, what was he chatting to you about before his big leap?"

"Complete nonsense, just trying to talk his way out of dying. Nothing to worry about. Shall we take a look around our new property?"

"And the vaults?"

Elton revealed the set of keys, jangling them in the air for dramatic effect, much to the others' pleasure.

"First task, we'll have to find a safe. I doubt these are the vault keys. Let's search his office."

The bank comprised five floors. The vaults were all underground, while the ground floor and first floor were designated for the use of the bank's customers, where the bank's staff would have been working. All had fled through a back entrance during the commotion outside. The second floor contained a staff lounge with a few various forms of entertainment, including a round table and an expensive painted marble chessboard, fixed to the floor. The pieces used for playing were not as expensive as the board, instead being carved from wood. There were also some meeting rooms littered with scrawled pieces of paper and chalk, as well as great slabs of slate attached to the wall for writing.

Finally, the top floor was dedicated to the manager's quarters and private facilities. A fully stocked and outfitted kitchen, complete with an extensive pantry and a door leading to an outdoor dining area on a balcony, which boasted a magnificent view of the city. Rafio's bedchambers were lavishly furnished, with a king-sized four-poster bed decorated in even pricier sheets than Elton's bed, with brown curtains, the edges of which were trimmed with gold silk. The bedroom had two more doors.

He opened the door on the left and found a personal bathroom, a rarity in Dannos. Most of the wealthy simply had a wooden bathtub which they kept in their bedroom. Rafio's bathroom, however, contained a spacious bath dug into the floor, a miniature version of the baths found in public bathhouses. He also had his own toilet which Elton reluctantly inspected; under the seat was a great drop, which was likely to lead to a cesspit underneath the building.

He continued searching the bathroom, looking in cupboards filled with expensive perfumes and soaps, feeling along the wall for any indents. He found nothing.

Concluding his search in the bathroom, he withdrew and opened the other door, revealing a small room which took the form of an extensive wardrobe, containing many outfits equally as obnoxiously opulent as that which Rafio had been wearing when he died.

A small wooden drawer hidden behind the clothes revealed an immense jewellery collection – rings, necklaces, earrings, bracelets, pendants, brooches of gold and silver, many inlaid with precious gems – diamonds, sapphires, emeralds, rubies, amethysts, topazes, opals, tourmalines and more.

Banking really is lucrative, Elton thought, pawing through the collection and picking out a few items he particularly liked. *Though this seems stupidly much for a single man to own.*

He opened another small drawer on the opposite side of the wardrobe, hidden in a similar fashion to the jewellery drawer, to discover a gemstone collection, even more exhaustive than the gems found inlaid jewellery. Inside must have been hundreds of large, flawlessly cut gemstones.

Elton quickly turned around to check nobody was on the same floor as him. Paul's booming voice could be heard from the stairwell, moving constantly closer as he and the others ascended. Elton quickly closed the drawer and rushed from the wardrobe.

He resumed searching the bedroom for a safe when Paul entered.

"Alright, boss? What's in those rooms then?"

"A bathroom and a wardrobe. Nothing of interest, the man certainly spoiled himself."

"Found that safe yet?"

Elton responded by pulling a small steel case from under the bed, locked. Methodically trying each key he found from Rafio's body, eventually one worked and the safe opened with a click. Inside was another larger set of keys.

"Boys, we've got 'em!" Paul hollered. Felix and Jerry were quick to respond and sprinted from elsewhere on the top floor. As a group, they travelled down the stairwell to the underground chamber containing the vaults. The underground air was stale, and it was pitch-black.

"Won't be a minute, boss," Jerry said, climbing back up the stairs to search for a torch.

They waited for a few minutes before he returned, torch in hand. The new light uncovered candles lining the walls between each vault, which they lit, allowing Jerry to discard the torch. There were seven vaults in total: one at the end of the room, opposite the stairwell, and three on each adjacent wall. Helpfully, there were also seven keys.

"Don't go pilfering from the accounts, I'm sure one of these vaults will hold the bank's own gold. Remember, we want to take control of these people, not drive them away," Elton instructed. He then opened each of the vaults, confirming his suspicions about most of them containing numbered slots. The vault opposite the stairs, however, contained a colossal mound of gold ingots, along with a great deal of coins littered on the floor around it.

"Jackpot!" Jerry exclaimed. "This is more than I thought there would be! I didn't even know there was this much gold in Dannos!"

"It is awfully suspicious," Elton pointed out. "I'm beginning to have doubts as to its origin."

"Bugger its origin," Paul bluntly said. "Look how much there is! We're rich! I mean, richer than we already were."

"Well, considering we control this building, there's no point in letting these safes go unused. Leave the ingots where they are, and we'll share out the currency. We also need to pay the guards."

Chuckling to themselves, Paul, Jerry, and Felix stuffed their pockets with as many of the gold coins as they could hold and hustled up the stairs to find sacks for the rest.

The vault, Elton noticed, contained no valuable gems like those he had found upstairs – a change from the banks he'd taken over in the past.

He couldn't have been keeping them upstairs to protect them, as they would surely have been safer in a sealed vault, Elton thought. *Wouldn't they?*

At this point, the guards marched inside to demand their payment.

"The banker paid us four hundred marks a month – each. You will pay us two thousand five hundred," the guard who negotiated earlier said.

Jerry, Felix, and Paul returned with numerous, reinforced linen sacks and began loading the coins into them, counting various quantities of coins into each one before handing them to the guards, who reluctantly accepted and promptly left. After the final guard was paid, they were left with a rather measly pile of coins, but the remaining ingots were easily worth more than the 125000 marks they had just paid out.

"Well, take the rest and share it out. I'm going to head home, there's been enough action for me today. Paul, come with me as a protector if you would."

"You need to grow a pair, boss. Nobody would—" he stopped short, frozen by Elton's paralytically hostile gaze. "Oh alright, I'm comin'," he finally said. "You better leave me some more loot."

"No guarantees," Felix teased.

Elton left the bank, guarded by Paul's somewhat-watchful eye.

"Oi, boss, where'd that Rafio's body go? It was 'ere a moment ago," he pointed out. Sure enough, the only reminder of Rafio's demise was a miniscule crack in the stone floor.

"Some scoundrel probably came and took it for the jewellery and his clothes. A shame we didn't get there first, I quite liked his pendant."

The journey home was trouble-free, which Paul didn't hesitate to comment about before rushing back to the bank.

He unlocked his door and stepped inside. The temperature immediately dropped unnaturally the moment he stepped through the doorway. To check he wasn't going crazy, he even stepped back outside – the temperature rose, then fell again when he finally went inside and closed the door.

A shiver ran down Elton's spine – and not from the sudden coolness. Something felt wrong, though everything looked in order. He even ensured the boot prints leading up the stairs were his own.

"I'm going mad," he said to himself, retreating to the kitchen. He quickly prepared a chicken sandwich, which he then cautiously took upstairs.

His paranoia only heightened when the temperature continued to descend with each ascended flight, from a slight chill on the ground floor to wintery on the top floor. Gripping the door handle to his bedroom, a pang of fear froze him in place, before he ran – he ran down the stairs, dropping the sandwich and grasping the front door handle.

Only there was no outside – Elton opened the front door and was met with a mirror, filling the entirety of the door's space. He tried striking it but achieved nothing besides bruising his knuckles. He removed his dagger from its sheath and tried to pierce the glass, but the mirror showed no sign of relenting. Cursing, he tried striking it again, kicking and punching and shoulder-barging, each impact leaving no trace of having occurred.

The grey hairs on his wrinkled arms stood on end as the chilly air grew colder. His frail heart pounded, blood rushing to his head as his rationality crumbled, desperately trying to smash the mirror.

"Hello, Elton."

He swiftly whirled around and pointed his dagger at the stone-faced intruder, ruby eyes, matching the pendant hanging from his neck.

"Put that down before you hurt yourself," the intruder spoke, in an accent Elton had never heard before. "It certainly can't hurt me."

His hair, jet-black, complemented his stony skin, and emphasised his choice of wardrobe – raven-black trench coat and boots.

Elton didn't falter, keeping his dagger raised, but pacing backwards as far as space would allow.

"What are you, monster?" he spat. "What have you come here for?"

"I thought I made myself clear at the bank. I gave you a choice and you let your arrogance get the better of you. I must say, it's something of a relief to finally be changed from that disgusting form, although you have ruined my career." The intruder threateningly deepened his voice as he spoke the last line.

"You're Rafio?" Elton queried. "I have trouble believing that."

The intruder's hands contorted to form a symbol, and a dark tendril shot from his fingers, stealing the ornate dagger from Elton's hand, which he clumsily attempted to take back. Elton returned to the mirror while the intruder clutched the dagger and admired the blade's decoration, running an elongated finger along its edge.

"A beautiful weapon. Come, let us find somewhere to sit, and if you behave rationally, I may be inclined to return it."

Beckoning Elton to follow, he ascended the stairs. Elton had no choice and speechlessly followed, articulating a plan to fight or escape. The intruder led Elton to his office, where he had planned the bank raid, and took a seat at the table, the bank's floorplan still present. Elton sat down opposite.

"Burn," the intruder whispered. Flames erupted from the table, reducing the floorplan to ash, before extinguishing themselves.

"What do you want?" Elton growled.

"For you, human, to listen, and observe. You clearly worked out that I am, or was, indeed, Rafio Benito, manager of the Dawn Bank. As I had been for three hundred years, as Elito Benito, Mateo Benito, Javier Benito and so on. Then you came along and put an end to a 'family' business, one which had acquired me significant wealth, as I'm sure you discovered."

"You don't look like an elf."

"Because I'm not. I'm far more interesting." Rafio's intense gaze never broke, his reflective, soulless eyes boring into Elton's conscience. "Luckily for me, humans are foolish and allow themselves to be slaves to fear – and fear drives people to irrationality. When it comes to believing my kind exist, that irrationality transpires as denial. Tell me, Elton. Look into my eyes, observe my figure, my abilities, and tell me what you see."

Elton didn't need to spend any more time observing, having been doing so since the moment he had first walked through the front door.

"You're a monster. In Valoria, they have the Dead, or Corrupted, or Cursed Ones – I've heard them be called many things. You don't seem like a mindless corpse."

"You know what I am, but you allow fear to dominate your rationality. Break through your pathetic emotional barriers and control your own thoughts." Again, he contorted his hand, but into another new shape. Dark tendrils, similar in appearance to the one which he had created earlier, shot from his fingers at great speed and impacted Elton. Though causing no physical damage, he immediately fell to the ground, writhing in pain. The dark tendrils stayed anchored to Elton's thigh, chest, and temple, causing immense illusory pain to erupt through his body, centred around those three locations.

"Stop! Please!" Elton begged, crying with pain.

"I will stop when you tell me what I am!" Rafio barked, his voice again deepening with anger.

"A vampire! You're a vampire!" Elton sobbed.

The sensation vanished and left no remnants of its existence. Elton, still on the ground, tears falling from his eyes, stopped crying at once and cleared the moisture with his arm. He then stood up and returned to facing the vampire.

"Good," Rafio said, sounding congratulatory. "You conquered your denial. After all, you always believed vampires to be the fabrication of fairy tales, am I correct?"

"It's the sort of shit I hear the idiots in the Syndicate spread. Never believed a word of it, and neither did they."

"Well, how much have you heard about vampires? I'm very interested." He reclined in his seat.

"Well, I never really bothered with listening, but I can tell you as much as I remember...

"From the fairy tales, I've heard there are two different types of vampire and they both do different things. But as I said, I never bothered listening. So I don't know what you expected from me."

After Elton had finished speaking, there were a few moments of silence while Rafio stared at him, looking deeply contemplative. Elton thought better than to make a remark and instead stayed silent, growing annoyed but continually fearful.

"Lesser vampires are the most common," the vampire suddenly began. "Though they aren't created through the bite of another, but by conception under the shadow of an eclipse. Once born, they grow like normal humanoids, but their heart doesn't beat. They breathe, though they do not need to. They feel the same emotions as a humanoid and can survive a long time without even knowing of their gift. In this cruel world, though, that isn't common. As their friend falls in the street and cuts open their knee, the blood which seeps from their leg seems so terribly appetising. They try, just a taste, and it's joy, an extravaganza of flavour, and it is then they make the decision – whether to pursue an uncontrollable desire for blood, or to overcome their nature and treat is as a delicacy, a luxury. Many lesser vampires can do this with ease, as their natures are weak. They go on, living humanoid lives, relishing their biological immortality.

"Malevolent vampires, less common, are not so strongly willed. They, like lesser vampires, are created under the shadow of an eclipse – but they have a much more tragic story. In order for the unborn vampire to become malevolent, their mother must be slain before she can give birth, her blood, cursed by the eclipse, seeping into the womb and infecting the unborn vampire. This process strips the vampire of its capacity for emotion and they quickly – and I mean quickly – evolve and develop in the lifeless womb, destined to become mindless, violent beasts, ravaging towns and cities, bathing in blood. They gain incredible magic abilities which only the most experienced humanoid mages would be able to cast – unconcentrated invisibility, imperceptible speed, fluency in near every form of destructive magic – pyromancy, cryomancy, haemomancy, for some examples. Keep in mind that these classes of magic are not necessarily purely for destruction – the ability to control fire can be a magnificent tool. They don't understand this, though, and are only given the knowledge of destruction. It's a shame they cannot choose how they use their gifts, as their actions are driven by their insatiable bloodlust. Unlike lesser vampires, who I've explained treat it as the finest delicacy this world has to offer, malevolent vampires feel as if they cannot live without its taste. They are insane. And they're also quite a nuisance, because it gives us a deplorable reputation among believers."

"Rafio – whoever you are - why are you telling me this?" Elton interrupted.

A mistake.

The vampire's ruby eyes flared in anger and he again summoned the dark tendrils, this time extending them to reach Elton's throat, wrapping around it and subsequently tightening. Elton, gasping for breath, tried grabbing at the tendrils to no avail, as they were unbelievably strong despite being as thin as strands of yarn.

70

"Please, my name is not Rafio. If you are going to address me, my true name, in your unsophisticated tongue, is Kalahar Kefrein-Lazalar."

Elton's face took on a collection of shades of red as he failed to breathe. Kalahar menacingly watched as the reds faded to purples and blues, before finally releasing the spell. Elton dropped to the floor, wheezing, regaining the natural tanned colour of his cheeks.

"I am telling you this, Elton, because you are my prisoner and I decide your fate. If your fate is to listen to my explanation, my story, then that will be what happens. Remember, I need only say a single word and you will die a painful, torturous death.

"Now, where was I? Malevolent vampires – a nuisance, yes. They do, in fact, have a weakness, and it isn't sunlight. See, I would be reluctant to divulge such sensitive information, but malevolent vampires really are a burden, so if they were to be exterminated, I can't say it would greatly trouble me. It would clash with my honour somewhat but, well, I've never let that stop me before...

"I've allowed myself to ramble. Malevolent vampires – they're near invulnerable, succumbing not to fire or aspen wood or garlic – I find the fact that people who believe in vampires actually accept the last two quite insulting – instead, you need an alchemical concoction. No simple formula, either – a solution of swallow's bones, myrtle berries, whale fat, humanoid blood and one final, vital ingredient – vampire dust. Those ingredients then must be grinded together and heated over a fire. The final result will be a deep, enticing red, reeking with death. Take care not to touch the elixir, as it is terribly corrosive, and your frail skin will not be able to withstand contact with it. Instead, use the concoction as a grease, applied to a weapon – the blade of a sword, the tip of an arrow. Either way, as long as that formulation is able to make contact with a malevolent vampire, they will become vulnerable. Ah, yes, I can see in your surprised expression that you expected this to kill them. No, no, no. They are far more resilient than that.

"You see, every legend, every tale, every story is based on a truth. That truth may have been manipulated and fractured to be almost non-existent, but it will always remain as a critical part of the story's foundation. The story about vampires being vulnerable to silver, while having been manipulated, still has a ring of truth. You must first weaken them with the solution I just described, however, before they can be struck down. And that will be the most dangerous aspect of defeating a vampire. For if they do not obliterate you from afar with their magic, by the time you can come close enough to strike the killing blow, you will also be within range of their vicious claws, their deadly fangs. Malevolent vampires are swift, but their insanity also weakens them.

"Should you get into a position where you can land a blow, all it takes is to pierce the weakened vampire's body with an instrument of silver."

He concluded his speech and stared intently at Elton, who was still processing the sudden deposit of information.

"What about you? Are you a lesser vampire?"

"Ah, no, not at all. I'm very unique, the only one of my kind. A chaotic vampire. I've been active for at least two thousand years, by this point, and not once has another chaotic vampire crossed my path. If I'm going to be blatantly honest with you, I'm not entirely sure myself how I was created, though I assume it wasn't natural. All I remember is waking up on a cold, stone table in a cave deep underground, various surgical implements littered on the floor around me, no memory of anything. It was all incredibly odd, but I quickly discovered my abilities when I tried to feed on the creatures living in the cave. It took a hundred years or so before I discovered another vampire, who took me in and introduced me to our hierarchy, teaching me about who I am. At first, he assumed I was a lesser vampire due to my control over my emotions, but then I showed him my shape-shifting abilities and my unparalleled skill in magic, and not just destructive. I can easily cast illusory, destructive, restorative spells and anything else I desire. I appear to have been given the best of both categories of vampire. And as the only active member of the category, I took it upon myself to give it a name, which I find quite neutrally fitting, as I don't necessarily mean by chaotic that I cause chaos, but that I have the capability to create an infinite number of scenarios and can respond effectively to infinitely more."

72

"Are all vampires this talkative?" Elton asked.

"No, but it's not every day I get to explain to someone about my species. I never usually talked to anyone, running that bank. I found human topics of conversation dreadfully dull, and I've always despised the northern Santerosi accent. Lucky for you, you only have a soft touch of it."

"Probably because I'm Salyrian by blood and childhood."

Surprise spread across Kalahar's face. "I would never have thought you a Salyrian. You look about as average an old Santerosi man as you can get. And I spent some time in Salyria, part of King Valkard the First's royal guard. That was some time ago, for I hear that only recently King Valkard the Third was slain and in his own throne room, too.

"Ah, I've allowed myself to ramble again. Now, you've already asked once, and I'm terribly sorry about my reaction – I can be short-tempered at times. Why did I tell you about vampires? Well, I'm sure you'll find it terribly beneficial. After all I've said, I'm sure you're wondering why there haven't been any reported massacres at the hand of one of these violent beasts, correct?"

Elton nodded.

"It's because the last total eclipse was hundreds of years ago. At the time, a group of elven mages across every continent had banded together to form a crew of vampire hunters, which evolved into the faction known as the Nightwatch. They were incredibly efficient in their methods of capturing the vampires, combining their magical strength to outmatch their prey. However, none of them knew the specific method of killing them which I described to you today. So instead, they created a small alternate dimension – this cost many lives – and trapped every vampire they caught inside it. Those vampires will still be in there today, but nobody knows how to access the realm, as the Nightwatch was disbanded when their necessity ended, and funding halted.

"Now, I still haven't told you why I'm telling you this, and I will stop my blathering and tell you now. As I said, the last total eclipse was several hundred years ago. Well, I was granted the power of foresight as part of my creation, and I know exactly when the next eclipse will come. When the leaves are reborn in the Salyrian forests' trees, the world will be drenched in darkness. In one month. And given the current state of the world, with war and conflict occurring on all fronts, I'm afraid it's terribly likely that catastrophic numbers of malevolent vampires will be born. I'm sure the elves and dwarves in Fenalia will gracefully handle it, as they embrace the unlimited possibilities of magic in their cultures, while humans archaically decide to label anyone practising it as worshipper of demons and has them systematically executed. I'm afraid your blindness will be your undoing, which is why I've chosen to warn you, a human, about the threat. Another reason human civilisation will be hit hardest is a result of your barbaric behaviour. The elves and dwarves – elves in particular – are very civilised and more often resolve matters diplomatically. There are also far higher levels of education in elven culture, so people are unlikely to commit vicious crimes like the murder of a pregnant woman. Humans are sadly easily capable of such a deed."

Elton stood, speechless, understanding the severity of Kalahar's words.

"What am I supposed to do? Have you forgotten that you're talking to the leader of a crime faction? I'm known for many things, and good will is not one of them."

"That is where you're wrong, Elton," Kalahar declared. "You may well be a criminal, and abominable to many, but in your heart lies generosity. When you raided my bank, you could easily have taken the gold all for yourself and ran off with it. But you didn't. You shared it among every man working for you in this city, not something many crime lords are known for doing. And let's not forget my guards, the traitors – you could have easily betrayed them and slaughtered them when they came to demand payment, but instead you happily paid them six months' wages – an astounding sum for fifty expertly trained mercenaries – and let them go on their way. You're not evil, Elton, and you never have been."

"I'm not very generous, either. I found your collection in the wardrobe and my first instinct was to prevent my closest allies from knowing about it. Those gems must have been worth more than everything in that vault."

"Those gems are no longer in your possession, either. They belong to me and I plan to keep them that way."

74

He contorted his hands and conjured a medium-sized steel case, light enough to hold in both hands. Uttering a word in a language unknown to Elton, the box opened, revealing all the gemstones and pieces of jewellery which were originally in the wardrobe.

"Your immediate reaction wasn't anger, greed or jealousy. It was admiration. You are capable of greatness, Elton, but you allowed yourself to travel a dark path."

"The gems, the jewellery – why did you keep it in the wardrobe? Why not keep it in the vault?"

Kalahar whispered another word and the box closed and vanished. "I have an inexplicable attraction to them. But enough about gems – the world faces a terrible threat in the increasingly near future. The Nightwatch are now merely a chapter in the history books. So I sought you, and I told you about the threat, because people trust you. People rally under your command. People believe in you."

"You can say all you want about believing in me or whatever, but you said I need vampire dust for the oil. I don't know how I'm to get that or how I'm to get a supply of it, but it doesn't seem like a tangible plan."

Kalahar retrieved Elton's dagger from behind him, where he had placed it down earlier. Holding it in his right hand, he raised his left hand and gazed almost longingly at it, before abruptly slicing it off. The hand fell to the floor, and his forearm immediately began to show signs of regeneration.

Kalahar once again set the dagger down and concentrated on the severed hand, contorting his still-attached right hand and whispering more spells in the unknown language. He then blasted it with a stream of fire before it exploded into a pile of fine, ash-like particles, which he levitated into the air and placed into an adequately sized wooden bowl, conjured from nothingness.

He gripped the stump, over which a layer of grey flesh had already grown. Discomfort, rather than pain, was the only expression visible on his face.

"Vampire dust," Kalahar stated. "Enough for a good dose of oil."

Kalahar handed Elton the dagger, which he tentatively took and returned to its sheath.

"I've done my part, Elton Redwinter. I've betrayed my species to help yours. Only I will know the reason why, but only you will live with the consequences, for I survive no matter what you choose. Farewell, Elton."

And with that, he was gone. The window to the office flew open and Kalahar vanished.

CHAPTER 9

The moon was high over the Old Keep. Richard was fast asleep in Jade's bed. He had been heavily inebriated by the point at which she had invited him to stay and dozed off within minutes, but Jade's senses remained sharp and undeterred.

She walked over to Richard and whispered a spell to ensure he would stay asleep until an hour after dawn, before changing outfits. She was now dressed completely in black, tight-fitting linen, including a cowl which shrouded her face in shadow. She then walked to the window, which was just wide enough to fit through, and jumped out.

She softened her landing with another spell and then debated whether to cast another to muffle her footsteps but decided she would be quiet enough as it was. The only obstacles between her and outside were two sentries atop the ramparts, who appeared to be falling asleep as opposed to watching the streets.

She silently climbed the steep, rickety stairs to the top of the ramparts.

"Elegance," she whispered, before leaping into the moat.

The spell allowed her to smoothly penetrate the water's surface without so much as a ripple, and she swam to the other side, thoroughly drenched.

"Dry," she whispered, and the water immediately evaporated from her clothes, forming a cloud of vapour over her head which she directed back into the moat.

Her destination wasn't far.

77

Upon reaching Joseph Fletcher's house, her theory that he would have stayed was proven to be true. Although the house appeared uninhabited, her enhanced hearing allowed her to hear the merchant's soft snoring.

"Open," she whispered.

A pitiful mistake. She had forgotten to first muffle the spell's effect and the lock clicked open at full volume, amplified by the night's tranquillity. She held her breath and listened carefully as the rhythmic snoring was momentarily interrupted, but soon resumed. Jade breathed a sigh of relief and gently pushed the door open, slinked inside and closed it behind her.

Once inside, vision became much more difficult. Much of the house was carpeted in complete darkness, with moonlight illuminating patches of tables, carpets and at the end of the main corridor, a staircase. The first step she took on the stairs resulted in a horrendous creak which sounded intensely louder than it really was. To be completely safe, though, she cast a spell to lighten her footsteps.

She ascended the stairs and crept across the landing, which overlooked the ground floor. Only one door lay at the end of the landing, hanging slightly ajar. Through the crack between the door and the frame, Jade could see only Joseph, fast asleep. She was in luck – unusually, the merchant appeared to live alone. Regardless of why this was the case, she was glad, as it meant only he had to suffer the consequences he faced.

Remaining completely silent, she softly pressed the door open just enough to squeeze through. The room was shrouded in darkness – there were no windows and the only light came from a candle which illuminated the merchant's wrinkled visage.

She took one pace into the room and immediately regretted it. Her leg caught a tripwire which had been stretched invisibly across the floor. It was connected to an urn, which fell to the ground and shattered.

This was loud enough to wake him.

"So you came for me after all, you dogs!" he shouted, leaping from the bed and grabbing a sword, unsheathed, from under the bed before Jade could even react to the situation. Now defended, he took a moment to use the weak candle burning at his bedside to light more, bigger candles, increasing the visible proportion of the room.

"Invectus," Jade whispered.

A dark, translucent blade with a cloudy texture materialised in her hand. Though a conjuration, it was wickedly sharp.

She emerged from the shadows and confronted the merchant, lowering her cowl. "We warned you, Joseph."

"You! What in Lanthanis's name is that?" His eyes were fixated on the texture-shifting sword in her hand, as if dark clouds were actually trapped within it.

"My weapon of choice," Jade responded. "Among others. Disarm."

The merchant's sword flew from his hand and lodged in the timber wall behind Jade.

"Accursed witch! A pox on you! May the Lord rise again and strike you from existence, vile bitch!"

Without a word, she struck swiftly and cleanly, severing the merchant's head. The headless body subsequently collapsed to the floor, a stream of blood gushing from the wound. Her sword evaporated from her hand as she picked up the severed head and shrunk it to a size where she could carry it in a small satchel attached to her belt. She then found the broken tripwire and incinerated it, leaving the shattered pot. Finally, she removed the sword from its original position in the wall and coated its edge in the merchant's blood before placing it haphazardly on the floor.

Apart from the headless corpse, Jade left the house as she had found it, locking the door from outside and briskly walking away, towards the other targets' residences. The other two had been much more compliant with her request in the day and she hoped for their sakes that they had followed through.

A quick check on both houses revealed both to be completely deserted, only items of little value left inside. She had been gone from the castle for around an hour now and decided to head back, her task completed.

She approached the castle walls feeling physically drained. The assortment of spells combined with the traversal across the city had been exhausting, so she decided to re-enter with an easier, riskier method.

Searching a patch of greenery next to the castle produced a large stone. Using no magical enhancement, she threw the stone as hard as she could, and it just landed on top of the lower rampart where a single guard was watching over the raised drawbridge. It landed with a crack as it clattered against the stone and the guard jolted awake, having dozed off on lookout. He called to his comrades who joined him on the lower rampart, and they surveyed the area but did not act any further. One stone wasn't enough. She found another, smaller stone in the patch of greenery and threw it at the soldiers, and it instead collided with the wall behind them. This was enough to draw them out.

The drawbridge began to lower and a group of five soldiers sauntered across and began to search for their anonymous attacker, concealed in a bush. She took one final stone and threw it in the opposite direction to the drawbridge, causing the soldiers to turn their attention. Seizing her opportunity, she sprinted across the drawbridge, light on her feet, and made it to safety. The soldiers quickly gave up their search and resumed their positions on watch, raising the drawbridge.

Jade returned to her bedroom and, as expected, found Richard still deep in magically induced sleep. She changed back into her original outfit and placed the satchel containing the merchant's shrunken head on the table. She uttered one last spell to seal the satchel, in case Richard tried to open it, before falling onto the bed, finding sleep in moments.

It was late morning when she awoke, and Richard had beat her to it. Everything seemed to be in order, though, and his eyes glimmered when she sat up, a genuine, warm smile beautifying his normally stern expression. He had taken a seat across the room and was reading from a book about illusory magic.

"Sorry if I wasn't supposed to read this, I just—"

"Don't worry, Richard. You can read whatever you like."

"I don't understand why magic is banned. By the looks of all this, magic-wielders could be really helpful."

"Humans will always scorn that which they do not understand. We are no exception. As long as old wives' tales are allowed to pass from generation to generation, magic will remain outlawed."

"I would love to learn," he said, taking on a wishful expression.

"Perhaps one day," she said. "The elven countries in Fenalia teach magic to a great degree, though they would never take on a human. If you ever are truly ambitious about learning magic, the night schools of Canaris would be your safest option. That's where I learned, many years ago. They're very secretive and manage to survive through bribes and coverups – they only ever accept those who have a reference from an ex-student or another associate."

"Canaris is quite the way to go. I'll stick with the bow for now. What are we doing today, then?"

She snapped her fingers and the candle burning at her bedside was extinguished, a thin strand of lavender-scented smoke trailing from its wick.

"What you are doing is up to you. I will remain here, creating replicas of the heads we need. Actually, you could go and check on the people, ensure their houses are deserted. We wouldn't want any trouble."

"Right, I'll get going. Anything I need to know, like, getting past the guards?"

"They know you're with me. Just don't say anything to them lest you sound too offensive – it's a fine line between life and the scaffold with the Sanskari."

Richard picked up his weapons from a corner of the room and fastened his sword to his belt, his bow and quiver to his back, and then briskly walked towards to exit. As he reached for the door handle, he abruptly stopped.

"Jade?"

"Yes?"

"Thank you."

He then awkwardly rushed from the room, overflowing with emotion. Jade smiled and turned her attention to recreating the heads of the targets, only two now necessary.

As Richard almost jogged through the Old Keep's corridors, he fought a losing battle against his feelings.

Attention to the task at hand, Richard, he thought to himself, regulating his abnormally fast breathing and raised heart rate. *You just said thank you, as any normal human being would do.*

Jade was right – every guard he passed on his way out of the castle simply nodded while he remained silent. As he approached the drawbridge, he slowed his pace, eavesdropping on the two guards manning it.

"...and then another stone nearly hit him. Would have been one of the locals."

"Blasted rogues. Ought to learn their place. I take it that they never found the scoundrel?"

"Well, the scaffold remains unused for the past couple days so yes, you would be right. They're sure to get a thrashing when they wake up. Francis isn't wont to kindness when he deals with us, but he's a blasted dog to Jade. Be a wish come true if she was sent back to Virilia."

"I must agree."

Richard strolled up to the drawbridge and made eye contact with the guards. "Bounty hunter, you may pass."

He curtly nodded, feigning gratitude, and left the castle.

He knew what the three houses looked like and vaguely remembered how to reach them. Being alone, though, he found his confidence with navigating an unknown city to be lower than he would have liked.

He tied his hair up with a band of cloth, leaving it hanging behind his head. Joseph Fletcher – the merchant. He had been the only target who didn't want to cooperate and hopefully he had changed his mind.

It wasn't far to travel. He arrived and the house looked deserted – no lights, no sign of activity, though all his possessions appeared to still be inside. If he was roaming around the town, his job would become much more difficult.

A beggar sat on the cobbles across from Joseph's house, dressed in rags but clearly generating enough money from the passing merchants to buy new clothes. He was smart – hopefully, this would work to Richard's advantage.

"Hey, excuse me," Richard said.

"What you want?" the beggar harshly responded. "Spare a coin?"

"Possibly – though I need information. The man who lives here – have you seen him leave the house today?"

"No sir, I've been sat here since the sun rose and not a peep has come out of those walls. No fat merchants either. He must be inside, though I bet something's happened to him."

"What makes you think that?"

The beggar put a finger to his lips and instead gestured his collection bowl in Richard's direction. He tossed a coin in.

"Right, yes, you understand me. Last night, there I was, asleep in that alley there, right next to the house, when I heard the door open. I thought, that can't be right, why is the fat man leaving the house at this time? So I peeped my head round the corner and what do I see? There's a person dressed in black – a woman, to boot! You couldn't see her face for her outfit, but she were skinny and curvy like a woman be. Anyways, the woman walks into the house and I hear the fat man shouting a couple minutes after. It were a bit hard to hear what he were saying, the thick wood and whatnot, but he didn't sound very happy. Then he was silent, and the woman walked back out a couple minutes after that. Then she turned to the door and I swear my eyes must have been deceiving me, but I think she locked it with magic! She didn't have any lockpicks or fancy stuff like that, just waved her hand and whispered something. I even tried opening the door when she left and sure enough it were locked! Who would've thought – a witch in Limara!"

"You're sure you didn't see the woman manually lock the door? After all, you said it was at night."

"I may be poor, sir, but my eyes can see as good as a hawk. I know what I saw, she didn't lay a finger on the lock."

Richard tossed him another coin, which was met with a nod of gratitude.

"Thank you," he said, walking away.

The first person to come to mind was Jade, but he dismissed the thought, knowing she was there with him all night. Though he didn't doubt her capability for stealth. He decided he would keep a closer eye on her and continue working.

He quickly checked the other two houses to find that the inhabitants had thankfully made the decision to leave town. That concluded his job, but before returning to the garrison, he thought he would explore first.

It was Sunday morning, a fact that hadn't been missed by the crowds who had begun to swarm through the streets following the weekly church service. Merchants frantically set up their stalls in the best location they could find, leading to squabbles about who had the fairest claim over a specific patch of land, while another equally adequate plot was snatched by someone else. Peasants had come from villages beyond the hills to sell their excess produce and envy the rare trinkets on display from across the region. Nobles purchased the rare items, strolling through the streets with pockets bulging with gold, completely oblivious to the pickpockets slowly relieving them of it. Mercenaries and bounty hunters took the opportunity to look for work and some even staked themselves a plot of land to display their trophies – heads of dire wolves from the southern tundra, of defeated Corrupted from anywhere a person died and wasn't burned, even of wyverns from the mountains in the East. As could have been expected, some were trying to pass off the wyvern heads as dragon heads, despite the fact that dragons were known to be a myth. Smooth-tongued traders always managed to convince at least a few gullible nobles, though.

At one point, the idea of hunting a dragon fascinated Richard. That was a long time ago, when he had only recently begun a career in bounty hunting and didn't know that dragons were the invention of a raving bard. For a fabrication of the mind, tales of dragons were described by minstrels the world over in great detail. They sang of a far-off land, deep beyond the reaches of man, dwarf and elf, deep in the ocean's clutches, a tropical island dominated by looming stone formations, plant life fighting to survive on its surfaces. The island was protected by fierce stormy weather which never ceased – monstrous waves forty feet high swallowed any ships that dared enter the waters.

Legend told that dragons used to live across the world in every kind of continent, and that there originally were dozens of different species of them. This has always been regarded as complete nonsense, though, as it left many questions unanswered, such as to where they disappeared and how humanoid races were able to colonise the world. And why the dragons from the far-off land stayed there instead of flying back to the continents and settling.

Most of the traders in Limara still used Miradosi rions as opposed to Sanskari pestas, which the authorities were trying to introduce across the newly inhabited areas, though not providing any incentive to make the switch. As he had a few rions to spare, he thought he'd take a look around.

Appetising smells first drew him to a plot where a well-to-do-looking local was frying a Miradosi special in a large pan – wild boar and apple glazing. He didn't hesitate to buy some which was enough to nearly sate his suddenly enormous appetite. Another stand was selling toffee apples, which left him feeling completely satisfied.

A bard strummed a lute atop a small wooden stage and sang his own ballads to the delight of a sizeable crowd. Richard recognised him – Master Ferris of Arbeford, something of a Miradosi celebrity. He always wore the same white jerkin over a bright lemon-yellow doublet and a beret of the same colour. He continued this garish style with his matching baggy breeches and snow-white boots.

Apparently, Ferris recognised Richard in the audience as well, as he brought an abrupt end to his song and called his name.

"Master Ordowyn! Ladies and gentlemen, please, the finest bounty hunter that Mirados and the ever-so-glorious Sanskari Empire has ever witnessed! Master, join me on the stage, for I never rewarded you properly for the job you did for me."

Puzzled, he took a few mindful steps towards the stage as the audience cleared a path directly to its centre.

"I'm sorry, Master Ferris, but I don't recall working for you."

"Nonsense! You rid my tavern of what we thought to be a small rat infestation, but you instead discovered to be a bloody network! The original reward was far too modest, but my innkeeper is one devilishly uptight man, so allow me to weight your pockets with adequate compensation."

Ferris grabbed a large handful of coins from his donation pile and placed them into a pouch, which he extended in offering to Richard.

"Forgive me, master," Richard said. "When exactly did I take this job?"

"Why, it can't have been more than two moons ago. You remember my tavern, the Canary? One of the finest establishments in Merana."

Richard thought hard about the time he spent in Merana a couple of months ago and began to recall the tavern, particularly how it stood out from the surroundings – the walls on the inside were painted a bright yellow colour in coordination with Ferris's outfit, creating a small pocket of life in the dreary streets the tavern inhabited. After remembering the inn, the events of the job came flooding back.

"Now that you mention it, I do remember. That was odd."

"It matters not whether it slipped your memory before, master, for you remember now! So please, do me the courtesy of accepting this compensation!"

Richard accepted the coin pouch and stepped away, while Ferris resumed strumming his lute and finished the song he had previously interrupted. Richard stayed and listened for a while before moving on.

A man claiming to be a bounty hunter caught his attention, particularly the way he was talking to a couple of young-looking nobles about his work.

"You see, good sir, good madam, it's common knowledge that the Corrupted are hideous creatures, but what isn't as well known is that there's much wealth to be found in their slaying. For you see, the dark magic which creates the abominations also has a silver lining – every single Corrupted has a diamond conjured deep in their unbeating heart. And it's not too difficult to extract, either – you just need to hire the right person for the job. Which is where I come in. At the right price, I can eliminate a whole horde of Corrupted with only my trusty crossbow. Then you are free to send in your men to collect the diamonds.

The nobleman and noblewoman, presumably husband and wife, looked at each other with assent.

"How big are the diamonds, master bounty hunter?" asked the noblewoman.

"My fair lady, they are not to be scoffed at. By my reckoning, each must be the size of the tip of my little finger."

"Extraordinary! How much would you ask for?"

"Well, my standard rate stands at a hundred rions per Corrupted that I eliminate. I must say that despite how expensive this may seem, I assure you that nobody else in these lands is as adept at killing those beasts as I. And by extracting those diamonds, you're almost sure to—"

"Master charlatan, please do us a favour and stop swindling innocent people," Richard interrupted. "Sir, madam, I'm sorry to tell you that this man is a liar and a thief. He was correct about the Corrupted being abominations, but that's about where the truth ended. They do not have a diamond embedded within their hearts – only filth."

"And just who do you think you are, drifter?" the charlatan angrily asked. "What right do you have to intrude and accuse me of such wrongdoing?"

"I have the right because I have actually killed the beasts before. Hundreds of them. Not a single one had a diamond in their heart. If you are so adept at killing the Corrupted, sir, then tell me – how do you do it?"

His expression changed from anger to worry as he struggled to invent a story.

"W-well, I, as you probably do, well, not as you do, because I can see you use a bow. But I use my crossbow, and I place a bolt right in their heart! It's their only weak spot, as I'm sure you well know."

"Have you ever used a crossbow?"

"Of course! What do you take me for, wretched drifter? Begone and mind your own business!"

Richard, scowling, was undeterred. He turned his attention to the nobles, who were taken aback by the two bounty hunters' sudden argument.

"Sir, madam. Allow me to introduce myself. Richard Ordowyn – bounty hunter. This man you are speaking to – a fake. Not once has he killed a Corrupted and if you were to hire him, he'd have disappeared by the time you went to visit the bodies."

The man turned to the fraud with a stern expression.

"Is this true? You would dare attempt to swindle us in broad daylight?"

"S-sir, I assure you, my trade is true. This man here is the true fake. For it is not he who has an impressive collection of trophies, no?" he stammered, frantically gesturing to the collection of heads pinned to a few planks behind him.

"Hmmm... the trophies do appear authentic..."

He turned back to Richard. "Master bounty hunter, how are we to believe that you speak the truth? For you have less evidence of your experience than the man you claim to be a thief."

"Well, if we were in a better location, I'd demonstrate my marksmanship. A crowded marketplace isn't exactly appropriate. So, unless you'd like to visit the local archery range, you'll have to take my word for it."

The nobleman muttered something to his wife before furrowing his brow and facing Richard.

"I'm sorry, master, but we simply cannot have this. After all, it was you who rudely intruded while this polite fellow was explaining his business. I must ask you to leave."

Richard, unwilling to argue, simply sighed and turned around, only to be met by the vast grin of Ferris.

"Good sir, my fair lady." He winked at the noblewoman, who blushed and giggled like a schoolgirl. "Is something the matter? Surely Master Ordowyn isn't the root of it."

This time it was the nobles' turn to stammer.

"M-master Ferris! It's an honour!"

"Now, now, good sir, you needn't treat me as if I'm not human. I asked a question."

"I-I'm sorry, master. Do you know this man?"

"Why yes, Master Ordowyn assisted me a short while ago with a problem I had and I must say he was stupendously efficient. If you were to look for a bounty hunter, I couldn't recommend a better man. Now, Richard, I left the stage in search of you. May I take a moment of your time?"

Richard nodded and walked away, trailing Ferris, who briskly made his way to a bench occupied by more nobles, though upon sight of Ferris they happily liberated the seat and stared in awe from a short distance away. He took a seat and motioned for Richard to sit beside him.

"Now, I know your kind generally stay apolitical, but I've got a job for you – one which involves a hefty reward. Tell me, Richard, do you align yourself with either side in this war?"

"If I told you, would my head end up on a spike?"

He folded his jerkin out to reveal a small badge bearing the Miradosi coat of arms – two silver roses entwined around a golden rose on a sky-blue field. "Have I guessed your allegiance correctly?"

Richard subtly nodded, not willing to give away too much.

"Then perhaps you will be interested in my proposition." He lowered his voice to a whisper. "Have you ever killed a man, Richard?"

"Before you ask, I'm not a hired assassin."

"Please, answer my question."

"I've killed brigands – outlaws. But I'm not a hitman."

"Even if the individual in question is, in the eyes of some, an outlaw? For example – a Sanskari advisor?" His eyes glistened with vice, completely contrary to his public impression.

Richard's silence gave Ferris enough information to carry on with his proposition.

"In the Old Keep, which has been desecrated by those dogs' presence within it, is a woman who at this point is in charge of Limara. She's wickedly good at her job – pretending, successfully, to be less influential than she really is. Posing as a simpleton sent simply to ensure order among the soldiers, but she instead controls the entire city. Even this marketplace today has been strictly regulated on her command and many peasants and their families will go hungry as a consequence. The Empire just takes and takes and takes, always employing the pathetic cover of 'providing unity and strength.' Limara is my true home, and it needs to be free."

"Even if I was to assassinate this advisor, nothing would change. Limara is deep within occupied Mirados; this war is a lost cause. Nothing is stopping the Sanskari and a city certainly won't be freed simply by chopping off the hand which chokes it. Because that hand will just regrow stronger."

Ferris smirked and sharply exhaled through his nose in amusement. "Have you ever tried poetry? I daresay you'd be rather good at it. Back to the point – I'm not stupid enough to think that killing one person would free a city but it's not about that at this point. It's about sending a message. If one person is able to kill the controller of this region's biggest market town and get away with it, what does that say about the Sanskari? It makes them look weak. It makes them look fallible."

"And the advisor's name? I can't kill somebody without knowing who they are."

"I'm afraid you're going to have to do this by my description of her – none of my sources have been able to discover her true name. Turns out she has many aliases – Jeyna Samarion, Keira Roseheart, Anya Townsend – she's unlikely to be using any of the ones we know about. But I've seen her, personally, when I was taken to the castle for questioning – bastards accused me of spreading slander about them. Which I have, just not in the manner they accused me of. She's certainly unforgettable – raven-black hair cascading over her shoulders; bright, emerald-green eyes which glint with such passion it's as if they physically penetrate you. By anyone's standards, she's very beautiful. But her heart is as black as her flowing locks."

Jade, Richard thought. *I have to warn her.*

"Master Ferris – how long are you planning to stay in Limara?" he questioned.

"Ideally until this job is done, though I tend to move around every couple months. If you don't want to do it, then I'll keep looking for someone who will, but if nobody wants to do it, I'll head back to Merana in a few weeks. Please, Master Ordowyn. I trust in your abilities and I've confided this much in you. It's one target. One loosed arrow and you create a rift. A rift which will be fed. And if you don't want to do it for the good of the people, then at least do it for the money. Fifteen hundred rions."

It was a lot of money – Richard physically expressed his surprise, leaning slightly backwards, a glint appearing in his generally expressionless eyes.

"You make a good case, Master Ferris. I'll think about it, and I'll give you my answer tomorrow. And that is my only offer."

"It is agreed. Until tomorrow, Master Ordowyn."

90

CHAPTER 10

CAMELION, SALYRIA

"Your Grace, I come bearing gifts."

The dark-skinned woman, dressed in vermilion robes with a large, brown, gold-buckled belt around her waist, stepped forward with a package, concealed with a layer of fabric. Her defined, extravagant curls ended just below her shoulders and bounced when she curtsied.

"Get on with it, then," Hortensio said, uninterested, choosing instead to fiddle with a few strands of hair which had fallen onto his face from beneath his crown. The woman, unoffended, pulled back the layer of fabric to present a ceramic bowl filled with precious gems – rubies, emeralds, sapphires, among others – and a rolled-up piece of parchment, sealed with the insignia of the Redwinter Syndicate. Hortensio, eyes wide, glanced over the bowl and its contents, the strand of hair with which he was previously toying held frozen in the air.

"A lovely little collection. Although old Valkard left me plenty more than that."

"This is the first instalment of what we hope to be a fruitful relationship," the woman explained. "Please, Your Grace, I urge you to read the letter."

Hortensio sighed and snatched the letter from the bowl, hastily removing the seal.

"You're a thief?" he queried, unfurling the letter. The woman didn't respond.

Dear King Hortensio, the letter began.

"Whoever wrote this letter could at least have used my full title of 'King Hortensio of Heathervale, first of his name,

91

Kingslayer and Saviour of Salyria' if you're trying to suck up to me."

The woman remained silent and watched intently as Hortensio reluctantly returned his attention back to the letter.

It is regrettable that I was unable to visit you myself, but I'm sure we can work out an arrangement through messengers. I reach out to you on behalf of the Redwinter Syndicate and all its child organisations across the continent. Let me first express my congratulations at your success in the capture of the Salyrian throne; it was due an overhaul long ago. I look forward to seeing progress under your enlightened leadership. Perhaps now, the King of Santeros will finally turn his pitiful attention from futile diplomacy and be forced to pay attention to Salyria and its majesty.

My main cause for writing this letter, however, was to ensure a lasting peace between your new reign and the Syndicate's activities. As I'm sure you are aware, the Syndicate carries out numerous operations across the land in secrecy and privacy – we aim to work for the benefit of everyone who deserves it. At no point do we demand or seek conflict – our secondary objective, after ensuring the happiness of our employees, is to avoid bloodshed at all costs. I am not a wasteful man.

You may see my organisation as an unruly band of thieves and brutes – this may be true in some peoples' perspectives. However, what sets us apart from common bandits and cutpurses is our value for honour – those who fall among the ranks of the Syndicate would never betray one of their own, and if we were to come to an agreement which means both your court and my organisations can work in peace, then it would be mutually beneficial. Therefore, this document serves as both a letter and a contract – by signing my name, I agree never to run any operations which would undermine the authority and supremacy of the Salyrian throne. If you choose to return this letter to me with your own signature, you agree to allowing the Redwinter Syndicate to survive in peace, and to turn a blind eye to their activities where we are upholding our end of the agreement.

This promise will not be without its benefits, either: my messenger brings a gift of substantial value which I hope you will understand the meaning of. If you agree to these terms, monthly instalments of payments similar in size will arrive at your court with my seal.

Thank you, Your Grace, for taking the time to read my letter. I sincerely hope you will agree to a future where we both may thrive.

Yours faithfully,

Elton Redwinter.

Hortensio snapped back to reality, absorbed by the letter's contents – it had been the most interesting item to arrive at the court all week.

"Good read, that," he said, shifting to look back at the woman. He beckoned to a couple guards, lining the walls like statues, and they came to collect the bowl with the gems, heavy metal-clad footsteps clanking against the marble floor. "Have that put in the treasury. And show our guest to the dungeons – we don't tolerate lawbreakers in Salyria."

One of the guards retrieved the bowl while another two reached for their swords, the screech of steel echoing across the throne room. They were unable to approach the woman, though, as she unveiled a hidden dagger of her own and rushed up the few steps between her and Hortensio. The King tried to react and leapt from his lazy slouch across the throne but was forcefully thrust back into place as the woman brushed past and knocked him backwards with surprising power. She then positioned herself behind the chair and reached around, placing the sharp edge of her dagger against Hortensio's throat. He frantically motioned to the guards with his hands, ordering them to stop. They stood still, beady eyes glaring at the woman through thin visors.

"Regi won't be pleased when I tell him the news," she hissed, her voice completely changed from the formal tone heard only minutes before. "He doesn't appreciate it when people disagree with him. Most of them don't stay alive very long to see the impact of their mistakes. Would you care to join them?"

Very careful not to accidentally slit his own throat, he gently shook his head, pressing it painfully against the throne.

"Tell your guards to piss off and allow me to ask you again whether you want to sign that letter. You're free to say no, of course, and I would leave. But if any of your guards make a move to kill me, then they die. Along with you." She then slowly backed away, trailing the tip of the dagger along Hortensio's throat as she went, before returning it to concealment beneath her robe. Hortensio rose from the throne, this time expressing no sign of ignorance.

93

"I think you'll find that I'm the King," he taunted. "I will be the one giving orders, not pretentious little bitches like you who manage to sneak a weapon past my guards." He slowly drew his sword, glowing blindingly bright in the sun shafts floating through the windows. "And when my guards fail, that's when I have to take command."

He rushed forward towards the woman and swung wide, underestimating his opponent. The woman swiftly ducked the blade and once again retrieved her dagger. Hortensio was quick to react and stepped backwards, taking on a defensive position, sword held across his body. Some of the guards lining the wall motioned to step forward and join the scuffle but were met with a harsh rebuke from Hortensio.

Holding the sword with both hands now, he rushed forward again and attempted to disarm the woman with brute force. He failed – she dodged his overhead blow and stepped forward, her dagger-wielding hand shifting dangerously close to his neck. Hortensio reacted quickly and brought his sword back up and traced a semicircle in front of him, forcing her to move her hand back. With cat-like elegance, she twirled and quickly stepped backwards in a predefined move, while whispering something inaudible under her breath. She then froze on the spot, deep brown eyes glistening. Hortensio didn't hesitate and lunged forward, striking her through the heart.

Except his sword never met her heart or even her skin – all he pierced was the limp fabric which now hung from the end of his sword. There was no trace of the woman – all that was left was her clothes.

"A bloody witch!" he cursed. "Not only have we got to exterminate a nest of thieves, but they've also got bloody witches!" He angrily thrust his sword back into its sheath and paced back and forth behind the throne, while the guards watched in silence. "One of you – go fetch me Sir Jannis. I've got a job for him."

The guards glanced at each other before one marched away. Hortensio resumed a lazy position on the throne while he waited, idly snacking on a plate of grapes provided by a servant. Some time later, the guard finally returned alongside a tanned man with similar traits to the dark-skinned woman – warm brown eyes, curly hickory hair. He was notably taller and older, though the woman was likely to have magically enhanced her features so as not to have any of the wrinkles exhibited on the man's face.

"You called, Your Almighty Magnificence?" the man drawled.

"I've got a problem for you to sort out, Jannis," Hortensio replied, ignoring his sarcasm. "I need you to raise an army. We're going to Dannos."

CHAPTER 11

DWARVEN ENCAMPMENT, HAMATNAR

"Estirit!" Tynak barked, grabbing the attention of the lightly armoured dwarven mage who had originally transported them to the camp. He scrambled towards them, almost tripping over a stray bucket but making a miraculous recovery.

"Kanstizit?" he asked.

"Nimmin ust til Lirkiff. Rikksgirit."

Estirit nodded and – after taking a deep breath – traced a circle in the air and pressed open a window revealing a monstrously large stone castle. Tynak ushered Elaeínn through without any chance to even think of escaping.

Her immediate reaction was a coughing fit in response to the acrid stench of smoke which seemed to outweigh breathable air. Tynak, on the other hand, was unaffected.

"Welcome to Rockfell," Tynak explained. "The beating heart of Hamatnar. Lirkiff, in Dwarven. Literally meaning Rockfell. And this magnificent construction is Castle Rockfell, one of the finest productions of dwarfkind. It's at least two thousand years old and yet it still grows and evolves over time. A suitably apt metaphor for the relentless pace of our development."

"Who lives in it?" Elaeínn queried as she was led towards a three-carriage-wide stone bridge over a vast moat of polluted water. "Surely not just the King? It's... enormous."

"Don't be ridiculous, of course not just the King lives in it. It's also the military centre of operations, the centre of the city's flow of trade, the location of operation of not just the executive but also the legislature and the judiciary. It's home to the ancient Rockfellian forges, where the majority of the land's steel is crafted – don't listen to any nonsensical blather about it being made up in the mountains in the north. It houses the military training facilities for the Rockfellian branch of the army and also a number of monarchy-run or owned institutions, including the Royal Bank of Rockfell. This is all, of course, public knowledge."

"That sounded rehearsed," Elaeínn mused.

"As it should," the captain responded proudly. "I've been alive for a fair while and I've been Captain of the Elites for five years now. It's only expected that I would have an adequate knowledge of the workings of my country."

"What use does your king have for me, then?" she questioned further as Tynak was recognised by the guards at the first portcullis, leading to a drawbridge.

"That there is confidential until we reach him. And then it is up to him to decide whether he really has use for yous."

The drawbridge was lowered over the second half of the moat, equally as polluted, and they crossed in silence, Elaeínn observing the columns of smoke rising from seemingly every direction she looked. The sky was mercilessly grey, complementing the monotony of the dwarven architecture.

The guards at the drawbridge recognised Captain Tynak and sharply saluted as they passed. The gates to the castle creaked open and they continued into a dreary, poorly lit hall only decorated by a gold-trimmed green carpet. The stone appeared to take on an even darker hue than its exterior counterparts.

"If it's that much effort to enter the castle, why is it such a hub of activity?"

"Because there are different sections accessible from different entrances," Tynak stated, as if it was obvious. "Ye can't get into one quarter of the castle from within another. And we've entered the Royal Quarter. The most tedious to enter."

"If it's so tedious then how have we managed to pass so easily? Surely someone could pretend to be you and achieve the same?"

"They could, but they wouldn't have one thing. Ye see the badge on me spaulder?"

She glanced at the armour covering the dwarf's shoulders and on his right was indeed a gold-and-silver brooch with the letters 'K.H.F.G.' moulded into the metal.

"K.H.F.G.?"

"Kanstizit Hamatnar Firat Gantra. Captain of the Hamatnarian Elite Division."

"Why can't intruders just make a copy of the badge?"

"Because I've got the only one. And its design is changed with every new Captain of the Elites. And even if they did manage to make an up-to-date copy of it, there are further security measures in place, don't ye worry. And anyways, it'd be bloody difficult for an intruder to imitate me and manage to go unnoticed. Security is tight around the King. They'd have to be a bloody brilliant actor."

Tynak led her through a cold, drab corridor – in which Elaeínn had to bend down to be able to walk through – into a busier room, secured by, as he had suggested, far more guards than before. They were stopped as they attempted to enter while Tynak said something indecipherable that didn't sound particularly Dwarven, or any language Elaeínn had ever heard of or read about. One of the guards closed their eyes and placed their hand on Tynak's shoulder before murmuring something incomprehensible. They were then allowed to pass.

"A secret code," Elaeínn deduced as they continued further into the bowels of the castle.

"Incorrect," Tynak said. "What the guards just did is read me magical signature – which is as unique to me as me fingerprints. Ye can imitate me voice, me beard, me charisma, but ye can't imitate me signature. Everyone's is unique."

The room they entered next was abuzz with the clanking of armour as dwarves marched in formation through wide, empty corridors. After that it was another long, uncomfortably claustrophobic tunnel through which Tynak laughed as he turned back to see Elaeínn struggling to fit through the entrance.

"We're nearly there, don't ye worry," he affirmed.

The corridor finally opened up to another green-carpeted hall. On their left was a throne constructed from the very same dark grey stone comprising every other part of the castle thus far, and on the throne sat upright an enormously broad dwarf, with wavy grey hair flowing to his waist. He was busy quietly addressing an audience of two important-looking soldiers, and Tynak waited patiently for him to finish before entering the throne room. Elaeínn noticed that they had come through from a side entrance, instead of the much more obvious archway directly across from the throne.

The dwarven captain dropped to one knee and insisted with an intense gaze that Elaeínn do the same. She did, but only to be courteous.

"Mi rikk," Tynak said.

"Sant," the King responded commandingly. Tynak stood and motioned for Elaeínn to do the same.

"My king, I humbly request that we converse in High Elven for the duration of our conversation."

"Request accepted. I had already gathered that our company in her youth would be incapable of the dwarven tongue."

"Ye assumed correctly, as should be expected, Yer Highness," Tynak flattered. "I bring to ye today a fighter of the FTA. Interested in bringing down the government of Tyen'Ael. I thought ye may be interested in a conversation with her."

"I would very much be interested. Please, let us continue in the war room."

King Kagyan stood and strode to an iron-reinforced door on the right side of the room and twisted the handle under the close watch of two neighbouring guards. He then led Tynak and Elaeínn into a room no more spectacular than the rest of the castle's innards, housing only a round table, four chairs and a large, imperfectly rectangular sheet of slate on one of the walls. On the table was a remarkably detailed map of the countries west of the Great Channel, a stretch of ocean dividing the continent of Fenalia in two.

Elaeínn wanted to look closer at the illegible markings on the map, because although she couldn't understand the language, it wasn't just writing. She decided against it, feeling the penetrative gazes of the senior dwarves on her.

"Yer name, lassie?" the King asked abruptly, standing across from her at the war table.

"Elaeínn Tinaíd, Your Highness," she provided.

"Captain Llavadi here says that yer in the FTA. I might just be interested in someone with yer allegiance. Tell me, lass, would yer boss be interested in some... financial support?"

"I'm certain he wouldn't turn it down," she responded, intrigued. "If I may ask... why are you offering to fund our cause?"

"That, lassie, is confidential. And the money won't be coming from the Royal Treasury, it will instead be coming from a private, independent, politically neutral organisation operating within Tyen'Ael. Do ye understand?"

Elaeínn nodded.

"We will need to arrange some details, in that case. I'll need to meet yer boss, lassie. Would ye be able to arrange a meeting here?"

"Ah," Elaeínn mouthed. "Slight problem on that front. We were attacked – our headquarters ransacked and he could be anywhere. What doesn't help is that my identity has been compromised. And Kí— an ally of mine was abducted. I need to find her."

"Surely that's one of the dangers of yer line of work? Much like a soldier must be prepared to see his comrades lay down their lives. Yer ally made a sacrifice, and now we need yer boss's help in furthering our cause. Because if we work together, it will be mutually beneficial, I assure ye."

"I... I guess it was a risk she willingly took," Elaeínn choked. "I'll need assistance from a mage of yours – I'm incapable of magic. If you, I don't know, look inside my mind? You might be able to talk to Berri? I have no idea how this magic business works."

"Ye can grant one of our mages knowledge of the character in question – I'm assuming this Berri is yer boss," Tynak chimed in. "Should be capable of such a feat without magic – just don't resist, else it'll be mighty painful for ye."

Tynak left the room and returned shortly afterward with a relatively slim dwarf, dressed unconventionally in elven-style robes and a hood. The captain quickly briefed him in Dwarven, and the mage looked at Elaeínn for her confirmation.

"Go ahead," she proceeded.

The mage extended his hand, closing his eyes and muttering a spell. A strange, indescribable sensation enveloped

Elaeínn's consciousness, and she was almost certain the walls had begun to move when the dwarf drew back his hand and spoke first to Tynak before switching to High Elven.

"I can speak to yer Berri. As Tynak says ye've been attacked, perhaps it might be an idea for me to tell him something to make him trust me? Otherwise we risk him severing the connection before we can agree on anything."

"Tell him 'Our day draws near.'"

"As ye wish. I'll contact him now."

The dwarf closed his eyes and furrowed his brow in concentration. Beads of sweat formed along his forehead and this time, he didn't speak a word. Silence ensued for what felt like much longer than it probably was as they waited eagerly to hear the mage's response.

"We're to meet Mr Berri at the southern mouth of the Darklight. No convoy, just one dwarf with confirmation of the King's involvement. And Miss Tinaíd. If he is convinced, he will come to Rockfell."

"Then let us make haste," Tynak asserted. "My king, may I request I escort Miss Tinaíd?"

"Ye may," the King permitted. "Ritter, how energetic are ye feeling? Can ye transport these two to the Darklight?"

"I can take them as close as possible to the mouth as I've been. A little village near the forest, Glandas."

"Right away, please, Ritter. Now, I must return to the throne. Good luck, Captain Llavadi."

"Thank ye, Yer Highness."

Ritter grunted as he opened a portal revealing an unimpressive village comprising an arrangement of rundown thatch-roofed houses.

"May ye be successful in yer endeavours, Captain," Ritter encouraged.

Tynak led Elaeínn through the portal and they landed in the middle of the village, under the inquisitive gaze of a group of dwarven children as they pointed and whispered to one another.

They left the village heading north, the dark green, almost black horizon of the forest within sight. It wasn't a lengthy walk by any means and they even encountered some of the villagers on their way back, wagons laden with mushrooms, herbs, and other pickings.

"They're awful bold, these folks," Tynak exclaimed. "Walking unarmed into the Darklight? Not advisable."

"That sounds like it's coming from experience," Elaeínn noted.

"It is," the captain grunted. "Not anything I'd happily relive."

They arrived at the mouth of the forest, the beaten road continuing into its boundless reaches. A quick survey of their surroundings proved them to be alone, until Berri stepped out of the brush, having been completely concealed.

"Elaeínn, what's going on?" Berri chastised. "You gave me up to a foreigner? They could very easily go straight to Jaelaar with that."

"Except that isn't what King Kagyan has in stock for ye, Mr Berri," Tynak chided. "Let me grant ye knowledge of Castle Rockfell and we shall return to allow ye to conversate with the King himself."

"I'm not going anywhere until I get an explanation," Berri demanded. "Elaeínn?"

Elaeínn briefly summarised the events leading up to her present position, provoking numerous different reactions from the older FTA leader. But he was understanding, and under the circumstances agreed to teleport to Rockfell.

"This better not land us in trouble, Elle," Berri warned, opening a portal after having gained the knowledge of the target destination from Tynak.

Upon arrival, Berri reacted in rather a similar way to Elaeínn, his body in complete disagreement with the air quality. But as they crossed first the bridge and then the drawbridge, then manoeuvred through the series of corridors, he adjusted, much like Elaeínn had already done.

Elaeínn was made to wait while Berri spoke in the war room with the King, a conversation that lasted remarkably long. But eventually, Berri emerged, his face dressed with confidence.

"We've no need for Garaennía anymore," he beamed. "Our most generous investors are to fund an entire new settlement right next to the southern border. We'll have more than enough space. Not only that, but we'll be able to house every single member of the FTA and arm them, too. We're finally a force to be reckoned with, Elle. No longer do we have to fight from the shadows."

Elaeínn shared in her leader's joy, but there was still one thing bothering her.

"Berri, I'd like to be sent to find Kíra," she stated. "I don't know where to start, I don't know where she could possibly have been taken. But I want to find her."

"You're a free woman," Berri chimed. "Just know that you're taking a great risk if you do go to save her."

"That's one of the risks of our line of work," Elaeínn recited. "And it's a risk I'm willing to take."

"If it means that much to you, then go. But we cannot claim responsibility if you're found. And I don't know where you could possibly begin."

"Take me to Sanaíd," she requested. "I'll start at the Tyen'Aíde."

Berri flourished his arms into a circle and cursed about not opening another portal for as long as he lived.

"Good luck, Elle," he wished.

She stepped into the relatively quiet Sanaían streets and quickly surveyed her surroundings. Her first alarming sight was a group of six soldiers marching in formation from an adjoining street. Instinctually she tried to fit in, but there were so few pedestrians with whom to do so. It was however clear that these soldiers had an alternative agenda and they marched straight past without batting an eye.

Elaeínn focused on the distantly visible Tyen'Aíde and set off towards them, facing the lowering sun.

"Alright," she whispered to herself. "Let's see how this goes."

103

CHAPTER 12

"How are the preparations with the Elites coming along, Captain Llavadi?"

The King closed the door to the war room after having offered their elven visitor accommodation within the castle for the night, which he had graciously accepted. He had then been escorted away by a servant, leaving King Kagyan alone with Captain Tynak.

"I would say they're all ready, Yer Highness," Tynak confirmed.

"Ye can drop the formalities when yer just with me, Tynak," the King asserted. "Now, our little alliance with the terrorists is going to be our key to taking Tyen'Ael and Teneth. Teneth is reliant on Tyen'Ael both economically and militarily: our sources reckon they send at least three tonnes of silver in heavily guarded shipments once a month. And this means heavily – bandits have had a crack at taking on the shipments and not ever managed to take out a single escort or nab so much as a stray coin. We, however, are going to take advantage of their confidence, as confidence leads to complacency. That, Captain Tynak, is the Elites' first assignment. However, not as the Elites. Ye will be disguised. During the attack, the elves should not recognise ye as any more than another bandit raid. A bandit raid of far larger and more organised proportion.

"After our new allies cripple the foundations of stability, we will then formally declare our intentions. By which point the Elite Division will already be stationed within the new settlement we plan to establish for the FTA. Ye will have the perfect opportunity to strike swiftly at Sanaíd – they won't expect it coming and the majority of their army will be at the border, fighting off the majority of our army – more of a distraction. Have ye understood, Captain Tynak?"

Tynak nodded.

"Excellent. In which case, it will only be a matter of time before we extend our reign and take back from the elves what rightfully belongs to us. They can bugger right off back to the Eye, where their kind came from.

"So ready yer men, Tynak. The next shipment of silver is due to cross the Aeli-Tenethi border in two days' time."

CHAPTER 13

Elton stood at his desk, trying to focus on something other than the small bowl of ash-like particles which he had placed onto a nearby shelf and covered with a cloth. He was still in the process of transferring the ownership rights from the deceased owner, Rafio Benito, to himself. By this point, a sizeable portion of the spoils of the bank raid had gone into paying off various authority figures in an attempt to speed up the process.

What didn't help with being constantly distracted was when he heard a sound behind him and swiftly whirled around, unsheathing his dagger, before averting his eyes in embarrassment.

"You need to give your attackers more time, Regi," a feminine voice spoke between gasps of breath. "Now keep your eyes off until I get dressed, you old git."

"Why did you choose to come here instead of your own house?" he asked, training his eyes on the desk's surface. He reached for a goblet of wine and sipped from it.

"Thought it'd... be a laugh. Which... it was," she teased, still struggling for breath. "Don't suppose you have a... women's... section in your clothes warehouse?"

"Just teleport home and come back."

"As if I wasn't knackered enough already."

A word in a language which Elton didn't recognise and a sound like a sudden gust of wind and she was gone. Elton found a seat and took a few minutes to smoke his pipe. She then arrived once again in no longer than a quarter of an hour, this time choosing to climb the stairs. She was visibly

106

exhausted, sweat streaming down the side of her face and darkening patches of her beige linen tunic.

"Is magic really that draining? You can only manage two teleports before conking out?"

"I haven't been a sorceress for that long. You sent me to that Lazerian academy. A lot of becoming a powerful sorceress is practice and growing old."

"Right. I take it that King Hortensio didn't take to our offer very well?"

"The halfwit attacked me in his own throne room. I decided against killing him after holding my dagger to his throat."

"I suppose we can expect to be meeting him again soon. I hope he enjoys the gems. Now, Rosa, I have a problem which I think you can help me with."

"Oh really? Me? What could it possibly be?"

"Grab a seat. It's a lengthy explanation and you'll probably think me insane, but I insist that you pay full attention. Every word I'm about to say is truthful."

Through multiple goblets of wine and a lot of ridicule from Rosa, Elton completely recounted his meeting with Kalahar Kefrein-Lazalar the chaotic vampire, having painstakingly remembered the formula for the oil in particular.

"Regi, you're telling me that someone who claimed to be a vampire mysteriously appeared in your house, which was significantly colder than outside, he chopped off his hand and vaporised it? Seems a bit far-fetched, boss."

"You see this bowl?" he stood up and carefully grasped the covered bowl from the shelf. Removing the cloth reminded Regi of how frankly dull it appeared and Rosa's reaction matched his thoughts.

"I think you've had too much to drink," she drawled.

"Rosa, I told you, every word I've spoken is true. I thought you, as one of my closest associates who also contains a scrap of intelligence, would be able to help me. The magical ability is a bonus."

"How long did that geezer say it was until the next solar eclipse?"

"A month. When winter's passed."

"And he expected you to turn the Syndicate into a bunch of vampire hunters? I dunno, boss."

"We may be a guild of thieves, but I'll be damned if I let the world I inhabit be overrun by bloodsucking freaks of nature. Obviously that vampire saw something in me. He could have gone to anyone in the world. I told you about the Nightwatch; he didn't go to the elves. He came to me – the self-appointed leader of this rabble we called the Syndicate. The Syndicate thrives on the successes of others. If all the others are slain by vampires, then there is no way for us to survive. It's our duty as human beings to prolong our race's existence, and our duty as thieves to make sure there are still others to steal from."

Rosa pondered for a few moments before instantly resuming her sarcasm. "Quite a speech. Plan on giving it in front of the rest of the org? I wonder how they would take it. Why do you care, Regi? You're bloody old, surely you'll piss off in a few years anyways."

"I have my reasons to keep going, Rosa. But my reasons are my own, and I intend to keep them that way. Even if I am bloody old."

"Right, well, we can try brewing a batch of that oil, I suppose. Shall I also order for our silver storages to be melted down into swords?"

"Place an order for Thornish swords. I'm sure they've never made silver ones but whatever they come up with, it'll be a damn sight better than any smith in this wasteland can make. We're prepared to pay the price for five hundred of them."

Rosa's eyes widened and her jaw physically dropped. Any semblance of amusement disappeared from her attitude.

"Five... hundred?"

"Five hundred," Elton reaffirmed.

"You know how much that'll cost?" she ridiculed. "I know we're bloody rich, Regi, but I don't know if we could sustainably afford that."

"I'm aware of the possible expense but I'm also aware of how it won't even be enough to arm one-tenth of our entire organisation. Now go, find Master Larron and give him the order. I'm willing to pay a maximum of two hundred thousand marks for the whole order. Try and see if you can get it for less, of course. And while you're at it, visit the apothecary and see if they've got any of the ingredients we need. Meet me back here in a couple hours."

Rosa sarcastically saluted and strolled from the room. A few minutes later, Elton followed but set off in the direction of the Redhouse, accompanied by two guards which were stationed outside his front door. They arrived with no trouble and Elton paved a way through the throng of people milling around as usual.

Off in a corner, one hand occupied with cards and the other with a tankard of ale, he spotted Felix, gambling against someone he didn't recognise. It was clear from the other man's distressed expression that Felix was winning. Elton strode over and Felix's attention dropped from neither the cards nor the ale.

"Felix," Elton said.

"Yeah, boss? What you want?"

"Where's Paul?"

"Think he's out. Knowing him, he'll be at the brothel. That's where I'd check."

"Right. When did you last see him?"

"Couple hours ago." He took another swig from the tankard. "Why?"

"Doesn't matter. Which brothel?"

"His favourite is Pillared Paige's. Apparently the best value for money. His words."

"Pillared? Not even a bloody word. Sounds about right for the imbecile."

"Whatever. Your guards ought to know where it is."

Elton looked from side to side at his escort and they nodded sheepishly. He sighed and turned back towards the exit. The guards not only knew where Pillared Paige's was but also knew a number of shortcuts to reach it in the quickest time. Elton realised he shouldn't have been surprised.

The decrepit-looking building they reached bore a tilted sign above the door on which the words 'Pilared Paiges' had been scrawled.

"Best value for money, my arse," Elton muttered as he pushed open the door, which was only attached to one hinge.

He was met with a provocatively dressed woman acting as a receptionist.

"Hey, Regi," she said, lingering on the word 'hey'. "I never thought we'd get anyone quite as important as you visiting our little esat— estabil— place." Her eyes constantly fluttered as she subtly bent down to exhibit more of her chest than Elton was comfortable with.

"Paul – name mean anything to you?" he asked, fixing his eyes on her face.

"Oh, he's one of our best customers. Upstairs right now, as it happens."

"Which room?"

"First on the left once you go upstairs."

Elton stomped upstairs followed slowly by his guards, who took their time admiring the women downstairs. The sandstone stairs were visibly worn and dangerously slippery. The first door on the left wasn't actually much of a door as half of it was missing, looking as if it had been sheared off at some point. Elton pressed it open with his foot and found Paul with two nearly naked women on his lap, who constantly shared the attention of his eyes, which couldn't decide where to focus. Once they found Elton in the doorway, they fixated on him.

"Not a great time, boss," he mumbled, idly fondling one of the women's bare breasts.

"You two," he said, grabbing the attention of the prostitutes, "get out." He tossed a pouch across the room which landed on the bed with a clink. One of them grabbed it and both hurried out, covering as much of their bodies as was possible with only their arms while staring at the Syndicate leader, who didn't look amused.

"Come on, boss, they were a couple of the best I'd seen in ages!" Paul whined, putting on a shirt. "And I'd already paid 'em, so you didn't have to waste your coin."

"I've got plenty to spare. Now, I have a job for you, so come back to the Redhouse with me. I've got a lengthy story and I'll dumb it down enough for you to get it through your head."

Elton rushed from Pillared Paige's despite Paul's complaints and ignored the receptionist on the way out, who was

110

trying her best to wheedle a tip out of him. Elton grabbed him and thrust him out the door.

"You really don't listen to a word I say, do you?" Elton said as they walked through a quiet alley.

"That'll be 'cause most of the words you say are borin'", Paul retorted.

"You'll wish you listened one day. Especially if you frequent establishments of that disgusting condition."

"That I doubt very much."

When they reached the Redhouse, Elton led Paul into the basement and found a room outfitted with a rectangular wooden table and seats on three of the sides. He waved off his original escort and tossed each of them a ten-mark coin which they eagerly shoved into a pocket.

"What's all this about, then?" Paul asked.

"Well, let me tell you."

Elton recounted a much briefer, simplified version of his encounter with Kalahar Kefrein-Lazalar the chaotic vampire than he did to Rosa. Regardless, Paul still looked confused for most of the explanation's duration.

"You're tellin' me," Paul said in a bewildered tone, "that vampires are real?"

"All of the things I just told you, with vampires existing being the first of many points, and that's what you ask me about? Yes, they exist and that's not to be argued against. I told you what it did to me – that was absolutely real."

"Right, right. So you want me and the lads to teach all the boys how to fight vampires? Instead of just how to gut nobles and merchants?"

"Every member of the Syndicate who visits this building on a daily basis should be taught how to wield a sword. Which you, Felix and Jerry are in charge of."

"Right, gotcha. Not sure we've got enough swords for that."

"Use whichever we have in the armoury, steal some from the smiths around here, whatever. I've also asked Rosa to contact Master Larron and place an order for five hundred silver swords."

"Five... hundred? Five hundred Thornish swords and made from silver to boot? That'll cost a bloody load!"

"Up to two hundred thousand marks, yes. But it's a price I'm willing to pay. And don't be ridiculous, they aren't solid silver, just coated."

"Dunno what that means, but I'm guessin' it makes 'em cheaper. Whatever, as long as I still get paid."

"And go wasting it on shitholes like Pillared Paige's?"

Paul smirked. "If that's the word you would use to describe it, then yes. Though I can't say I agree."

"Well, your primary focus is on swordsmanship from now on. There are a few fencing instructors in the city – hire them. They can help you three. Make sure to tell them that the men won't be fighting humans, and make doubly sure that they understand that. Our Thornish suppliers are a reliable bunch so hopefully we'll have that shipment within two weeks' time. Meanwhile, Rosa and I will work on the alchemical side of this problem."

He rose from his seat and opened the door to leave, followed by Paul. They strolled towards the stairs which led back to the main hallway and found Felix in the same place as he had been earlier, with a significantly larger pile of coins and a new opponent.

"Oi, Felix. We've got a job," Paul announced.

"Oh, good," Felix responded. "I was getting bored here." He revealed his hand of cards to his opponent's dismay, took the pile of coins from the current betting pool in the middle of the table and shovelled them, along with the rest of his winnings, into a sack which he had brought with him.

"Where we off to, Regi?" Felix asked.

"I'm off to my house. You are going with Paul to find Jerry, and you'll get everything explained to you. Perhaps telling Paul first wasn't the best idea, but I hope he'll get the general message across."

They split and Elton grabbed two sentries from the Redhouse's exterior to act as his guards for walking back to his house. When they arrived, he paid them both a small sum and shooed them away.

When he opened the front door, he was hit with an appalling smell coming from upstairs. Then there was a small bang followed by a series of curses. Elton sighed and trudged up the stairs to the alchemy lab, where Rosa was boiling a strange

112

crimson solution among a mess of glass shards, scattered specks of blood and other, different-coloured liquids.

"You've made rather a mess of my lab," Elton remarked.

"I'm ever so sorry," she snapped, her focus not dropping from the boiling solution.

"Is that the oil we need, then? You found all the ingredients?"

"It is indeed – only a small amount, don't worry, you still have plenty of vampire dust left. Though I discovered something quite interesting when I tried experimenting – come look here."

Elton stepped closer, avoiding the shards of glass which littered the floor. He carefully rested his hands on the table after clearing an open space.

"You see, this bubbling right now isn't actually the potion with the vampire dust." She grabbed another crimson solution from a shelf above her which Elton hadn't noticed in the room's dim lighting. "But this is the real thing. Looks the same, dunnit?"

"If that's not the real thing"—he pointed to the solution bubbling above the fire—"then what is it?"

"Well, as we only have a little tiny bit of this vampire dust, I thought it would be wholly... impractical, to only have a little bit of the oil in total, given how dangerous you said this eclipse would end up being. I would've done a touch of research if it were any other type of concoction, as usually there's a fair bit of info documented about ingredients which can be swapped around, useful tips about certain things, etc. Our case is a little different, though, so I had to find things out myself. And in this case, I think I'm onto a winner. My, uh, previous attempts"—she motioned to the mess which encapsulated them—"weren't so successful. I tried swapping the dust out with oak ash, coal dust, gravel, sand, just other things with a similar texture. Then I had a thought – what things are vampires traditionally weak to in legend?"

"Don't tell me that you've put garlic in there," Elton muttered, sniffing the concoction. He wrinkled his nose in disgust and violently coughed into his elbow. It didn't smell of garlic.

"Funny you should say that, because I did try garlic. Popped to the market and found some sap who'd evidently already been robbed, so I took pity on him and paid for a couple bulbs. Grinded it into a powder, shoved it in the kiln for a bit to dry it, put it in the potion and bang – literally. That's what you can see here.

"By this point, I was close to giving up 'cause I'd used more of my blood than I was happy to, so I thought to try one more thing – aspen ash. As you may well know, not many places to buy aspen but some Salyrian merchant was pawning its bark off as having magical healing powers. I nabbed some of that, rushed back here and woe is me, I forgot to wash the garlic off my hands. Another bang. I tried again after thoroughly cleaning my hands in the basin over there and here is our result – smells just as delightfully potent as the real thing, is the same disgusting blood-red. I reckon it'll be just as effective."

Elton leaned against the wall, crossing his arms. "Well, you've outdone yourself. But Kal said in slightly different words that aspen wood is about as effective against vampires as a slap in the face. How can you be sure it's not just a fluke?"

"I'm pretty sure, judging by the fact that it shares the exact same colour and gods-forsaken stench, that it'll be just as effective."

A shiver ran down Elton's spine.

"Well, this is interesting," a deep voice spoke from behind them. Rosa whirled around and ran at the intruder who casually raised his arm, causing her to stop in her tracks.

"Rosa, stop. There's no point in attacking."

"And why's that? A wizard has broken into your house and you're telling me not to attack? I can't move, Regi!"

"That's no wizard," he said, glancing at the dark-haired, stone-faced intruder.

"Is that—" she was speechless as she turned her head to face the vampire, who cocked his head and stared at her with opulent ruby eyes.

"It is, so please, don't attack me. You couldn't harm me anyways." He dropped his arm and Rosa regained control of her limbs.

"Not even with that?" she turned and pointed at the red solution which Elton had removed from the fire.

114

"Don't make me laugh. Of course not. You really think I would freely divulge information to a human or anyone for that matter if they could use it to harm me?"

"Hold on – what's the mixture for, if it has no effect on you?"

The vampire looked at Elton, who still stood against the wall, arms crossed. "Elton Redwinter – I assume you've told her about me, then? Ah, what am I saying, I know you've told her about me. In rather remarkable detail, as well. I must admit, I was somewhat disappointed with how many details you omitted when telling that bald 'imbecile' as you referred to him."

"How do you know all of this?" Elton questioned, somewhat annoyed.

"I have my ways," the vampire stated. "Now, let me take a look at this filth you've concocted. You – Rosa, was it? – you said you replaced the vampire dust with aspen ash?"

Rosa, rubbing her hands against her arms, nodded.

"Interesting. It amazes me how much peasant nonsense turns out to actually work. Now I may have understated the whole 'doesn't affect me' thing; it does affect me. Just doesn't make me vulnerable to silver as it would a malevolent vampire. Please, pass the true concoction."

Rosa reached for the glass beaker and, shivering, handed it to Kalahar.

"Sorry, I forget how cold it gets. Afraid there's nothing I can do about that except start a fire. Actually, that's a lie. I just don't want to do anything about it. Now, this is going to hurt."

Grimacing, Kalahar poured a tiny amount of the mixture onto a patch of exposed skin and roared in pain. His upper canine teeth even elongated into wicked fangs while he doubled over, convulsing.

"Yes," he huffed. "That worked. Now, the one with the aspen ash, if you would."

This time, Elton grabbed the flask and handed it to the vampire, as Rosa shivered rapidly in the cold, the chattering of her teeth making more noise than the bubbling of the solution. Elton opened the door for her and she didn't hesitate to run to the warmth.

"I'm terribly sorry about that," Kalahar reiterated. "If I could forgo any of my abilities, that would be the one. But no matter what I do, whenever I'm in this form, I give off that unbearable chill. Unbearable for you, anyways."

"Why not shift into a different form? Seems easy enough."

"It would be terribly uncomfortable. I hated being Rafio Benito but I had to put up with it and honestly, when you came and liberated me, as disruptive as it was, it was more delightful than a sip of fine elven blood. Oh, take that expression off your face. I may be cooperating with you, but I'm still a heartless beast. I couldn't care less if she doesn't take well to the cold. I'm not sacrificing my own comfort for her benefit."

The vampire poured a small amount of the new liquid on a different patch of skin. The original patch, Elton noticed, had darkened in colour and was now closer to coal than stone. When the liquid made contact, Kalahar reacted similarly to the first test.

"I must say," the vampire coughed, "that is remarkable. I thought I would've known about this by now. Even the elves of the Nightwatch never discovered this. It's terrific! Truly terrific!"

"You are a strange fellow," Elton mused.

"And to think that some good-for-nothing human in this dusty hellscape came up with it!" Kalahar continued to himself. He stopped talking to himself and turned his attention to Elton, fiercely gripping the flask in one hand.

"It seems I was wrong, Mr Redwinter. You and your bandits have a fighting chance against the hardships to come. It still won't be easy and it was never going to be – but this has just given you perhaps the step you needed to have a fighting chance. If I were you, I'd give that young woman a holiday. She's just saved all your hides."

Rosa peeked her head round the corner, grinning from ear to ear. "Hear that, boss? The vampire says I deserve a holiday. What do you think? The eastern isles, the Salyrian forests, the Thornish mountains? So many places to choose..."

"Don't get ahead of yourself," Elton interjected. "Perhaps after we've dealt with the problem, we can talk about getaways. For now, you need to go join Paul, Felix, and Jerry in

116

swordsmanship training – primarily as a babysitter, I imagine."

"You got it, boss," she said, turning to leave the room.

"And one more thing," Elton remembered. Rosa cocked her head back and scowled.

"Buy and steal as many of the ingredients we need as you can. Order apothecaries pillaged; ransack transports coming into the city; if you feel to need to kill anyone while stealing, collect as much of their blood as possible. The world is about to witness the might of the Syndicate as they've never seen before. And to think that it's for their own protection.

"Go to the Redhouse. Give the order."

The following week, Dannos fell into a state of chaos.

CHAPTER 14

LIMARA, OCCUPIED MIRADOS

Ferris stood up and instantly resumed his bright, bubbly façade. The nobles who had given up their seat in the first place
approached and asked for signatures, having rushed off to
quickly buy quills and pots of ink, as well as high-quality
parchment. Ferris took this in his stride, glowing with happiness and enthusiasm.

Richard turned back in the direction of the Old Keep,
wanting to check on Jade's progress with the heads, but he was
mainly curious about the actual process of their creation.

It was nearing noon and the market had only grown busier,
so it was something of a struggle to make his way back to the
castle. Sanskari soldiers patrolled in pairs, completely oblivious to the hostile glares cast from most of the streets' occu-
pants. But glares were as aggressive as they were ever safely
going to act.

The streets remained busy the entire journey to the Old
Keep, though Richard noticed the increasing numbers of soldiers patrolling the areas closest to the drawbridge, which remained raised. A pair of archers stood atop the ramparts, arrows nocked. They saw Richard and called to someone below
who lowered the drawbridge.

As he crossed the moat, he could feel the venomous glares
penetrating the back of his skull. Francis was waiting on the
other side and escorted him across the courtyard, occasionally
glancing at his hands, his sword, and his bow.

"Have you fed Rosie?" Richard asked.

"Only the finest horse feed we have available. Worry not, bounty hunter, for we have just commissioned the construction of a brand new stable, so your mare may live in luxury while she remains here. Tell me, how goes your task?"

"Still gathering information while the sun is up. I'm going to go for them come nightfall. If they're still in Limara."

"For what reason would they not be in Limara? It's their home, after all."

"Oh, I guess it's just a possibility." They passed through the doorway into the castle's main lobby and ascended the stairs.

"Are you working together with Lady Jade?"

"Yes."

"She's a very capable woman. I'm surprised she was stationed here – this city doesn't have much to offer."

"Well, at least she's doing a good job."

"In fact, she's doing almost too good a job. Some of the things we would like to do to the folk here, she won't let us. If you understand me."

They reached the floor on which Jade's bedroom was situated and Francis turned around to walk back down the stairs.

Richard's sword hissed as he drew it from its scabbard and plunged it between Francis's chest plate and right shoulder plate, though it wasn't enough. He cried in pain and swore in Sanskari before drawing his own sword, longer and heavier than Richard's.

"You blasted rogue! I knew I was right not to trust you!"

He struck methodically and calculatedly, yet clumsily. His wounded shoulder made his movements slow, so Richard easily avoided his strike before returning one of his own. Francis parried and punched with his left arm, which caused Richard to stumble backwards before regaining his balance and holding his sword across his body defensively.

Francis held his sword above his head, attempting a feint, but Richard knew better. He counter-feinted by thrusting his sword forward before bringing it up to collide with Francis's. The clang of clashing metal rang throughout the hallway. Richard then used the momentum he had gained to try to disarm Francis, but he was strong and knocked him back again.

Jade burst from her room, eyes wide.

"Lady Jade!" Francis panted. "Stand aside!"

119

"Stop!" she called. Richard almost obeyed her command but instead chose to continue fighting and regain some of his lost ground. He made three quick swings, each of which Francis blocked, but only just. He feinted another swing from the right before kicking with his left foot, which caused Francis to topple backwards and crash to the floor. He still valiantly held his sword and attempted to get up but struggled, weak. Blood stained the area around their scuffle and trickled from his shoulder at an increasing rate, leaving a crimson streak down his black breastplate. A small pool began to form on the floor.

"Lady Jade, please! Do something!"

And she did. She ran towards Richard and grabbed the hand which held his sword, prying his strong fingers from its hilt. Richard struggled in response, trying to shake her but she held on tightly, aided by magic. Francis managed to regain his footing and raised his sword in one hand, removing his shoulder plate with the other. It clattered to the ground and he used the free hand to clutch the open wound which now produced a steady stream of blood, the colour draining from his face.

"Your head will decorate a spike outside this castle."

He then collapsed, losing consciousness.

"Sleep." Jade said, brushing Richard's wavy hair, which caused him to crumple to the ground, knocked out. She immediately rushed to Francis's side and began reciting healing spells, which she had never spent extensive time researching. Her basic knowledge at least was able to temporarily stop the blood flow and return colour to his face, though she still had to conventionally cauterise the wound. Luckily, he didn't wake as she heated her hand and pressed it against him, but he wouldn't stay unconscious for long. She tried to pick Richard up, but he proved too heavy for her physical capabilities so she resorted to rolling him into her bedroom, just able to push him onto the bed from the floor. Three severed heads sat on her desk, two new magically conjured heads joining the real one which she had returned to normal size. To the untrained eye, they looked exactly like real heads, just as grotesque as if they had been removed with a blade. Jade could spot some imperfections, though – the skin was unnaturally clear of blemishes in some places, the hair not dishevelled enough, the eyes lacking the same reflective qualities of real eyes. But they

120

were, without a doubt, good enough. The real question was whether they would come in use after that catastrophe of a fight. *Probably not,* she thought.

There were a number of ways through this situation. The easiest would be to partially erase Francis's memory, though memory erasing spells fell under a category of magic which was strictly forbidden by mages' codes of conduct everywhere, simply due to their potential evil applications and the horrendous nature of the spell itself. It would also mean removing the event from Richard's mind as well, and she could easily accidentally erase too much and miss learning some valuable information that he may have gained while he was out.

Another option, much riskier, would be to trick Francis into thinking he imagined the event. To do this she would need to put both him and Richard to sleep for even more time while she studied restorative and healing magic to accelerate his shoulder's recovery. The main risk wasn't Francis discovering the truth, but instead taking too long before waking him up. The rest of the soldiers would begin to suspect something was wrong if he went missing for a couple of days.

But there was also a third, easier option which would also serve to strengthen her position within Limara.

Night fell and Richard still slept. Jade had used a much more potent version of the spell and she expected he would remain completely dead to the world until first light or later. At any rate, she could forcefully wake him if the sleep lasted longer than expected. During the day's preparations, she had taken Francis into her room and painstakingly cleaned the floor of the bloodstains, leaving the stone suspiciously smooth and polished. She was ready, but still contemplative about how to go about taking him outside. It would be impossible to drag him out through the main gate and into the water without being noticed. Instead, she described a circle in the air in front of her with her hands and then pushed forward. A portal opened, showing her target destination in perfect clarity – a darkened alley just out of view of the castle. Grabbing a dagger from a drawer in her desk, she shoved Francis's unconscious body through the portal and jumped through after him.

121

It was quiet – the main roads were occupied by drunks, thugs, and the occasional patrol, but the alley was quiet.

"Kan'ze van deth los," she whispered. "Vallan ze nav les nam'fanath."

Francis jolted awake, but under the effect of a trance. His chestnut irises were drained of colour, turning ashen-grey as his pupils steadily dilated, eventually occupying the entire area of his eyes. The voids which now occupied his eye sockets reflected no light and he began to wheeze as if struggling for breath while someone pressed down on his chest. His now pale skin was darkened by streaks of black as his blood vessels changed colour. One of his armoured hands stretched forward, clawing at invisible salvation, while the other buckled under his weight, trying to keep his body propped up. Moments later, he collapsed, wildly convulsing, making far too much noise for comfort as his armour clashed with the cobbles. Jade quickly cast a muffling spell and tranquillity returned as Francis suffered in silence.

The convulsions lasted for around five minutes, before he abruptly stopped, though the physical changes exhibited on his face remained. A wispy cloud of grey mist seeped through the chinks in his armour and from the pores of his face. Jade produced a small, jagged crystal the colour of amethyst from a pouch on her belt. The mist reacted to the crystal as if alive, rushing away from it in erratic jumps, but staying near Francis's lifeless body. The crystal began to glow, producing a soft purple light, which made the mist's movements even more erratic. Jade began murmuring an incantation which further unsettled the mist, which now rapidly circled the crystal, steadily nearing though attempting to move further away, accelerating with every revolution. The distance between the mist and the crystal became so small that it travelled so fast as to appear stationary, before it was absorbed into the crystal. The crystal flared up for a moment, giving out an intense burst of light before fading, assuming its original appearance.

Jade ended the incantation and surveyed the surroundings. Nobody had noticed – not even the burst of light towards the end of the spell.

She used the dagger to slice off the cauterised scab and sat his body upright, allowing blood to spill from the new wound.

She assisted by also stabbing him in the neck and the leg. It wasn't long before a thick layer of blood coated his armour. Her work was done – she left his body to be found by the Sanskari, but not before taking the gold wedding ring from his right hand and searching for other valuables. Apparently, Francis was a very practical man, or was sensible enough to keep his dearest possessions locked away.

She turned back to the portal, still open, showing Richard fast asleep. There was no hesitation before jumping through and closing it behind her.

"Rise," she said, gesturing towards Richard. His eyes shot open and he began breathing heavily through his nose, showing signs of panic as he remained on the bed. "My bad," she muttered. "Free."

"What did you do?" he asked angrily, immediately after his mouth was able to be opened.

"I saved your life," she spat back. "I expect you to show a bit of courtesy in return. Why did you attack Francis?"

He sighed and looked away. "I was left alone with my enemy, in a position of power. I took advantage of it. Do I need to leave now?"

"No such thing will be happening. Though a new officer is required, and I don't suppose it's likely that this new one will be quite as hopeless as Francis. I will have unrestricted control over this garrison until they arrive, though, so that is a positive."

His eyes widened as he realised the gravity of her words. "You killed him?"

"First, I healed him. Then, I killed him. I had you put to sleep for the entirety of it in case you acted irrationally, which you've proven on multiple occasions to be perfectly capable of doing. You need to understand that the only way to undermine these people is to work with them – a direct affront will only lead to failure. Now, I have a new outfit for you."

She opened the wardrobe and retrieved a black linen shirt, its edges laced with red thread, as well as a black cloak complete with a hood. The finishing touch was a small red phoenix pin.

"If you want to defeat the Sanskari, you will wear these instead of your current attire. The black isn't entirely necessary, though they will appreciate the choice of colour. The badge, however, is essential. It signifies your position within the hierarchy here and grants you access to any of the garrison's supplies. Nobody should get in your way, though you might fall out of favour with the locals."

He unenthusiastically removed his hunting jacket and shirt, revealing a collection of scars decorating his chest, varying in shape and size.

"How did you get your scars?" Jade asked, walking closer.

"It's not very interesting," he began. "This one here"—he pointed to a long, thin scar running from his right shoulder to his lower back—"was from a bandit contract. Usually I manage to take them out without a scratch, but that day I was careless. I thought I had killed them all and went into the camp to collect the ringleader's head, before a young child jumped out from a tent, landing behind me. He couldn't have been older than ten. Despite his age, he was happy to wield a sword, though a small one, and managed to strike me when my guard was down. I whirled around, drawing my own sword before I realised who had attacked me. I couldn't kill him. I disarmed him with ease and told him to run off. Maybe it would have been kinder to kill him – I heard the wolves howling later that night."

"What about this one?" Jade questioned, touching a larger, oddly shaped scar on his upper right arm.

"That was a present given to me by a Corrupted. Big group of them in an abandoned hamlet. If I had to guess, it had been raided by bandits and the villagers were killed and left to convert. I took out a good number of them with my bow before running out of arrows. The remaining three or so lumbered towards me, as they do, and I couldn't have outrun them if I tried. So I drew my sword. Fighting three Corrupted in close quarters definitely wasn't something I'd ever hoped to do, but I managed to stab one through the eye before another got my arm. I drew my dagger to deal with that one and once they had fallen, I could focus on the last one, who I painfully managed to kill, but it was close. I remember collapsing after that fight and waking up a few hours later, the bite wound looking even worse than when it was fresh, and I ended up having to spend my money from the bounty on treatment. The apothecaries and medics in Mirados are extortionate, but I guess it's better than dying."

She brushed her hand delicately across his body, causing him to subtly tremble. Her hand stopped over a scar located between his two of his ribs on the left side of his body, about the width of a dagger's blade. "And this one?"

He craned his neck to be able to see it and took on a puzzled expression.

"I... I'm not sure. Most of my scars I remember getting, but I have no memory of that one. I have no idea how that happened."

"It looks like the result of a deep stab. Are you sure you don't know?"

"No... I know that sounds odd, but I really have no idea."

She withdrew her hand from his chest and allowed him to put on the shirt and the cloak. The red lace on the shirt clashed with his brown breeches, so she also gave him a black pair from the wardrobe, looking away for a moment while he quickly changed into them. Now all he needed to finish the set was a pair of black boots, which he insisted on needing to be as comfortable as his old, worn-down pair of hunting boots which were in desperate need of replacement. They agreed to visit the nearest shoemaker and order a new pair.

"From the ankles up, you look rather elegant," Jade exclaimed in admiration.

"I feel sick," Richard responded drily. "It'll get stupidly hot in this."

"But you look so dashing in black. Your hair just goes perfectly – you look the image of a vigilante. Now, put the badge on. It's not compulsory to be visible, you could conceal it on the inside of the shirt if you wish. As long as you can show it to the guards when they need to."

He followed her advice and pinned the badge on the inside of his shirt.

"You can wear your bow and quiver as you would normally, but your cloak will be draped over them. So, make sure that if you ever need to access them, you leave plenty of time between the thought of grabbing them and loosing the arrow."

"This doesn't seem very practical," he complained.

"Practicality always comes after image. Think about the most well-known people – they don't gain fame for their actions; they gain fame for their perceived actions. The King of Mirados, for example, is thought to be a kind, generous king. Why? Because he's paid great amounts of money to travelling bards to sing tales of his deeds, which are complete fabrication. I've spent time at the man's court, and he is nothing like what people think. He's emotionless, selfish, and driven by personal gain. He cares nothing for the people of his kingdom, even those like you who would die fighting for him. Similar to most kings, I suppose."

"You're committing treason by saying that."

"Speaking the truth is committing treason? Forgive me if it doesn't appeal to your narrative, but I prefer to view the world without bias. Let's not elaborate on this subject. It's only a matter of time before someone finds Francis's body tomorrow, and then we'll have to deal with that. It's grown late. Let's go to sleep."

Richard walked towards the door, ready to go to the room which Francis had first designated him upon arrival to the castle but into which he hadn't yet even been.

"Richard," Jade said as he grasped the door handle. He turned around.

"Stay."

He obliged without hesitation.

CHAPTER 15

After having quickly paid a visit to Kíra's empty house for supplies and a change of clothes, using a spare key she had been given when Kíra had first purchased the property, Elaeínn reached the side entrance to the Tyen'Aíde. It had been installed for use by politicians who didn't want the attention of entering through the main entrance, and therefore saw more use during peak times than the main entrance. Unfortunately for her, though deserted by politicians, it was still guarded by two sentries.

"Help me!" she cried, running towards the sentries. She feigned a stumble and reached the guards, who had drawn their swords and watched her apprehensively.

"The FTA! One of the traitors!" she cried with a convincing layer of anguish. "They just tried to attack me!"

The guards looked at each other wordlessly and one of them turned and jogged in the direction from which Elaeínn had arrived. The other, however, stayed diligently watchful.

"I, uh, I don't know if you're the right person to ask," she began, looking at the expressionless guard, who stared straight ahead. "I've always wanted to look around the Houses. Would you... be able to show me?"

The guard, as she had expected, retained the appearance of a statue.

"Listen here." She looked the guard in the face, changing her tone. "I've wanted to look inside this place for my whole life. Can't you just tour me?"

"Our day draws near," the guard spoke quietly.

127

Elaeínn's eyes expanded as the guard allowed her to pass, shielding her from view as he did so.

The Houses seemed to be mostly abandoned and she was able to traipse through the blue-carpeted halls without overwhelming fear of capture. But at no point did she drop her guard.

She reached the room normally occupied by legislation writers. It was empty and unlocked. She graciously entered.

It was Tyen'Aeli tradition since the founding of the democratic system that new legislation passed in the year was announced in a king's address. That day was upcoming, which meant almost a year's worth of legislation went unknown by the public. She was curious to have a look beforehand.

As could have been expected, bound scrolls were meticulously organised according to date in a filing cabinet designated for only the current year's legislation. Once the year had passed, they would be moved to storage elsewhere in the Houses where they would be left to collect dust, but still meticulously organised.

She first reached for something at random from early in the year – the note attached to the binding on the scroll read *January 31st, 2M220*. Elaeínn removed the binding and briefly skimmed over the contents of the *High Elven Union Ascension of Power Act*, detailing the new sovereignty of Elven Union law over Tyen'Aeli statute, which Elaeínn took to mean as Tyen'Aeli dominance of Tenethi and Tyen'Ardi law. According to the little wording that she did bother with reading, she appeared to be mostly correct.

The next few scrolls she skimmed over were equally uninteresting and of varying importance. Then she opened one labelled *November 29th, 2M220*.

"The Military Expansion Act," Elaeínn whispered to herself, unravelling the parchment. "Additional thirty thousand soldiers to be conscripted... investment in destructive and restorative trees of magic... new military tax to be levied on every citizen at one aerrin per month to provide funding for the purchase of new, progressive siege weapons and cavalry... what the bloody hell? This is a clear breach of the terms of the Peace Treaty..."

128

She bound the scroll and placed it in her satchel, not overly worried about maintaining its exquisite condition.

Satisfied with the find, she left the room and continued skulking through the barren corridors of the Tyen'Aíde. She climbed the stairs to a corridor which acted as a viewing platform of the Common Chamber. The empty blue seats were eerily ominous, and she was cautious about how abnormally loud her careful footsteps seemed to sound in the emptiness of the House. She stopped for a moment to look through the enormous window occupying the entire wall opposite the horseshoe arrangement of seats, observing the waves of people heading home in the sunset.

She snapped to attention and withdrew from the rail on which she had briefly rested, realising she had allowed her guard to momentarily drop. She needed to find more – a single piece of legislation about an expansion of the military wasn't going to be of any use in finding Kíra.

Having already studied a floorplan of the entire complex, it didn't take long to navigate to the open Common Chamber. The window wall made her feel extremely exposed, so she took as little time as possible sprinting, head lowered, to the largest seat on the right hand of the horseshoe, designated for the leader of the largest party.

On the podium were a number of pieces of parchment, which Elaeínn roughly grabbed without first scanning over before running back to cover. Taking shelter behind a door, she strained her eyes to read the almost unintelligible handwriting, hindered by the dimming light. But she managed to start piecing it together.

"Recall the Nightwatch for deployment in two weeks' time... what the hell is the Nightwatch? Delay shipment of financial aid to Teneth by one week... what do the Tenethi need with our silver? Tayannan delegation to arrive in Kaelestia by mid-week... not of much use to me... expedition team set to dispatch by beginning of next week... expedition?"

She added the papers to her satchel and swore, coming to the realisation that the operation in which she and Kíra had been abducted was too confidential even to be a matter of the party. It must have been a personal order, no matter if Jaelaar's party would have supported it, which she suspected they would have done. Alongside the subordinate minority parties.

She formulated a new plan as she crept back through the ornately decorated wooden halls and found her way back to the side entrance both sentries were outside again, but she managed to grab the attention of the mole and he was then able to distract his cohort, allowing her a moment to slip outside.

The Regal Guard, the city's official security force, was headquartered within the Serenna Palace, which presented the first obstacle to the completion of her plan. The Serenna Palace was the most heavily guarded structure in Sanaíd, and unlike the side entrance to the Tyen'Aíde, there would be more than two guards. That left the option of blending in. But for that, she would have to wait, as the gates closed in the evening.

She visited Kíra's house again and stayed there overnight, taking more of her friend's supplies and clothes that she was sure she wouldn't mind her using.

And she waited.

*

She awoke in the morning to the sound of marching and the loud cries of what turned out to be generals, after briefly looking out of the window. The generals were in turn directing hordes of uniformed soldiers, brandishing swords. Behind those in heavy metal armour were what must have been mages, in much more traditional clothing.

The spectacle lasted for at least half an hour, which she spent couped up in Kíra's bedroom, unconfident to go onto the streets while they were there. Eventually, the soldiers cleared the area and she left.

Apart from the morning's unexpected military parade, the day proceeded as could have been expected from then. Elaeínn had no trouble walking to the palace, situated at the very centre of the city, and utterly unmissable.

For the second time since returning to Sanaíd, she was in luck, as the palace gates were wide open and allowing a constant flow of civilians inside. She simply merged with the crowd, and, without even batting an eye at the two guards either side of the entrance, she made it inside.

At least, she had made it inside the walls. She now had to walk through the extensive palace gardens with the crowd, who were taking an irritatingly long time admiring the exotic flora, imported to the country over centuries, maintained and replanted by the gardeners. The Issalandish cherry trees had blossomed for the second of two times in the year, basking the sky in bright pink. Many of the flowers, primarily from Tayanna, home of the light elves, the dwarven kingdoms and insignificant neighbouring islands, were also in bloom, decorating the beds with explosions of deep indigo, vibrant scarlet, bright yellow and every conceivable colour in between. It was a wonder to behold.

But not her reason for being there. That was why she was relieved when the iron-studded wooden palace doors finally came into view and were pulled open by another pair of guards. After a crew of eight guards appeared from within the palace, she suddenly wasn't so relieved.

"We are about to carry out a mandatory search of each person willing to enter the palace," one of the guards boomed. "Please do not resist – it is for your own safety. We request that anyone wearing a hood or cowl remove it so we may view your faces."

Elaeínn contemplated a number of options, including running back through the gardens and running through the blockade and into the palace. As the guards stationed themselves to efficiently search every visitor, she decided against both options and warily lowered her hood, undoing her braid and tucking her hair inside the neck of her robes.

"Your name, please?" the guard said when it came to be her turn to be inspected.

"Delía Hatten," she provided.

The guard quickly noted something down on his clipboard, presumably the given name, and then quickly patted her down. He stopped upon reaching the sides of her chest, feeling the hard outline of her knife.

She blew past the guard and immediately triggered a caucus of alarmed cries. The crowd who had been successful in entering the palace provided excellent cover and she swerved through them, ducking low so as to avoid line of sight with the guards. As she was now inside the palace, she raised her hood and continued running through the swarm of visitors.

"Everyone on the floor, now!" one of the guards cried. The crowd complied without contemplation, including Elaeínn. Her heart pounded as their heavy footsteps engulfed the crowd, who were perhaps as terrified as she was.

Her restricted field of view provided only a view of the time-worn marble floor and fractions of the people cowering next to her. As the rattling of metal armour drew nearer, she reached her arm into the pocket on the left side of her robes and fondled the handle of her knife, its blade retracted.

The physical position of the trembling woman to her left gave her an idea after she quickly glanced up to notice the guards searching everyone once more.

She pulled her knife from her pocket, flicked open the blade and slid it gently towards her neighbour, where it settled next to the woman's loose-fitting robes, draped across the floor. As she had hoped, one of the guards noticed the blade as their search moved towards them and they violently dragged her up, at which point she screamed in terror.

Elaeínn realised at that point how helpful it was that she and the woman shared a remarkable resemblance to one another.

The woman was dragged away, crying about her innocence, which fell upon the guards' deaf ears. They confiscated the knife, which was inconvenient. It would also mean having to plead the blacksmith into making her another.

The guards signalled that the event was finished, and she rose with the crowd, brushing the dust from her robes and straightening them. Then she made a beeline for the Regal Guard.

It was the first of two areas she hoped to visit and was far easier to access than the second location she had in mind, as it was open for tours. All she had to do was quite simply join the group of other visitors who had beaten her there and wait for a guard to guide them through the complex.

She didn't pay much attention to the guard's rambling about the history of the Regal Guard – or something along

132

those lines. The people she walked alongside seemed unbelievably fascinated by the collections of identical interrogation rooms, meeting rooms, storage rooms and many more arbitrary, uninteresting rooms.

They approached a corner and Elaeínn used the opportunity to hang back from the group and she slipped away, unnoticed, as the tour continued onwards. They had just passed a particular door which caught her attention, bearing a brass label reading *Record Storage* and then one below that reading *STAFF ONLY*.

She twisted the brass doorknob and crept inside. The heavy silence was rapidly uncomfortable, and she felt the same sense of dread as she had before in the Tyen'Aíde. Except this time, she knew there were people around.

The room was occupied only by a number of large filing cabinets, inside which were a collection of pitifully boring, extraordinarily detailed reports and records, as was implied by the name of the room. As was custom with the High Elves, the records were sorted neatly by date. Hoping to find a record relating to Kíra's abduction, she began searching the records from the drawer labelled *December 2M220*.

After a panicked ten minutes of skimming through various legal documents, she accepted that her efforts were in vain. It was clear that whoever was behind their capture, she would not find out about in the Regal Guard or the Tyen'Aíde – the only places where official, governmental documents were stored. Jaelaar wasn't behind the capture.

Unless the capture wasn't to go on record.

Elaeínn returned to the door and listened carefully, her heart pounding. She heard only the heavy footsteps of armoured guards marching through and the softer footsteps of clerks and other staff on their way to do something other than file a report – at least, that's what Elaeínn deduced from the fact that she wasn't discovered. She breathed a silent sigh of relief when she heard the horde of footsteps meaning the tour had returned and slipped almost invisibly from the room, rejoined the group, and left.

On their way out, they observed the woman Elaeínn had framed, in tears, being interrogated in one of the chambers. She heard a number of derogatory whispers primarily from the older elves and stifled a scowl. Their tour guide wasn't keen on allowing too long for observation and quickly ushered the group towards the exit, but not before quickly glancing himself through the soundproof window.

Her next option was the trickiest, as it involved access to an area certain to be out of bounds. The area being the residence of the Prime Minister of Tyen'Ael – an entire section of the palace dedicated specifically to Jaelaar, his predecessors and his successors.

She set off across the lobby, keeping a close eye on the guards stationed periodically around its perimeter. Then, when she thought nobody was looking, she darted through the corridor leading to the western wing of the palace.

It led to a door, which was, unsurprisingly, locked. This is where Elaeínn had talents which other elves lacked – she couldn't open a door by magic, but with a lockpick, nothing stood in her way.

Thirty seconds later, she had it open. The lock was underwhelmingly easy to break through – clearly, the palace's security hadn't been updated in centuries. Which was believable – there was never any threat of trespass until recently. But she was still astounded by the lack of guards.

She tiptoed into a chamber which acted as the Prime Minister's personal lobby and it occurred to her that he might very well be within the palace at the current moment. In fact, she thought it likely, and she hoped it to be the case.

Another door led to an opulently decorated bedroom – an enormous carved wooden bed draped with an immaculately neat blue silk duvet, a silver chandelier topped with fake candles emitting magical light, an expansive wardrobe outfitted with a variety of expensive clothes.

She quickly searched the bedside cabinets and came up empty. At one point, she accidentally knocked a book from one of the cabinets and it slammed to the ground dramatically loudly, spurring her heart into a sprint. But nobody arrived to arrest her, and she calmed down and continued.

Before she entered the Prime Minister's office, she decided first to obtain a weapon. A ceremonial sword on a plaque above the fireplace proved excellently convenient. The symbol-etched blade was still surprisingly sharp and the textured, moulded golden hilt fit remarkably comfortably in the shape of her hand.

She slid through the door to the office and raised her sword, cutting the air with a metallic hiss. But there was nobody inside and she was free to place the blade on the desk while she examined the strewn pieces of parchment.

And once again, she was defeated by a lack of information.

"Shit!" she whispered aggressively, clenching one of the papers in her fist and allowing it to drop to the floor.

She picked up the sword and held it weakly as she traipsed back into the bedroom.

"I wasn't expecting company at this time."

CHAPTER 16

Through night and day, shadows crowded the streets. Shadows which broke down doors, harvested blood, slaughtered swallows, built bonfires with aspen wood, ransacked carts coming from the East and the West. The usual busy market was raided in full. After that, no merchants were brave enough to attempt to pawn off their goods, no matter where from.

The ingredients were kept in a storage cellar in the Redhouse, organised into large containers. The desert heat was repelled by the magical abilities of Rosa Feranimor who, along with learning to wield a sword, had been practicing vigorously as a sorceress. Without her, the ingredients would have quickly rotted. The containers' capacities were significantly filled with every day as Elton Redwinter watched over the city from the front balcony of the Dawn Bank, having been officially recognised as Lyrio Benito, the younger brother of Rafio Benito.

Kalahar Kefrein-Lazalar hadn't been seen throughout the duration of the week, but Elton knew he was watching. Whether it was the occasional chill which ran down his spine or the times where he would wake up at midnight drenched in a cold sweat.

"How much of the grease can we make with all this?" Elton asked Rosa, who stood in the refrigerated cellar alongside him. He lifted one of the lids of the containers to reveal it was filled to the absolute brim with aspen ash. Another container couldn't even completely close as it was overfilled with whale fat.

"By my reckoning, a bloody lot," Rosa replied confidently. "Enough to kill a Salyrian army's worth of bloodsuckers."

"How has the swordsmanship training gone?"

"There's been plenty of complaining from the lazy ones, which is most of them, but they're all in order. All it takes is to remind them who gave the order and who pays them."

A scruffy young boy burst through the door, out of breath. Elton and Rosa turned their attention to him as he regained the ability to speak.

"Mr Regi, sir, I come bearing news from the western Trail. It's not good sir, not good at all."

"Well, spit it out, then," Elton ordered.

"It's the Salyrians, sir, they're killing all our men stationed on the Trail. Even the ones who don't make a move on them, sir. If they see a Syndicate badge or emblem then they slaughter 'em, sir."

"And why are they doing that?"

"Well, my negotiations didn't go swimmingly, may I remind you," Rosa said.

"It's the King's orders, sir. He's riding with them, sir."

"And why are they riding on the Trail?"

"I wish I could tell you, sir, but they're coming this way. That's all I know, sir."

Elton grimaced and looked at the floor. "How far away are they?"

"If they are indeed coming to Dannos, sir, I reckon they're about half a day's march away based on what I've been told, sir. They don't show any signs of stopping, sir."

"It seems I was right, then. I suspect he'll start his conquering of Temerios with our free city. Though Rosa, if you end up with your dagger to his throat again, don't hesitate to open it this time. I assume this new king is some snotty little brat who never actually served as a knight?"

"He was young enough," Rosa supplied. "I'd say late teens, early twenties. Irritatingly handsome. And yeah, from the rumours I heard from merchants, tavernkeepers and the likes, it seems our King Hortensio is a bastard. Nobody knows his mother or father, for that matter. The story goes that a peasant woman from Heathervale found him in a basket at the side of the highway and took him back to the village. That

137

peasant woman raised him until he was old enough to become a squire in the capital but apparently he was banished when he was only thirteen for treason. For most people that would've meant hanging but Hortensio got away with exile thanks to old Valkard's softness. Then he came back one day and chopped old Valkard's head off in his own throne room."

"However much of that is true, I don't want to guess. But it seems reasonable. I take it we won't be able to reason with him when he stomps his shiny cavalry past the gates?"

"That won't happen. If I were you, Regi, I'd have us go into hiding until he gives up. Would certainly be the safest move."

"Or we could eliminate the biggest— second biggest threat to stability in the continent. The Benetian Civil War was bad enough for trade in the North but this lunatic will plunge everything into chaos."

"If he's marching with an army, we stand no chance. Especially not against knights of Camelion. You forget, Regi, we're a bunch of nobodies. Just a lot of them."

"And that will be what gives us an advantage," Elton said smugly. "Allow this Hortensio to find the Redhouse. There will be nobody there. But the Syndicate is always watching. Watching for just the right moment to let loose an arrow or a throwing knife which embeds itself in his skull."

"So, basically, my plan but a bit looser. Works for me."

"In that case, let's go upstairs."

Elton generously tipped the message boy, to which he responded with glee and numerous thankyous. He and Rosa then made their way upstairs, noting that every Syndicate henchman they passed was equipped with a sword at their belt, although each person seemed to have a different variety.

Paul, Jerry, and Felix were found in the training yard – a large, open, stone-floored area behind the main hall where primarily straw-stuffed dummies had been set up for swordsmanship training. One of the walls had also been fashioned into a fake building exterior to practice climbing. In the corner was a pile of broken pieces of wood and a target, which would have once been used for marksmanship practice. Though among the ranks of the Syndicate, someone carrying a ranged weapon other than a throwing knife was about as common as an honestly earned coin. There were plenty of bows, crossbows, arrows, and bolts in the Redhouse's armoury, but they usually remained untouched.

The training yard was crowded with people practicing a defensive fighting style, guided by five instructors who stood in front of Paul, Jerry, and Felix.

"It seems to me that they've forgotten the part about not fighting humans. For god's sake, they're practicing parrying now! I need a word with them three," Elton stated.

"You alright, boss?" Jerry asked upon Elton's approach.

"No, not really. We've got a bit of a situation on our hands. Do you remember when the City Guard marched on the Redhouse a few years back? They used all their resources on trying to root us out of Dannos once and for all, and were nearly successful as well."

"Of course we remember. I killed the Captain of the Guard!" Felix responded.

"Yes, that was a bloody good move. Well, we've another, similar problem of far grander proportion. One which we won't be able to deal with as simply as sending in a boy with a shiv. The Salyrian army is marching on Dannos."

"You what? What are those honourable freaks doin' comin' 'ere?" Paul ridiculed. "With their fancy knights an' everythin'?"

"According to the message boy, yes. It seems like a full-fledged invasion force. And, uh, some more info about it. They'll be here before sundown."

Paul, Jerry, and Felix all broke out into uninterrupted, imperceptible speech, trying to shout over one another. This grabbed the attention of not just the people training in the courtyard but also the instructors, who stopped sparring and turned around just to observe the commotion.

"Alright, you lot," Elton called to everyone in the yard. "A Salyrian invasion is on their way to this very city and it's likely that their only objective is to defeat the Syndicate after our failed negotiations. We cannot meet them in battle, so our only option is to hide. The Redhouse is to be deserted; every room locked, every vault sealed. All symbols which could finger you as a member of the Syndicate are not to be worn or displayed in any way. If a clear path to kill King Hortensio of

Heathervale reveals itself, we will not hesitate to walk it. Otherwise, we remain in the shadows until the impatient young bastard grows bored of searching and moves on."

His announcement was met with a murmur of assent throughout the crowd and frantic glances between the instructors.

"We go into hiding from now. Go, spread the word to the rest of the Syndicate in Dannos and allow no one to be slain by a Salyrian blade."

The crowd all sheathed their swords in relative unison and dispersed. As Elton and his seniors walked through the Redhouse, it seemed that everyone was having a conversation about the event to come. Many were discussing their plans on obtaining a Salyrian sword, which Elton dismissed as foolish nonsense. *If they wish to get themselves killed, let them,* he thought.

Within the hour, the building was deserted except for the occasional rat. The main hall could still be accessed through the open entryway but any areas requiring a door to be passed were inaccessible without a key or brute force. There were no sentries outside the compound – instead, they watched from a Syndicate-owned apartment complex across the street. The members of the City Guard which were loyal to Elton were also informed of the coming mission and told to do everything in their power to mislead the Salyrian King.

"Y'know, boss, I dunno if it's the best idea you've had to hide out in your own house," Paul said. The five of them were watching from the window of Elton's study on the top floor of his house. Usually, it would be alive with both merchants and members of the Syndicate. Instead, neither were to be seen, as the merchants were too afraid to leave their homes after the week-long pillaging.

"If everything goes according to plan, then there will be no way for him to know that I live here. And if he does find out, then what's he going to do? Send in the cavalry? I trust in you four to do a good enough job of protecting me."

Felix smirked and twirled one of his expensive knives on a finger, lazily slouched on a wooden chair.

"Yeah, but what if he chucks a bomb through the window? That'll kill us all without a fuss," Jerry suggested.

"They're knights, not smart. Their first priority is honour and glory, which involves a one-on-one showdown in which one of the combatants provides an excellent display of their valour or whatever. They don't use bombs."

"Eh, I dunno, boss. Didn't that Hortensio geezer decapitate Valkard in his own throne room? And apparently his men used crossbows to kill the King's Guard, who didn't stand a chance."

"I'm hoping he wouldn't compromise traditional Salyrian values in favour of his massive ego. But you make a valid point."

The next few hours were dull and uneventful. They all attempted to find something with which to amuse themselves, which included an alchemy tutorial on behalf of Elton and Rosa. At first they tried to demonstrate the basics, but gave up and instead just created a potion with the most dramatic-looking reactions between the ingredients, which went down far better than the informative lesson. After that, Felix bragged about his skill with the throwing knives and they drew a crude target on Elton's wall with a piece of chalk. Felix hit the bullseye every time and even allowed Paul and Jerry to try his knives, though only the plain Thornish blades. He wouldn't allow anyone to so much as breathe near the decorated Kinan ones.

Eventually, the city's silence was broken by the loud echoing of a horn from the direction of the West Gate. The group of five immediately stopped what they were doing and gathered at the window, eagerly peering through the shutters. It seemed to the merchants that the Salyrians' arrival meant the streets would be safe to return to and they flooded the streets to quickly set up stalls in Silverstone Square. It didn't take long for lowlifes to arrive soon after, though none which found their places within the Syndicate.

Rhythmic clops sounded from down the street, rising in volume as the knights drew closer atop their snow-white mares. It was clear that the large crowd which arrived in Silverstone Square was merely a detachment, as the King was nowhere in sight. Instead, they were led by a helmetless man who otherwise looked identical to the men trailing behind him. They stopped in the square and called out to gain the attention of the merchants. The helmetless man began shouting something which they couldn't hear from their current location.

"Rosa – can you, like, make him louder or something? Is there some way you can let us hear him?" Elton asked.

"Afraid I dunno how to do that yet, bossman," she responded.

"I'll go and listen," Felix said. "After all, the best way to hide is to blend in, right?" He jogged from the room and could be heard running down the stairs. A moment later, the four which were left in Elton's study observed Felix jogging towards the square, where the helmetless knight had finished shouting and was now instead talking to individual merchants at their stalls.

They watched as Felix went over to one of the merchants and had a brief exchange with them, after which he went and talked to the knight.

"What the bloody hell is he doing? I thought he was gathering information, not talking to them. What happened to blending in?" Elton scorned, scowling.

"Maybe he's tryin' to throw 'em off," Paul suggested.

"The only thing he'll achieve by talking to them is letting them recognise him in the future. That's if they don't take him in as— shit!"

They watched in horror as the helmetless knight drew his sword and placed its tip against Felix's throat, as he dropped to his knees and raised his hands above his head. Even in that position, it looked as if he was still talking. The knight allowed him to stand but placed the tip of his sword against Felix's back, barked an order and Felix began to walk from the square in the direction of Elton's house, hands still above his head. They then turned away and went along a different street in the direction of the Redhouse, which is where Elton assumed Felix was leading them.

"We have to follow him. He's expecting them to act like a Dannosi citizen, but the Salyrians are a different breed. He's going to get himself killed."

"Looks to me like they already expect something of him. I'll go, boss, you should stay here," Rosa said. "Salyrian or not, they're still men. As long as they've got a cock, I can have my way with them."

"A good thought, but have you forgotten what they're like? They'll see a woman dressed in something other than a maid's long dress and instantly assume the worst. You look like the picture of an undesirable rogue, Rosa."

"How sweet of you. I'm going."

"Then I'm goin' too," Paul added.

"I may as well," Jerry said, before noticing Elton's icy glare. "On second thought, I'll stay here. Or Rosa could stay here, as you said she wouldn't be a very good idea— and she's gone."

Rosa had indeed quickly run from the room, leaving the door swinging on its hinge. Paul was quick to follow.

"I suppose I am a tad older than them," Jerry said, shrugging. They peered through the shutters as the last of the Salyrian knights exited the square, casually followed by Paul and Rosa who appeared to be putting on a great impression of a young couple, arms linked and feigning friendly conversation. They all disappeared in the direction in which Felix had gone and the sound of the horses' hooves against the cobbles grew quieter. They opened the shutters and allowed light to flood the previously darkened study.

Elton and Jerry stayed there for an extended period of time, periodically checking outside for further developments. They spotted the occasional patrol accompanied by City Guards, some of which they assumed were fulfilling their orders to mislead the knights. This assumption was reaffirmed when they saw the same patrols crossing through the same streets, led by guards which confidently strutted between insignificant market streets and unknown back alleys.

The sun's light was dimming when they finally caught a glimpse of a bald man jogging towards Elton's house. He was alone. Elton and Jerry both assumed the worst and rushed downstairs to unlock the door and undo the many latches. Paul slammed against the door and leaned against his knees, completely out of breath.

"It's... it's the King!" he wheezed. "They took Felix to him an'... managed to get Rosa as... well..."

"How did you get away? How did they get Rosa and not you? Where did they take them?" Elton interrogated.

"The City Guard... that crazy git strolled in an' slaughtered the Captain of the Guard... before he could even say 'ello! He's taken over the City Guard for his own use now and he's claimin' to be the new King of Dannos."

"And he's taken Rosa and Felix there? Why?"

"Someone ratted 'em out, boss. Obviously they didn't know that much otherwise you would've had the knights comin' to your door."

"You're telling me that some fucking peasant pointed at them and cried 'Syndicate'? And they took them away?"

"These aren't the good-hearted knights we thought they would be. They're bein' much meaner and harsher than any knight in the past ever was. I think it's to do with this Hortensio geezer, he must've sacked all the old ones and got his mates to wear their armour and be at his beck an' call."

They once again heard the distinctive clopping of hooves coming into Silverstone Square. It was another patrol, larger than the previous and led by another helmetless knight who, if he wasn't clad in decorated iron armour and bearing the Salyrian coat of arms on a shield hanging from his horse's saddle, they would have thought to be a local, as he looked like the male equivalent to Rosa. They stopped alarmingly close to Elton's house to address the crowd, after ordering them to be silent.

"Elton Redwinter! I hope you are listening, for we know of your presence here. We have two of your associates in captivity and they are currently enjoying the full extent of the array of torture implements we inherited from the guards. So far, they've had some very interesting things to say," he boomed.

"You don't think they ratted us out, do you?" Jerry asked, clearly concerned.

"They couldn't have. They wouldn't," Elton responded with relative confidence.

"Please, give yourself up and leave your home or we will be forced to search every one. The citizens have been kind enough to give us a full description of your decrepit appearance, so the only thing left for you is to willingly come with us, or your friends will taste steel in their hearts instead of their joints. You will not be killed immediately, for the gra-

144

cious King Hortensio of Heathervale, first of his name, Kings-layer and Saviour of Salyria would like to share a word with you beforehand. Now, you have until the contents of this hourglass drain into the bottom before we find you by force."

The tanned man with curly, hickory hair cut above his shoulders revealed a small hourglass in which they couldn't see the contents. He made a show of turning it upside down and looking confident.

"We need to go."

CHAPTER 17

LIMARA, OCCUPIED MIRADOS

Richard and Jade awoke the following morning to the sound of shouting in the courtyard, followed by the frantic creaking of the drawbridge's cogs. Simultaneously, they rose from bed and didn't bother with getting dressed, instead choosing to peer through the thin window above the desk. A group of soldiers stood in the middle of the courtyard while another two dragged a body across the drawbridge before it was promptly raised again. The group jogged over to look at the body and stepped back in revulsion, though Jade thought she noticed a hint of elation on a few of their faces.

"Report to Lady Jade!" one of them called, and two of the other soldiers rushed towards the castle.

"That's my cue," Jade sighed, pulling on a black robe from the wardrobe, decorated with the same red lace as Richard's shirt. Unlike Richard, she wore her pin facing outwards.

No more than ten seconds after pulling on his boots, there was a banging at the door. Jade sauntered over and opened it to find the two expected soldiers, on their knees, out of breath.

"I'm sorry... to intrude... my lady," one panted. "We found Francis in an... alley... near the castle. He was murdered. You will want to look at the body – something strange has happened."

"Lead the way," she ordered, gesturing Richard to follow.

The soldiers turned around and marched at a much more relaxed pace towards the stairwell, descending them at an even slower pace. They arrived at the courtyard and the crowd around Francis's body had grown, with nearly every soldier in the garrison trying to look.

146

"It would appear to just be an attack with a dagger – he was stabbed here"—he gestured to Francis's neck—"here"—he gestured to Francis's shoulder—"and here"—he pointed to his leg. "We've sent a detachment of soldiers to search for any clues, but the most concerning discovery is this." The soldier then leaned over and raised Francis's eyelids to reveal his expanded pupils. By this point, the dark streaks had disappeared.

"Good work, soldiers," Jade stated. "Do any of you have any idea what happened?"

"I've never seen anything like it in my life," one of them said. "He must have been possessed by a demon! Certainly looks evil!"

"Or," Jade countered. "Francis here could have a secret. Shall we check his quarters?"

The soldiers followed without question. Francis's room was found with the rest of the soldiers' sleeping quarters, though slightly more luxurious. The door was locked, so one of the soldiers rushed off to find the master key and upon his return, she opened the door to unveil a well-equipped alchemy laboratory, complete with a collection of exotic ingredients.

"That would explain it," Jade stated. The other soldiers looked shocked, mouths agape.

"A blasted alchemist!" one of them finally found the ability to speak. "He was a witch! Or a... err... witchman! We've had people burned at the stake for this!"

"It does appear that way," Jade calmly said. "Remind me, where did you find him?"

"A local found him, my lady. They found the body and told Darryl and Luca, who took him back to the castle. He was in a dark alley in between the rows of houses just visible from the drawbridge. It's all very confusing, my lady, because he was never reported to have left."

"Alchemists are capable of many feats, including teleportation," she explained. "I imagine he will have done that. If I had to guess, Francis had some dubious business outside of the castle to attend to and leaving via the drawbridge wasn't an option. He will have taken a night vision potion to avoid using a torch, which caused his pupils to dilate to the size they are now. Then whoever he was meeting probably killed him. The price of disloyalty."

147

"Beg my pardon, my lady, but how do you know so much about alchemy?"

"I've had a formal education, my dear, which included learning about things which are illegal to practice. It's beneficial to know about things that others would do, even if you would not."

The soldier nodded and stepped back sheepishly.

"That would conclude our investigation, then," Jade dictated. "As advisor to this garrison, I claim sovereign control of this castle and the city it inhabits. Everyone, back to your posts. Send out another five detachments, each with ten men. We will find Francis's murderers, even if they were doing us a service in eliminating a traitor."

The soldiers saluted in unison and marched back out to the courtyard, organising fifty soldiers into groups, who then left the castle in opposite directions, ready to scour the city. The castle was left relatively undefended, as many soldiers were already patrolling the streets on guard duty. Around twenty remained in charge of guarding the castle itself.

Twenty became nineteen when a crossbow bolt found itself between a guard's eyes.

They fell from the rampart with a metallic clattering and the remaining guards burst into rehearsed battle plans and the drawbridge was immediately raised as a few more crossbow bolts made their way over the walls, not finding a target.

"They're crossing the moat!" one of the soldiers shouted from atop the ramparts. "They've got ladders!"

"And we have archers. Kill them!" Jade rasped.

Half of the soldiers retrieved a bow from the courtyard's weapon rack, also carrying buckets full of arrows. They lined up along the rampart and began to trade arrows and bolts with the attackers, who had begun to place long wooden boards across the moat. Once the boards were placed, more invaders appeared with ladders. Slowly, the Sanskari forces were depleted as, one by one, the invaders' crossbow bolts landed in the archers' heads. This gave plenty of opportunities to place ladders against the outer walls, which they did, and began to climb onto the rampart.

"Someone sound the blasted horn!" Jade hollered, temporarily dropping her consistent formality. One of the infantrymen sprinted away and moments later, the thunderous boom of the invasion horn was heard across the city.

Another soldier rushed over to Richard and Jade. "My lady, it would be in your best interests to find shelter. We cannot hold them off for much longer – there's not enough time for the rest of the soldiers to arrive. His message was reinforced by the first of the invaders' foot soldiers leaping over the parapet. They were dressed in a light leather tunic with steel plates on their arms and legs, face covered by a mask concealing everything beneath their eyes. A thin rapier hung from their belt, which also displayed a small badge bearing a blue coat of arms decorated with two silver roses entwined around a golden rose. More ascended the ladder, outfitted the same as the first and they all drew their rapiers, menacingly advancing on the remaining Sanskari archers. They valiantly continued to defend their positions, even until the point where their bows were knocked from their hands, before being slain, bodies thoughtlessly shoved into the courtyard.

"My lady, you really must retreat!" the soldier affirmed, drawing his own sword and rushing off to join the remaining infantrymen, who were outnumbered by the countless invaders climbing over the parapet. Jade grabbed Richard by the arm and motioned towards the keep but they were cut off by three invaders who had climbed into the castle over the wall adjacent to the main structure. They were surrounded. The Sanskari footsoldiers continued to fight bravely even as their numbers dwindled. The invaders took control of the drawbridge mechanism and ensured it stayed raised, while the boards and ladders they had used to climb into the keep were retracted. A few of the detachments sent out before the attack had returned, but they quickly dispersed when they realised they had no method of entering the castle and set out to find materials to allow them access.

The last Sanskari soldier was slain and the group of uniformly dressed invaders stepped forward to encircle Richard and Jade.

"Master Ordowyn!" a voice boomed from the rear wall. Atop the rampart stood a figure dressed similarly to the other invaders, but not carrying a weapon. He also wore a black beret, while the rest of the invaders allowed their hair to flow freely. Richard recognised the voice. "You said you would give me your answer today. Today has come – I still await your answer. It's in your best interests to be quick about it."

"Master Ferris – you don't know what you're doing. Please, let us talk to you without swords at our throats," Richard pleaded.

"I know enough," he sharply responded. The Sanskari soldiers outside the castle had grown in numbers and Ferris stepped down from the rampart so as to avoid the arrows which started to fly over the walls, met with bolts from the invaders' crossbows.

"Master Ferris – the troubadour?" Jade ridiculed. "Richard, what have you been doing?"

"I meant to tell you. He wants to kill you, so you better say something fast."

Ferris cleared a path between the invaders surrounding Jade and Richard, standing with his arms crossed. "Master Ordowyn, you surprise me. You are in cohorts with this crone?"

"Yes, but if you tell your men – and women, by the looks of it – to step away, we can resolve this peacefully. At least, Jade can stay alive." He motioned to Jade.

"Jade, hmm?" he probed. "What makes you choose that name now?"

"Because it's my true name, Ferris. Tell your men to back away and I will explain myself, and then maybe you can have control of this garrison. Believe me, it's better than the alternative, because at least if you let me live, I'll authorise you to eliminate every last Sanskari soldier in this city. That will allow you perhaps two weeks of free reign over Limara before a small army is sent in to reclaim it. However, if you kill me and leave enough soldiers alive to flee and tell the Empire, then expect to be overthrown in no more than two days. Make your decision."

"Hold your tongue, hag. I am the one who offers ultimatums in situations such as this. And please, if you are to address me, I appreciate the use of my full title."

150

"Your full title will be appreciated when you instruct your band of rogues to stand down. Go ahead, slaughter the troops outside, fighting to save my life. Spare me and you will understand why Master Ordowyn didn't take you up on whatever offer you gave him."

The troubadour snickered at her boldness and gestured to the other invaders, who turned their attention to the drawbridge. At least seventy of them had entered the castle, outnumbering the fifty remaining Sanskari soldiers desperately trying to cross the moat, many falling prey to their well-aimed bolts. Fewer invaders fell prey to the not-so-well-aimed Sanskari arrows.

"Kill every last one of the dogs!" Ferris ordered, before leading Richard and Jade into the keep. Although he tried to maintain an aura of confidence, he soon became lost, so Jade subtly guided him towards the interrogation room where Francis had first taken her and Richard upon their arrival in Limara. He took the interrogator's seat and rested his legs on the table, while Richard and Jade took the other two seats as they had done once before.

"Talk," Ferris said bluntly.

"Master Ferris – I assume now that playing the banjo isn't your only talent?" Jade prodded.

"Walking on thin ice, scum. Explain yourself."

"First, I'd like you to explain why you've attacked this castle. It serves no benefit to Mirados and will only cause unnecessary deaths for your own people. Why sacrifice their lives like that?"

"Why do you care about Miradosi loyalists? I would've thought your first concern would be losing your head if you continue in your current manner. I said explain yourself."

"I'm not working for the Sanskari."

Ferris was silent for a few moments before a grin crossed his face and he snorted in disbelief.

"Good try. Richard, will you tell me something valuable? You seem to care about this sorry excuse for a woman so please, enlighten me on why you're wearing that hideous getup. Otherwise I'm afraid it will be both your heads on a pike."

"She's telling the truth, Ferris. When we first met, I was hunting bandits who turned out to be working with the Sanskari. Jade was among them and she confided in me. She's working for the Miradosi and she even helped me complete my initiation task without killing any of my targets, though I was never able to officially complete it as the officer who assigned me the task was killed – by Jade. I attacked the officer in a fit of anger and wounded his shoulder – he would have had me killed if Jade hadn't stepped in and killed him. Then she lied to the soldiers who your men just killed and sent them to look for his murderer, which I guess is what gave you the opportunity to attack."

"Actually, you're wrong on the last count. We were going to attack regardless, though the removal of defence beforehand was a fantastic surprise. Now, Richard, do you really expect me to believe all that nonsense you just told me?"

"It's all true! I swear, Ferris, I swear it on his majesty King Herford's life, and all the lives of his successors."

Ferris mused about whether to believe Richard, staring absentmindedly at the rough surface of the table. He stayed like that for a few minutes before finally returning his attention to reality.

"Alright," he began. "I'm ready to believe you – but I'll need proof. Richard – you said she helped you complete your initiation task without killing. I'm curious as to what that means."

Richard awkwardly fidgeted in his seat and glanced at Jade, who had remained cool and collected for the entire duration of the affair, her steely gaze fixed on the troubadour.

"What it means, Master Ferris, is that through one way or another, I was able to assist Richard in killing three targets who the Sanskari had marked for death. He didn't do the killing. I did. Because I recognised his potential to help me in my own mission, which I'm sure shares many traits with yours. Though mine has worked far more successfully than yours."

"It is clear you have a way with words. Enough to have fooled Richard into believing whatever codswallop you placed into his head. Words, my dear, will not suffice. I believe Richard said that the targets were not killed at all. Now, you tell me that you killed them in his stead. Time is ticking." He took his legs down from the table and for the first time since entering the room assumed a serious expression, leaning forward in his chair.

An invisible force promptly threw him back, taking the chair with him. Him and the chair crashed into the wall, the back chair legs snapping off and leaving Ferris pinned to the floor.

"Who would have thought?" he laughed. The muscles in his arms tensed, trying to raise him from the floor but achieving nothing. "A damned witch, taking the role of lawmaker in this city. How many innocent women have you drowned who you claimed were like you?"

Jade clenched her fist and his ability to converse was lost. She rose from her seat and strolled to the other side of the table, staring down at Ferris like a cat over a mouse as his face began to turn red.

"Do you have enough proof now, Ferris?" she calmly asked. She relaxed her clenched fist just enough to allow him to mouth the word 'yes', before relaxing her fist entirely. The troubadour gasped for breath and allowed the red colour to drain from his face. He then returned to his position at the table and remained standing, leaving the broken seat on the floor behind him.

"Wouldn't it just have been easier to say 'This is Jade, she's a witch! That's how she helped me!'?" he ridiculed. "That display was entirely unnecessary. Though I'm still interested as to how she helped you with your initiation."

"I magically constructed three replicas of the targets' heads, which at this moment sit on the desk in my room upstairs. Happy?" Jade falsely smiled.

"Interesting," Ferris shot back. "Now, Jade, or whatever your true name is, what exactly would happen if word were to get out about your abilities? If I'm not mistaken, it's a crime against the gods, whichever of them you believe in, to practice magic."

"Or, Master Ferris," Jade argued, "you could instead use my abilities for your own cause. If not my abilities, at least my authority. People listen to me – they won't listen to a ragtag group of bandit lookalikes who miraculously captured the second-oldest structure in the city. It may have slipped your mind, but I am, in fact, on your side."

Ferris paced back and forth across the room, looking contemplative. Jade and Richard patiently stared until he returned to the table.

"As I understand it, Jade, you're posing as a Sanskari official, but secretly trying to undermine them?"

"Correct."

"And what exactly have you done to undermine them? Do you even report to anyone in Mirados?"

"Empires don't fall in a day, Ferris. Perhaps they do in your ballads, but we live in the real world, where knowledge holds more power than an army of five thousand men. What if I were to tell you that the emperor himself counts me among his closest confidantes?"

"Normally, I'd laugh in your face. Though after that demonstration, I'm willing to allow myself to believe you. Provided, of course, that you tell us something to reinforce such a bold claim." Ferris's question was followed by Richard perking up, clearly interested.

"Varanus the Vanquisher – an imaginative name, as they happen, and it boasts the advantage of alliteration. He is a memorable man, even if you haven't met him. The name is enough. If you do meet him, though, then you really can't get him out of your head. Do you sometimes wonder how he's been able to rule Sanskar for as long as he has? By my estimation, it must be close to fifty years. Fifty years without competition, without threats to his life, without passing from old age. He was only twenty when he ascended to the throne of the Kingdom of Sanskar. He was twenty-five when he commanded a vast army through Jakaris, razing the country in his wake. This was the beginning of the Empire. By thirty, he controlled all the land surrounding the Redwater Bay. The kingdoms of Canaris and Mirados were the most powerful on the continent, and both were controlled by fools who failed to recognise the rising threat of Nendar Varanus, yet to be known as the Vanquisher. In the years following the conquering of Jakaris, he also captured other neighbouring states – Handor, Floria, Kelmar, Rendon, Senna. Years of striding

154

from victory to victory, implementing control like you see now in this city.

"He was forty when he finally hit a wall in his northern conquest – the Canarian border. By this point, the King had noticed Varanus's actions and sent an army of six thousand soldiers, mainly infantry, to the Cayna River. From the Red-water Bay to the Cayna, there had been no impassable bodies of water – there are narrow, shallow rivers in Jakaris and the Gherad passes through both Floria and Handor. Canaris didn't have this problem – what they did have, however, was a lack of skilled soldiers. You see, one of the things which made Varanus so successful was his method of raising an army – instead of just rounding up all the peasants and sending them to war with minimal training, minimal pay and minimal motivation, like most kings, he instead heavily taxed his subjects and paid for an army of elite mercenaries. It didn't go down so well when he first rose to power but really, there was nothing the people could do. The tax collectors made the rounds and allowed for the first army to be raised. The rest was history. His invasion armies will always outperform his enemies' which is why the Miradosi army is being so viciously destroyed in the current conflict. They are simply incapable of successfully defeating the skilled swordsmen, rangers and cavalry hired by the Sanskari."

"You're telling me," Ferris interrupted, "that those numbskulls we just mowed through were trained soldiers? We slaughtered them."

"No, Ferris. If you listened carefully, you would have noticed that I said Varanus's invasion armies comprise mercenaries – the soldiers he stations at garrisons and as guards are the less skilled ones who would otherwise be working in the fields."

"Okay, I understand that. At what point are you going to tell us this great secret about him instead of teaching us a history lesson?"

"Considering I'm the one with information you need, I suggest you keep quiet and let me finish. Nothing but good will come from learning about his history and perhaps you'll understand him more if I do teach you a history lesson.

"Now, when he began conquering land across the continent, many of the Sanskari people began to grow happy or at least content with the tax. Perhaps it's because it had been in place for a number of years or perhaps because they were proud of their country's progress, considering it once used to be an insignificant backwater which might have had to be passed through to reach more interesting destinations. When he finally crossed the Cayna, the ensuing battle was a bloodbath – the Sanskari forces slaughtered the Canarians. They subsequently marched north and many of the eastern Canarian vassal states backed down even before the Sanskari came close, simply to avoid unnecessary bloodshed, much to the King's dismay. Before you know it, half of Canaris was taken. The only thing which stopped the Vanquisher's conquest in the North from then was and still is the Irena Mountains, which isolate the rest of Canaris from the continent. He tried to pass through the unguarded valleys but was generally stopped by nature before the Canarians – northern wyverns are much larger and fiercer than the ones in the east. And then many of the valleys' exits were blocked by landslides. The final nail in the northern conquest's coffin was an outbreak of plague among his main army, eight-thousand strong. Only four thousand were left after it had run its course, and many were in no state to fight for weeks after the disease had infected them. The Canarian King took the opportunity to bring his troops in and finally, the Vanquisher faced his first defeat."

"When did he turn his attention to the South?" Richard chimed in.

"Not long after his failure in the North. The Redwater Bay had become the main hub of trade on the continent which, as a result, made the region very wealthy. Virilia in particular became the primary destination for merchants around the Bay and even travelling from the Isles with exotic goods. This made it very easy for Varanus to quickly raise a substantial fund for another army which he promptly sent south and this time, they were met with stronger resistance. King Herford had directed all his focus into defending the border and maintaining a strong connection with the Isles – that's where most of the country's trade came from. Myana has always been the

156

capital of Mirados, though never the most influential city –
seaside cities which fell under Sanskari control were always
the King's priority, as that's where most of his wealth was extracted from. When the time for battle did come, there were
great casualties on both sides but Varanus constantly hired
more and more mercenaries from everywhere he could find
them, even the Isles and the World's End Mountains. Despite
this, the two sides remained relatively evenly matched, which
is why it's taken him ten years of far more lucrative plans to
get to the point where he is today, when the scales have finally
tipped in the Sanskaris' favour."

"You're well acquainted with the man's successes," Ferris
concluded. "What's the big secret?"

"What's the life expectancy of a human, Ferris? Sixty, at a
push, when you live in total luxury? Varanus is seventy years
old and still the picture of health. Maybe you can guess how
that's come to be."

"Aromatherapy? Meditation?"

Jade rolled her eyes. "He's a sorcerer. An adept one, at that.
I can assure you that his real age is far more than the one he
exhibits. His exceptional magical talent is the reason why all
the poisoned drinks, assassins' blades and unfortunate acci-
dents have left him unscathed. He is, to most humans, untouchable. Only another mage could take him on, which is
why I grew close to him. Growing close to him was one half of
the equation but the other half was growing strong enough to
rival his abilities, which I'm yet to achieve."

"I get it," Ferris exclaimed. "That old bastard has outlawed
magic and encouraged witch hunts as a method of protecting
himself."

"This is where your talents become very useful, Ferris. The
people love you and your ballads – if you were to sing about
Varanus being a mage, it would spread like wildfire across the
continent and the bards of Virilia would be singing about it
before long. He may be ruthless, but if enough people talk
about it, he can't execute them all. Which leaves him vulnerable."

The troubadour smirked. "Forgive me, Jade. It appears, after all of this, that I indeed misjudged you. Come, let us see

how the Sanskari soldiers are faring in retaking the castle – while I come up with a few verses for my next poems."

Ferris, already standing, walked towards the exit, followed by Richard and Jade – this time, they happily joined him. When they walked into the courtyard, it was clear that the Sanskari had made no progress in recapture – the invaders had suffered a few more casualties but no more than they had inflicted on the Sanskari soldiers.

"We need to do something to get them to stop that. Jade, may I invite you to the ramparts? Hey, you, give me your sword." Ferris retrieved a rapier from one of the swordsmen idly waiting in the courtyard for something to happen and clumsily twirled it around like a young boy, in awe. He then led Jade up the cracked stone stairs and held the rapier's blade dangerously close to her throat for the soldiers to witness. At once, they all stopped their efforts to re-enter the castle and lowered their weapons. The Miradosi invaders did the same.

"Sanskari dogs," Ferris taunted. "This would be your advisor in my clutches at this moment, no?" The soldiers frantically looked at one another, unsure collectively how to respond. "I don't dare think what would happen to you if you allowed her to die. I give you a choice. Drop your weapons and surrender yourselves to us – we will throw you in the dungeons along with this traitor, but you will live. Or your blood will dye the moat red. Make a decision, quickly."

The Sanskari soldiers, those left numbering around thirty, gathered into a tight group and whispered amongst themselves before their weapons clattered against the cobbles. Ferris ordered them to move towards the moat and cautiously allowed the drawbridge to fall. A group of swordsmen surrounded the Sanskari and led them into the courtyard, across the moat while another group collected the discarded weapons.

The Sanskari, helpless, stood in a tight huddle, now surrounded by all the invading swordsmen. The rangers on the ramparts also trained their weapons on the Sanskari. Ferris's expression turned cold and he made a brief gesture to one of the swordsmen with his hand, dragging a finger across his neck.

Blood spurted from every accessible vein and artery, leaving a pool on the dusty floor. Immediately after the onslaught began, the defenceless Sanskari soldiers rushed forward, fighting hopelessly for their lives, fists flailing. Jade watched from the rampart, emotionless, while Richard watched from a corner of the courtyard, feeling a mixture of hatred and shock as the Miradosi forces hacked and slashed through the Sanskari like a pack of wolves to a flock of sheep. They didn't relent until the last, crying in anguish, was cut down. There was then a period of silence as everyone – Ferris, Jade, Richard, and the invaders – took in the sight of the pile of lifeless, mutilated bodies.

"Well," Ferris commented. "Somebody best have them burned."

CHAPTER 18

VIRILIAN PALACE, SANSKAR

Nendar Varanus eagerly opened the scroll as it materialised on his desk, having been thoroughly pleased with the previous three. It hadn't been more than two days since the last letter and he was worried that he would grow impatient.

Your Grace,

All still goes well. I've witnessed no signs of him regaining his memory and I'd like to believe that soon, we can bring him to Virilia. He's splendidly impetuous, which will work in our favour. He's definitely the one – just being around him fills me with magical pleasure which you simply don't feel around anyone or anything else. I'm deeply jealous. The crystal is an improvement over the pitiful boundaries of human capacity, but to be born with his gift would be a blessing like no other. And to be born with such an incredible gift and not to know, how it hurts my heart.

I should hope that you've prepared a team of mages to capture and convert him. This part of the task I will leave up to you, as I'm not foolish and arrogant enough to try to convert him myself as Lynn did, landing us in this mess to begin with. Just trust in my abilities to bring him to you unharmed and unaware.

– Val

Nendar completed the letter and incinerated it with a command which left no remnants other than a pile of cooled ash in the palm of his hand, which he brushed into a container at the side of his desk. He then picked up a looking glass just bigger than his entire hand and mounted it in a metallic frame decorated with various dried herbs and roots intertwined through the structural and decorative connectors of the frame.

"Es tar, galar," he said. His reflection in the looking glass slowly faded from its surface and was replaced by an unnatural shimmering and pale blue sheen. A faint ring of mist poured from the centre and surrounded the mirror's edge, constantly revolving around it.

An image slowly appeared, resembling a blurry construction of black and red before completely appearing as a person – a dark-skinned man with short-cut hair who looked no older than forty. Nendar knew for a fact that he was at least three hundred years older than that.

"Hep tar, Varanus," the man greeted.

"Hep tar, Lopan," Nendar responded, bowing. "I require the Council's assistance."

"For what do you need us this time, Nendar? Have you not risked our existence enough times already?"

"I need a team of mages to help with a conversion. We believe it's the one."

"You jest, Nendar. The Council has been searching for the Child of Fate since its establishment. And you come to me saying you've found them?"

"They're not a child anymore, Tregor. Valerie has done an excellent job in winning his trust thus far. I've received a string of letters detailing her work and I commend her for it, as the Fateborn appears to be rather the difficult individual. A conversion is difficult enough with a weak-willed being, so I'll need more help with one as headstrong as Valerie has described."

"If it really is the one, you will have every member of the Council on standby for your command – with the obvious exception of Ríyael. We wouldn't hesitate to see the Fateborn become ours. Ours, Nendar. Not yours. We will not allow such a vitally important character to become a pawn in your pathetic conquest of the continent."

"Perhaps we could make this work for the Empire as well as the Mages' Council – I could make the use of magic legal—"

"No," Tregor interrupted. "The Council are a separate entity to the guilds and nations of people. We have no interest in the control of land and people as you do – only the safeguarding of magic. You will find and capture the Fateborn and we will convert him and train him in the ways he was destined to

161

be. He will become the leader of the Council and live forever, the first immortal man. The first living deity. He will ensure the world does not fall to anarchy under liberal use of magic."

"So be it." Nendar scowled. "Hep tar, Lopan."

"Hep tar, Varanus. Es tar, closs."

The image of Tregor Lopan dispersed much quicker than it had originally appeared along with the mist revolving around the looking glass. Nendar's reflection replaced the pale sheen and he turned with a sigh to the paperwork to which he had been attending before the scroll appeared.

"Servant!" he called. A young woman in a long, plain beige dress appeared quickly from the corridor outside.

"Yes, milord?"

"A camomile tea, please. And make sure we have plenty in stock. We'll be needing it."

"As you wish, milord."

"And," he continued, "plenty of Virilian Red. That's vitally important."

"Of course, milord."

CHAPTER 19

SANAÍD, TYEN'AEL

Elaeínn leapt over the bed and held the tip of her sword to the Prime Minister's throat.

"Are you going to kill me?" he asked plainly.

"I would certainly like to," Elaeínn seethed.

"But you would like something from me that my dead body won't provide?"

"Where is Kíra?"

"Withdraw my sword from my neck and perhaps I will talk. Without ordering a battalion of guards in here."

Elaeínn cautiously drew the sword back but held it across her body in defence.

"Kíra... that would be one of your allies?"

"The one you abducted who wasn't fortunate enough to escape."

"Abducted? Miss Tinaíd, I believe there has been some misunderstanding. I have ordered no such barbarity. I prefer to see my enemies rot in prison, publicly trialled. Fairly or otherwise. Silent removal of opposition? Not my method of choice."

Elaeínn scowled.

"You don't believe me?" he inferred. "I don't blame you. You've conjured me to be some evil man who oppresses the masses. But tell me, Elaeínn – Who is the true oppressor? The man who suppresses the dangers of democracy, or the woman who would willingly murder their leader in front of a crowd?"

"I have two problems with what you just said," Elaeínn retorted. "Well, more than two, but two that can be easily expressed.

163

"Democracy exists in this country because King Elgaer realised the injustice of the monarchy. Yet you choose to erode the system put in place to ensure a fair society to maintain your own position of power. That sounds oppressive to me.

"And my other problem – you call yourself my leader. That you are not."

"King Elgaer was an eccentric," Jaelaar hissed. "The cretin was just as incapable as his brother. Wrong in the head, mentally instable. His unrestrainable mind generated these radical ideas which, to an average mental patient, wouldn't be so harmful. However, in the mind of a king, they were. Democracy was just one of Elgaer's wild ideas and it should be put down as he was by the Monarchists."

"Have you not noticed how his reign changed society for the better? We are a prosperous people – poverty is almost non-existent! People are happy, they feel a sense of freedom that is exclusive to Tyen'Ael! Had they been unhappy, they would have quite happily fled to Tyen'Ard."

"Correlations. Not causations. The reduction in poverty came as a result of the founding of the free magic schools. Before then, it had been very much an elitist skillset, being able to cast spells. But you didn't read that part of the history book, did you?"

"And what makes you so fit for rule? Why not simply pass a law which returns power to the King if you're so opposed to the very democracy that had you voted in in the first place?"

"Power centralised within an external House that avoids the obnoxious nature of the monarchy is very favourable to me," Jaelaar explained. "I've lived in Tyen'Ael my entire life. I was almost around to see Elgaer and the sacking of the palace. I have a great understanding of the tissues of our society and I know what's best for the future of our nation."

"Including war?" Elaeínn provoked.

"Including the prospect of conflict with foreign nations," he said unassumingly, as if just continuing his explanation.

Elaeínn readjusted her footing and loosened her muscles, which had been intensely tightened since the Prime Minister had appeared from the balcony.

"I didn't really come here to argue about preferred systems of government. I came here to find something, just a clue, that might lead me to Kíra. Does the name 'R' mean anything to you?"

"Absolutely nothing," he insisted. "As I said, I've not ordered for your abduction. I don't know who did, but I have no connections to them. Or if I do, then I don't know who."

"So you haven't funded any hidden dungeons near the Hamatnarian border?"

"A ludicrous proposal. I can understand it might well be secretive, but that's the inherent nature of a dungeon. And I would have far less control over a not just a dungeon, but anything positioned at such a distance."

A frosty silence ensued as Elaeínn contemplated her enemy's words.

"I'm willing to leave without decorating your bedroom with your own blood," she finally allowed. "But not without gaining at least something. So, if you truly don't know anything about Kíra and my abductions, then tell me something else. About the expansion of the military, perhaps. The one that breaches the ancient Peace Treaty."

"The Peace Treaty, dear child, expires this year. On the 31st of December, two hundred years after its signing, both the dwarven and High Elven kingdoms regain the right to expand their military in any way they want.

"Now, I request that you leave. I have nothing more to tell you, nothing that would help you find your companion. I've complied entirely with your conditions, so the least I ask is the same courtesy in return."

"Open me a portal and I'll leave without complaint," Elaeínn demanded.

"As you wish." he performed the same action as every other mage she had ever seen open a portal and she carefully examined the image of the exit destination while the elderly Prime Minister stepped back, giving her sufficient room to feel comfortable ending her venomous glare.

"I'll be keeping this, too," she stated. "Compensation for your guards taking my knife."

Jaelaar didn't argue and Elaeínn stepped through the portal, realising she would have the hold the sword until she could acquire a scabbard from a leatherworker. It might look odd to passers-by, but it wouldn't be anything anyone would worry about. It was common for elves to carry weapons, especially in the city.

She could determine that Jaelaar had sent her to Sanaíd's market district when she turned the corner and was subject to the bustle of distastefully dressed merchants fighting over locations to set up their carts and stalls, while shop owners at the street side united against the travelling merchants to scare them away from the shopfronts. It was actually a fairly generous place to teleport her, as the activity made it easy to blend in and avoid the authorities.

She thought back to the other discoveries she had made in the Tyen'Aíde – mentions of the Nightwatch, a Tayannan delegation to the state of Kaelestia and an expedition. She hadn't ever heard of anything called the Nightwatch, so she thought she would start there.

Her first port of call would normally have been the library, but that was, for obvious reasons, out of the question. Her next idea was, for the second time in the past two days, to seek Caeran.

Despite Caeran's young age, he was extraordinarily knowledgeable and had spent his youth under his mother's strict ideas about raising a wise, respectable child. She was successful in this objective – Caeran was exceedingly intelligent. However, it also meant having raised a son that detested his mother and left home at the first opportunity.

"Caeran," Elaeínn sang as she strolled into his office. The day being a Sunday, there were once again no classes.

"What do you want now?" Caeran sighed sarcastically, not removing his focus from his search through a filing cabinet.

"The Nightwatch – have you heard of them?"

"Of course – old fairy tale. An organisation of vampire hunters that supposedly reconvene every several centuries."

"Jaelaar doesn't seem to think it's a fairy tale," she countered. "Take a look at this. Straight from the Common Chamber."

She opened her satchel and produced the page of notes she had swiped from Tyen'Aíde. Caeran looked over it scathingly, making various expressions as his eyes passed over each individual note.

"Perhaps it's in reference to something else," he concluded. "This expedition – this ought to interest you more."

"Why's that?" she stepped closer.

"Because this, unlike the other things on the list, is due to be announced publicly. A friend of mine, a frequent visitor of the palace, told me how he overheard two Nationals discussing it. Apparently Jaelaar himself is going to be on the trip. And they're going to the West – he didn't hear any more about why, but it's unexplored ocean. There could be anything there. And they seem to think it's important, which is why the Prime Minister himself is going. And announcing it publicly, too – but we haven't worked out why that is."

"To raise morale, I imagine," Elaeínn suggested. "It's a plot to embolden nationalism. It's all a part of his plan."

"What plan?"

"I spoke with Jaelaar. Personally," she explained.

"That presents a number of questions," Caeran interjected. "But... continue, and I'll see if you answer them."

"I went to the palace, looking for answers to Kíra's disappearance. There was nothing in the Regal Guard, so I managed to slip into the Executive Wing. Jaelaar was there. And we spoke. He knew nothing about Kíra, or if he did, he was doing a bloody good job at hiding it. But he did tell me about the military expansion I found... here, I also snatched this from the Tyen'Aíde."

She produced the scruffy piece of legislation from her satchel and allowed the teacher to skim over it.

"He said about how the Peace Treaty with the Dwarves expires this year. He's preparing for war – as are the Dwarves."

"What makes you so sure? Of the Dwarves, at least – I can quite clearly understand the elven perspective."

"Kíra and I were abducted from Garaennía," she began. "Masked figures, very secretive – they never revealed their identities or their motives or their employers. They knocked us out and took us away – to separate locations. I personally ended up in a dungeon past the Hamatnarian border and was interrogated by a lovely man called R," she placed emphasis on the word 'lovely'.

"To my luck, a dwarven patrol found the dungeon and rescued me, but not until just after R and a subordinate of his had teleported away in the nick of time. I'll spare you the unnecessary details leading up to my presence in Castle Rockfell and a meeting with the King."

"This story sounds more like something I would tell my pupils," Caeran chuckled.

"Well I haven't embellished it in the slightest, so shut up and listen," Elaeínn snapped.

"I talked to the King, and the captain of the patrol that found me – the Hamatnarian Elite Division. Have you heard of them?"

"Of course. They're the Dwarves' most skilled soldiers."

"Well, I spoke with him and the King. And they essentially described plans to fund us through a proxy. An entire project in the South. It's excellent news, and by the look on Berri's face when he went in the speak with them, it really is more funding than we've ever known."

"Be wary, Elle," Caeran cautioned. "You're right to assume that the Dwarves must be preparing for war – but they're using you as cannon fodder. They're avoiding wasting any of their own resources and paying you what is probably to them a pittance, and the FTA is quite happy to throw their limited men armed with dwarven money at the system. Berri is intelligent – but anyone can be used. Especially if they believe they are the ones benefiting."

"Well it's something," Elaeínn mused. "Doesn't help me find Kíra, though."

"I just thought," Caeran perked up. "I'm quite surprised the idea didn't come to me sooner. If you want to find Kíra, it's quite simple. Go to an astromancer. If you bring them something from Kíra's body – a tuft of hair, perhaps – they'll be able to track her. They've been trained specifically to be able to do so."

"Where's the nearest?" her eyes lit up.

"I don't know any personally, but I'm sure you can find one if you ask around at the University. They've got departments for every bloody branch of magic ever to exist. And, also, bring a pretty penny. Their services don't come cheap."

"Thanks, Caeran!" Elaeínn beamed, already halfway out the door.

She almost sprinted back to Kíra's house and raided her once again, pilfering her hidden cache of emergency funds. It wasn't much, but hopefully would be enough to pay however exorbitant a price the astromancer was going to charge.

*

"Fifty aerrins?" Elaeínn blurted, her jaw dropped. "That's daylight robbery!"

"It's a valuable service," the astromancer drawled, readjusting his glasses and smoothing down his robes. "One that costs me a great deal of energy. And, perhaps more importantly, one that only I, Vaerron Híanen, am at this moment providing in the entire city."

"You've certainly taken the liberty of hiking the price," she chided. "If you think I'm paying that much, you can shove that up your arse."

"I beg your pardon?" the old man raised his voice, astounded. "I shan't be talked to with such disrespect!"

"When you charge such a ludicrous price for such a pitifully niche service, you damn well will be talked to in such a manner. Tell me, when was the last time someone came to you for your services?"

"Two days ago," he responded drily, with plenty of venom behind each word.

"Ah," Elaeínn faltered.

She contritely produced the meagre funds she already felt bad about having taken from Kíra and spread them across the table. The end result of a quick count was a total of thirty-one aerrins and ten naemmons, or simply thirty-three-and-a-half aerrins.

She looked pleadingly at the astromancer, whose wrinkled face showed absolute displeasure at the situation.

"I can pay you back," she bargained. "With interest. I just really need this."

"I will take thirty aerrins now, and thirty more are to be paid back over the course of the next three months," Vaerron asserted. "For every week you haven't paid me back, the amount owed increases by five aerrins. Do we have an agreement?"

"Absolutely," she didn't even think about it.

As she moved forward to give the man the single black hair she had been lucky enough to find near Kíra's bathtub, he put a hand up for her to wait and rummaged around in his desk for an empty piece of aged-looking parchment and a quill. He dipped the quill in an ink pot on the corner of the desk and began to write.

"Sign here, please," he said after covering half of the page in almost illegible scribble, offering the quill to Elaeínn. She quickly scrutinised the contract before signing the bottom of the page as *Delía Hatten* after concluding that nothing was amiss.

"This way, then, please, Miss Hatten." He gestured for her to follow, rising from his chair with a creak.

"Tell me, then – who is it you seek?" he asked, closing the door behind her after entering a barren room lit only by what looked to be real candles.

"A friend – Kíra Karíos," she provided uneasily, having considered using a fake name, but deciding that she didn't want to risk anything going wrong.

"And what made you look for the assistance of an astromancer? Is she that lost?"

"She went missing. Nobody knows where she is. I've made it my job to find her."

"Very noble. Please place the hair in the centre of the circle."

A perfect circle had been traced on the stone floor from chalk and she placed the hair in the absolute centre of it, as instructed. The astromancer stepped forward and motioned for silence as he stepped into the chalk circle and knelt down on both legs, placing his hands on his knees and bowing his head. Elaeínn retreated to the corner of the room and watched, her curiosity piqued.

Vaerron began murmuring something incomprehensibly quietly – it looked to Elaeínn as if he was just moving his mouth without speaking. But whatever he was doing, it was having an effect – particles of the chalk comprising the circle in which the astromancer sat started to float, only a few centimetres off the ground. The overall scene was enchanting as the chalk particles remained suspended above the floor, creating a halo-like mist.

The candles positioned in the corners of the room flickered as if struck by a sudden gust of wind and the volume of Vaerron's murmuring grew to an audible level. The roof boards creaked under an invisible strain and Vaerron raised his arms as if cradling something. Then, he reached his arms out to his side. And then the candles went out.

The room was bathed in darkness. Out of instinct, a rush of adrenaline shot through her and she felt the urge to flee. But then the candles relit themselves and she slowly breathed out, focusing her eyes on the rising astromancer.

"Well?" Elaeínn asked pleadingly.

"I successfully saw your friend," Vaerron confirmed. "Come this way, I'll mark it on the map."

The astromancer directed her back to a map dated to 2M135 in his office, already covered in numerous crosses and markings across the continent of Fenalia and the insignificant neighbouring islands.

"The images I saw of your friend were blurred, distorted," he explained. "She was clearly in distress, fading in and out of consciousness. Surrounded by people whose identities managed to evade my vision. And not simply due to the likes of a mask, no – these mysterious figures are well versed in illusory magic. To the degree that they've protected themselves from what I expect to be any sort of magical vision. However, I was able to piece together her location. Based on the various scenes I witnessed, I would say she's about..." he swept the quill over the map, a drop of ink falling to the floor, "here."

Vaerron confidently marked a cross on the map in the middle of the ocean to the far west of Tyen'Ael, lined up almost perfectly with the Hamatnarian border.

"The ocean?"

"She's on a ship," he stated without a trace of doubt. "Travelling west."

"But... there's nothing to the West."

"As far as we know, that's correct. Which is why I find it odd that whoever is currently in control of your friend is taking her there. And I have a number of other questions that my curious side would like to ask. However, I am a professional, and I have completed my part of the contract. Remember, I'm expecting the other half of the payment in full – thirty aerrins."

"You will receive it," she agreed. "Now, thank you for doing this... and I'm sorry for insulting you. I have to go."

The old man waved her off and she left in silence, clambering down the university stairs and racing to the exit, securing a number of inquisitorial looks from the various university staff.

*

"Caeran!" she exclaimed, slamming open the door to the teacher's office. He begrudgingly turned around, tilted his head at her and raised his eyebrows.

"That expedition," she huffed. "When are they supposed to leave?"

"Funny you should ask – one of my colleagues just told me that Jaelaar himself was spotted heading towards Common Square. With an escort, naturally. That could very well be the announcement."

She was gone quicker than she had arrived.

CHAPTER 20

Elton, Paul, and Jerry rushed down the stairs to the ground floor before exiting the house through the kitchen, aiming to escape out back via the outdoor area. The area itself overlooked a narrow alley and it was a significant jump to get down, as the area was found atop a steep wall. Paul and Jerry jumped without hesitation, surprising a nobleman and his wife, who quickly leapt aside and hustled further along the alley. Elton looked down nervously and attempted to climb down instead, finding loose footholds within the cobbled wall.

"Come on, boss! Anyone sees us is gonna go straight to the Salyrians!" Jerry urged. "And it definitely seems like we can't pay 'em off to get lost!"

He dropped to the floor, knees creaking, and took a moment to find his footing. Paul and Jerry tried to urge him on and the three of them broke out into a run at first, but Elton couldn't maintain such a pace for longer than a minute and dropped to a gentle jog.

"We can't stick around, boss! We need to go save Felix and Rosa!"

"I don't think we'll just be allowed to waltz past an army and release their binds. We need to take time about this," Elton asserted through long-drawn breaths. "They think we're just an honourless group of bandits, albeit a large one. They will therefore treat us like they would any bandit. They won't rely on emotional blackmail to lure us to the City Guard, because they don't think we care. We will use that against them."

"You sure, boss? These new Salyrian geezers don't seem like the most brainy 'emselves. Praps they'll misjudge us – after all, we do make ourselves look like a proper organisation thing," Paul said.

"No matter what they think, going to them is suicide. We'll have our heads chopped off and put on spikes as a warning to others who would dare offend that brat's ego. We need to find another way."

"I've an idea, boss," Jerry said. "What if we sneak into the Redhouse—"

"They'll have the whole place on lockdown. If someone gave them an accurate description of me, they'll also have known where I tend to do my work."

"Lemme finish. So, as it'll be on lockdown, we'll *sneak* past whatever guards they put outside. If you're right about how they judge us, Regi, then surely they'll trust a minimal amount of guards to defend would be enough? They'll think we're too stupid or weak to defeat even one knight."

Elton raised his eyebrows and nodded.

"You may be onto something. What next?"

"We'd have to get some supplies – shivs would be ideal, since they're small and easy to hide. And then a whole load of explosives, as many as we can carry without being spotted. Make an explosion at somewhere out in the city and get whoever of our lot is nearby to blame it on you. They'd send a load of knights to check it out and that would be our ticket into the City Guard."

"That might just work. And then we can kill the lunatic."

Paul and Jerry both grinned confidently in response.

"Then let's go. We'll take the back way to the Redhouse."

The back way involved a number of narrow, dilapidated alleys which were often useful for escaping disgruntled victims and do-gooding guards. Some of the alleys were already occupied by members of the Syndicate in hiding, looking as if they had used their time to make a small profit, judging by the pouches of coins dangling from their belts. They briefly exchanged nods before Elton ordered Paul and Jerry to move on.

They reached the end of the final alley, which opened up onto the street of the Redhouse's residence. They stood between two apartment blocks, covered overhead by a wooden walkway connecting the two buildings. Shadows of footsteps were cast down upon them by people standing atop the balcony, who they could see through the thin gaps between the planks.

"Jerry, peek round the corner and see if you can see any guards."

Jerry tiptoed to the edge of the alley's shadows and slowly peered around to the right. He then came back with a malicious grin across his face.

"Just two knights. I told you."

"Have you got weapons on you?"

Jerry raised an eyebrow and unveiled a dagger from his waist, before also pointing out a second and third hidden on his back and on his chest. Paul also had two shivs tucked away in his pockets.

"Okay, you two go ahead and take out the guards. If sneaking isn't possible, use words. I'll let Jerry be responsible for that, should it come to it."

They both briskly walked from their spot in the alley and kept their backs against the wall as they left onto the wider street. Elton peered around the corner as much as he could without revealing himself to any passers-by and watched as Paul and Jerry slinked around against the sandstone walls of the structures lining the road and managed to slip into the entryway beneath the low roof. The guards, oblivious, stood in front of one of the carved sandstone pillars, engrossed in an apparently hilarious conversation. A conversation cut short by the blades which suddenly found themselves against their necks. Once the guards clattered to the ground, Paul and Jerry motioned to Elton to join them and he jogged over, carefully avoiding stepping in the growing pools of blood.

"Hide the bodies. We really don't want anybody joining us," Elton commanded. Paul and Jerry each grabbed one of the heavily armoured corpses and dragged it loudly into the building with them.

"I hope you know how to unlock all the doors, boss. Every-thin's shut good an' tight," Paul said, leaving a body in a dark-ened corner before briskly walking through the main entry hall.

"There's a set of hidden spare keys. Go to the armoury, I'll be with you in a moment."

They split off in different directions and Elton made his way up a flight of stairs to a corridor decorated with paintings. He removed one of the paintings from the wall, a defaced portrait of Ramsey, former self-proclaimed King of Dannos. Behind the painting was a safe, secured by a permutation lock. Elton had never entrusted the code to anyone.

He twisted the code into place and it clicked open, reveal-ing the deed to the Redhouse and the set of spare keys. He grabbed it, the many keys jangling noisily, locked the safe and returned the painting to its original position.

Paul and Jerry hadn't gone to the armoury as instructed and instead were watching outside the main entryway. Elton stopped in his tracks and backed behind a pillar as Paul and Jerry frantically waved at him and put a finger to their lips. Outside the grand entrance was a group of ten knights, all as heavily armoured as the two which they had killed. The Rosa lookalike was among them, knelt down, inspecting the ground on which the guards had been standing when their throats were cut. He removed one of his iron gauntlets and brushed the ground with a gloved finger, inspecting the fresh, crimson pool of blood. He scowled and brushed his finger against a dry patch of ground to remove the blood from his finger.

"It appears we have an insurrection on our hands," he said. "The bloody bandits thought they would be clever by hiding the bodies. Probably taking their armour and swords as well, the dirty scoundrels. Split up and search the area. Exterminate the vermin."

He organised the gathering of knights into four groups of two, sending them off in different directions, even in what looked like the direction of back alleys in which Syndicate henchmen were hiding. Elton cursed under his breath before panic set in on the knight's next words.

"Sir Yaris, you're with me. There's probably some inside by now."

Elton exchanged an uneasy glance with Paul and Jerry, who mouthed the word 'run'. They took off in one direction, making more noise than necessary and grabbing the attention of the dark-haired knight. Elton quietly moved in the other direction, making a beeline for the location of a secret bunker installed specifically for times like these. It would be only the second time he had ever needed to use it.

Alone, panicking, afraid. The fearless, ruthless, and emotionless façade Elton had formulated for himself disintegrated in the face of such sudden danger.

He reached the bunker, hidden deep within the labyrinth of corridors in the Redhouse's underground level, without trouble. The only signs of life besides him had been mice, looking for scraps in the wrong place. Controlling his breathing, he forced himself to be calm and inserted the largest of his spare keys into the right-hand keyhole of three keyholes in the bunker door. Twisting the key produced a satisfying 'chnk' and he quickly turned a large metal wheel to completely unlock the door. It was heavy and he had to use substantial force to push it open.

Inside the bunker was a dreary, dungeon-like room with minimal decoration. On the roof there was a small vent to allow for air to circulate, but not large enough for a person to fit through. Despite the vent, the air in the bunker tasted stale and it wasn't even far underground. In terms of seating, there was a wooden bench which left much to be desired. A lonely, rickety shelf attached to the wall was littered with a few dusty tomes which hadn't been opened in decades. In front of the bench there was a small table, in a similar condition to the shelf, though it didn't serve much purpose.

Elton stepped into the depressing room and slammed the door closed. He shuddered at the thought of the vibrations it would have caused throughout the building, but was calmed by the fact that there was no feasible way to enter without a key – or an exceptional lockpicker. He didn't think the Salyrians had either.

Sighing, slouching down onto the bench and finding a use for the table as a footrest, he closed his eyes and pondered as the temperature sharply began to drop.

"Vampire?" he said, not opening his eyes.

"This accursed 'ability' is getting on my nerves," Kalahar replied.

"What are you doing here?" he inquired, still not opening his eyes.

"Noticed you were in a bit of a pickle. Would have been terribly disappointing to miss out on the entertainment. You know how long we sometimes have to go without a good show?"

"I can imagine. I'm afraid down here isn't the best place to go. If you want to watch people suffer, go have a look at the City Guard. They're torturing Rosa and Felix there."

"Oh, I've already been. Is that what the knights told you?"

Elton opened his eyes. Kalahar was levitating directly across from him in a position imitating his own.

"Yes... why?"

"I'm afraid it's a load of codswallop, dear Elton. I thought it would be interesting to have a look at the new King of Dannos, and I explored the rest of that crumbling excuse of a building while I was at it. Don't recall seeing your buddies."

"I'm a bloody fool. Of course they were bluffing. How did you get in here?"

"Teleported. Why?"

"Paul and Jerry are in trouble. Do you know where they are?"

The vampire instantly transformed into a cloud of black mist, exiting the bunker through the vent in the ceiling. He returned a few minutes later in his original form, teleporting instead of moving as a mist.

"In response to your question, yes, I know where they are. I suppose you want to know?"

"Just get on with it, for god's sake."

"Well, the bald one was duelling one of the knights on the upper level of the complex. It seemed like rather a fair fight. The ugly one – well, neither of them are pretty but the other one is particularly hideous – he was fighting the dark-haired knight, the one who looks a bit like he comes from around here. Now, that was not an even fight, and it had concluded before I even got there. The ugly one is dead."

"Fuck!" Elton angrily rose from his seat. "Why didn't you do something? Why didn't you kill the arrogant bastard?"

"Oh, no, my friend, you don't seem to understand how this little arrangement works. I don't help you, I merely observe from the shadows and make the odd appearance to give you my opinion. I'm not your plaything and I never will be."

"If you won't kill him then could you at least, like, revive Jerry? You seem to think your powers are so boundless, can't you bring him back to life?"

"So Jerry is the ugly one? I'll remember that. Or maybe not, I have a lot of things to remember. In response to your questions, the short answer is no. No I cannot."

"Why the bloody hell not?" Elton fumed.

"It seems you don't understand how necromancy works, either. Now, I'm not against necromancy, as many human mages seem to be. In fact, I've utilised it numerous times in the past for particular issues. Or just for a bit of fun – you should see the look on a man's face when he sees a lifeless corpse walking towards him. Though on the other continent they get those naturally, the poor souls. I tried to convince the Council not to do it, but they were an evil bunch. Forgive me, I've allowed myself to ramble. Necromancy, you see, is not quite as simple as politely asking a corpse to wake up and poof, it's like they never died. No, no, no. Although it does often involve the reanimation of corpses, you can never recover their soul. They're particularly volatile constructs, souls, and if you don't capture it the moment it's free of its living prison, then there's no point in trying to capture it again. It will have long since disappeared into who-knows-where. Even I don't know."

"Sounds like a load of superstitious nonsense," Elton grunted, unsure of how to offload his anger when locked in a bunker with a vampire. He chose to forcefully remove one of the books from its place on the shelf, shifting the thick layer of dust from the shelf's entire collection. He threw it as hard as he could, groaning in the process, and the pages detached from the spine mid-air as it flew towards the wall and landed with a thud. The floor and table were covered in ancient manuscripts and fictional stories, historical documentations and other things that could have been in the books as he threw another two at the same spot, achieving a similar result to the first.

"You really believe that after everything I've said, I would be capable of spewing nonsense? I'm a fierce opponent of misinformation, my dear Elton. I would be quite the hypocrite to spread it myself. Your ugly friend is gone. His soul has escaped and if I were to resurrect him, you would be left with a lifeless shell of a person. Ironic, I know. I think you have bigger problems to worry about, though, as the bald one will be next on the chopping block."

"You need to help him! There's no chance I can get there in time! And even if I could, what would I be able to do against a Salyrian knight?"

Kalahar shrugged and mockingly unfolded his legs out to rest on the table as Elton had done.

"This is your fight, not mine. As I said, I'm just observing. Human quarrels are terribly entertaining. So petty yet so intense."

"You're fucking useless," Elton said, going to unlock the bunker. He started to unlock the heavy door before his breathing was halted by a dark tendril wrapping and tightening around his throat. The tendrils forced him to turn around and face the vampire, whose ruby eyes appeared to be glowing much more intensely than before.

"I will help you just this once, Elton Redwinter," Kalahar hissed. "I mean, it's not as if I've already helped you by chopping off my own hand for the survival of your race. But don't overestimate how far my help extends. Nobody will die by my hand, so it will be up to you to finish the job. Get moving."

The vampire vanished and Elton doubled over, gasping for air. He then swiftly opened the door, checked that his dagger was still at his belt and jogged from the bunker, fuelled by adrenaline. Regardless of whatever chemicals were assisting his body, his physical fitness was still far from able to sustain a sprint. And if he tried to sprint, it wouldn't be much faster than a jog. So he jogged upstairs, listening to the crescendo of clashing steel and shouting. One more flight of stairs put him face to face with Paul, who was under attack by the two knights, one of which had tripped and dropped their sword. Elton rushed towards the fallen knight like a rabid dog, dagger drawn and aiming for his neck, but he was too slow and the knight picked up his sword in time to block the blow, before

180

pushing forward with enough force to cause Elton to land on his back. He struggled to his feet as the knight aimed to swing his sword again – but instead, he dropped it. Elton seized the opportunity and charged, using his weight to his advantage and knocked the knight to the ground, landing on top of him. The knight's eyes grew wide with terror as the Syndicate leader plunged the dagger into his throat without hesitation.

The fallen knight gurgled on his own blood as it erupted from the wound and Elton wasted no time in rushing to assist Paul, who was moving at incredible speed to dodge or parry the dark-haired knight's sword, which moved with a hypnotic elegance. Moving quickly came with the penalty of being desperately tiring and it showed – Paul's face was coated in a thick, reflective layer of sweat and his heavy, rapid breathing was clearly audible. Elton tried to make the dark-haired knight train his attention elsewhere by taking the fallen knight's sword from his unmoving hand and clashing it against his breastplate. The knight did not lose focus. Instead, Elton's noise caused Paul's attention to falter and the knight used the moment to his advantage, punching Paul in the stomach with a steel-plated knuckle and kicking him to the floor. Paul's shivs pathetically clattered against the floor. He crawled backwards, clutching his abdomen where he had been struck as the knight raised his sword to deliver the final blow.

"No!" Elton cried, sprinting forwards at a speed faster than he had ever travelled on foot. He didn't make it.

Instead, as the blade fell, tip towards the ground, Elton and Paul were both shocked as it flew from the dark-haired knight's solid grip and smashed a window as it sailed through the air, landing outside. The knight swore and looked to the stairwell, where Rosa stood, completely naked. She looked as exhausted as Paul and their breathing was in sync. Elton quickly kicked the fallen knight's sword towards Rosa.

"You sons-of-bitches are in cahoots with witches, are you?" The dark-haired knight spoke. His words were delivered with a strange sense of power. "I know when I'm outmatched. I'll be leaving now."

He rushed towards the stairwell, shoving Elton and Rosa out of the way as he went, catching them off guard. Rosa was about to chase but Elton stopped her and they heard his metallic footsteps grow quiet as he left the Redhouse and they watched as he mounted a white mare outside. He promptly spurred the horse with his heels and galloped in the direction of the City Guard.

CHAPTER 21

"I wager you have three months left to live, bard," Jade announced. She, Richard, and Ferris rode together atop their horses – Ferris had purchased a seemingly unremarkable chestnut gelding from a stable outside the gates of Limara. It had turned out to be much more valuable than first thought, being extraordinarily calm and faster than both Rosie and Jade's mare, of which she had neither claimed ownership nor given a name. Ferris had instructed the Miradosi insurrectionists to stay in Limara and control the keep for three days or until the first signs of a potential Sanskari retaliation before returning to their homes and carrying on with life as normal. But not before causing as much disruption as possible.

"Ahah, but they can't kill me if they can't catch me!" Ferris taunted, spurring the horse forwards to demonstrate its speed. He then brought it to a halt after a reasonable distance and allowed the others to catch up.

"They can catch you if they have soldiers everywhere who are capable of blocking your path. Speed won't be of much use when the road is impassable."

"If people get in the way, that would be no problem at all. I'm sure Breeze won't have complaints about mowing through a few dozy soldiers."

"He might have complaints if said dozy soldiers impale his flanks with arrows and spears," Jade argued. "Why are you even travelling with us? I feel like your bravery borders on stupidity. You would be entirely safer if you went south."

"Ah, but I need new material! What better place to find it than in the occupied lands of the North? There will be no

shortage of suffering, corruption, and destruction – perfect for what I need. And you happen to be some of the most interesting people I've travelled with – well, particularly you, witch. I mean no offense to you, Richard."

Richard waved it off and continued onwards without a word.

"To write about travelling with a witch, though – people will come flocking to see me!" Ferris continued.

"Don't they already?" Richard muttered.

"You're even more foolish than I thought if you would actually write that," Jade scorned. "You'd be killed for having travelled with a magic-wielder, no matter which side of the border you were on. Unless you were planning to spread your ballads to the Canarian night schools?"

"Killed? Not a chance. You see, although my ballads are wonderfully moving and capable of entrancing an audience, they're also usually riddled with fiction. That doesn't escape the attention of boring, do-good authorities, regardless of which side of the border they're on. I have free reign to spread my stories. Usually the authorities appreciate me coming to their towns and villages too, because it brings in plenty of travellers and travellers means tax. Not for me though, I manage to be exempt most of the time."

Jade scoffed and turned her attention to a horse-drawn wagon heading towards them. It was loaded with various furs and the man mounted on the horse dressed like a typical Miradosi merchant.

"You still haven't told me where you're heading, witch," Ferris exclaimed, inspecting the furs on the cart in greater detail as they passed.

"And it will remain that way, for you are not accompanying us. However, I will at least say as far as possible from Limara after that disaster you created. Hell, I won't be able to show my face there again."

"What will you do if I follow you, then? You say I'm not accompanying you, but it seems very much that way at the moment."

"I have my ways," Jade drawled, shooting the troubadour an icy glare. He finally chose not to respond.

After a lengthy distance travelled in silence, the highway led through a small village. They watched from atop their horses as at least half the village's population came to beg for food or money. They were exceedingly thin and frail, their cheeks hollow, fingers akin to twigs.

"Please, sirs. They took everything from us," an old woman spoke.

"Who? Bandits?" Richard asked intently.

"No, sir. The blackplates. They said they needed it for the war. They left us and our young 'uns to starve!"

Richard rummaged through Rosie's saddlebags and found an apple and a wedge of cheese and tossed both to the old woman. Her eyes lit up as she caught it and the rest of the villagers were quick to gather around.

"Thank you, kindest sir!" she beamed. "May the Deities grant you safe travels."

Richard nodded and carried onwards, scowling. He considered tossing a small pouch of rions as he left but was unsure of whether it would be of any value.

"I thought they would want the people to be on their side?" Richard asked, agitated. "How can they expect to peacefully rule anywhere if they steal from helpless peasants in much the same way as a common cutthroat?"

"They don't expect support because they know they don't have any," Ferris supplied. "They will benefit more from ruling through fear, as that allows them to gather resources in whichever way they see fit. I heard that they even employ the use of slaves in the far North."

"You don't have to go that far north before you see slaves," Jade stated. "But the Miradosi aren't so innocent. They will loot and rape in just the same way as the northern soldiers because regardless of what colour they wear, they are all men. Miradosi villages near the border will be in much the same condition as the one we just passed through. I even visited some which had been plundered by the Miradosi forces while I was supervising my Sanskari detachment – the bandits we worked alongside wanted to raid a village nearby but we got there to find a Miradosi detachment already there, loading a cart with supplies from the village under the watchful, angry eyes of villagers which might once have supported them.

Along with the tears of mothers and the loud curses of fathers locked outside their own homes as their only daughters took turns being defiled by each forsaken soldier. There was nothing they could do as they were left with nothing. Much like we just saw."

Richard and Ferris were both taken aback by how emotional the sorceress had become.

"What... did you do?" Ferris asked uneasily.

"We slaughtered every last one of the vile creatures and gave the people back what they rightfully owned. I've never seen a group of people change their allegiance so quickly. We managed to convince the bandits to ask for compensation instead of committing the same atrocities. Nobody was going to get hurt that day," she recounted.

Richard looked straight ahead as he had done for most of the journey and felt a sense of dishonour. Ferris's usually jubilant expression had also turned to stone as they returned to silence.

At one point, the highway split in two and they chose to continue travelling north, perpendicular to the sun's path across the sky.

"Are you planning to continue north until you reach Vivian waters?" Ferris asked.

"I want to go to Virilia," Jade announced.

Richard brought his horse to a halt. Ferris and Jade followed his example.

"What? Virilia is at least a week's journey away and also happens to be the capital of this blasted empire. What are we going to achieve by going there?"

"I have a plan," Jade said. "Involving you, Richard. Bard, if you must, you can come along, but don't get in my way."

"And what is your plan, O mysterious witch?"

"To kill Nendar Varanus."

"Woah, woah, woah. Hold up, there. If I recall correctly, you lectured us about how the man is untouchable back in Limara. And now you tell us you want to travel into the heartlands of the enemy and kill him? Surely if he's as omnipotent as you describe then your quest is a suicide mission?"

"I believe I said he's untouchable to *most* humans. I am not most humans. I've thought this through rather thoroughly."

"Well, do feel free to explain," Ferris patronised.

Jade rolled her eyes. "It will be getting dark soon – we'll find a tavern and I will explain then. For now, focus on the road. I'm surprised we're yet to be attacked by some form of menace."

Around ten miles further along the country highway they began to lose light as the sun sank below the horizon. They had reached a gloomy oak forest with no signs of human activity nearby and the already dark forest was no more inviting with the complete loss of light.

"Come on, we have to keep going," Jade ordered. "Grab a branch each, we'll make our own light."

"Why don't we just make a camp for the night, witch?" Ferris suggested.

"Because we've reached the Kal'sennar Forest. We do not want to make camp here, or anywhere nearby. There's a fortified town on the other side of the forest – we can stay there overnight."

"How do you know all this? What's so special about the Kal'whatever forest?"

"I travelled along this very highway on my way south with my original mission. And the Kal'sennar Forest is named after the people that live in it – but they're more akin to creatures than people. We do not want to cross paths or have them find us. Make haste."

Jade found three sizeable fallen branches at the mouth of the forest and lit one end of each. Her chilling warning encouraged everyone to ride their horses at a canter as the mighty oak trees appeared to constantly encroach upon them more and more as they continued along the well-worn path. It was clear by the thick, undisturbed layers of brush lining the path that nobody travelling along this stretch of highway strayed from the beaten track.

At one point, a raven suddenly flapped its wings and flew off into the night sky, startling all three members of the party. Richard and Jade's mares had become increasingly skittish and were showing signs of fear while Ferris's gelding plodded onwards with no reaction to the sudden sounds and eerily quiet atmosphere.

Richard spotted the giant reflective eyes of an owl in the canopy overhead before it gave out a hoot and vanished into the darkness, presumably having spotted some form of rodent scuttling amongst the dense foliage. The owl's eyes were replaced by a smaller pair of eyes from lower down on the tree and they traced the trio's every movement until having gone past.

"Did either of you see that as well?" Richard whispered. Jade nodded in response but carried on without a word.

Another pair of eyes identical to the last appeared on the other side of the road, even lower than before. They were strangely humanlike apart from their unnaturally bright reflections. The pair of eyes was joined by another from deeper in the thicket and it wasn't long before a third pair appeared. Jade silently instructed them to slow their horses as more and more pairs of eyes appeared all around them and even in front of them on the road. Richard hesitantly looked behind him to find an army of eyes peering through the thick blanket of darkness in their direction, advancing at the same speed as their horses.

Jade raised her fist to tell them to stop and they came to a halt, having already been travelling at a walking pace. The eyes also stopped advancing but continued to multiply in number until they were entirely surrounded and phenomenally outnumbered.

"Witch, I'm freaking out," Ferris announced.

"If we act wisely, we will survive. We will not try to fight the Kal'sennar."

Eventually, one of the pairs of eyes moved forward into the dim light of their torches to reveal a short, human-like creature which treaded without making a sound. The creature was completely covered in short grey hair, apart from its ashen face, palms, and feet. Its eyes were indeed a similar size to a human's but shared features with those seen in cats – its large pupils narrowed to slits when it came into the light but were capable of expanding to occupy the entire area of the eye. It also had distinctly large ears which looked comical aside its relatively small head.

What the trio didn't fail to notice was that the creature was wielding a crooked spear crudely fashioned from a sharpened branch.

"I've heard of creatures like these! Apparently they live in the Lavinian jungles!" Ferris quietly exclaimed.

"No, Ferris. These are not apes. These are the Kal'sennar – the original human-like inhabitants of this continent. But the Temeriosi settlers scared them away into isolated pockets like this forest. And they have found us."

"Do they speak?"

"No. But we will understand them."

The spear-wielding Kal'sennar almost unnoticeably shifted its padded foot against the ground and two more Kal'sennar appeared from the darkness behind him, both holding rope made from plant fibres they had managed to craft in the forest.

"Get off your horses," Jade instructed. Richard and Ferris did as they were told and Jade followed suit. The spear-wielding Kal'sennar flicked its eyes between the three before choosing to focus its attention on Jade and thrust the spear in her direction as the other two Kal'sennar walked cautiously towards Richard and Ferris.

"Witch, they're tying us up. Is this supposed to be happening?"

"Yes, and they will tie me up as well. Allow it to happen and trust me."

The Kal'sennar made swift work of binding Richard and Ferris' feet and hands, completely immobilising both. Jade was then also bound and after all three were incapable of moving, the rest of the Kal'sennar flooded from the shrubbery in a swarm of grey. They worked together to pick up the trio and carried them from the beaten path, bringing the horses along with them. Somehow, the horses didn't need to be bound and instead just followed without any instruction.

Perhaps the most surreal part of the experience thus far was the complete and utter silence. Even as the colony of primitive creatures liberated themselves from the shrubbery, they did so without so much as rustling a leaf. Their collective footsteps' volume rivalled that of a stalking cat's, and they didn't grunt or make any noise breathing when they picked up the comparatively heavier humans. They trudged through the ghostly forest and could hear every nocturnal creature whether it was near or far – hearing was not obstructed in any way.

Richard realised that in the darkness, he had no real idea whether he was still accompanying Jade and Ferris. He gently called their names but received no response. He called their names louder, trying not to provoke the strange creatures. Off in the distance he heard Ferris call back, but Jade didn't respond. Or if she had, Richard couldn't hear her.

Eventually, the creatures stopped moving and set Richard down on the ground. He realised that at no point had the creatures taken his weapons and this gave him the confidence that he could fight his way out if Jade had made a mistake. It was still pitch-black and the only sounds were still those of the natural world – until nearby, one of the Kal'sennar began rubbing two pieces of wood together. Within moments, Richard saw the first light since being abducted from the forest path as the Kal'sennar worked together to swiftly build an impressive fire.

It appeared that the creatures had taken Richard to what he would have described as a ritual site – the fire was being built within a circle of stones which itself was the centrepiece of a large clearing. Logs placed in a ring around the circle were being used as seats. The ring of logs was interrupted at one point where a makeshift podium had been constructed from logs, stones, mud, branches and even a few flowers. A barrier had been lashed together with more of the rope which had been used to bind the trio and a single Kal'sennar stood atop it, larger and more imposing than the rest. It wore a wooden crown decorated with flowers and carried a branch which split into two at its end before curving back around to form a circular shape.

The roaring fire was joined by two more, each acting as a vertex in a triangle. The shadowy outlines of more Kal'sennar could be seen crowded around the other two fires as Richard was hauled up and carried towards the podium where the crowned Kal'sennar awaited, dramatically twirling its staff-like branch above its head. Before they reached the podium, more of the creatures arrived with long, straight branches and rope and they quickly lashed together a platform onto which Richard was placed. They then worked together to lift the platform onto the podium.

Panic began to set in as the beady-eyed creatures stared eagerly at the helpless bounty hunter. The crowned one, which Richard assumed to be the leader, slammed its staff down against the podium, creating the first loud noise since having captured the three humans. What followed was as if something had tripped in their brains.

The crowd of Kal'sennar erupted into noise: hollering, hooting, cheering, crying, shouting, and howling. All indistinct, unbearable slurs of whatever their unevolved bodies could produce. Richard realised the reason why these creatures were so easily deterred by the early human settlers. They were intelligent enough to work together and create structures and even apparently perform rituals but Richard realised at this moment that they were controlled by deeply primal instincts. Now, their comprehendible intelligence was comparable to that of the Corrupted.

They continued waking the forest as the leader of the tribal creatures stepped towards Richard and raised the circular end of its staff above him, running it over the length of his body. He hummed ominously while doing so but it was almost inaudible over the screeching of the audience. It then raised the staff towards the full moon overhead and without warning, slammed it down as hard as it could.

Richard jerked forward, but only out of anticipation of the impact which never came. Instead, the falling staff reached just above his hunting jacket and bounced off as if there was an invisible shield in the way. The leader gave out an ear-piercing shriek and ran from the podium.

Thanks, Jade, Richard thought.

But he wasn't safe yet. Although Jade had protected him with a spell, he was still tied to the podium. This became more problematic when the Kal'sennar leader approached with a much more dangerous-looking utensil than a staff-shaped branch.

The creature wielded the dagger which looked more like a short sword in its relatively short arms. It must have been sal-

191

vaged from previous victims as it appeared to be the only object made from something other than whatever could be found in the forest and Richard couldn't see any forges. The creature stepped forward and drove the tip of the sword directly towards Richard's stomach but achieved the same outcome as had occurred when using the staff. It shrieked even louder and even more ear-piercingly and furiously drove the sword down again and again, hollering in sync with the crowd the whole time. After enough failure, the crowned Kal'sennar abandoned the use of a weapon entirely and began frantically beating its fists against the invisible barrier as if it had gone mad.

Richard didn't know how long the shield would last but he wasn't confident it would be enough. He thought about trying to roll over and land on his feet but there was no feasible method of escape without being caught again. That was, until the Kal'sennar leader began to float.

It was very gradual, but the confused creature was lifted into the air by an invisible force. It started to frenziedly convulse, trying to escape the unknown entity which carried it into the air. Meanwhile, the Kal'sennar audience had stopped their screeching and looked up in awe as the full moon illuminated their leader while it continued to float. Its eyes then suddenly glossed over and it began to drawl something in an unknown language which sounded mostly slurred. Judging by the reaction of the other creatures, it was significant news and they started to panic, running around aimlessly while the leader continued drawling about whatever end-of-the-world scenario to which the other creatures were reacting.

The leader then said something in a much harsher tone and the others immediately scattered into the brush. Now that they were gone, Richard was finally able to observe the surroundings in more detail. He wished he hadn't.

Littered around the campfire where the Kal'sennar had been sitting were bones. Human bones. An assortment of bones from the legs, arms, spine and just about anywhere else on the body. Human skulls were implanted in holes which had been carved from the logs they used as seats. His stomach felt a particular stir when he saw one femur which still bore gnawed flesh.

The Kal'sennar leader dropped from the sky, landing in the middle of the roaring bonfire. The hairs on its body were instantly set alight and Jade appeared from the shadows, refusing to watch. The creature cried in agony, trying hopelessly to escape the fire's grasp before its cries eventually dwindled in volume and died out completely.

Jade whispered a spell and cut the ropes which bound Richard to the makeshift platform. He stood up and immediately nocked an arrow, preparing to fight. Jade gestured him to remain calm and put the arrow away. He obeyed.

As they hacked their way through the dense shrubbery, Richard noticed they weren't being watched by any glowing eyes. They made their way to the last bonfire where Ferris was still tied up in a similar predicament to how Richard had been earlier. Also like Richard was earlier, he was alone with no audience and a burning Kal'sennar leader's corpse in the middle of the fire.

Jade whispered the same spell as she had done when releasing Richard and set Ferris free. They wasted no time in escaping the forest, navigating as best as they could back towards the highway. The creatures had led the horses to a smaller clearing which was completely devoid of light, but Jade applied a spell to herself which allowed complete night vision and she became their navigator.

Richard and Ferris couldn't be of any help, so they followed Jade's every move as the brush became less and less dense. They hoped she knew what she was doing, and they were right to do so – she led them onto the worn stretch of highway within minutes. Having spent time in the forest's depths, the moonlight now made the road seem infinitely brighter, but they still lit torches for optimal vision anyways.

It was a while before anyone said anything, but Ferris couldn't help himself.

"So... what exactly did you do, witch?"

CHAPTER 22

SANAÍD, TYEN'AEL

The closer Elaeínn managed to get to Common Square, the thicker the crowds became. Which was tedious and a hindrance, as she wasn't quite able to hear Jaelaar's speech. It just meant that she would equally have to be a hindrance to the others who were interested in hearing what he had to say.

"—and those selected to take part in the journey were hand-selected from a large pool of all incredibly talented mages, all of whom exhibited phenomenal talent and knowledge. But we managed to pick out those who we believe would be the greatest assets to our mission – the exploration of new lands. New lands, I might add, that we believe hold great magical significance. New lands which could be the key to unlocking the future of High Elven society."

The crowd clapped politely.

"Therefore, the team leaving on the twenty-seventh will comprise the following accomplished mages: Fura Aeríard of Sanaíd; Kaesta Haettís of Henvaer; Seríen Díefren of Kalanor..."

Jaelaar rattled off a list of what must have been no fewer than thirty names, before coming to the last name on his list.

"—and finally, Delía Hatten of Garaennía."

At that moment, the Prime Minister's eyes fixated on Elaeínn, who had been continuing to shove her way through the crowd. She froze and returned the gaze before frantically searching for the oncoming guards, thirsty for her arrest. But there were none. And a few seconds later, Jaelaar continued with his speech.

"Congratulations to those who have been selected, and condolences to those who were not. You are all valuable contributors to the Tyen'Aeli cause – your country is proud of you. Your people are proud of you. Please, a round of applause to all of our benevolent mages."

The crowd clapped again, this time for a longer duration, but no louder than before.

"To those of you who were successful in auditioning for a place on the expedition, I'd like to thank you personally. As such, I invite you all to the Serenna Palace, from where we will travel directly via teleportation to the docks in Laethyvaerd. It is from Laethyvaerd that we will depart on our journey, which is expected to last a week. With the might of the grandmasters who will also be joining us on the mighty Aeli galleons, we will breeze through the journey and the perils of the ocean will be no more than an afterthought.

"If there is someone from the list that is not here today, I ask that anybody who knows them inform them at the earliest opportunity. It is imperative that we are ready. Those who are here, please, visit the Serenna Palace at the most immediate notice."

Jaelaar stepped away from the podium and drew a hand into a fist, concluding the effects of the pathetically weak volume-increasing spell he had been utilising throughout his speech.

The crowd dispersed orderly and Elaeínn was left with two options. It only took a moment's contemplation to choose between them.

She headed off in the direction of the Serenna Palace for the second time that day, still dangerously handling the unsheathed sword. Along the way, she paid a quick visit to an FTA-sympathising blacksmith.

"Aegard," she stepped onto the patio of the blacksmith's shop, greeting Aegard, who was in the midst of sharpening a standard-looking, unimaginative steel sword.

"Elle," he responded, stopping for a moment to wipe the sweat from his brow. He eyed up the ornate sword she held carefully in both hands with a sharp look of appraisal.

"That's quite the blade," he commented, looking scathingly at the one he had paused sharpening. "Better than the tripe

I've been tasked with making. In the hundreds. For shit-all. I barely have the metal for it, as they're damn touchy about my use of their resources."

"For the government, I take it?" Elaeínn inferred, taking a seat on the wooden bench lining the patio.

"Yeah... out of nowhere, a delegate from the palace comes and gives me an order, signed by the Defence Secretary. Five hundred steel swords. Nothing worthy of a craftsman, just bog-standard cheap garbage. The pay seems hefty, but as much can be expected of such an enormous order. Individually, I'm getting paid next to nothing."

"And you're making it for them?" she ridiculed.

"I have to make an income, Elle. And besides, don't go thinking I'm putting my full effort into this. Because I'm not – in the slightest. Whoever uses these swords will be lucky to keep themselves alive with it. There's certainly no pleasure in using such abysmally poor steel. Anyways, where did you get that?"

"It's a long story. I'll tell you inside. I also need something – a scabbard. It didn't come with one, so to say."

"Do you know the dimensions?"

She shook her head.

"Well, anything to take a break from... this." He gestured agitatedly at the unsharpened steel sword.

"What you've got there is a relic, by the looks of it," he continued, leading her into the workshop. Various swords of various shapes, sizes and materials were hanging from the wall or placed neatly on shelves, along with an assortment of other weapons and pieces of armour – war axes, halberds, spearheads, arrowheads, knives, scythe blades, war hammers, helmets, breastplates, pauldrons, spaulders, gauntlets, cuisses, and greaves.

"So? What is it?" she asked, laying the blade on the table indicated to her by the blacksmith.

"Let me have a look." He crouched down, closely scrutinising the various markings and carvings on not just the hilt, but also along the blade.

"I... don't recognise it," Aegard concluded, after turning the sword over and examining its entire surface area. "None of

196

these symbols – they aren't Elven. Or Dwarven. I've never seen anything like this."

"I found it above Jaelaar's fireplace," Elaeínn stated proudly.

"I'm sorry?"

"Above Jaelaar's fireplace, in the palace," she reiterated. "Somewhere I am apparently visiting again after I get a scabbard for this thing. I take it you weren't at the square, so I'll tell you what happened. Jaelaar announced the names of the 'mages' accompanying him on some expedition to the West. My code name was among them."

"Delía?" he queried.

"Delía Hatten," she confirmed. "This could end up very bad. Because my real identity has already been found out – and now, apparently, so has my fake identity."

"You're also not a mage," Aegard pointed out, sauntering towards a cabinet and retrieving from next to it a measuring stick, which he brought back and placed alongside the blade of Elaeínn's sword.

"Seventy centimetres," the smith remarked. "It's also"—he picked up the blade in one hand and whirled it around—"incredibly light. Like nothing I've seen before. But I've already said that."

"Do you have a scabbard spare?"

"I do. One moment."

Aegard disappeared into what must have been a storage room and came back a minute later cradling a simple brown-leather sheath, complete with a strap to attach to her belt.

"How much?" Elaeínn inserted the sword into the scabbard, and it fit perfectly. She fit the strap to her belt and practiced unsheathing it, finding a comfortable position on her waist to do so.

"In honesty, I've had that lying around for months. A half-aerrin would be more than enough."

She fished through her robes for the few remaining coins after her experience with the astromancer and tossed him two naemmons.

"You be careful, Elle," Aegard warned, ushering her to the patio. "But if you're going to risk yourself, I trust you'll make something out of it."

"Without a doubt. Thanks, Aegard."

The new weight on her side, although Aegard had insisted it was light, would need getting used to. She shifted her satchel to the right side of her waist in an attempt to counterbalance the weight of the sword, and that helped.

She reached the first set of gates to the palace as a group of discontent others were being told to move along. The guards, the same as had been stationed earlier in the day, noticed her approach and allowed her through without so much as a confirmation of her identity.

She breezed through the gardens, not interested in any further admiration of the flora.

She reached the door to the palace, where she thoroughly expected her sword to be taken from her person. It wasn't and she was allowed to pass and even told where Jaelaar was waiting for her – by the very guard to whom she had lied about her identity and run from. But either he didn't remember her from only a few hours ago or he had been told not to apprehend her. Either way, the situation was surreal. And she couldn't help but feel that she was walking into a trap.

Jaelaar was waiting for the expedition invitees in the palace lobby, protected by a pair of guards at his sides. He noticed Elaeínn's wary approach and whispered something to his guards, after which they stepped back and allowed him to walk away. Towards her.

"Miss Hatten," he exclaimed. She felt herself hunching over out of instinct.

"Prime Minister," Elaeínn replied politely, straightening her posture and fondling the carved golden pommel of her sword. "I'm sorry, but I'm not quite... prepared, for the expedition. In fact, I had no idea it was possible for my selection."

"No, you didn't," he smirked. "You were one of the few 'Unity' candidates. This was not something the public was made aware of, and you were passed off as a mage. Miss Hatten, I'd like to introduce you to your counterparts – Karek, Laettía and Períen to me, please!"

His bellowing to the crowd produced three individuals – an exceptionally tall man, at least two metres. With a full head of ashen hair, he managed to look simultaneously fifty and one-hundred-and-fifty. Though there wasn't much difference, by High Elven standards.

There was also an older woman, with a nick on her left ear and a scar running across her right eye. She bore the signs of a hardened warrior and kept her hair tied neatly in a bun, while her face was dressed with a grin.

The third man Elaeínn could only describe as the physical embodiment of anger – whether it was his scraggy, unkempt auburn hair and beard, his furrowed brow, his resting frown, or his uninviting physical stance. His skin was also an unusual off-white tone and his ears slightly shorter than that of a normal high elf.

"Karek Hyggavaerd," Jaelaar began, motioning to the ashen-haired man. "Before your time. But back when I was merely a representative for my district in the Common Chamber, he was infamous. He committed the October Killings – are you familiar with them?"

"I've heard of them, but I'm not familiar."

"The October Killings were an atrocious event in which this man before you set out with a clan of believers across the country and systematically slaughtered villages and towns of Raerists, sparing the Lirdían population. He, like you, believed in overthrowing the system. And he was defeated. But many still exist who believe in his words, and we have released him from his life sentence to bring him along. In an attempt to show that there is no feasible reason to segregate society based on religion, and that the Lirdíans can coexist peacefully with the Raerists."

"I could fucking throttle you this moment, Jaelaar," Karek warned in a gravelly voice.

"You could," Jaelaar agreed. "But that would benefit nobody, and would only fuel hatred against the Lirdíans. It is of mutual interest that we work together and present a united front."

Jaelaar moved on to gesture towards the woman, who sniggered as he stepped in front of her.

"Laettía Irgalín," Jaelaar pronounced. "Another infamous criminal, and I'm sure you have heard of her this time."

Elaeínn nodded.

"The ringleader of the Jesters," Jaelaar explained anyways. "The rationality of their motives was comparable to the laughability of the job from which they derived their name. Incapable of viewing any situation as remotely serious and exhibiting a complete disregard for the basic concept of empathy. Wholly and utterly convinced that those around them whose lives they made a misery supported their constant murder and thievery. What a shame it must have been for you, Laettía, to find out that it was your own neighbours who betrayed you to the Guard."

"It was a laugh," Laettía retorted. "I knew I wasn't to be killed. It was a fun little game. And before you sent in your second batch of guards, I even managed to catch the rat."

"Moving on." Jaelaar moved abruptly to stand next to the other man. "Períen Fyríard, Folantan exile. A crossbreed between a high elf and a light elf. Shunned and rejected, he decided his best choice was to turn to blindly hateful terrorism, against anyone unlucky enough to cross his path. He's exceptionally knowledgeable about explosives, and the implications of that were what led to his exile from Folanta. Because apparently they can't be bothered to deal with their own criminals, so they send them elsewhere. Which, in this case, was Tyen'Ael, where he continued bombing regions of governmental significance. And very nearly managed to take down the Bank of Sanaíd. But then he was caught, and landed here, in the palace's dungeons."

While the previous two insurrectionists had provided something of wit to say to the Prime Minister, Períen remained eerily silent. And he, Elaeínn thought, was the scariest of them all.

"You referred to them as my 'counterparts'," Elaeínn drawled. "In what way does that describe any of them?"

"You four"—Jaelaar stepped back to face them as a group —"are all terrorists. Convicted terrorists, too – that includes you, Miss Hatten. Hatten, Tinaíd – regardless of which name suits you, the only way you are leaving this palace is through a safeguarded portal which our mages are to open to transport us to the docks at Laethyvaerd. The palace was put on lockdown the moment you stepped through the gates, and the guards have been instructed only to let through the expected remainder of the expedition team, the appearances of which they have been described to in immaculate detail."

"That's why it was so damn easy!" Elaeínn hissed as her right arm twitched, anxious to grasp the hilt of her sword and make first use of it.

"Before you do anything rash, please know that we don't mean to detain you. In fact, the opposite. We have made it our mission to unify the citizens of Tyen'Ael under our belief that there is no better place to live in the world, and to do that we must work with those who oppose us, to convince them and their followers that they are wrong. So while you aren't the leader of the FTA, Elaeínn, you are high-ranking enough to set an example. And I truly hope that you'll fulfil your role to its capacity, and embrace a future of peaceful coexistence, instead of irrational violence and terror."

"The only future of coexistence I'll accept is one of freedom," she barked. "That means that unless you plan on radically changing your way of thinking, we will never get along."

"We'll see," Jaelaar silenced her. "Come – it's time to leave."

He turned and began to walk towards the main group of mages. Períen roared and careered towards the seemingly defenceless Prime Minister, who pivoted to face the charging cross-elf and extended a hand, uttering a spell. Períen's momentum was eliminated and he simply tripped, stumbling over his feet and landing face first on the floor, inviting a round of laughter from the entire capacity of the palace lobby, whose attention had been caught by the initial burst of sound.

Jaelaar leaned down to speak to the incapacitated elf.

"That," he drawled, "is not a good start."

Períen regained his footing and sauntered away, evidently uninterested in interaction with the rest of his counterparts, as Jaelaar had described the members of their little group.

"FTA, eh?" Laettía asked, drawing Elaeínn's attention from Jaelaar, who was organising the mages into groups of their own. "I thought about joining you lot when I got out. But then I realised that I really don't give a toss. And that I would probably end up in that cell until the day I die."

"Noble," Elaeínn responded drily.

"Oh, you really believe in what you do? I have to admit, I wasn't entirely convinced. And what, you think the best way to go about getting what you want is to kill those who stand in your way?"

"Well—"

"Because you're right," the Jester cut her off. "Diplomacy is a myth – achieves nothing. When you want something, you need to take it by force. As you've worked out. Smart girl."

The corners of Elaeínn's mouth raised in an uneasy smile as Karek stepped closer to join in on their conversation.

"And what exactly were your motives, clown?" he grated, directing a glare at the ever-smirking Jester.

"Self-benefit, nothing more," she supplied matter-of-factly. "I got rich, my allies got rich, we had a boatload of fun in the process. Then the government in their almighty wisdom decided that our methods were wholly unethical and ordered us imprisoned. I was actually meant to be hanged but the Liberals managed to garner enough support to miraculously avoid it. That's your generation, girl, saved me from the noose. I thank you for that.

"As for you, Lirdían – you're a right bloody moron. You went out killing off the majority religious population of the country and expected to get away with it? You incompetent fool. And you call me the clown."

"I'll have you know the Lirdíans are the only ones to believe in the true God, unlike your false prophet," Karek hissed, bristling with rage.

"And I'll have you know that I don't give a shit about whichever probably made-up fool followers of either religion believe in. Because I don't believe in any god or prophet."

That quieted the Lirdían, who stepped back and followed the same thought path as Períen, leaving the two women to themselves.

"Looks like we're on our way," Laettía remarked, watching as old men dressed lavishly in heavy, broad, fur-trimmed robes sporting a variety of dark hues of traditionally garish colours opened a series of room-length portals. They were clearly straining under the effort, though trying exceptionally hard not to let it show.

"I like you, girl," Laettía then revealed to the abnormally quiet Elaeínn who had since Jaelaar's departure still been reeling in a minor state of shock.

202

"Thanks," she whispered distractedly, glancing quickly between Karek and Períen, who appeared to have been naturally drawn to the shadiest areas on opposite sides of the lobby.

The last of the mages filed into the portal and Jaelaar beckoned for Laettía and Elaeínn to follow suit, while the other men had to be coerced with help of the Guard. Períen put up a fight and forced another trio to help the first guard wrangle him under control.

"Prime Minister, I'm not sure this is a good idea," one of the guards stated after having shoved the wild-haired cross-elf through the portal. "You're sure to be killed. Magic is only so useful – for people like that, you need a blade."

"It'll be quite alright. Return to your post," Jaelaar dismissed as Karek was encouraged through the portal by a surly guard.

A perky man clutching a clipboard and quill approached the remaining three expeditioners.

"By some miracle, everyone is accounted for." He smiled to Jaelaar. "Good luck, Prime Minister."

Jaelaar nodded in assent and ushered the two women through the portal before finally stepping through himself.

CHAPTER 23

"Odd fella," Paul remarked, having returned to being himself. "Thanks for that, Rosa. Never had my life saved by a naked lady."

"You bloody dog," she snipped, covering her breasts with her arms. "Really, I don't need to do this anymore. One of the Lazerian illusionists got in contact with me recently. Look what I can do now."

She murmured something under her breath in a language which neither of the men understood and a set of robes quickly materialised over her bare body. Paul's eyes remained fixated on the exposed areas for as long as they remained exposed, which wasn't long.

"Ta-da," she said, bowing.

"You said 'illusion' or something, right? Does that mean if I touch it—"

"You won't dare try," she interrupted, smiling with a paralytic glare.

"Have we forgotten something?" Elton asked, gesturing towards the dead body swimming in a pool of blood. "We need to go back into hiding before that peacock comes back with the King and his army. He just failed to eliminate the sole target they came to this city for, and I doubt he's going to omit that to his king. Rosa, did you find Felix?"

"I found him, alright. He'll probably be here any minute. I just took the quicker route. Turns out that we worried for nothing – he was taken to the City Guard and told to give a statement but they didn't do anything to him. He was let free after telling them a load of bollocks about you."

"But that knight that just ran off came to the square some time after you left and said that he had captured... wait a minute. Yeah, that makes sense. He said he had captured two of my associates. Lucky choice of number, I suppose."

"Well, everyone is safe. Except poor old Jerry. Suppose we'd better bury him. Shit, if one knight can do that then we've got no chance!"

"Which is why we must hide and bide our time. They will not remain here forever."

The group gazed at Jerry's lifeless body and Elton asked Rosa to get some supplies to stitch up his wound. She complied without question and they stopped the slow trickle of dark blood from his leg and chest, where the knight had delivered the finishing blow. Once the bleeding had stopped, they carried his body to a small, sandy area in the back of the Redhouse which, in other, more forgiving climates, might have been called a garden. The only contents of the area, apart from the sand, were a rusty shovel leaning against the sandstone wall and an old headstone, engraved with the names of all the fallen members of the Syndicate. It had been Elton's idea to bury all the dead here, but it had since been reserved for only the most important, as they discovered in horror that the bodies often didn't decompose as quickly as they had expected. Now, Jerry was given his own spot in the corner of the garden and he was memorialised on the tombstone with the etching of *Jerald Gondas – B. 1313, D. 1348. A valiant, reliable member of the guild and always a good friend. Died in battle at the hand of a Salyrian knight. Forever strong.*

As they finished carving the message on the headstone and prepared to re-cover the body with the coarse soil and sand, they heard shouting from near the entrance of the Redhouse.

"Rosa! Elton! You there? I've got your robes, Rosa!"

Elton motioned to go to find Felix but Paul was faster and instructed him without words to sit down. They were back shortly thereafter and Felix realised the gravity of the situation upon seeing the look of sorrow on the others' faces.

"The bastards. The absolute bastards," Felix mumbled, idly twirling one of his expensive, gemstone-encrusted knives with his fingers. He abruptly stopped its spinning and held it in his hands, gently placing it next to Jerry's body in the ground.

"There you go, mate. You can finally have it. At least one of them. Whatever you're able to do with it when you're dead, do a bloody good job of it."

Together, Elton using the shovel and the rest using their hands, they finished covering Jerry's body and stood in silence for a minute before Elton was forced to interrupt.

"We need to go. That bloody knight will long have gone and reported to his king and we'll hear the war cries within minutes. Let's go back to mine, I doubt they'll search there again."

The others nodded, staying silent. Elton thought he saw a tear escape Felix's eye, which he swiftly and subtly wiped away. They were all armed now – Rosa, who had previously been relying on magic, undid the illusory outfit and dressed in her real one. She then took the dark-haired knight's sword with its scabbard from where it had landed outside, affixing it to her belt. It was almost comedically large, but she wore it with pride.

"You ever, uh, used one o' those, Rosa?" Paul asked, gesturing to the beautifully reflective sword.

"Are you really that dense?" she replied. "Tell me, Paul. How old are you really? Because your memory is about as good as a decrepit old man's. No offence, boss."

Elton rolled his eyes.

"What am I forgettin'?" Paul asked in genuine confusion. Rosa simply sighed and put a hand against her forehead, covering half of her face.

"Never mind. In answer to your first question, yes, I have used a sword. I spent a week learning how to rather recently."

"Did ya? I did too! Boss told me I had to instruct all the lads how to use a sword to fight off the vampires."

They trudged onwards, away from the loudening hubbub of crowds which gathered in increasing sizes to survey the scene which had been left outside the Redhouse. Many gasped in awe upon seeing the pools of blood and as they looked behind them, many gathered the courage to check inside the entry hall. They came out with as much of the dead knights' armour as they could carry, and the previously observant crowd erupted into a mad rush as they all tried to get their hands on expensive pieces of plate armour.

They arrived back at Elton's house having had to duck into a few alleys along the way to avoid passing Salyrian patrols. However, as predicted, it didn't look as if there were any knights in Silverstone Square for them to worry about. A few doors had been systematically broken down, but it seemed they had given up around halfway through the residences on the square's perimeter. Elton's door had been left intact, and he fished for a key in the pocket of his gambeson, which he used to unlock the door after a cautious knock. As might have been expected, nobody responded.

Instead, when they gathered inside, they were met with the stony face of Kalahar Kefrein-Lazalar, who smirked upon seeing the sudden wave of terror upon all their faces.

"Bloody hell, vampire, you don't seem to leave me alone!" Elton asserted, though coming across as angrier than he really felt.

"If I have the power to meddle in human affairs and get away with it, then why would I give up the opportunity? You're the only people I've made myself known to, so I'm a bit limited when it comes to options of where to go."

"Fine. What are you doing here?"

"Thought you could use some assistance. How long you have before the Salyrian army enters and pillages the Redhouse, for example."

"We'll be quite alright without your information. We just need to stay in hiding."

The vampire shrugged. "If you say so."

The group of four returned to their position in the study where they peered through the shutters to observe the events in the square, before Felix had run off and the situation spiralled out of control. Now, they were relaxed, though missing one of the original members of the group.

Not much had changed from the first time they had sat in the study, disinterested, watching outside for new occurrences. They still spotted Salyrian patrols roaming through the streets but none of them stopped at Silverstone Square, instead always passing through.

"So, what happened to them knowing about me living here?" Elton said.

"I reckon," Felix replied, sinking a throwing knife into the bullseye of the target which had been etched onto the wall, "that they thought you had moved somewhere else. They probably got bored of smashing down the doors of unhappy rich folk."

"If they had any sense in the world, they would at least check the house. Instead, they left my hinges intact."

"Well," Felix said, sinking another knife into the bullseye directly next to the first, "guess they don't have any sense."

A loud crash resonated from downstairs as an unhinged door collided with the floor. The four instantly jolted upright in alarm and found places to conceal themselves within the room. Elton and Felix stood on either side of the doorway, brandishing their weapons. The intruders were not interested in stealth as they clanked up the stairs, shouting something unintelligible. As they moved closer, their words became clearer.

"Cellar and ground floor clear, sir!"

"Did you find anything noteworthy?"

Elton recognised the voice, and the looks on Paul and Rosa's faces showed that they did too.

"A lot of alcohol, sir. Including Camelian vintages. Nothing to report on the ground floor."

"We'll drink when we find the bastard. For now, search the first and second floors!"

More crashing and louder metallic footsteps.

"I think they're gettin' closer, boss," Paul whispered from behind a solid oak chair. Elton glared at him in response.

"We've found something, sir! You might want to have a look!"

"Looks like our fat bandit is into witchcraft. I shouldn't be surprised. Burn the lot."

The organised shuffling of footsteps resonated through the walls as the knights caused a commotion in the alchemy lab. None of the four knew for sure what they were doing, but they assumed the first step was to drench it in oil.

"I hope your aspen wood definitely does the trick, Rosa," Elton whispered to her as they heard the dark-haired knight chant some denunciation about dispelling magic. This was followed by a cheer as they presumably set fire to the contents of the laboratory.

"Erm, boss? Where's the lab in the house compared to us?" Paul asked.

"It's right underneath us. But it's stone, and only dragonfire can melt stone. We're fine."

"You believe in dragons now, boss?" Rosa teased.

"I believe in a great many things now, after recent events in my life. Now shut up."

"Nothing else to report on this floor, sir," one of the knights exclaimed.

"If the rat is here, then we must be close to finding him. I'll go myself," the dark-haired knight replied.

"As you wish, sir."

After a few moments of silence, a chorus of heavy footsteps thundered up the stairs and Elton wasn't ready for the sudden charge. Led by the dark-haired knight, the door was battered down and heavily armoured men rushed into the room, swords at the ready. Within moments, Elton, Rosa, Paul, and Felix were at their mercy.

"You!" the dark-haired knight growled, looking at Felix. "You were the one who 'led' us to this vile pig!"

Felix shrugged sheepishly, grinning.

"You may be amused by this now, but you won't be laughing when we stick your head on a pike. And you! I believe that belongs to me!" he boomed, looking at the sword on Rosa's belt. "Sir Dennar, please retrieve the weapon from the slut's filthy waist. And be careful, for she is a witch."

One of the knights who weren't holding a blade to someone's throat stepped forward and ripped the sheathed sword from Rosa's belt, fixating his eyes on hers for the entire duration of the action.

"You are all under arrest for treason. Sir Harrod, disarm and shackle our prisoners."

Another unoccupied knight stepped forward, carrying four pairs of clean steel shackles. First, he patted down Paul, finding his shivs and tossing them aside. After disarming him, he forcefully placed his hands behind his back and tightly locked the shackles. The knight did the same to every other prisoner and once they were all lined up neatly, the knights led them from the house and out of the front door, which was intact. They had scaled the wall to get in through the back door and Elton cursed as he realised the people that they had passed in the alley must have reported them.

The knights marched with them at a fast pace in the direction of the City Guard, and the prisoners were being as difficult as they could, by constantly causing them to slow down through 'tripping' or refusing to honestly answer any of the questions the dark-haired knight could think of.

"It was you, fatty, that killed Sir Yaris, wasn't it? That alone ought to have you subject to death after intensive torture. He was a good knight."

"Evidently not good enough," Elton remarked. His comment was met with a harsh, steel-plated smack across the face. It was immediately painful and Elton could do nothing about it with his hands bound behind his back as the skin on his cheek burned. He heard Paul snicker behind him after the exchange.

"There'll be more where that comes from if you choose to be antagonistic for the duration of my questioning. We have been authorised to do whatever we like with you."

"Isn't it breaching your code of honour to treat prisoners in this way? Doesn't your charter mandate that you keep silent and refuse to acknowledge your prisoners if they choose to be argumentative?"

"You poor old man. Our gracious young King Hortensio has reformed the millennium-old charters and laws which restricted us. Now, knights are more than ornaments at a banquet."

"You're right, now they invade shitty desert backwaters because a criminal got on your angsty king's nerves because he sent him a bowl of gemstones and a peace offer. But the ever-wise young King decided that instead of peace, he would inflate his already gargantuan ego by spending the country's money on invading the shitty desert backwater for no reason other than killing a thief."

"You do not get to question our king's motives. He knows what is right for Salyria and freed us from the tyranny of King Valkard. Now we will spread the rightful reign of our glorious

210

king so others may be free of tyranny. And this 'shitty desert backwater' will be the first to benefit."

"I've never heard such delusional tripe in my life," Elton muttered.

As they walked through the streets, Elton caught the eyes of a number of City Guards who he knew worked for him. He knew better than to make them attack for him and made sure his expression made that very clear. Nobody came to his rescue.

Some Syndicate henchmen were also positioned off to the sides of streets, blending in with crowds or hiding in dark alleys. Some of them motioned to step forwards and say something but Elton shot them the same icy stare that he had given the guards and they too backed off.

"I thought the Syndicate was huge in this city," the dark-haired knight said. "I don't see any of your friends coming to help."

"Well, obviously it's as you say. There's no honour among thieves."

"Hah! That there isn't. Which is why we expunge them all from society to allow breathing room for the good and the honourable."

From the shadows, a group of three hooded figures dashed forwards, daggers in hand. The dark-haired knight immediately called for the knights to circle the prisoners and they did, drawing their weapons. The hooded figures wasted no time in attacking and were immediately on top of the knights. Elton watched as their overconfidence caused them to find their swift end by a clean, steel blade.

"Three incompetent fools. Are there any more? That certainly livened up my day," the dark-haired knight said, sheathing his blood-soaked sword.

"They weren't mine," Elton grumbled.

"No? They were just anonymous vigilantes who stepped in to save the biggest crime lord in not just this city but this poor excuse of a country? Hah. You amuse me, fatty."

The commotion had drawn a sizeable crowd who were aggressively dispersed. Elton and the other prisoners noticed a number of their own within the crowd and made sure they understood not to try the same through exchanges of glances, careful not to be spotted by the watchful eye of the dark-haired knight.

The rest of the journey to the City Guard was uninterrupted and spent in silence, apart from the loud shifting of metal plates. The dark-haired knight's appetite for conflict had been sated and even he didn't interrogate or provoke any of the prisoners, who were thoroughly thankful.

The City Guard building was as rundown as every rumour and story portrayed it to be. Although it was relatively large and dwarfed some of the smaller shops and houses in the vicinity, there was no correlation between its size and its quality. On a platform which housed four sentries, guarding the entrance, were four thick, decorative carved sandstone pillars which supported a roof overhead. One of the pillars had long since toppled over, the rubble removed but the memory of the pillar still remaining in the form of a small, atypically shaped sandstone anomaly and a cavity in the roof overhead. All three of the other pillars were damaged in one way or another, each exhibiting a collection of dents, scratches, cuts, and other blemishes where the stone had been chiselled or eroded away.

They passed through the damaged oval-shaped entrance, acknowledging the increased presence of knights, and passed through a dingy entry corridor with minimal lighting and no windows. The knights had to duck to avoid a small beam hanging from the ceiling, attached to a few resilient strands of wood. They stopped and the dark-haired knight looked back at the beam and tore it from the ceiling, tossing it aside. The hole in the ceiling allowed some light in from the floor above, which must have had windows. They continued on, passing a number of doorways which Elton noted were in a similar state to the ones in the decrepit brothel he had visited to find Paul.

The straight corridor led to an expansive meeting room which had been fashioned into a makeshift throne room. On the makeshift throne lazed a young, blonde man who matched Rosa's description of King Hortensio to the letter.

"Is this him, then?" he asked.

"Indeed, Your Magnificence," the dark-haired knight replied.

"Sir Jannis, please, while we're in front of these gentlemen – and lady – ensure they learn to use the correct titles. Criminal scum – you shall address me as Your Grace, or my king. Oh, would you look at that. It's you again." He looked at Rosa, who was clearly unamused. "She understood courtesy when she came to visit me in my palace – at least, she did until she tried to kill me. Yes, she'll be the first to be executed. And who are these other two misfits?"

"Just who we rounded up in the fat cretin's house. You, speak." The dark-haired knight, Jannis, prodded Elton in the back. "Of what relation are these people to you?"

"Brothers and sister," he spat.

"Hah! As if. Now tell the truth or your execution will be particularly gruesome."

"They're my children. From different mothers. I've been at this game a while."

"More plausible, but still complete bollocks. I guess we'll have to force it out of you later. You Grace, what shall we do with them?"

The young King pondered for a while before coming up with an answer.

"Take those three to the dungeon. Shackled to the wall – we don't want to take any unnecessary risks. Leave the fat one with me."

The knights saluted and roughly grabbed Paul, Felix, and Rosa, dragging them in the direction of a shadowy set of stairs. Hortensio watched as they left before turning his attention to Elton.

213

CHAPTER 24

KAL'SENNAR FOREST, OCCUPIED MIRADOS

"I cast a spell on the leader. What did you think I did?"

"Well, I gathered that much. But, like, what was he saying? What did you make him say?"

"I didn't specifically make him say anything. I merely forced him to recite his greatest fear as if it were coming true. It appears that his greatest fear was shared by the rest of the Kal'sennar."

"I see."

They continued to the forest's boundary where the expanse of trees gave way to a grassy meadow which would have been bursting with wildflowers had it been spring. On the far side of the meadow, clinging to the edge of the tree's protection, was a single well-sized doe. Richard immediately left his position atop his mare and whipped out his bow, nocking an arrow in the process.

He quickly shuffled towards the doe before he saw its ears prick up and then stopped. He waited for it to return to feeding on the grass before creeping closer, waiting for the right moment. The doe raised its head again and turned to look behind itself. That was the right moment.

The arrow pierced the doe's eye and it collapsed.

He dragged the carcass out of the forest to meet Ferris. They heaved it back to the horses and Jade made the decision to make camp for the night in the meadow. They found a hefty branch from the forest's edge which was sharpened into a stake and driven into the ground to which to tie the horses and Richard, having done so many times before, quickly butchered the doe. They ate well that night, feasting on juicy venison steak before laying their heads down on the soft, grassy floor and drifting off to sleep.

Richard's slumber was plagued with nightmares. Nightmares which he had never had before. He was revisited by the Kal'sennar and eaten alive, still able to feel as they gnawed on his bones and mutilated his flesh. He saw visions of fire and destruction, a group of sorcerers and sorceresses commanding an army of Corrupted through a city which he helplessly tried to defend. The monstrosities didn't attack the magic-wielders and instead ran around them as if they were an obstacle – they acknowledged their existence but made no move to attack them. Something Richard had never seen the thoughtless creatures do before.

He emptied his quiver of arrows into the skulls of each Corrupted beast, but for every one he took down, two more bounded towards him. He was forced to draw his blade and dodged falling planks alongside the beasts' vigorous lunges and swipes. He deftly placed his sword in front of him as one of the Corrupted launched themselves at him and promptly swallowed the sword, pushing Richard backwards in the process. He planted his feet and narrowly avoided falling but was knocked down by a second Corrupted who batted away the body of its fallen comrade with the sword still inside it.

Richard fought for his life: kicking, punching, squirming, clawing, even biting. But the beast was too strong. It pinned his arms against the ground while another group of the creatures came to reinforce the first. But they didn't obliterate him there and then as he would have expected. Instead, the creatures somewhat scarily waited for the group of mages to approach Richard while they prevented him from moving, which was perhaps more frightening than being killed on the spot.

No amount of writhing loosened their grip and he stopped resisting, defeated. The group of mages, dressed in opulent furs and golden jewellery, looked down at him. At least, he thought they did, as they had no faces.

Where normally one would have eyes, a nose, a mouth, eyebrows, wrinkles, freckles and other common features of a face, these abominations were blank. They walked like humans and Richard assumed it must have been some form of illusion, one of the most terrifying he had ever seen.

One of the faceless mages leaned down and placed their feminine hand against Richard's forehead. He immediately lost all feeling in his chest before the numbness snaked through the rest of his body and he was left completely devoid of physical sensitivity. He could hear the mages uttering spells in mysterious languages despite their lacks of mouths, but he noticed their speech becoming harder and harder to perceive, before realising that all sound was dampening. The foundations of a bridge which crossed over the street collapsed and he heard none of it as the wood splintered and crashed against the cobbles.

The next of his senses to be taken was sight and soon the Corrupted joined the mages in being faceless. What were hideous, decomposed recollections of deceased humans faded to vague, unassuming grey apparitions before everything in sight faded to the same blurry, grey view.

The dream must have lasted longer but he couldn't remember any further than that the next morning as he tried to recount it to himself in his head while he nibbled on a deer rib. Ferris and Jade had awoken before him and saddled the horses, returning all the items they had taken the night before to the saddlebags. They had also eaten already and so were only waiting for Richard to be satisfied. He inhaled the rest of the meat from the rib and tossed the bone aside, wiping his hands on the dewy grass.

He felt a jolt as he mounted his horse and the chilly air attacked his bones. The others were also visibly cold, and Jade even whispered a spell to magically insulate herself. Richard contemplated asking her if it was possible to apply the effects of spells like that to others but decided the cold would do him good.

Ferris wasn't so quiet when it came to his feelings surrounding the temperature and made sure to comment on it seemingly every five minutes. Eventually, Jade grew so tired of his whining that she offered her cloak to him, but he refused, stating that it wouldn't make any difference. The sorceress then snapped at him to shut up and he didn't complain about the cold again.

As the day progressed, the combination of travelling north and the sun progressing through the sky resulted in a change in temperature anyways. Jade undid the insulation spell and Ferris was satisfied with the newfound warmth.

Richard never mentioned his dream. It was still vivid in his mind as if it was a memory – he could recall every individual detail about the Corrupted he had killed with his sword and the other Corrupted which had knocked him to the ground. The dark hair of the faceless woman who had erased his use of the senses.

That was a new detail. Previously, he hadn't been able to distinguish the gender or any defining features of the mage which crippled his hearing, vision, and touch apart from their feminine hand. Now he could remember it was definitely a woman. She still had no face and her hairstyle was blurred, but it was new, nonetheless.

They travelled all day without a break, and it was both dull and exhausting. The most exciting thing to happen was when a platoon of mounted Sanskari soldiers thundered past at full gallop, not even batting an eye at the travellers. They soon disappeared and a mile later, they came across the site to which the soldiers must have been sent. The highway led through a village which was now swarming with soldiers in black armour. Behind them was a mighty oak tree, surrounded by a low stone wall, the centre point of the village. From the sturdy branches hung at least a dozen peasants.

"Miradosi sympathisers?" Richard asked quietly.

"No," Jade replied. "We're too far north. If I could get a closer look, I could tell you why they've hanged. For all we know, they could just be criminals. Plenty of reasons to commit a crime when you live like this."

The following few days were filled with plenty of similar sights and the week slowly passed as they repeated the same routine of waking up, travelling north, finding a suitable place to stay and sleep. Luckily, they weren't ambushed by forest creatures again or anything of the like, but Richard couldn't

help but feel that it would have livened up the journey somewhat.

Richard and Ferris realised that they were truly clueless as
to their location, having blindly followed Jade along the endless stretches of identical highways. They passed through numerous meadows and forests, across the River Jallian, and
made it to the seaside city of Kalsefar – hungry, dehydrated
and in desperate need of a bed.

Before they could achieve this, however, they had an obstacle to overcome first in the form of a queue to enter the
city. Being a seaside city and the capital of occupied Kelmar, a
great deal of wealth constantly circulated through its gates on
its way to and from the Vivian Isles and Virilia. Traders from
far and wide made the arduous trek with wagons laden with
goods, many of which were in the queue with them.

The gates were heavily manned by Sanskari soldiers, the
same as they had seen throughout their journey to reach the
city. From a distance, it was hard to distinguish exactly what
they were doing but they could see that every cart of goods
was being inspected and people were only being let in one at a
time. They couldn't deduce the reason for the inspections, but
it probably wasn't reasonable.

They waited. They waited as the queue gradually progressed forwards as the moon crept into the sky and had to
wait even longer as the guards changed shifts. The new guards
on duty were even slower and even more thorough with their
inspections but finally, it came to be their turn. As their only
luggage was in the form of the horse's saddlebags, it didn't
take long to inspect but they were also asked to step down
from the horses for their clothes to be inspected.

"May I inquire as to the necessity of the inspections?" Jade
asked.

"Shut your trap, wench," one of the guards retorted. "Isn't
your place to ask questions like that."

"Oh, it's alright," another guard chimed in. "Plenty of people in the city already know. What's the harm if one more
knows? At least that way she'll know the truth, instead of whatever blather the peasants go on about."

"I suppose. We've got a bit of a raging problem in Kalsefar
with hevvie – the drug, that is. Blasted merchants have been

bringing it in under our noses and poisoning everyone with it which makes it significantly harder to collect taxes. Hard to collect taxes from people who are too far gone to go to work or people who took too much and died. Or the ones that are too fucked to think coherently."

"Well, I didn't even know of the existence of such a drug. Is this a recent problem?" Jade asked.

"The first few cases appeared about a moon ago and since then it's spiralled out of control. I'm starting to think the captain's wrong about people bringing it into the city. I reckon it's being made within. Anyways, that's enough chatter. I'll get you three a pass each. If you ever need to enter the city again, just cut to the front of any queue and show it to whoever's on guard. They'll let you straight through."

The guard strolled into the guardhouse at the side of the gate and came out shortly afterwards with three rolled-up pieces of paper.

"Here you are. Now, if anyone approaches you about hevvie, ensure you report them to the authorities immediately. If you don't and we find out you were in contact with them when we catch them, you'll be held responsible for allowing their freedom. You may enter."

The guard motioned for them to continue, and they mounted their horses and trotted through the gates. The gate opened to an expansive cobbled street which, even at that hour, was bustling with activity. A lot of which was obviously shady, but the guard patrols which rhythmically patrolled up and down turned a blind eye to the cloaked and hooded and sometimes even open-faced ruffians running between the dark alleys. The street turned out to run straight from the city gate where they had entered directly to the port. Richard, Ferris, and Jade weren't particularly focused on the details as they passed but instead prioritised finding a tavern which looked reputable enough to warrant choosing to spend the night.

As it was the main street, many of the buildings they passed looked well-to-do and lawful. They didn't have to look far for an inviting tavern by the name of *The Siren's Tears* which advertised *Beer and Beds, Plenty of Both!*

They found a spot to tie up the horses nearby and walked over to the tavern, carrying the saddles and saddlebags with them.

The atmosphere inside was an entirely different world to the cold, daunting darkness of the street and the encroaching buildings which lined it. The tavern was alive with life of the best kind – people guzzling tankards of beer, slurping bowls of broth, slamming cards against tables, and engaging in rowdy debates. A band in the corner played an upbeat folk song and gestured everyone who so much as glanced at them to toss a coin into their tipping basket. Perhaps not the classiest of atmospheres, but the merriest. Richard and Ferris entered with joy, while Jade reserved her excitement and made as quick a job as she could with paying for a room and retreating to it. Ferris and Richard gleefully joined in with the revelry for a while before also doing the same.

They didn't spend any time in Kalsefar the following morning and instead left the tavern at first light. The city was easy enough to leave with their new passes and the journey continued, tracing the highway along the oceanside. They were in permanent view of the crashing waves as they travelled and the constant flurry of ships travelling between Kalsefar and the distant mouth of the Redwater Passage, which they couldn't actually see due to the fog which rested over the ocean's surface and the fact that the Redwater Passage was still hundreds of miles away and Virilia still further than that.

The temperature warmed up again as they approached the Desnari Desert. An ancient, cobbled path appeared as the grass disappeared, and they made sure to stop and find a stream to fill their water reserves before heading into the desert's clutches.

"Hey, witch, I'm not really sure why I haven't thought of this yet, but why didn't you just teleport us to Virilia?" Ferris complained.

"Too much risk for something like that," she responded. "Numerous officials are very aware of my absence from the capital. If I were just to appear one day, they would immediately know something was amiss. It needs to be realistic."

"Why not just teleport us outside the capital and we can walk in?"

220

"You think they would believe us if we said we walked on foot from Limara to Virilia?"

"Teleport the horses too!"

"Just how boundless do you think my abilities are? We've got maybe a week's journey left. Let's hope it passes quickly. In fact, we could even catch a ferry to Virilia from one of the ports in the Bay. That will only shorten the journey. For now, let's get through this desert."

For a desert, it wasn't as hot as Richard and Ferris had expected. They were still blessed by the cool ocean breeze which counteracted the scorching of the sun overhead.

"Hey, look at that!" Ferris called, pointing into the desert on their right. Jade and Richard turned their heads and at first, they couldn't see anything but then it burst from the sand: pure white scales interrupted by red rings, resembling an overblown snake, as well as mouth full of razor-sharp teeth. It captured and instantly killed the lone camel, dragging its carcass beneath the sand and disappearing from view.

They returned their gazes to the troubadour whose face was now white as a sheet.

"Well, I was pointing out the camel. That, uh, wasn't what I meant to show you."

"The thing which ate the camel is a red-ringed lenkraad. It's very much like a snake in the fact that it's cold-blooded, predatory and relies much on vibrations to locate its prey. However, they have no relation. We will be fine as long as we stick to the path. They don't travel far from their hunting grounds."

"It doesn't seem like we're very far in the first place."

"I guess you'd better hope you don't get eaten by it then," she teased.

So began the arduous trek along the desert coast. Jade warned them to be conservative with their precious water supply as Ferris pointed out his sudden thirst. They didn't encounter any more monstrous lenkraads but did see some more camels of varying numbers of humps as well as smaller creatures – scorpions, lizards, hares, foxes.

"What exactly is it about ocean water that drives men mad?" Ferris asked, gazing longingly at the crashing waves.

"Salt," Jade responded. "It's very salty and makes you thirstier than you were originally. Enough salt water and you go mad. If we were to run out of water, we'd be fine. Would just have to boil the seawater first to distil it."

"Do you know this much about everything?" the troubadour asked.

"Only what's important. I haven't a clue about music, which I assume is your area of expertise."

"That it is, that it is."

Richard stayed mostly silent throughout the journey, only raising his voice on the rare occasion to point out something which he didn't recognise or to ask about the geography of the land they were travelling through. Jade explained how the Desnari was the western component to a tropical zone which separated the southern forests and the northern savannas. In the East were the rainforests, encompassed entirely within the Sanskari vassal state of Lavinia. Politically and economically insignificant, not many people visited Lavinia. The only people who lived there were those who lived close to borders with other countries and were only interested in cultivating crops which grew exclusively in the tropical heat and humidity.

When he wasn't asking questions, he was reliving the nightmare from the night in the meadow. He still hadn't told Jade or Ferris, primarily because more and more details revealed themselves as time went on. The mages' faces began to appear in his recollection, and he wasn't sure if he was inventing it or whether something unnatural was occurring. Whatever it was, he kept it to himself.

The moon rose once again, and they stopped to make camp. They moved down towards the beach and stopped where the sand became damp. They found a piece of driftwood which looked like it had come from a wrecked ship and used it as a stake to which to tie their horses before creating a weak fire out of whatever other damp driftwood they could salvage from the falling tide. Cold deer meat was the only option for now, as it needed to be eaten soon before it went to waste. They were famished and too impatient to try to heat it over the already dying fire, so it was quickly devoured before they put their heads down to rest.

Richard awoke at the crack of dawn, this time before the other two. Not by choice – near their camp was a large pile of rocks from behind which he could hear a woman's beautiful voice – singing.

The bounty hunter had heard countless tales of fishermen who'd been lured towards what they thought was a lone, helpless woman with a voice of silk. He didn't want to become the subject of such a tale and grabbed his bow and quiver of arrows before treading carefully towards the rock pile.

He nocked an arrow as the singing grew louder. Its source was still out of sight but he drew the bowstring back to his cheek and stepped around the perimeter of the rocks. The source of the singing finally came into view: from its waist up was a shapely woman's body and freckled, pretty face with sea-green eyes and short-cut cedar hair. Below its waist was a large, green, fishlike tail which shimmered in the early rays.

The bounty hunter released his bowstring. The creature was left unharmed because no arrow was ever loosed. Instead, Richard had dropped both his bow and arrow on the sand and walked towards the beautiful creature as its singing grew ever louder and more intense.

He could do nothing. He had lost control of his mind as the creature's magical influence forced him to keep walking, closer and closer. He noticed how closely the creature resembled Linelle. And then, a moment later, it didn't resemble her in the slightest.

What had been the picture of unimpeded beauty transformed into a monster: its attractive face turned a dark shade of green as its eyes turned red and its mouth erupted into an array of vicious, serrated teeth. Its flowing locks writhed and turned ink-black as its shapely figure flattened and turned the same shade of green as its face. Long, talon-like claws grew from what were previously fingertips.

It leapt towards the entranced bounty hunter with incredible speed given its lower body. As it had stopped singing, he had regained control of his mind and dodged out of the way as the hideous monster crashed into the sand. His primary focus was to retrieve his bow and arrows, which were currently between him and the creature.

223

"Jade! Ferris! Wake up!" he shouted, dodging again as the creature careened in his direction, furiously swiping with its curled claws. "Get up! We're being attacked!"

He didn't know if his warning was heard but he dived for his bow and arrows, grabbing them as he rolled forward and stood up again. The creature hissed, its hair hardening into clumps and vibrating as it did so.

Richard nocked an arrow and sent it at the creature's head. It didn't move, but instead deflected the projectile with its claws which were apparently left unimpacted.

"Wake up!" he cried again, sending another arrow at the monster. Again, it deflected it into the sand and then leapt towards the bounty hunter, who rolled out of the way. He wasn't cunning enough: when he stood up, the creature swept its tail towards him with immense force and knocked him off his feet. Within a second, it was on top of him, staring into his eyes, thick saliva dripping from its deadly mouth.

"Richard!" Jade cried.

CHAPTER 25

The cold sea breeze was favourable to the grandmaster mages who ended up the last to arrive at the Laethyvaerdian harbour, as it helped to eliminate the traces of sweat they had fought so hard to conceal. To everyone else, it was quite simply cold.

Tyen'Ael was by no means an exotic country. But here, in the North, in the height of summer, it was remarkably cold, and Elaeínn found herself immediately yearning for the uncomfortable, humid heat of Sanaíd. Unlike the lesser mages, however, she managed not to let her discomfort show, while they huddled together in groups, crossing their arms and making snide remarks about the weather and some even loudly, obliviously spouting their discontent about the accompaniment of the four convicts. Elaeínn made a mental note of a few faces.

"They haven't been tight with whatever it is we're doing, if those are the ships we're going on." Laettía pointed to the waterside, where five enormous wooden galleons were being prepared by teams of muscular sailors, hoisting white sails probably large enough to cover the surface area of the lobby in the palace, had it been cut into pieces and rearranged.

"Those are new models – still good old Tyen'Aeli galleons, but with hallmarks of newness. I mean, anyone can tell that they look remarkably clean and the sails are as white as a newborn light elf. But these here models have got an extra deck and an extra sail to compensate. We'll be flying across the water on these, and in comfort, too."

"How do you know so much about boats?"

"Ships," the Jester corrected. "I used to be a sailor, once upon a time. Worked aboard a merchant's freighter travelling between the Eye and the Shield. At least that's what we called them – the Eye is the land east of the channel, and the Shield is everything 'west'. Even though parts of the Shield are further east... it doesn't matter. I was fascinated by ships, even wrote a little encyclopaedia for myself, if you like. Documented all the different ships I saw coming into port from all the different countries."

"What made you leave? How did you end up as a Jester?"

"Pay was shit," she laughed. "Oh, yeah, it was awful. I liked the ships, sure, but I had to survive, and staying on that ship wasn't how. Didn't help either that every time I turned to look at my boss, I'd catch him staring at my backside. So I left, and ended up in the Shield. I actually was born in Ferloris."

The enveloping shadows cast by the sails of the galleons eliminated light from the area of the harbour in which they stood. The sailors gestured to Jaelaar and a few other senior officials he had brought along to say that the ships were ready.

"What's your deal then, girl?" Laettía inquired as they were corralled towards the ships, behind the sailors now loading the last crates of supplies into the cargo bay. "What does the FTA do? And why are you so quiet?"

Because I don't feel the same constant need to talk, Elaeínn thought.

"It stands for 'Free Tyen'Ael Army'," she explained. "A little bit on the nose, but it gets our point across."

"In what way do you need to 'Free Tyen'Ael'?" Laettía ridiculed. "Place is as free as it gets. You can do whatever the bloody hell you want and get away with it. Most of the time."

"Maybe for now, but Jaelaar and his National Party are chipping away at our democracy piece by piece. And if we're to stop him, we need to do so fast. And by force, because peaceful protest and petition won't get us anywhere."

"I'll agree with that last point," she smirked.

Elaeínn stepped onto the deck of the third galleon and was almost toppled by its gentle rocking, being caught by Laettía. She seemed keen to remain at her side, though perhaps more so she could constantly ridicule her seafaring ineptitude. It

226

then spread a smile onto her face when Jaelaar also stepped onto the deck and faced the same trouble with imbalance.

The last to join their crew were Karek and Períen, who once more had to be coerced, this time by the sailors, who had apparently retrieved spears from somewhere. They were immediately unhappy.

"You're telling me that we have to be on the same boat as that fucker?" Karek scowled in Jaelaar's direction, where he had taken cover behind a barrier of armed sailors.

"I myself am interested in working alongside you folks," the Prime Minister alleviated, parting the sailors. "This is a national effort, which wouldn't be particularly national without my support. And my active participation only makes it more... dedicated, for want of a better word."

"I think the word you were looking for is convincing," Laettía piped up from Elaeínn's side, where they had found a seat atop a pair of barrels loaded with supplies.

"I would like to convince all of you that the country you seek to destabilise is not worth doing so," he continued, ignoring the comment. "And I cannot do that through a medium. I am doing it myself.

"Joining us on this galleon is Grandmaster Arrayanor." Jaelaar gestured to the pale-skinned elf as he dragged himself and his heavy fur robes onto the ship.

"He's a fucking light elf!" Karek swore.

"And yet, life goes on," Jaelaar mused sarcastically. "Mr Hyggavaerd is certainly not incorrect in identifying the race of our grandmaster companion. I see no relevance to such a conclusion, though, as Grandmaster Arrayanor is here to oversee guidance of our ship throughout our journey. He is our protector and our support. We could not continue without him."

Arrayanor traipsed up the stairs to the top deck without even so much as a glance at the crewmates whose protection he was apparently in charge of.

"With that, I believe we are ready to set off," Jaelaar announced. He turned around to signal to the captains on the other galleons, who were equally as ready.

"Captain Rikkard is the captain of this vessel," he declared to the convicts as the sailors untied the galleon from the harbour and allowed it to drift into the open water. "What he says

227

is authority – higher than mine when we're sailing. Now, let me show you where you're staying."

Jaelaar entered an open archway leading to a set of stairs to the area below deck. They stopped at the bottom of the first flight of stairs, though there were at least another two, by Laettía's reckoning, which the Prime Minister didn't particularly care for.

"These are your chambers," he stated. "Each of you have your own room in this corridor here – Mr Fyríard, you're at the far end, then Mr Hyggavaerd, then Miss Irgalín, and finally Miss Tinaíd."

"And where are you staying, Jaelaar?" Karek growled. "Some makeshift palace below deck, I assume?"

"The opposite side of this deck," he replied monotonously. "Please settle yourselves – you've been given essentials. For now, I recommend we retire. Tomorrow we will resume conversation and I will get you up to speed on the nature of this expedition."

Tomorrow came, as could have been expected. But all plans of explanations or pacifications had to be allayed.

"Pirates!" the sailors called, wresting the sleeping crew from their slumber. Jaelaar was the first to appear, sharply dressed in a way which made him look comparably similar to a commoner. If you didn't recognise his distinct facial shape, you would never have thought him to be a person of significance.

"Dwarves?" Jaelaar asked, Elaeínn being the first to appear from the chambers on the other side of the ship.

"Yes, Sire. Sahloknirians, if I'm not mistaken."

"Dwarves are dwarves, their specific country of birth doesn't matter. To your stations! Load the ballistae!"

The sailor rushed further into the bowels of the ship as more of the crew arrived from their chambers. Karek and Períen were notably absent.

Elaeínn rushed up the stairs onto the deck and nearly had her head taken off by a flying stone the size of a fist. It was almost dawn – the pirates were difficult to see in the dim moonlight, as were the projectiles with which they were pelting the galleons. Their exuberant cries, however, were audible for miles around.

228

More rocks showered the deck before being joined by flaming arrows, the dwarven pirates having lit fires aboard their ships, making them immensely easier to track.

They targeted the sails with the flaming arrows, a fact which didn't escape the attention of Jaelaar and Grandmaster Arrayanor. The mage expended a lot of energy catching the arrows mid-air and dropping them into the ocean before they had a chance to find a place on the sail. But for each arrow the mage caught, three more were loosed and eventually, one of the sails were hit, the flame catching and spreading like an epidemic.

The sail was lost, leaving seven remaining. The other galleons were facing similar trouble, one distant ship even bright with the ferocity of fire burning through their two main sails and also having worked its way onto the mast, which appeared, worryingly, to also be happening on Elaeínn's galleon.

"Where are our defences?" Jaelaar howled in the tone of an army commander.

His question was answered when a heavy spear was ejected from the side of their ship, crunching through the shoddy material comprising the pirates' ship. The pirates' cries changed tone and they paused their assault to assess the damage, but soon resumed pelting them with what seemed to be endless ammunition.

A specially crafted ballista bolt pierced the hull of the pirate ship and exploded, dealing catastrophic damage. The pirates stopped their assault entirely and quickly deployed a handful of smaller rowboats onto which they jumped, some missing and landing in the freezing ocean water.

"Sherrikas!" an alarmed voice called from above. Elaeínn looked up to see a sailor occupying the crow's nest frenetically gesticulating to the waters behind them. She looked in the indicated direction and at first saw nothing, but then the pulsating glow of bioluminescent white strips around the sherrikas' dorsal fins lit up the dark waters as they converged on the ships.

The pirates who had fled from the now sinking ship began to row towards the galleon, some towards Elaeínn's galleon and some towards the one on their left. Both were already travelling far faster than that with which they could have hoped to keep up. They were left stranded, near the water level.

Elaeínn saw one of the enormous shark-like creatures breach the water, leaping over the lone rowing boat. Its mouth of monstrous fangs flashed the same brilliant white as its glowing ring on its dorsal fin as it ripped the life from one of the pirates, snatching it from the boat and dragging it beneath the water, spraying blood through the air as it made its re-entry.

The second, third and fourth rowboats were all annihilated in moments and the sherrikas advanced past the floating wreckages and placed their focus on the pirates who had refrained from abandoning the sinking ship, now half-submerged. One of the creatures bolstered the courage to attempt to attack one of the dwarves leaning over the side. Wide-eyed as death catapulted from the water and swiped him clean from the tilted deck, the sherrika plunged beneath the water with a tremendous splash as the ballista operators readjusted their aim at the remaining stragglers trying desperately to find a way off the ship.

Another ballista bolt pierced one of the pirates and the force dragged his lifeless body along with the trajectory of the projectile, but a white stripe moved with imperceptible speed to grab and swim away with the body as soon as it made contact with the water.

"Tell below deck to start shooting the sherrikas!" Captain Rikkard ordered from the bridge, located on the galleon's elevated stern. "If they aren't scared off now, they'll only turn their attention to us! And they're not to be underestimated!"

A sailor rushed downstairs to issue the captain's orders and Elaeínn turned to find Laettía at her side, crossbow in hand.

"Where did you get a weapon?" she asked incredulously.

"Well they left so many lying around, I thought it wasteful not to help."

Laettía aimed the crossbow at one of the sherrikas, their dorsal fin slicing the surface of the water. She pulled the trigger and her bolt pierced the creature, which recoiled and fell back, its white ring shifting colour to a bright rose.

"Captain! There are more ships ahead!"

230

Elaeínn glanced at the waters in front of the ship, where the intensity of the waves was increasing as clouds rolled in overhead. Hurtling over the waves with no effort were several warships, smaller than the galleons and seemingly not much of a threat.

An explosion reverberated across the water as a cannonball careered through the air, crashing through the hull of Elaeínn's ship. That was only the first of many, and the backup from the mysterious warships fuelled the pirates' morale, as they strengthened their own assaults.

A pirate ship appeared to starboard, its sails in line with the top deck of the monolithic galleon. The top of a ladder appeared on the side of the deck and Elaeínn sprinted across the ship with unwavering determination. She reached the ladder and pushed it down without a second thought, looking over the side to see a black-haired dwarf crash back down to the deck of his own ship.

The other pirates saw Elaeínn and nocked their longbows, this time aiming at her instead of the galleon's sails. She quickly ducked and flattened herself against the deck as a volley of arrows sailed over her head, continuing on into the sky.

Several more explosions resonated from the warships, with the harsh crunching of wood indicating a couple had found their marks on Elaeínn's galleon.

"We need to turn the ships to return fire!" Captain Rikkard ordered. "Mage! Tell your associates that we're turning to starboard!"

Grandmaster Arrayanor closed his eyes and knelt next to the captain, rising a few moments later to indicate that the message had been received.

Captain Rikkard sharply spun the wheel, careening the ship in a ninety-degree turn. The pirates on their right were quick to respond and imitated the turn, still attempting to find a way onto the ship while the starboard-side ballista operators finally began to defend against them.

"Tell below deck to stop shooting the sherrikas and put all focus on getting rid of these attackers! We'll be reduced to scrap if we continue to take any more cannon fire!"

A volley of flaming ballista bolts soon sang through the air, a few making their marks on the warships but fizzling out.

Cannon fire came swiftly in return, further bedecking the hulls of the galleons with holes.

"The pirates are moving back, Captain! They're... retreating?"

The pirate ships, seven remaining in total, had fallen back behind the elves. But contrary to the lookout's speculation, they were not retreating, but regrouping, and sailing towards Elaeínn's galleon, isolated at the far right of their five-galleon-strong convoy.

The sherrikas were also still in pursuit, evidently not yet satisfied. Normal sharks would have given up by now, or not even have attempted the fight in the first place. But that was what differentiated the bloodthirsty creatures – sharks hunted to survive. Sherrikas hunted for sport.

The sherrikas leapt from the twilit water, sliding onto the decks of the redirected pirate ships. They thrashed their muscular tails, knocking several of the fiercely defensive pirates off their feet. Those who were unfortunate enough to be near their mouths were viciously lacerated by their despicably sharp teeth and inevitably dragged into the water as the sherrikas bounded with unimaginable strength across the decks and back into the water.

At last, Períen and Karek made an appearance, bursting through the door from below deck. They were armed to the teeth, evidently having found a cache of weapons and armour – both were dressed in light plate which protected the broader stretches of their legs, arms, and torso. Períen was wielding a sabre and Karek a rapier. Their intentions were immediately evident.

They quickly surveyed the chaos encapsulating the deck and found their target. Splitting up, they cut off Jaelaar, Grandmaster Arrayanor and Captain Rikkard's access to the stairs.

Blood spattered against those very stairs as a bolt from Laettía's crossbow found its way through Períen's unguarded neck. He collapsed, futilely grasping his throat and choking as the blood poured out.

Karek growled and set his sights on the Jester, temporarily diverting from his original plan. In two quick bounds, he was across the width of the ship and with one precise swipe of his sword would have disembowelled her, still reloading the crossbow.

But this wasn't the case, and as the Lirdían retracted his arm to strike the blow, it was frozen in place. Just long enough for Laettía to finish reloading the crossbow and, without hesitation, place a bolt between his eyes.

His body collapsed onto her and she disgustedly threw it overboard, to be quickly snapped up by the ever-pursuing sherrikas. Looking up to the stern, she nodded in gratitude to the grandmaster, whose expressionless countenance betrayed nothing.

Fires had begun to spread on the warships, but the pirates had caught up to Elaeínn's galleon and converged around it. Ladders were placed everywhere there was free space and Elaeínn drew her sword, ready to defend herself. The symbols etched into the blade were glowing gold.

"Yaharrrr!" a pirate cried, being the first to successfully board the galleon. He was almost instantly skewered by a prepared sailor before being thrust overboard.

He was quickly replaced by another two pirates, who fell almost as quickly. The crew were overwhelmed, unable to keep up with the ladders constantly being placed against the side of the hull.

As the next two pirates fell, another four replaced them. This time, they weren't slain so easily and the extra time taken in a quick duel with the surprisingly adept sailors was critical in allowing more and more pirates to board the ship.

They shouted to one another in Dwarven and Elaeínn dived into the fray. Her sword danced through the air and sliced clean through their feeble excuses for armour. She was a frenzy of gold, from which sprang fountains of crimson.

The spectacle inspired the rest of the crew, who cheered in unison as they battled off the pirates, who were still relentlessly climbing aboard, the ships rotating around to provide a constant fresh supply of new attackers. The clanging of steel drowned out all other sounds of the morning.

Elaeínn stepped back for a moment, realising what she had just accomplished. She was fairly skilful with a blade, but not to the degree that she would ever have felt confident taking on such a multitude of enemies. And she had done it anyways.

The ship rocked, causing the battlers to sway, some falling over and being defeated by their opponents. Including a couple of elven sailors.

It rocked again, this time even more forcefully. Elaeínn ran up the stairs to the stern and looked over the side of the ship where the glowing white strips of the sherrikas could be seen systematically slamming against the galleon's side.

"What the fuck is our grandmaster even doing at this point?" Laettía joined her, directing her question at Jaelaar. Grandmaster Arrayanor and Captain Rikkard were there as well, as they had been for the duration of the dawn.

"He's saved you from certain death," Jaelaar said coolly against the backdrop of a cannonball crashing through the ship's hull. "If it weren't for Arrayanor, we would be sinking right now."

"Take a look around you! We're a lost cause!" she swept her hand at the bloodstained main deck, where the pirates had begun to win out against the sailors and were advancing steadily towards the bridge.

"If he's such a master of magic, he can bloody well do something about the attackers! Or perhaps there's a reason he isn't!" Laettía continued.

She marched across the bridge and placed her crossbow against Grandmaster Arrayanor's head – between the eyes, the exact place where she hadn't hesitated to pull the trigger against Karek.

"Why aren't you helping us?" she seethed.

The sun's rays finally rose from beyond the horizon, illuminating the entire scene in brighter light than the twilight they had been using before.

"Captain!" the sailor in the crow's nest cried. "I can identify the warships! They're Tayannan! Yellow eagle on a navy field!"

Laettía pulled the trigger.

Jaelaar extended his hand and forced the weapon from her hand with a gust of magical force. Instead of running to grab the weapon, as Jaelaar seemed to have expected, she grabbed the Prime Minister by his collar and raised him into the air with surprising strength.

Captain Rikkard then stepped in, leaving the wheel with his eyes set on Laettía. That was when Elaeínn raised her sword to protect her, pointing its tip at Captain Rikkard's unarmoured chest.

The ship rocked again, harder than it had any of the previous times. Laettía dropped Jaelaar and he hit the deck hard, grunting. Captain Rikkard used the opportunity to duck under Elaeínn's blade, but she stepped back and lacerated his outstretched arms in a quick flourish of gold.

Captain Rikkard was stunned as blood spurted from the wounds. He retreated as the few remaining sailors defending against the pirates were backed onto the stairs, the number of casualties steadily increasing.

"I don't see a way out of this," Elaeínn shouted over the perpetual din of battle.

"Nor I," Laettía echoed. "I guess we're hoping for a miracle. Or for someone to take charge."

Captain Rikkard was too busy bleeding to death to steer the ship, so Laettía happily took to the wheel. She swerved hard to the left, sending nearly everyone on board tumbling to the floor if they were unable to find something with which to steady themselves.

"What in Raeris's name are you doing?" Jaelaar lost his composure, trying hard to fight against the swaying of the ship.

"Relax, I know what I'm doing," Laettía reassured, directing the ship towards the galleon on their left, the captain of which looked on with wide eyes. He responded by quickly spinning the wheel in a similar fashion, disrupting the array of flaming ballista bolts which had been fired at the still-present Tayannan warships.

"Go now, jump!" Laettía ordered not just to Elaeínn but to Jaelaar. The pirates hacked and slashed their way through the last of the sailors guarding the stairs and stampeded towards the bridge.

Elaeínn sheathed her sword and jumped, clearing the small gap between the ships with ease. Jaelaar followed suit just as a pirate's sword closed the same gap. None of them would attempt to jump – the gap was too far for a dwarf.

"Laettía!" Elaeínn cried as the dwarves surrounded her, producing a cacophony of cackling.

"It was nice knowing you, girl," she shouted at the top of her voice, still smirking. "Even if it was just for a day."

As the pirates converged on her, she turned and jumped overboard. She didn't even manage to reach the water before being snapped up by the voracious jaws of the sherrikas.

CHAPTER 26

"You're not from here, are you?" Hortensio asked. Elton was surprised that his first question hadn't been loaded with ridicule.

"You're correct, Your Grace."

"Where are you from, then?"

"Salyria, Your Grace. A small market town north of Camelion – Gatherford."

"I know it. Very close to my home village of Heathervale. I remember visiting Gatherford with my mother on Sundays before I was shipped off to be a squire."

"What's all this peasant rambling about you being a bastard from the side of the highway, then?"

The King's casual expression hardened, and he sat up straighter in his makeshift throne.

"It's exactly that – peasant rambling. I would've thought a man like you would be able to deduce such a thing. Why did you leave Gatherford, scum?"

"It wasn't right for me there anymore. Though I feel like I might have a reason to go back at last."

"Oh, really? I'm afraid it's too late for that. Your final resting place will be whichever scaffold is nearest. I'm merely interested in who you are, given how much of a big deal you are on this continent. I must say, I haven't been very impressed."

"I'm sorry to disappoint, Your Grace. Tell me – what drove you to decline my offer which would not only have benefited us but also you? I daresay it would even have catalysed the rate at which you could generate armies and extend your

237

reign. Instead, you chose unnecessary losses and wasted resources through invading a hopeless desert city."

"Unnecessary losses? Wasted resources? You're mistaken. What we're doing here is sending a message that your kind will not be tolerated in the Kingdom of Salyria, regardless of the generosity of your bribes. We fight for honour and strength, not for personal gain or money. Besides, we can simply raid your coffers after the Redwinter Syndicate is destroyed."

"My men would flee with all the wealth we control before you could even set eyes on it. But that's fine, I suppose, because you don't care about the power of money."

"This – this is why one of our main priorities is to rat out filth like you. Those who spend their whole lives focused on the accumulation of wealth are wasted men who will never visit the clouds after they pass. Now, you're boring me. Guards!" he clapped twice, "Take the scum to the dungeon with the rest. Announce his capture to whichever crowds are largest and gossip will do the rest of our job for us. The execution will be tomorrow at noon."

Noon of the next day came soon. A crowd thousands of people strong had gathered in Megaross Square, in the city centre – it was the largest open area in the entire city. Even so, it simply didn't have the capacity to contain all the people which pushed and shoved their way to acquiring a good view of the newly installed scaffold and the four prisoners standing defeated behind it. Rosa had to be permanently held by a knight so as to prevent her from teleporting away.

The dark-haired knight, Jannis, stepped onto the platform to address the crowd, waving and planting a long wooden pole adorned at the top with a Salyrian flag, drooping lousily in the windless air. His enthusiasm was curbed by a sudden stone which sailed through the air from somewhere in the crowd and landed at his feet. It was soon accompanied by another volley of three stones which he saw were thrown by a group of two hooded individuals. They noticed Jannis had spotted them and immediately ran away into the throng of people. To chase them would have been futile, so he instead returned to addressing the crowd.

238

"Oppressed people of Dannos!" he bellowed. The volume of the crowd lowered in order to be able to hear him but a faint chatter still reverberated through the crowd. "For too long your city of great potential has been prevented from achieving great things because of the actions of this man, who many of you will know – Elton Redwinter, the head of the Redwinter Syndicate."

A mixed murmur of assent and dissent rumbled through the crowd in response.

"Today, the might of the enlightened Kingdom of Salyria will put an end to your oppression and make a damned good show of it, too. For before we execute Elton Redwinter for his treachery, we must first deal with his comrades, who will face a trial by combat!"

The crowd cheered as Paul was freed of his shackles and thrust forward to face a knight, who had walked to the other side of the execution platform. Paul glanced around, trying to find a way to escape. But every direction was under the constant guard of a statue-like knight. He contemplated jumping off the platform and into the crowd but there were two knights standing at the head of the crowd, below the elevated platform.

A Salyrian sword was placed gently into his hands and Paul allowed himself a few moments to familiarise himself with its weight and length. It wasn't much heavier than the swords with which he had trained in preparation for fighting vampires. But he wasn't fighting vampires now.

A gong sounded and his opponent rushed forward, sword drawn across his body. It was an unfair battle from the start – the Salyrian knight was clad in an almost full suit of heavy armour. Only his head remained exposed, while Paul was left unarmoured – but this worked in his favour. He'd never liked the idea of wearing armour as not only was it noisy, but also unbearably heavy. His father, a criminal like him, had always told him: 'Lightly armoured means light on your feet, son. Remember that.' He had died with a blade through his heart after being captured by the City Guard before the founding of the Syndicate.

The knight was strong and his blade moved fast, but he did not. Every predefined swing gave Paul an opportunity to duck

239

out of the way and readjust his position to force the knight into moving. He was hoping he would eventually be able to tire out his opponent, but after a lengthy period of exchanging swings and parries, both were feeling the effects of fatigue creeping in.

"Sir Renard! Finish him off!" Jannis called.

Jannis's cry gave Paul the opportunity he needed. His opponent, distracted, wasn't watching closely enough as Paul kicked him backwards and, with a calculated strike, decapitated him. The crowd gasped in unison as the head flew forward and landed at the feet of the knights at the fore of the crowd. They immediately rushed to pick it up and conceal it as Paul stood victorious over the corpse of his opponent, recovering his breath, while the crowd erupted into cheers.

Jannis uneasily stepped forward and retrieved the sword from Paul's sweaty hands.

"You're free to go," he growled. "But I don't ever want to see your face again. Leave Dannos – and if you remain, I won't hesitate to kill you myself."

He turned to face the crowd.

"Wasn't that quite the fight?" he boomed, "The gods in all their wisdom have deemed this criminal to be worthy of life. The gods' wrath is to be feared, so we will obey their command. This associate of the Redwinter Syndicate—" he dropped his voice to a whisper, "what's your name?", he raised his voice again after receiving an answer, "Paul Harriwood, is now a free man. But make no mistake, if he commits another crime, he will answer for it. Now go, Paul Harriwood. We have another trial to carry out here."

Paul shot a quick look at the other prisoners waiting patiently for their turn to fight a knight. Elton nodded as if to say 'go' and Paul nodded in response before turning and briskly walking away from the execution platform. He didn't look back.

The crowd still remained as enthused as ever and they cheered as Felix was pushed forward in much the same uncaring way as Paul had been, while a fresh gleaming steel sword reflecting noon's bright sun was placed gently into his hands.

"And now, ladies and gentlemen," Jannis cried, "we have a handsome young buck. He's almost certain to be agile and dazzling with a sword, so his opponent must be adapted to compensate! Our next accused criminal"—he looked back at the young Syndicate henchman for his name—"Felix Anderassan, will face Sir Goron, referred to among the Salyrian knights as 'The Bear!' Folks, you will soon see why! Sir Goron, please step forward!"

A hulking mammoth of a knight revealed himself from behind the execution platform. Felix's eyes grew wide as the knight towered over him, clad in armour which must have been a special order to be able to protect his immensely broad shoulders, frighteningly muscular arms and each leg sharing a circumference with that of a young oak's trunk. He drew his menacingly long sword, which must have been thrice as heavy as Felix's own and glowed blindingly bright. He didn't trust the now pathetic-looking blade in his own hands to be of any use against the beast of a person before him.

Felix backed away and the gong sounded. He barely had time to recognise that the fight had begun before the colossal sword whizzed past his left ear, smashing into the sandstone platform. Felix sprinted to The Bear's right and attempted to find a chink in his armour but was unsuccessful, with each strike only finding a sharp retaliating clank of metal against metal. The Bear swept Felix aside with a single blow from his paw-like fist. A jolt penetrated his spine as he landed hard on the ground, feeling the impact on his tailbone. The huge knight raised his sword again and planted it where Felix had been a split-second before rolling over and painfully jumping to his feet.

Now on level ground, Felix had an opportunity to analyse his opponent's weaknesses as the knight turned around again to face his much smaller opponent. The giant sword came down again in a diagonal movement before rising and falling in the opposite diagonal, both swings easily avoided. The Bear angrily squinted at Felix through the thin visor in his helmet and swung his sword over his head as fast as he could – Felix was still able to step out of the way in time. As the sword collided with the ground, he used his newfound opportunity to run straight forward and went unexpectedly between his opponent's firmly planted legs. Mustering all his strength, he dived at one of them and pulled, attempting to make the enormous knight lose balance and fall over. *The bigger they are, the harder they fall*, he thought.

But fall, he did not. The Bear's tree-trunk legs remained planted and he leaned over to view his assailant who was quickly losing faith in his ability to win the battle. Felix slid out of the way as the knight brought his sword down between his legs, narrowly avoiding collision with his own groin. The nimble thief leapt onto The Bear's back and clung onto whatever pieces of armour weren't fused together. The Bear immediately reeled up, trying to shake him off and Felix reached his sword as far ahead as he could, pointing it back at himself. He then drove it with maximum force through the visor of The Bear's helmet. All resistance came to a halt as the gigantic knight collapsed to his knees and fell to the ground with a crash, sending a weak tremor through the platform. Felix, panting, clambered from his back and collapsed to his knees himself, but alive, and victorious.

Jannis was visibly furious. His eyes burned with rage as he stepped forward to drag the thief to his feet.

"The gods have also judged Felix Anderassan to be worthy of living another day! Please, cheer for your victor!"

The crowd burst into applause and cheered louder than before. Felix merely smiled, still regaining his breath.

"However," Jannis began. The crowd immediately went silent. "Felix Anderassan is not guilty of the same crimes as Paul Harriwood. Instead, he is guilty of not just thievery and assisting a master criminal but also of misleading the King and his subjects. In other words, Felix Anderassan is guilty of treason – and even the gods may not interfere in the rightful punishment he deserves. Sirs Hallor and Gerard, please take hold of our prisoner!"

Felix wasted no time in leaping from the platform. He landed in an area occupied by a group of bedraggled men and women who must have been at the front of the crowd begging before the event had even begun. They were quick to move out of the way after the young thief had nearly landed on one of them.

As Felix pushed his way through the vastness of the crowd, he noticed their collective jeering and wasn't sure whether it was directed at him or the Salyrians. He hazarded a guess that it was at the Salyrians due to the lack of resistance he faced as he moved through the crowd and even the fact that some people purposefully moved out of the way to allow him through. When he thought about it, he was surprised the opposition to the foreign invaders hadn't come earlier.

A quick glance behind found a number of knights making quick progress through the crowd as they chased him. They utilised their strength and hardened exteriors to remove any resistance with force and Felix also noticed some knights running around the edge of the crowd to cut off the exits.

There was one choice which he saw working. His hand moved almost invisibly fast to snatch a sheepskin hat from someone near him and he suddenly ducked low, placing the hat on his own head and rising again after sidestepping from his previous trajectory. He stopped moving, his heart beating madly.

The knights drew closer and were constantly calling to each other. His deception had worked and he tucked the loose strands of hair which escaped the hat's grasp back on top of his head. He looked around so as to give the impression of looking for the missing criminal and the knights paved onwards, moving past him and eventually reaching the rear end of the crowd before giving up the hunt.

"Good trick, bossman," a bald man beside him said. "Can I have my hat back now?" Felix recognised him as a member of the Syndicate who he had trained in swordsmanship practice before the invasion.

"Yeah, after all this malarkey is finished," Felix whispered in response.

The crowd had grown restless with mixed emotions as Jannis once again took to the execution platform, brimming with anger. This time, when he made his announcement, he didn't even try to conceal his fury.

"Now, exalted citizens of Dannos, we have our last dirty criminal before the grand finale. Don't get excited, as she will not face a trial by combat. Instead, she will burn at the stake, as she is a gods-forsaken witch! Sir Hallor, bring forth the stake! You lot, bring forth the wood and the kindling!"

A crew of knights quickly assembled a stake behind the scaffold at a safe distance so one wouldn't burn down the other. Rosa was gagged and violently picked up as she tried her best to resist, to no avail. She was thrust against the stake, her hands and legs bound and attached to the long wooden pole found in the centre of an impressive, organised pile of fuel.

"We waste no time in striking this filth from our world! The witch will now burn!" Jannis cried, sounding more and more insane with each announcement. He began to chant 'Burn the witch! Burn the witch!' and the crowd gradually joined in, though more of them were growing displeased with the Salyrians' actions and refused. Some also jeered, which surprised both Felix and Elton, as they knew that witches as a concept were still feared by much of the Dannosi population.

A torch-wielding knight stepped forward and lit the lower layers of kindling in the wood pile. The fire immediately grew as the chanting grew louder and Rosa grew more restless. The flames now enveloped half of the pile and the blaze only grew faster as it devoured more of the fuel. The wood crackled and popped as Rosa feared for her life, seeing no way out of her situation.

The flames slithered around the sides of the wood pile and snaked around the wooden pole to which she was tied. The heat had grown unbearable, as had the volume of Jannis's chant. His voice had stopped sounding human and was now simply a faint, incomprehensible noise in Rosa's ears before she finally felt the flames lick her bare feet. She cried in pain before all her senses felt relief.

She was no longer crying in pain atop a stake. Instead, she was in a cold room with Elton, Paul, and Felix. She surveyed the surroundings and found there was one more person in the room, sitting lazily in his chair and surveying a map of the continent.

Elton looked around the room and immediately located a weapon rack. He grabbed a sword from the rack and rushed forward, placing it against Hortensio's neck as he stood up and turned around the face the intruders.

"How the bloody hell did you get in here?" he said, careful not to raise his voice. He gazed worryingly at the sharp edge of the blade which was only inches away from ending his life.

"Rosa teleported us in, I presume," Elton responded. "But that doesn't matter to you."

"I didn't do it, boss," Rosa corrected. Elton didn't take his attention from holding the sword against Hortensio's neck but gradually looked to his side as if to ask for more information.

"I thought I was dead, boss. Then we got put in here."

"How the bloody hell is it so cold?" Hortensio complained. "A moment ago it was baking!"

"No idea," Elton said, while the other three exchanged knowing glances, "but you're not going to say another word unless you want your blood to soil the contents of that table."

"Hah! Jannis will already be on his way here to report. You're dead, Redwinter."

Elton drew closer with a menacing glare.

"I meant what I said," he growled. "Now, I need you to answer a few questions completely honestly. If you comply, we'll let you go. Don't, and I'll put you down. I'm not known for making idle threats."

The young King of Salyria didn't respond.

"Good," Elton continued. "First question – are there guards behind that door?"

Hortensio nodded.

"How many?"

"Just two."

"Felix, Rosa – block the door. Quietly."

Felix and Rosa found various large items of furniture and other objects from around the room to create a substantial barrier between them and the door which would take tremendous effort to break through.

"Second question – who really are you? Who are your mother and father?"

The King looked down in shame and pondered his answer for a few moments before looking back up.

"It's all… it's all true. I have no idea who my mother or father is. I make sure to spread that Maria and Jacob Riff of Heathervale are my true parents. That I'm not a bastard, even if I am just a peasant boy. But my mother— I mean Maria, she told me everything before I was sent to Camelion to become a squire. The rumours aren't far off – I was found in a basket on

245

the edge of the forest near Heathervale. No sign of my true mother and father, the imbeciles."

Elton turned away, his eyes suddenly glassy.

"Your real mother is dead, Hortensio. Her name was Violet, and she was beautiful. Truly, astonishingly beautiful – cascading blonde hair; eyes as soft as a newborn's skin and the colour of a summer day's sky; full, enchanting lips and a nose which fit perfectly in her symmetrical face." Tears formed in the old thief's eyes.

"How do you know all this? How can I know you're not making this up?" Hortensio interrogated.

"Because I am your father," Elton growled. "I was the imbecile you speak of who left you on the edge of the forest. I was the one who couldn't bear to bring you up alone, couldn't bear to watch you grow up in this unforgiving world. Couldn't bear to be the man who you would call father."

"You? Some old man who doesn't share a single feature with me? Well, it's all very nice you saying this, but it sounds like bollocks to me. You're going to have to do much better than this," Hortensio said, standing up. Elton realised he had drawn the sword away in his story and returned its tip to Hortensio's neck. The young King returned to his seat.

"You want to know why I did it? Of course you do. I don't know if you've realised it yet but I'm not a very nice man. And I never was. I didn't deserve your mother but she married me anyways and I could almost put my past behind me until they came one day. My rotten luck that she was alone in the street, having bought a lovely amethyst necklace from the market. Some lowlife also wanted that stupid necklace and decided that they would take it from her without asking. And put a knife in her gut at the same time. Well, I'll tell you what I did after then. No thief in all Gatherford was safe when I found her. That night, I went out alone armed only with a relic of my past. That relic claimed the lives of dozens of wanderers and hell if I knew if they were innocent or not. I just kept killing and killing and killing because I didn't know what the hell else I could do because all I felt was rage and fury and nothingness.

"I eventually found someone in possession of the necklace and asked them where they found it. They said they had

246

bought it from the market. I put the relic through that bastard's heart without a second thought and took the necklace, leaving the dagger behind. I didn't return to Gatherford, I merely took Violet's cold, lifeless body from our little market house and buried it in the meadow outside the city walls. Then I took you, our newborn baby, and placed you in a basket. I took you through the forest and braved the dangers within. Then I left you near a lonely little village so that I could continue my life where it had left off before meeting your mother. Without corrupting your life. Thus, the Redwinter Syndicate was soon born."

An aura of uneasiness hung over the room with nobody speaking or moving for a while. Elton quivered, nearly killing Hortensio with the sharp tip of the sword.

"Do you still have the necklace?" Hortensio asked.

Elton fished into a buttoned pocket on the inside of his gambeson and retrieved a small, tarnished silver necklace holding a pendant containing a flawlessly cut amethyst.

"Well, I'll be," Hortensio said, leaning back as far as could be allowed.

"I need you, Your Grace," Elton said. "I need you to trust me."

"Why do you need me to trust you?"

"You've noticed the chill in the air already. Would you like to know why it's so suddenly cold?"

"Enlighten me. And then start a fire to warm up this bloody place."

"Kal, I assume you're still there?"

The vampire emerged from a shadowy corner of the room. Hortensio raised his eyebrows in surprise but didn't show any signs of fear.

"Are you just telling everyone about me?" Kalahar mused. "I suppose it's for the best. Let me guess – you want to recruit the use of the Salyrian army in your upcoming fight. In fact, don't answer, because I know the answer. Benefits of telepathy."

"Oh, fantastic. He can read our minds as well as make rabbits appear out of hats."

"Can someone please explain what's going on here?" Hortensio asked, flustered.

247

"It's a long story. Where should we start—"

Kalahar cut him off with a wave of his hand and muttered something in an ominous, guttural language which he had used before. Hortensio's eyes glazed over and Elton tried to regain his attention but he was completely detached from reality.

"What did you do that for?" he demanded.

"Just give it a moment, you impatient old man."

After more than a moment, Hortensio blinked and looked at the people in the room with him one by one, with an expression as if he had never seen them before. He blinked again and shook his head before returning to full confidence.

"Vampires? You want me to use my army to fight vampires? And… they're real? What have you just done, wizard?"

"I'm not a wizard, I'm a chaotic vampire," Kalahar corrected. "I've transferred a copy of part of my knowledge into your brain to skip the tedious monologue which would have ensued should we have chosen to listen to Elton's explanation. Now, do you understand the gravity of the situation? I'll let you speak your mind instead of doing it for you."

"It all seems like a load of witchcraft to me. And vampires can't be real. This is all bollocks!" Hortensio rambled. "I'm King Hortensio of Heathervale, first of his name, Kingslayer and Saviour of Salyria. I will not be spoken down to by a group of cutthroats, one of which claims to be my father, and their pet wizard! If you're going to kill me, at least allow me to die honourably. But I will put up with this for no longer!"

The young King, disgruntled, rose from his seat and crossed his arms.

"Well? What's it going to be?" he demanded. "I trust you're not going to kill me, Elton Redwinter. That wouldn't be very fatherly of you. What about the others? Do they have the authority to kill me?"

"He certainly takes after you, Regi," Rosa snickered.

Elton sighed.

"You know why they call me Regi? If it's not boss, bossman or something else that isn't Elton, it's Regi. Have you picked up on that?"

"That witch called you that when she came to deliver the jewels."

"There you go. Regi is a nickname I picked up shortly after arriving in Dannos, a few months after I left Salyria. It's short for Regicide – a word I learned from a scholar I grew to be friends with before he went his own way. It only turned from a word I knew into a nickname I gave myself after I killed Bloody Ramsey – the 'King' of Dannos. He was a mean old bastard and this was reflected in the former half of his name. Believe it or not, crime was more rife then than it is now when I first arrived at the city. Unorganised, messy crime and even messier punishment by the corrupt King Ramsey. So I took it upon myself to kill him and take over, establishing a new, cleaner order. Corrupt in a way which would allow the streets to bathe in silver, instead of blood. I'll spare you the details of how I was able to kill him, but know that it's my most famous act – and one that I memorialised through a nickname which a much younger self thought was intimidating."

Elton paused and looked expectantly at Hortensio, who merely shrugged his shoulders and returned the expectant expression.

"My point, boy," he said, gazing at the sword in his hand, "is that I've killed a king before. I can bloody well do it again, whether you're my son or not."

CHAPTER 27

TYEN'AEL-TENETH BORDER

Erríl had guarded the silver shipment every single month. His blade had tasted the blood of many a dwarf and many an elf who were interested in robbing the convoy as they would a travelling merchant's caravan. And every time he had engaged in battle, he and his companions had emerged victorious. Naturally – three tonnes of silver wouldn't be shipped without adequate protection. And in the case of this particular monthly shipment, the protection wasn't just adequate – it was overkill.

Twenty armoured foot soldiers, six mounted cavalry and six chariot-riding archers. Their equipment wasn't the shoddy standard-issue steel, either – it was forged exquisitely so as to be light, but strong. Weapons capable of dealing large forces while remaining light to wield. Armour which was protective, yet manoeuvrable.

One might have thought that being tasked with guarding such an unimaginably large quantity of silver would have driven the guardians of the convoy to theft – even a small fraction of the amount they protected would have set anyone up for life. But this didn't happen – Erríl was a veteran of the Tyen'Aeli army, throughout peacetime being tasked with little more than protection of the realm and dealing with domestic affairs, like the October Killings. Erríl himself had taken on the infamous Karek Hyggavaerd in a duel and defeated him, leading to his arrest and imprisonment.

The foliage rustled in the wind as the convoy passed the south-easternmost treeline of the Darklight Forest. Passing through the Darklight was always the most treacherous part of the journey, for they often had to deal with threats armed with more dangerous tools than rusty maces and sharpened sticks. This time, however, it had been surprisingly quiet, without even so much as a whisper of a crawler – oversized, fatally venomous arachnids which haunted the depths of the Forest.

Now was usually the time that they would be ambushed by bandits – lying in wait at the only road through the forest for miles. This time was apparently no different.

Erríl drew his sword and turned to face the attackers. But as they emerged from cover, Erríl surveyed the relatively structured organisation of the ambush, the quality of their equipment and the sheer number of attackers. It was clear from the fabricated tears in the fabric draped over their shoulders and the stains on their blades that these dwarves were attempting to appear to be bandits. But they weren't bandits.

They were soldiers.

*

"No survivors!" Tynak cried, leading the charge against the convoy. "For the Ki— For our pockets!"

It pained Tynak to see his axe in such a state as he drew it from his back – normally, he was meticulous about ensuring it remained clean. Staining it on purpose had been one of the most painful things he'd had to do in his life.

The dwarves cried with energy and threw themselves at the High Elven guards, the six archers distributed across three horse-guided chariots being their first targets. The archers whipped the horses' rears and sped away, attempting to reach a safe distance from which they could begin to launch a hail of arrows. They never reached this safe distance when the other half of the Elites revealed themselves from the other side of the forest's exit, circling around to meet the first half and trapping the elves in a circle. The archers then made the quick decision to begin shooting, their arrows downing a number of onrushing dwarves. The deaths of their allies only fuelled the remaining further hundred Elites and they ravaged the archers and their horses before moving on to the mounted cavalry, who had feebly begun to hack away at the dwarves, their swords barely even able to reach. The horses were felled, and the riders fell with them, being finished off as they hit the ground and sometimes even before.

Tynak almost expected the remaining guards on foot to surrender, something he believed to be typically elven. But, to his surprise, they didn't, and battled just as ferociously as the dwarves.

No more than a minute later and the number of remaining elves had been whittled down to two. A war hammer split the skull of one of them, leaving only a startlingly old-looking man. But then Tynak realised that he must have been of a similar relative age himself.

Tynak raised his fist, signalling the Elites to stop. He lowered his axe and walked up to the last elf, who stared down at him with cold eyes.

"Have ye any last words?" he asked in High Elven.

"I've protected my land for a hundred years and I'll continue to protect it for hundreds more, even if I'm to fall today," the last guard replied. "But I shan't fall without a fight."

*

Erríl wiped his blade clean of dwarven blood for the last time.

"I wouldn't have had it any other way," the red-haired dwarf cackled.

*

"Right!" Tynak bellowed, pulling his axe from the elf's chest. "Let's see what we've got. Get these tarps off the wagon!"

The elves had been guarding a few caravans, drawn by sturdy horses, which they wouldn't be leaving behind. The soldiers unfastened the tarp from corners of the wagons and ripped them off before jumping onto the wheel to survey their prize.

"Captain!" one of the soldiers cried. "We've been had!"

"What?" Tynak responded in disbelief.

He joined the soldiers at the wagons and peered inside, where he had expected to see mountains of silver.

Instead, they were empty.

CHAPTER 28

The siren turned its attention for a moment to the sorceress, who stretched out her arms and began to chant an incantation. The creature recoiled and its hair writhed even more vigorously as it let out a head-wrenching scream. Richard attempted to push it off him, but it was surprisingly heavy and he could do nothing but watch as it gradually transformed back into its original form, squealing all the while.

"Quick!" Jade called. "Before it starts singing again!"

Richard was still unable to move and regretted not bringing his sword. The creature cried in pain as its shapely figure returned and its skin colour returned to being pale. Its red eyes were the last transformation to occur.

"It's too heavy! I can't do anything!" Richard hollered.

The creature smiled beautifully before its face was split in two by a thin, wickedly sharp rapier. Slime-green blood splattered across Richard's face and he huffed as the slain creature's weight removed the air from his lungs when it landed atop him. Ferris, wiping the blood from his rapier, moved to assist him and managed to roll the carcass onto the sand, allowing Richard to remain lying on the ground for a while as he took a number of deep breaths.

"Witch," Ferris began, sheathing his now clean rapier, "you're getting into a habit of not warning us about the beasts you want us to keep travelling near."

"I suppose I didn't expect to encounter a siren. Oh well, we managed to overcome it."

"I'm starting to think you're trying to kill us," Ferris muttered, running his fingers over the siren's scales.

253

"At least it's been an exciting journey," Richard said, standing up and placing his bow and quiver of arrows onto his back after retrieving the ones he had loosed in the fight.

"Perhaps too exciting," Ferris remarked. "Every cloud has a silver lining, though – I shan't run out of material for a long time, now."

"Come, let us carry on. We'd do best to set off now and avoid the coming heat," Jade instructed.

They travelled through the desert without a worry. Their conservative use of the water supplies meant that they had plenty leftover when plant life began to appear in greater quantities, followed by animal life. The Desnari of southern Sanskar gave way to savannas and grasslands south of the Redwater Passage, which they reached by nightfall.

They collectively decided it would be more comfortable to travel by ferry to the Sanskari capital and travelled to the town of Sellayi, where they booked rooms and passage aboard a ship to Virilia. Sellayi was by no means a bustling city but it had a suitable port and they set off that very night aboard *The Marigold* with a few other passengers. They were able to bring their horses, but they were made to stay in the cargo bay alongside a number of crates, the contents of which the captain had refused to reveal.

Richard had never travelled by boat across bodies of water larger than a river. He was lucky that the waters were gentle that night. Ferris was in a similar situation, while Jade had travelled across the Bay a number of times in the past. Still, despite the gentleness of the boat's rocking, Richard had to relieve his stomach of its contents twice throughout the journey, one of which times he was joined by the troubadour.

Strong winds in their favour the following morning meant that the grand port of Virilia, the sun-soaked capital of the Empire, appeared on the horizon. It was a long-awaited moment after the hardships of the journey, but they had made it and it was more than Richard had ever imagined. Idle chatter among the Miradosi betrayed the city to be a rundown arrangement of slums where the Emperor ruled supreme, extorting the already poor residents of the city of their last pennies to fund his war. It turned out that the idle chatter was complete nonsense.

The scene in front of him was a bustling metropolis. A constant flurry of merchants' large sailboats and fishermen's smaller rowboats in and out of the overcrowded dock which opened up to a fish market at a break in the carved stone wall which separated the port from the rest of the city. There were constant patrols of what looked at first to be Sanskari soldiers but their armour had slight differences to the traditional, cheaper-made uniforms of the soldiers they had encountered before – for one, the armour appeared much blacker and cleaner than the soldiers' armour, where the natural grey of the steel revealed itself in places. They wore plate armour which all interlinked to allow complete movement and protection, while the soldiers' armour sacrificed the complete protection to allow movement while still armouring the torso, the arms, and the shins. Richard noticed the armour was comparable to Francis's. He wondered if the sets shared the same weakness.

Unlike Francis's armour, the guards patrolling the port did not bear the Sanskari phoenix on their breastplates. Instead, they bore a symbol which Richard hadn't seen before, which looked like a shield with two swords crossed behind it. He pointed it out to Jade as they rode past a patrol in the port and she explained that it was the traditional insignia of the City Guard.

The exquisitely outfitted guards were only the first sign of the city's affluence. The buildings behind the port's wall were elegant, exhibiting modern architecture and constructed from expensive materials from across the continent. Notably the banks of the city were particularly opulent, with stained glass windows as would be seen in a church, but on a grander scale and featuring a number of statues carved from marble. One of which statues was of Nendar Varanus himself.

"Where exactly are we going?" Ferris asked as they walked past a market stall offering gem-encrusted gold and silver jewellery at exorbitant prices.

"I have an accommodation near the palace. Have you spotted it yet?"

"Is it that one?" he guessed, pointing at a distant looming structure rivalled only in size by the city's Lanthanist cathedral. Jade nodded in affirmation.

"I've also recognised a slight problem which might prove to be somewhat dangerous for us," Ferris stated. "We don't speak Sanskari."

"Hablar Sanskarra," Jade said, gesturing to both Richard and the quizzical troubadour. "Now it's not a problem."

"You just taught us how to speak an entire language with a couple of words?"

"As if," she chuckled. "No, you will still speak Miradosi. But everyone else will hear it in Sanskari."

"How long does the spell last?" Ferris inquired.

"A few days. Then I can just refresh it. Now, let us get going."

After more than a week of constant riding, they still had one last stretch to go. Fortunately, the palace wasn't particularly far from the port, and they were able to take in the delights of the heartland of the Empire. They passed through vast markets selling whole varieties of products which put Limara's Sunday market to shame – furs from rare animals native to the North and the Vivian Isles; assortments of exotic fruits and vegetables from all the different climates within range of Virilia; wine produced from the numerous vineyards found in the countryside surrounding the capital – including Virilian Red, a bottle of which Jade didn't hesitate to buy with the few Sanskari pestas which had somehow appeared in her bag. An array of chefs preparing examples of their finest work and offering free samples to the wealthiest-looking bystanders. Richard particularly took notice of a dish being cooked in an oversized frying pan – the main components appeared to be rice and chicken, all seasoned and spiced. He bought a portion with Jade's remaining money of which she assured him she had plenty more to spare at home.

"It appears we've been somewhat sidetracked," Jade mused as Ferris purchased a steak skewer from another chef.

"Oh, we may as well enjoy what we can while we're here," the troubadour responded, dramatically biting off one of the chunks of steak from the skewer and making a show of his pleasure.

"We must continue," Jade asserted. "We're nearly to the stable."

The stable in question looked less like a stable and more like a tavern for horses. Richard thought that the idea of a stable in a city would look somewhat out of place for an urban area but it contained all the necessary facilities to leave horses for extended periods of time and blended in perfectly with the urban environment. Constructed from stone bricks and wooden beams like many of the other buildings nearby and across the city, the only thing which indicated it to be a stable was the collection of carved wooden letters above the door reading 'Senna's Stable'. The reception looked more like that of a bank than of a stable and the receptionist assured them that their horses would be subject to the highest-quality treatment and even though he was in the heartland of the enemy, Richard didn't doubt it. Especially when he saw the price of keeping the horses there for even a single night.

"That was an odd sight," Ferris said as they walked away from the stable, holding their horses' saddlebags. "Whatever happened to a fence post and a roof over their heads?"

"Senna Visane is one of the most well-known businessmen in the city," Jade explained. "He owns a number of operations at the port and accrues astounding amounts of money from daily trade. He also has a stake in every bank in the city, so he makes money from interest on loans. Once upon a time, before he grew as wealthy as he did, he simply made his money by assessing the markets every day and buying and selling various items for a profit. He made enough money from that to start his own business and open a factory, which is where his wealth skyrocketed."

"What did he sell?"

"Weapons and armour to the Sanskari army. Swords, shields, lances, spears, bows, arrows, cuirasses, helmets, pauldrons, greaves, gauntlets, battle-axes, war hammers... everything they wanted, really. It was all in terribly high demand. Still is."

"And now he owns a stable which doesn't look like a stable."

"Correct."

"What you're saying," Richard said, "is that this Senna is responsible for the deaths of the Miradosi troops back home?"

"I wouldn't say that. Perhaps he plays a part in their deaths by supplying the instruments used for the practice. However,

257

it is the Emperor who declared war on Mirados, the Emperor who sent his armies south, the Emperor who ordered them to kill the Miradosi resistance. And then it was the generals of the Sanskari army who decided on locations to attack. And then it was the individual members of the army who chose to engage in battle with the Miradosi soldiers and chose to kill them when they had the opportunity. So no, I don't think Visane is responsible for their deaths. I think he merely saw a business opportunity and took it. As anyone else would have done."

Richard grunted but didn't argue. They took interest as they passed in a pair of Sanskari soldiers – not City Guards – banging heavily on the door of a rundown house. They received no response and broke down the door with a heavy kick before entering. It must have taken a while to find what they wanted, because they still hadn't come out when they reached the end of the road and were forced to turn and continue.

"I've just realised that everyone is speaking Miradosi," Ferris exclaimed. "Is that also part of the spell?"

"No, the entire population of Virilia has simultaneously decided to speak the language of the enemy," Jade replied, rolling her eyes. "We've arrived."

They turned another corner and were faced with a rudimentary multi-story stone brick and wood house which didn't look the tiniest bit out of place when compared to the other accommodations in the vicinity. Richard had expected a witch's den with blazing braziers hanging above the door and a pointed roof. Instead, nothing hung above the door and the roof was a simple slanted arrangement of wooden planks.

"Well, this is disappointing," Ferris blurted, voicing Richard's thoughts.

"Just wait," she snapped, inserting a key into the rusty keyhole. The door creaked open and the company went inside.

Once they were inside, Richard realised he hadn't seen any windows on the house's exterior and understood why. From the doorway, not much could be seen apart from another door and a right turn. The first thing Jade showed her guests was the contents of the room behind the door: a miniature library. Richard had been impressed with the collection of tomes in her room in Limara but evidently that was only a snippet of the true collection. In fact, Jade didn't even refer to the first room as a miniature library, but it was the only fitting description which came to Richard's mind. The walls were lined with ornate, carved hardwood bookcases which were much more appropriate for a sorceress. Not a single slot on any of the bookcases was left empty, each occupied by a thick hardcover book about any number of different topics. Unfortunately, there was no brazier hanging from the ceiling but instead there were steel sconces attached to the walls at even heights in the spaces between the bookcases. Jade lit them with a command as they entered the room and they flared up to an unnatural brightness before dimming.

They didn't tarry in the first room and were led around the corner where there was another door, hidden from view when standing in the doorway, and a staircase. Behind the door was an unexciting kitchen and dining table where they spent fifteen minutes in silence, pilfering Jade's aged supply of food found in a sealed stone container, the insides of which were frozen to the touch. She explained how Varanus himself had enchanted the container to be endlessly cold as long as it remained intact and she was able to keep food in it for months. The downside was that before they could tuck into a chicken drumstick each was that it had to be defrosted, which was, of course, accelerated with a spell. Hunger sated, their desire to see more of Jade's mysterious accommodation returned and they climbed the stairs to the first floor.

A chill hung in the air on the first floor. Richard shuddered as they ascended and turned into the first room on the left which looked the stereotypical image of a witch's brewery. The centre of the room was adorned with a grand, empty cauldron atop a firepit. There were shelves around the room teeming with a plethora of herbs and other alchemy reagents, neatly organised into categories. For example, one shelf only contained green-leafed herbs while another shelf contained the bones of various unfortunate creatures. Richard gulped upon sight of a collection of clear glass jars filled with red liquid.

"Is this more what you were expecting?" Jade asked, turning her head to Ferris.

"You even have a cauldron! I'm surprised it's not the centrepiece of a pentagram!"

"Oh, that comes later," she jested. "You expected a sorceress's abode and here it is. Now come, we have some plans to discuss."

"That's right, I nearly forgot why you dragged us here," Ferris said as they walked into a much more inviting reading room. "Are we going to meet the Emperor in person?"

"Richard will. You, my dear bard, will not."

"I have skills which will be of value to you, witch," Ferris exclaimed.

"Playing the banjo?"

"I'm very sociable. Much more so than your friend the bounty hunter, the number of words he spoke in our entire journey here I could count with my fingers and maybe a couple of toes. You really expect him to engage in a conversation with the leader of the people who he – and I – despise the most in this world?"

"I can speak for myself," Richard interjected. "I don't need you to do it on my behalf. However, Jade, I want you to take Ferris with us. He would definitely help us were he to come with us."

"Varanus is a very distrustful man. He would have him killed," Jade retorted.

"Why would he do that? He doesn't bear any connection to Mirados."

"He would be able to detect the spell which allows you to speak and understand Sanskari. He's much more powerful than I."

"But you cast the same spell on me. That means he would kill me, wouldn't it?"

Ferris raised his eyebrows and glared at the sorceress who increasingly tried to rummage for a response.

"I— I can manage to convince him of your defection," she stammered. "He would believe you, Richard. You don't understand why, but I do. I can't explain it."

The bounty hunter cast a steely glare upon the sorceress and backed away.

"You're lying to us," he enunciated.

"I assure you, I have only spoken the truth."

"You say you're working for the Miradosi cause. Yet you said how you and a band of Sanskari soldiers and bandits slaughtered a group of our boys. When I first found you, you were on an official assignment from Limara, but you said you weren't working officially for anyone in Mirados."

He began pacing up and down the room.

"You indulge in the delights of Sanskari wine, straight from the capital. You didn't let me kill Francis. Hell, you said you were making replicas of our targets' heads in Limara, but you went and killed one of them in cold blood! That's right, a peasant saw you go into that merchant's house without picking the lock. He heard his cries as you killed him. I didn't entirely believe it was you, but now I'm not so sure."

He stopped pacing.

"You demonstrate a comprehensive knowledge of Sanskari warfare and their history. You speak of your limitations as a mage, but I'm yet to see them. You bring us to Virilia without even devising a plan any more detailed than overthrowing the Emperor and putting me in his place!"

He stepped closer to the sorceress, who had remained silent, arms crossed.

"Whose side are you on?" Richard growled.

Jade sighed.

"I had hoped to have more time."

She pressed her palms against Richard's chest and her hands erupted with light, forming a large disc in the air. He flew backwards, colliding with the wall. He didn't get back up.

Ferris leapt into action and freed his rapier from its sheath, pressing forward at speed. The sorceress ducked his initial thrust and shouted a spell. The troubadour's sword arm went limp, and he quickly grabbed the rapier with his other hand before it fell to the floor.

"You bitch! I knew there was something wrong with you from the start!"

"Should have said something, then," she spat, raising her arms again.

Ferris threw the rapier like a throwing knife and it pierced her robe above the right arm, pinning her to the wall. He ran from the room and the front door subsequently opened and slammed shut.

Jade didn't worry as she heard the troubadour's cries of 'Witch! I was attacked by a witch!' outside. Instead, after trying and failing to reach for the handle of the rapier pinning her to the wall, she telekinetically removed it from her robe and allowed it to clatter to the ground. She strolled towards Richard's motionless body and knelt down to hear his faint breathing.

"I think we'll require an appropriate setting for this," she said, tracing a circle in the air.

A window opened, showing an empty operating theatre. She levitated Richard's body through and placed it upon the operating table before stepping through herself, just as her front door was kicked in.

CHAPTER 29

King Hortensio of Heathervale, first of his name, Kingslayer and Saviour of Salyria unhappily stood before his army alongside Sir Jannis in the very square where they had previously planned to execute the criminals of the Redwinter Syndicate. Though now, their plans had changed entirely.

"Knights of Camelion, guardians of the realm," the young King bellowed. "There have been some alterations to our original plan. We will still fight to shower this continent in the glory of Salyrian prosperity, but first, we must fight alongside our enemies. For there is a graver threat at hand. When you were mere children, you may have heard old wives' tales of blood-sucking creatures of the night. They are more than just tales. They are grounded in reality. Vampires are real, and they are soon to rise in great numbers. The Redwinter Syndicate has been preparing to fight a war of their own against the vampires and we would be foolish not to join them. For if the vampires rise and slaughter the continent, there will be nobody left to spread our core values to. Do not trouble yourselves with the fact that we are working alongside criminal scum. For they know they are not safe from our enlightenment. But the enemy of our enemy must be our friend, or we will all be destroyed."

The crowd of knights appeared unsure of how to react, exchanging perplexed looks with one another. The gathering had also attracted a number of prying onlookers who were much more dramatic with their reaction, frantically running away to inform as many people as they knew, or perhaps to quickly purchase as many bulbs of garlic, silver lockets, aspen posts and jugs of holy water as they could.

"You may be puzzled, upset, annoyed," Hortensio continued. "This is certainly not what I had planned for our conquest of the continent. But it is our duty as knights to protect the people. To fight honourably beside those who would otherwise stab us in the back for personal gain. To show that we are better."

Hortensio stepped back and left a space in between him and Jannis. A moment later, the space was filled by the menacing figure of Kalahar Kefrein-Lazalar who appeared ever so slightly taller than normal. The knights, who had been mostly silent and sturdy as statues until this point, recoiled in horror while the vampire laughed.

"Goodness me, I think I'm being blinded. I thought there was enough dust and sand in this wasteland to coat anything. Apparently your terribly reflective armour is impervious. Honourable knights, allow me to introduce myself. My name, or rather the name I go by most frequently, is Kalahar Kefrein-Lazalar. I am not sorcerer in the traditional sense, for I was born with my abilities. I am a chaotic vampire – the only one on this planet. Don't be alarmed, I'm not going to hurt you or anyone else. I'm not going to sink my fangs into your necks under the cover of night, as delectable as it would be. I'm merely going to help you. So listen closely."

CHAPTER 30

Since the morning of the attacks, the journey had progressed without a hitch. The pirates had made off with the battered fifth galleon, which Elaeínn's new captain claimed wouldn't make it back to dry land before sinking.

Her new galleon had a name: *HHS Wavestrider*. She was now under the command of Captain Varraed, a notably more outgoing man than the deceased Captain Rikkard. He didn't hesitate to boss around his crew, including Elaeínn and even sometimes Jaelaar.

She was also shackled to a post in the brig.

Her sword laid on a shelf across the corridor from her. She had been devoid of contact since being thrown in the jail on Jaelaar's orders, his diplomatic mission having failed. Now all he was interested in was reaching the geographical destination of their expedition.

The steps leading down to the brig creaked and she presumed it was one of two feeding times which occurred every day. Normally, it would just be a sailor coming to toss her some bread and fruit. Instead, it was Jaelaar who appeared from around the corner.

"We're arriving at the island," he announced. "Before we leave, I would like to discuss something with you."

Jaelaar picked up the sheathed sword and drew it, admiring the exquisite runes decorating the blade.

"When you attacked the pirates, this very sword glowed a vibrant gold."

"I was there," Elaeínn drawled.

265

"How? How did you make it do such a thing? I have owned this weapon for decades and never have these ridiculous markings meant anything. Why did it mean something to you?"

"I'm as clueless as you. Am I accompanying you to the island or am I to be left to rot in here?"

"I have had my people study it relentlessly. Historians, smiths, mages specialised in various trees of magic – nobody has been able to make sense of it. The symbols quite simply aren't anything we've seen before."

"Just what my friend said when I showed it to him. Where did you even get it?"

"It was a gift, delivered by a courier under a code name."

"What was the code name?"

Jaelaar squinted in contemplation and sheathed the blade.

"The name was R."

She jumped to her feet and grasped two of the bars of her cage.

"You told me that R meant nothing to you when I asked you about it," she hissed.

"Because I didn't believe it was in any way relevant. But now that the sword has clearly in some way reacted to you after you were, I'm guessing, captured by an 'R', I'm re-evaluating the situation."

Jaelaar retrieved the keys from a hook on the wall, unlocking the cage and freeing her from the post. She didn't abuse the freedom, intent on never having to go back to the brig again.

She was kept under close watch as Jaelaar guided her to the top deck where the first signs of land were appearing on the horizon. The sun was high, the air humid.

The landmass ahead stretched to the boundaries of view. A thin stretch of beach appeared to surround monumental, jagged stone formations and cliffs, and beyond the shore a mountain range stretched into the sky. It was a scene from a fantasy story.

As they sailed the remaining ocean between them and the island, Elaeínn provided yet again an account of her experience, and in the most detail yet.

266

"And then I went to see an astromancer, with the hopes that I would be able to find Kíra with his magic. He said that she was... travelling to the West..."

She looked in awe at the looming cliffs as the *HHS Wavestrider* reached the shore, the sailors hoisting an anchor over the side.

"The astromancer said that she was travelling West, aboard a ship. She could be here – on this island! It's directly to the West, and he said he couldn't really see much of the scene from Kíra's perspective. He only assumed that they were sailing because this land has never been documented before!"

The gangplank was lowered, and the crew steadily dismounted, the mages particularly joyous at the contact with dry land. The warmth of the sand was indeed pleasurable, as was its softness. Hard wooden planks had become somewhat tiresome, as had the persistent gentle – and sometimes not-so-gentle – rocking.

A deep rumbling reverberated from within the island and silenced the entire expedition. The dragging of crates and the rolling of barrels was paused, the chattering of excitement quashed, the lowering of sails interrupted.

"What was that?"

"I haven't a clue."

While seemingly everyone else was handed a rucksack filled with necessities and a hat, Elaeínn was excluded. She asked why but wasn't given a response.

As they walked up the beach towards the breaks between the cliffs, it was clear the heat of summer was only going to intensify in the dense, tropical foliage ahead.

She walked alongside Jaelaar, still under close watch. The sword hung from his belt, tantalisingly close. The thought of snatching it and running to find Kíra passed through her mind numerous times but in none of the imagined scenarios did she escape from the group.

It would also probably be safer in numbers, she thought – the rumbling they had heard earlier she had decided was likely to have been some fantastical creature, and jungles were full of deadly fauna regardless of their possession of magical capabilities.

The first signs of animal life they saw were, as could have been expected, in insects. Dragonflies the size of fallen twigs shining a brilliant teal as they buzzed through the brush. Spiders the size of flowers in bloom waiting in webs spun between trees. Luckily, these spiders appeared just to be natural, unlike the crawlers which occupied the Darklight back in Tyen'Ael.

Then there were the occasional rodents scurrying after one another across the treacherous jungle floor – treacherous in the fact that plenty of the expeditioners had already tripped on the many outstretched, tangling roots and the scattered stones and boulders.

As they continued, the humidity uncomfortably soaking Elaeínn's clothes, one of the mages pointed into a tree where a snake the same shade of green as the leaves above it waited motionlessly. It was at least two metres long and about as thick as Elaeínn's bicep.

The ground shuddered as they felt the rumbling once more, this time much more intense. They had now been hacking through the jungle for hours, stopping only twice for a drink and a rest. Jaelaar had been relentless in wanting to reach whatever had caused the source of the sound, a drive mirrored by Elaeínn, albeit for different primary reasons.

They came across a shallow river slicing through the jungle, its bed solid enough to tread through. Small groups of tiny fish, the sunlight reflecting off their silver scales, darted past their feet, heading downstream.

"Wait a moment," Jaelaar ordered as they were about to step onto the far bank. He tentatively left the river and closely examined the riverside, which Elaeínn didn't understand at first. But then she saw it.

Jaelaar evidently had seen it first and he drew his sword. She knew from the look in his eyes that he had been hoping for it to be glowing, but it looked, to his evident disappointment, as ordinary as any steel.

The Prime Minister extended the blade of the sword to an open space between two trees leading into the jungle on the other side of the river. Then he cut down.

The trap was triggered and the ground between the two trees crumbled, revealing a steep pitfall stretching the entire distance between them. Jaelaar was lucky enough to have been standing at its very edge and he backed carefully away, maintaining a defensive stance.

"Draw your weapons and be on your guard," he instructed.

Steel hissed as the sailors drew their swords, as well as the few mages humble enough not to leave all self-defence down to magic. Jaelaar stepped back towards the pit, studying it. Elaeínn broke from the group and joined him.

"If you give me back the sword, then perhaps I'll be able to make it glow again," she persuaded.

"Perhaps," Jaelaar responded. "However, this also presents another opportunity."

Before she could react, Jaelaar used a quick burst of kinetic magic to blast Elaeínn into the pit. She cursed profusely and tried to scale the walls but unfortunately for her, whoever had implemented it had done an excellent job and she was rendered truly incapable.

"Jaelaar!" she shouted as the Prime Minister appeared overhead. "You wanted this mission to be about establishing diplomacy, or whatever it was you rambled about. Whatever happened to that?"

"Oh, you bought that?" he said nonchalantly. "I'm glad, because it allowed me to get this far. I doubt I'd have got away from those pirates without you and the clown. That was coincidental, though. What did you think was really going to happen, Elaeínn? That I was going to forge some happy friendship with a group of terrorists? No. That was never the plan."

"So the plan was just to kill us? Well, you've done three quarters of the job. Why is it taking so long to do the last bit? Why have you dumped me in a pit instead of just fucking killing me? And what was the point of this bloody expedition?"

"Don't be so self-centred, Elaeínn. The expedition merely provided an opportunity to kill off some pests without arising any controversy. That wasn't the reason we set out – the reason was to find this source of magic our mages are so certain of to give us the upper hand against the dwarves in the war, which I can imagine will begin only days after the expiration of the Peace Treaty. They're preparing, just as we are. Am I correct in assuming that? Of course, you would be more knowledgeable, given that they're providing you with a stronghold and funding. Oh, don't look like that. You should know that I have eyes everywhere."

"Why aren't you killing me?" she reiterated.

"This sword"—he gestured to his belt—"is of great interest to me. It reacts to you and I'd like to find out why. Therefore I must keep you alive. And you're far too much of a liability to keep along with us as we go forward, which is why you'll be staying here. It's almost too perfect. You'll even have your own set of guards."

He pointed to what she guessed were people above the pit, though she couldn't see anyone except him.

"Kaesta, Erría, Lysíen and Ytríen will be here, twenty-four hours a day. You'll be fed, you'll have water. But you won't be going anywhere. You definitely won't be grabbing my sword and running off to find Kíra."

"Mind-reading scumbag," she remarked. "You have no right to enter my thoughts."

"I have every right, for I am above the law. Which means I can do as I please. Now, we'll be going."

Jaelaar called to the rest of the crew and they quickly departed. It didn't take long for Elaeínn's new squad of guards to take an interest in her.

"You're that FTA girl that tried to kill the Prime Minister, then?" the first guard questioned, popping her head over the pit. Elaeínn didn't grant her a response.

"Why would you do it? Why kill someone just to get your own way?"

"Because there is no other way," she snapped. "Look at what he's done to me – to avoid the bureaucracy of the system he's trying to whittle away, he's gone to such a measure as to take me out to a far-off island that we didn't even know existed just to have me put down.

"Tell me – what's your name?"

"Kaesta Haettís," the girl supplied.

"You look exceptionally young to be at the University. How old are you?"

"I'm fifteen. I was given a scholarship because of how well I did at the lower school."

270

"To practice magic at the University at your age means only that you must be truly gifted – perhaps capable of becoming a grandmaster. And yet, look where you are – you've been dumped on guard duty by someone who holds the genuine belief that he is superior to others. That isn't fair to you and it isn't fair to anyone on this expedition."

The girl looked hesitant and glanced around at what Elaeínn presumed to be her companions.

"In Elgaer's democracy, we are all powerful because we are all equal," Elaeínn continued. "Jaelaar seeks to remove your power, to set aside equality. Is that really the future you want to see? A future where you have no control over the structure of your own country? Where you are subservient to someone whose ego is on the verge of bursting from overinflation?"

"Stop talking to the prisoner!" Elaeínn heard someone above shout.

"I am not your enemy," she monologued. "We have only one enemy – the one leading your friends and companions into the jungle, where they are to be used as cannon fodder for whatever is to come. Because while Jaelaar is selfish, he's an excellent actor – and he's fooled all of you into believing that what you are doing is for the greater good. That this discovery will benefit all elfkind. But I guarantee you he would never put himself in harm's way for your benefit, so why should you do the same for him? This trap is obviously not natural – something intelligent resides on this island. And, as you can see by my situation, it isn't friendly. Your friends are walking into a trap, and I mean that in both the physical and metaphorical sense. And it's Jaelaar leading them there. But if you get me out of here, I can help you all – we can finally free ourselves of his command and work together, collectively. We can run this expedition in a way which works for all of us."

"Don't listen to her, girl," a gruff voice barked, the same that had spoken earlier. "She's trying hard to fill your head with nonsense."

The owner of the gruff voice appeared alongside Kaesta. He was one of the sailors, and by the wrinkles on his face and his seemingly involuntarily furrowed brow Elaeínn assumed him to have been at it for a long time.

"You," he grunted. "Keep quiet or we'll be finding something to make a gag out of."

"Did you vote for Jaelaar, then?" she ignored his threat. "Did you allow his Nationals to take control of the Houses?"

"I did, and I absolutely don't regret my decision in doing so. Jaelaar has been totally true to his word and is doing an excellent job at ensuring we respect the morals on which our country is founded. I couldn't stand to see the Liberals go on bastardising in the way they were."

"I can see we disagree in terms of ideology," she concluded. "However, I'm hoping we can agree that we both enjoy – or rather enjoyed – the freedom of democracy. Jaelaar is destroying that. Is that really what you voted for?"

"I'll be honest, girl – as long as Jaelaar does a good job at putting down the likes of you, I couldn't care less about what he does to the system."

"Well that's just damn ignorant," she snapped. "You know he's planning to go to war? That'll affect you as it will affect everyone else. He is going to bring destruction to our country, not prosperity."

"War with the dwarves, I presume? I can't say I have any problems with that. They need to be put in their place. Now, I remind you of what I said. Shut up or we'll force you to. Come on, Kaesta."

"I want to listen to her," Kaesta argued. "She makes a good point. I don't necessarily agree with Jaelaar in the same way that you do."

"For Raeris's sake, would you two shut up?" a third voice called. The third voice then also appeared above the pit, in the form of another mage, this time male. He was dressed in blandly coloured robes only a slightly darker beige than his skin. The bland brown appearance was further emphasised by his light caramel hair tied in a bun at the back of his head.

"Are you also of the opinion that a tyrant in the making shouldn't be impeded?" Elaeínn spat.

"No, actually. I plan to go into politics," the mage responded matter-of-factly. "So I agree with you to an extent, FTA girl. I think you'll find most of us do. It's the old you have to contend with. Erría?"

272

A third young mage, again only a girl similar in age to Elaeínn, joined the other guards. She exuded ferocity in her sprawling brown hair, her sharp jawline, her shadowed eyes.

"None of you are really here for King and country, are you?" Elaeínn interrogated. "Except for you, sailor."

"Ytríen. And I'll have none of this treachery. You three, go find something to gag her with."

The other man, presumably Lysíen, glanced at the two girls before puffing out his chest and arrogantly crossing his arms.

"No," he said. "I don't think we will."

"Think very carefully, boy," Ytríen growled, walking up to Lysíen while doing his best to appear menacing. But to his disadvantage, they were of the same height.

"I have thought. I've been thinking ever since Jaelaar left us here only minutes ago. I thought: 'Why, isn't this perfect? An opportunity to finally strike out on my own, do things my own way.' I wasn't made for blindly following orders. I'm independent, and I absolutely despise the hierarchy Jaelaar has us organised in. I say no to his superiority."

He looked towards Kaesta and Erría for support.

"As do I," Erría pledged.

"And me," Kaesta added, the most hesitant of the three.

"In that case," Ytríen hissed, drawing his sword. "I'll be happy to put you all in there with the traitor! Either with your bowels or without!"

He lunged at Lysíen, who quickly drew his own sword in time to parry. The sailor, despite his age, was remarkably quick. And immensely skilful.

"You crazy old fool!" Lysíen cried. "You first instinct was to attack us for disagreeing? I was between choosing who I supported but you've just gone and tipped the scales!"

They stepped away from Elaeínn's range of view and Erría could be heard drawing her blade to assist Lysíen, who was grunting furiously under the persistent effort of the practiced old man. Kaesta stayed behind and tried to help Elaeínn from the pit – first by physical means, but eventually she gave up and resorted to levitating her out with magic. It was clearly an exhausting procedure and Elaeínn made a note to thank her profusely after the scuffle's conclusion.

Kaesta offered her sword to Elaeínn, which she took with grace, joining the now heavily imbalanced fight. Ytríen had begun with confidence – now his face only depicted fear and struggle.

Elaeínn ended up being the one to disarm him – while her foe's focus remained on Lysíen, eyes burning with passionate rage, she managed to sidestep around the sailor, and, in a clean swing of her blade, sliced through his sword arm.

He wasn't finished and despite his wound, gushing blood, he stumbled towards Lysíen, shouting through the pain. The young mage was caught off guard and Ytríen grabbed him forcefully by the throat, at which moment Elaeínn skewered him with her sword.

Ytríen's grip loosened as the blood continued to pour from not just his stump, but also the newly opened hole. A red patch grew exponentially in size across his dirty yellow uniform which had probably at one point been white and Lysíen was able to push him away, forcing him onto the ground.

Elaeínn then raised her sword and drove it down into his skull.

CHAPTER 31

FREE CITY OF DANNOS, SANTEROS

The church bells rang out across the hollow streets. Not to call for a ceremony or a service, but to call for readiness.

The Knights of Salyria were prepared, having spent extensive time training under the instruction of Kalahar Kefrein-Lazalar before his sudden disappearance. Hortensio worked alongside his father in planning for the event, but still refused to recognise his authority. Rosa had spent days relentlessly brewing the concoction they were to use against the vampires. Paul and Felix had distributed the silver swords among those they could trust not to immediately sell them off. Primarily the Salyrian knights.

"We've left it too late now," Hortensio stated. "We should have sent our forces across the land a long while ago if we were to protect everywhere. It will be impossible to reach North Benetia and Lazeria now."

"North Benetia would never have allowed you access in the first place. They will have to fend for themselves," Elton dismissed. "Lazerians are supposed to be somewhat well-mannered. They're also supposed to have a number of reclusive mages living around the place. They will be fine. We can still send forces to Thorne, South Benetia, Salyria and Kina. We will have to concentrate what little we have in big cities, because we simply don't have enough men. And it would be ideal if Kal would reappear, because we'll need his convincing skills if the noble kings are to be wiled into believing us."

"As I understand it, your organisation already has control of most crucial trade routes across the continent? And facilities in numerous cities?"

"But we only have five hundred silver swords. And that's what counts."

"We can forge more. Order women to hand over their jewellery. Melt down coins. I'm a king of one country, and you're more or less the king of another. Tell me, Elton, how much power does the monarchy of Santeros really have?"

"Bugger-all," Elton promptly responded. "It will take too long to send yet another order to Thorne and wait for it to be completed. We'll have to make do with what we have."

"You're a thief, surely you understand compromise? Perhaps we will have to sacrifice the quality of the Thornish swords in favour of mass production. The Santerosi smiths must be able to accomplish something of value."

"They can't forge a bar of iron, much less a silver-coated blade for killing bloodsuckers. If anything, I would rather outsource such a task to your Salyrian smiths. They're far more competent."

"I shall send a detachment back to my land to give the order," Hortensio confirmed. He clapped his hands twice and Jannis quickly appeared from outside. Hortensio instructed him to send back a group of knights to Salyria and begin the taxation of every stray piece of silver. Every smith was also to be rounded up and sent to the biggest cities around the country and set about producing as many quality silver swords for the Salyrian army as they could.

"Have you delivered any of the anti-vampire juice to any other Syndicate locations?"

"Some, but not enough. Rosa is in charge of that – ask her about it. I'm only in charge of general organisation."

The days had passed alarmingly quickly. Probably because every day was the same – managing an assortment of requirements, sending letters to various Syndicate facilities across the continent, worrying about the lack of preparation, recruiting anyone fit enough to fight, spreading the word about the upcoming event, dealing with the obstructive intervention of the authorities... It all blended into one. Ever since Kalahar had disappeared, everything was the same.

They continued the few remaining days they had before the supposed day of the eclipse planning and spreading people and resources across the continent. Kalahar didn't make an appearance, but they managed to get permission from South Benetia and Thorne to station vampire hunters in their countries. As expected, the North Benetians completely barred access to their border and the Kinans were untrusting of the Santerosi crime lord, due to the active Santerosi offensive at the Kinan border. So they did what they could.

The Salyrian blacksmiths and tax collectors efficiently carried out their new job and within a week had smithed two thousand new silver swords of passable quality, which were handed out to the Salyrian army. Hortensio still didn't trust any Santerosi person to be in control of Salyrian property so they didn't allow the Redwinter Syndicate any extra swords, but they returned the Thornish swords Elton had granted to the knights. They were now distributed among the various groups of Syndicate henchmen dispatched across the continent, residing in every city with a population over five thousand.

"I don't get it," Elton announced, kicking his feet up onto the table. "The sun passes over us during the day, and then it becomes night. But somewhere else, it's still day. Doesn't that mean that even while we're seeing an eclipse, the other countries of the continent will be unaffected? At least those more easterly or westerly? Or even different areas of countries – Salyria and Santeros are large enough to see different stages in a day."

"I suppose that's a question you'll have to ask your vampire friend," Hortensio said contemptuously. "All this planning to defend an entire continent and you haven't even thought of the idea that the effects of this baneful eclipse might be concentrated in one area?"

"Kalahar told us to prepare for continent-wide destruction. He knows much more than any of us. He wouldn't have said it in mistake – every word he says is precalculated. Even when he pretends to make a mistake, it's usually to make a point."

The door to the Syndicate meeting room burst open to produce Paul, eyes alert and bald head shiny with sweat.

"Boss, we've a problem," he said. "The Santerosi army are here."

"What?" Elton ridiculed, standing up and stomping from the room, Paul and Hortensio trailing behind him.

"They're outside the city gates. Claimin' somethin' about retakin' Dannos. I thought it was an independently ruled city?"

"It is," Elton mused. "The word must have just reached the King of Santeros that Ramsey had died and the city was worth trying to rule."

"Should we go chat with 'em?" he suggested.

"Yes," Elton replied. "Yes, we should."

"Take some of my knights with you, Elton," Hortensio suggested. "They'll hopefully be discouraged by the presence of another army, even if it is just the cavalry."

"That won't be necessary," he dismissed. "Paul, get Felix and Rosa. We're going to say hello to our visitors."

"Right away, Regi," he complied.

Rosa was wrenched without any complaints and with unsurprising enthusiasm from the alchemy table and Felix was talked out of a round of cards in which he appeared to have swindled his opponents out of nearly every last coin. They left the Redhouse in the direction of the South Gate, where Paul claimed the army was waiting, currently being stalled by the City Guard.

"That's a bloody lot of soldiers," Paul remarked when the gate came into view. Through the great sandstone arch which allowed access to the city from the South they could see nothing but pointed helmets, gleaming spears, and spiked shields.

Elton proudly strode towards the impatient Santerosi captain, the only soldier with a sword at his belt. He was also one of the only Santerosi soldiers wearing extensively protective chest armour which actually guarded the shoulders and armpits. The rest of the soldiers weren't so fortunate and made do with a simple breastplate forged from cheap steel.

"Who is this?" he barked with a thick southern accent.

"Elton Redwinter. Pleased to make your acquaintance."

The Santerosi captain drew his sword in an instant and thrust it towards the Syndicate leader, but he jumped away in time to put some distance between them. Meanwhile, the onlooking members of the City Guard intervened and crossed their spears, creating a barrier between the captain and Elton.

"Move out of my way, heathen! You are guarding a wanted criminal!" the captain ordered.

278

"Your king has no jurisdiction here, captain. This is an independent city," one of the guards countered.

"One currently occupied by the Salyrians!" he shouted back, never seeming to lower his voice. "We know the new king currently resides within this city and it is our duty to rat him and his knights out!"

"The King of Salyria is currently under the protection of the City Guard. The Free City of Dannos remains independent and merely houses the Salyrian knights and their king. There is no occupation."

"I should think so! But regardless of what you say, the Salyrians' place is in the West and so to the West they shall go! Meanwhile, the criminal you defend shall go into the ground! I've had enough of this futile waiting – we march now! Soldiers, onwards! Capture Elton Redwinter and the Salyrian King!"

The guards jumped out of the way of the sudden rush of soldiers and retreated into the towers of the South Gate. Paul and Felix drew their swords; Elton drew his dagger. But in the end, the only option was to run.

They knew the city better than the invaders and this came as a distinct advantage when they ducked into a side alley and scaled a set of balconies which allowed them to reach the roofs of two townhouses. Elton had to be helped by the other three but they still made far quicker work of it than the few soldiers who had pursued them. Once on the roof, they leapt from rooftop to rooftop and were soon far enough away not to have to worry about the soldiers, watching as they finally reached the roofs of the initial townhouses. The soldiers spotted them and slowly began to progress towards them, but they were clearly inexperienced when it came to leaping between buildings, evidenced by one's unfortunate fall. After watching that, the other soldiers appeared to lose heart and some retreated back the way they had come while others relieved themselves of their burdensome armour and started to move quicker, weighed down only by their spears and shields.

"To the Redhouse," Elton ordered, to which the others nodded in agreement.

They abandoned their pursuers who, despite their newfound lightness, were still incompetently clumsy. The streets were flooded with noise and cries of terror as the Santerosi army swarmed through the Free City, doing as they pleased along the way. They watched from above as a group of merchants' wagons were relieved of their wares and a cluster of screaming women were corralled into a darkened side alley by a few snarling soldiers. The occasional pure-hearted city guard would spring into action and attempt to fight back the onslaught of enemies, but they were simply outnumbered, and those who did fight were cut down in a number of moments. The less pure-hearted guards quickly abandoned anything identifying them as an enemy and blended in with the crowd before racing away from the action as soon as possible.

"They're gonna take over, boss," Paul marvelled. "There's no way we can stop this."

"We might not be able to," Elton said. "But perhaps the knights can."

"The knights are bloody strong, bossman, but have you taken a moment to try and take in how many Sants there are? There must be thousands!"

"And we have a few hundred knights. It will be enough to at least stall them while we find the captain again and negotiate. If it's war they want, then it's war they'll have, and war we'll win. They may have manpower, but money wins wars. And we have money."

The army finished razing the street below and left it depressingly empty – a few blood spatters decorated sandy cobbles and walls, almost every last pedestrian had retreated from sight. Stalls and carts which previously stood proud were reduced to scrap, their owners sat behind them, miserable. The women who had been taken into the darkened side alley didn't return into the open, but their sobbing echoed from deep within.

"Bastards," Felix commented, scaling a wall down to the ground. The others followed.

"If your plan is to negotiate, Regi, that involves knowing where the captain is and knowing that he isn't going to kill you. Because I'm imagining that your original plan was to negotiate, and he seemed more interested in sticking a sword down your throat," Rosa said.

"Don't be a fool, I won't be the one negotiating," Elton derided. "I will send Hortensio."

"And if he kills Hortensio?"

"He won't. Hortensio is far too sharp for that skinhead. He will be safe. And I'm sure he's itching to do something other than sit around and discuss."

Hortensio, as expected, was more than glad to be asked and set out alongside Sir Jannis immediately. Felix, Paul, and Rosa were wary about just the two of them leaving by themselves to confront what could turn into the entire Santerosi invasion force, but Elton dismissed their concerns. He knew the young King would return.

"What the bloody hell do you think you lot are doing?" Elton shouted as they arrived at the Redhouse, pivoting around to address the current occupiers. "The city is under attack! Lock down, immediately!"

The majority of people simply flooded from the premises and weren't seen again, while others stayed to barricade the wide, open entrance. Elton grumpily trudged back into the planning room where he had originally been before deciding to convene with the southern visitors.

"And now, we wait," Elton instructed, locking the door.

They waited. They heard no commotion from outside, though the little room in which they hid was far enough away from the entrance to be exempt from exterior noise. Occasionally, the rattling of a Salyrian knight's armour would briefly pass the door. But otherwise, their wait was uneventful. And they waited.

They waited until a powerful armoured fist slammed repeatedly against the door and shattered the tranquillity.

"Elton! Let me in!" Hortensio shouted.

Elton fumbled in a pocket for a set of keys and leisurely undid the door's two latches and twisted the correct key in the lock. He stepped away as the door swung open and produced a ragged King of Salyria and equally untidy Sir Jannis.

"That's an awful lot of blood on your armour for a civil discussion," Elton observed.

"The negotiations proved to be more aggressive than originally intended," Hortensio rebuked.

"Who died?" Elton cut to the chase.

"The captain. And some other important figures. I'm not particularly well-versed in the rankings of the Santerosi army."

"More importantly, who's now in charge of the rabble?"

"I wouldn't have thought anybody is. Jannis and I killed everyone who wasn't wielding a spear."

"So now they're more or less brigands," Elton concluded. "If they aren't going to leave the city themselves, then we are going to force them out. Hortensio – you are going to round up your knights and I will round up my... associates. Ideally, we try and force a retreat before we slaughter them. But do whatever is necessary. Now go."

Emptying the Redhouse at their initial return proved to be a bad move, for now it was devoid of life. If Elton was to gather a substantial fighting force, he would have to send someone out to spread the word. He left alongside Paul, Felix, and Rosa in search of anyone they recognised.

"I remember when Dannos used to be pretty quiet," Paul said. "Nowadays it seems we can't stop gettin' invaded."

"Shit happens," Elton said.

The Salyrian knights soon charged through the streets on horseback. They met the Santerosi infantry as they entered Silverstone Square and the following engagement was a bloodbath. But mainly, it was the horses' white heels bathing in the blood of the helpless foot soldiers as they were slaughtered like livestock. The horses were too quick and had enough space to maintain speed as they ran circles around the frantic spear-wielders. They were lucky to be wielding spears in this situation and not swords, for it allowed them to create a decent range between themselves and the horses. But until they worked out how to group together, they would continue to be slashed to pieces from their completely undefended rears.

Bodies soon littered the cobbles of the square and gradually reduced the area in which the horses could traverse. This provided an opportunity for some of them to be struck down, knights thrown from the saddle and forced to meet their enemies at the same level. Money proved to be the winning factor and the shoddy Santerosi spears proved ineffective against the expensive plate armour worn by the knights.

Although the end result looked dramatic and the sheer volume of blood coating the normally silver pavements was enough to bring a strong-willed person to their knees, the fight wasn't over. But it soon would be.

The Salyrian knights had demonstrated their might to full effect: out of the twenty that had engaged in the skirmish, only one had fallen. Meanwhile, the dead bodies of a hundred Santerosi infantry were now in need of clearing out, but not before they were thoroughly looted by those not repulsed by the sight of blood and guts.

More knights on horseback entered the square, including the helmetless Hortensio and Sir Jannis. They surveyed the aftermath and showed no sign of remorse, instead nodding in approval at the knights who had lined up to wait for their next order.

"Elton, I should hope your men are ready," Hortensio called.

"Indeed they are, indeed they are," Elton cackled, withdrawing from an almost entirely concealed passage, accompanied only by Rosa.

"In that case, we are also ready. Honourable knights! Follow Elton Redwinter. He knows this rathole better than any of us. We will root out the Santerosi."

Elton and Rosa led the way along a carriage-width street heading north, already occupied by a number of fleeing pedestrians who had to squeeze against the buildings either side of the street in order to avoid being trampled by the horses.

The street gradually widened, first to the width of two carriages, and then three. The knights, who had originally been riding two abreast, could now spread out and appeared much more daunting.

Ahead, Elton spotted Paul leaning from a metal balcony and raised his fist in the air before pulling downwards. Paul recognised the signal and seemingly gestured at the neighbouring building. As planned, a swarm of armed Syndicate henchmen appeared and completely blocked the road.

As if on cue, a large detachment of Santerosi soldiers, even larger than that which had fallen in Silverstone Square, filed into the street from connecting roads. As they steadily filled the gap between the knights and the Syndicate henchmen, Elton saw that the plan had worked exactly as expected – the Santerosi soldiers had been pressed back by an array of Syndicate henchmen on either side, threatened with a line of swordsmen in the front row and crossbowmen behind them. They had linked their shields together to form a wall, through which they placed their spears. But they couldn't press forward – the circular shields weren't the right shape to provide protection against the guaranteed volley of crossbow bolts should they choose to attack.

Instead, they continued backwards. The two groups of Santerosi soldiers merged into one and they formed a tightly packed circle, shield walls linking together.

"Halt!" Elton called.

The Salyrian knights yanked the reins of their horses and brought them to a stop, while the Syndicate henchmen stopped moving forward and assumed a defensive position.

Elton sauntered towards the line of horses, their clean white fur stained beige by the sand. He approached the Santerosi soldiers, pushing through the two central horses rode by Hortensio and Sir Jannis respectively, and began to speak.

"Soldiers, footmen, farmers. Slaves. That's what you are. You're slaves to your Santerosi overlord. You've been wrenched from your life to fight for the desires of another. Well, you're no longer subordinates to your captain, because he's dead. Nor are you subordinates to your deputy captain, or commander, or whoever the bloody hell else you would have answered to. Because they're all dead. You soldiers are the only ones left. So I give you a choice. Leave Dannos. Never return. Or you will join your superiors in the afterlife."

Instead of a response, Elton received a revelation. That revelation being that the average Santerosi soldier's aim wasn't quite up to scratch.

284

CHAPTER 32

The operating theatre was sombre and practical. The only light was provided by a trio of candles atop a candelabrum on the shelf next to the operating table. Also adjacent to the operating table was an assortment of operating instruments and accessories – saws, scalpels, tongs, tweezers, tourniquets and more. She required none of the items except for an ovular mirror about the size of her head.

"Es tar, galar," she said. Her reflection in the looking glass slowly faded from its surface and was replaced by an unnatural shimmering and pale blue sheen. A faint ring of mist poured from the centre and surrounded the object's edge, constantly revolving around it.

A young-looking, light-skinned man with short-cut raven-black hair and piercing green eyes appeared in the looking glass's surface. His entire face was symmetrical and he looked unnaturally perfect.

"Valerie," he exclaimed. "Or should I say Jade? You finally contact me through the glass."

Valerie nodded.

"I assume you have made it to Virilia. I must say, far quicker than I anticipated. Did you travel by portal?"

"I did not. The Fateborn and I, alongside a meddling bard we picked up on the way, made the journey from Limara on horseback. It was quite the adventure, father. Have you ever been tied up by the Kal'sennar?"

"I must admit I haven't. But have you sparred with a vampire?"

"Unfortunately not. Though we did run into a siren at one point. Beast nearly killed the Fateborn."

"A siren?" Nendar laughed. "Of all the creatures to give you trouble, I doubted it would be a siren. The Kal'sennar are much more vicious."

"You're correct. But it was early in the morning and he woke up before us, only to be lured away by its dreadful singing. Does it really sound different to a man?"

"I couldn't tell you from personal experience as I'm immune to their magical influence. However, I can assure you that the beast we call a siren appears profoundly differently according to your sex. To you and me, it sounds like a hideous cacophony of guttural rumbling and grinding teeth, perhaps mixed with a touch of nails against a chalk board. To men, a siren's singing is as soft and gentle as silk. They also appear in the form of a beautiful woman before transforming into the creature which we always perceive them to be."

"Interesting. Thank you."

"Now, Valerie, the Fateborn! Where are you at this moment?"

"In the operating theatre of the palace."

"And you have him with you?"

"He lies on the table right next to me."

"We would be best to visit the Mages' Council. They will assist you with a conversion. Then they plan to take him as their own and promote him to be the leader of the Council."

"Hold on a minute," Valerie said, taken aback. "You're telling me that after all our work to repair the mistakes of the Council, they plan to just take him away?"

Nendar nodded with raised eyebrows and pursed lips.

"Believe me, I already made it very clear that I would like to make it work for both the Council and the Empire. They wouldn't have it, preferring to live in secrecy without ever interacting with the world."

"Why must we obey the Council?" Valerie scowled. "Their motives are incomprehensible and they would rather see the world burn than allow it to develop with their assistance and supervision. Why don't we convert the Fateborn ourselves and use him against the Council? We could eradicate them and build a new order of magic!"

"Be quiet!" he barked, looking at his surroundings. "I will teleport to you. Ensure the operating theatre is locked."

Jade looked at the closed door to the operating theatre and issued a command which caused the lock to click shut. She looked down at Richard's expressionless face as he was still knocked out from the impact. As she was about to caress him, a rift opened on the opposite side of the table and produced Nendar Varanus, sovereign Emperor of Sanskar.

"Oh, well done, well done indeed, my dear," he exclaimed, inspecting Richard's motionless body. "He certainly isn't a child anymore."

"Hasn't been for a long time. He wasn't even a child when we— when Lynn caught him the first time."

"Lynn was inefficient and costly. You have done a far better job – I'm proud."

Valerie beamed as her father prodded and turned Richard over on the table before acquiring a shady expression.

"You're also wiser than Lynn ever was," he stated. "You're right – the Fateborn will be much more use to the world in our hands. We shall perform the conversion ourselves."

Valerie smirked and approached the table again as her father had stopped pacing around it.

"You've never performed a conversion before, have you?" the Emperor asked.

"I have not. I have, however, studied plenty about the concept."

"It's a simple concept, but requires a damned amount of energy and concentration. Get some sleep, we'll do it later this evening. And Valerie – use no magic until we start the conversion. The Council will pick up our trail the moment it happens, so we must be swift."

"May I put myself to sleep?"

"You may. I shall do the same."

Richard was bound to the operating table and they found comfortable corners of the operating theatres before putting themselves to sleep with a spell. They then awoke exactly ten hours later.

"I do hope the illusion I left in my place is still working," Nendar muttered, approaching Richard. He had clearly regained consciousness but eventually succumbed to sleep at some point. He bolted awake at the sound of footsteps and writhed helplessly as the expressionless emperor stood over him.

"Who are you?" he seethed, struggling against the steel shackles which bound him to the table.

"I'm offended. Dearly. Did Valerie not mention me at all?"

"Valerie? Is that the backstabbing witch's real name?"

"Indeed. I would never have called her anything as tawdry as Jade. Definitely a southern name."

"Hah! Unbelievable. You're her father?"

"You would be correct, dear bounty hunter. Though I have much more important roles than the father of an aspirational sorceress in this world."

"Is that right?"

"Emperor of Sanskar, for one. I'm also a member of the Council of Mages, though that's lesser known. In fact, only known by members of the Council."

"The Emperor of fucking Sanskar. The all-powerful mage. I take it Jade— Valerie doesn't actually plan to overthrow you."

"Is that what she convinced you with? I must say, you really are easily manipulated to have believed that nonsense. And here I was believing you to be headstrong and stubborn. No matter, that's enough chitchat. We shall begin the conversion."

"Conversion?"

"A magical procedure to bend your will. Don't worry, you shan't feel a thing. If you don't resist, that is."

"You'll do no such thing!" he shouted, creating an echo across the theatre. "Where is the witch?"

"I'm here," Valerie mused, strolling casually towards the table. Upon sight of her, Richard's eyes reflected a combination of grief, anger, and regret.

"Why did you do it? Why did you betray me?" he choked. "I trusted you."

"Your unbending trust until the last moment was your downfall. I made numerous mistakes which could have betrayed my identity. I'm surprised you didn't just kill me at our first meeting. Instead, you were desperate for someone to replace dear Linelle and I exploited that vulnerability to the fullest extent. I made up the simplest of lies and presented them as secrets. I told you real secrets which had no impact on my position. All in all, this was a dastardly easy task compared to previous cases of espionage which I have completed, and it was all thanks to you being hopelessly lonely."

All signs of grief and regret disappeared from his eyes while the voracious anger burned stronger.

"And to think you might have had even a scrap of purity in your heart. You're very good at pretending, Valerie Varanus. If only I hadn't been such a fool. Go on, then, get it over with. Bend my will. Make me do your bidding."

"Gladly. Father?"

Nendar and Valerie Varanus stretched their arms out and began gurgling what was probably some form of archaic speech but sounded to Richard like pure gibberish. They looked noticeably drained already, beads of sweat forming on their foreheads. Their breathing also increased rapidly in both rate and volume along with their drivelling while Richard didn't feel a thing. The Emperor had made it sound like it would be a fight to stay in his own conscience, yet only he and his daughter were the ones struggling.

Finally, something began to happen as Richard's body was engulfed in light. Only subtly at first, enough to illuminate his immediate surroundings, but it quickly brightened, becoming unbearable to view directly. He was forced to close his eyes as he continued to wait for the promised struggle, the mages' drivelling having turned to chanting.

"At what point does the magic happen?" Richard teased, sensing something had gone wrong. The mages either ignored him or couldn't hear him, as they didn't respond. He assumed the latter was more likely.

The process reached another period of stagnation as he continued to emit a terribly bright glow and the mages continued to hoarsely chant their ancient incantation. He had even allowed his body to relax, partially enjoying the suffering of his captors. It surprised him somewhat that it wasn't the Emperor's struggling he enjoyed most but Valerie's, whose enthusiastic tone at the start of the spell had dwindled to pathetically panting every individual word.

"Varanus!" another voice cried. "Stop what you're doing immediately!"

Richard wanted to open his eyes but feared going blind. Instead, he continued to rely on his ears to hear more characters jumping to the ground from what he assumed was a portal.

Nendar didn't stop his recital, though he was fully aware of the intruders' arrival. It even propelled him to chant faster, despite the toll it took.

"Allezar! Je kennath!" the voice bellowed. Richard heard the pained cries of Valerie and Nendar as they collapsed to the ground, followed by the complete dimming of the light which had previously engulfed his body. He opened his eyes to see a group of five people walking towards him, carelessly stepping over the paralysed bodies.

He recognised the people. They were the mages from his dream – the ones whose identities had become gradually clearer over time. He spotted the dark-haired woman who had erased his use of the senses. She looked alarmingly similar to Jade – pale skin, emerald eyes. She showed a particular distaste for the helpless figures on the floor.

There was a man who looked to be middle-aged – dark skin, short hair, and faint wrinkles. He was leading the group and the rest of the mages remained mostly silent while he was doing anything as simple as breathing.

"Lynn – I entrust you with your kin's safe transport to the Retreat. They are not to be harmed," the middle-aged-looking man ordered.

"Only with words," the dark-haired woman responded.

"Only verbally," the middle-aged-looking man corrected.

"You're no fun," she pouted. However, she didn't maintain this attitude and immediately opened a portal through which she lifted Valerie and Nendar, less carefully than she could have done.

The middle-aged man stood over the operating table and inspected Richard from head to toe with his eyes.

"You were able to resist the unbridled might of two Varanuses?" he asked in disbelief. "Remarkable. Truly remarkable."

"All in a day's work," Richard seethed. "And I take it you're not my knight in shining armour?"

"A correct assumption, for I am not a knight, nor do I wear shining armour or any armour at all. I am Tregor Lopan of

290

the Mages' Council. I'm pleased to finally make your acquaintance, Child of Fate."

"What the fuck is a Child of Fate?" Richard exasperatedly asked.

"Beyond our complete comprehension, I'm afraid," Tregor replied. "What we do know about Children of Fate is that they break the boundaries of magic. You see, an adept mage is capable of elongating their natural lifespan by about a thousand years through the aid of magic. They are also capable of a great number of tasks, many of which they are unable to carry out without the aid of a lirenium crystal."

"A lirenium crystal! Jade— Valerie told me about those."

"They are exceedingly useful tools and vastly expand the boundaries of our capabilities. Every member of the council is in possession of one. Including Valerie, though her membership of the Council is soon to be re-evaluated. However, even with the aid of a crystal, a mage's powers are still limited. A Child of Fate's is not. Once they learn to harness their power, they can create and destroy worlds with a command."

"You're telling me that if you teach me to use magic that I could destroy this world if I happened to desire it?" Richard snickered.

"That is exactly right," Tregor confirmed without any hint of sarcasm in his tone.

"Who are the rest of your buddies?" Richard interrogated.

Tregor stepped to the side and gestured to the woman he had seen earlier who had apparently reappeared from wherever the portal had taken her beforehand.

"This is Lynn Varanus. The eldest daughter of Nendar Varanus," he explained.

"How old exactly is Lynn?"

"Asking a woman's age?" Lynn interjected. "Have you never been taught basic social expectations?"

"Lynn is one hundred and twenty-two years old," Tregor stated. "I assume you're more interested in the age of her younger sister? Valerie is only a mere eighty-seven."

"Pretty face for eighty-seven..." Richard muttered.

"As I'm sure you're now aware, many mages choose to mask their true age with an illusion and we naturally age far slower anyways. It's a fairly simple process—"

"Do you know what, Tregor?" Richard interrupted. "I really couldn't care less about what magical shit you've done to look pretty. What I care about is that I'm locked to a table, you've appeared out of a portal and wittered on about me having something to do with fate and that I've seen every single one of you before in my dream!"

Tregor raised his eyebrows and cast a tentative glance over his companions, who gradually backed away from the table.

"You've seen us before in a dream?" Tregor inquired.

"What does it matter to you?"

"Dreams have always fascinated me. Why do we dream? Of what substance are they? How do they intertwine with the real world? Is there any way to access the realm of dreams? All questions which I've had for decades, all questions which have remained unanswered. The fact that you say you've seen us all before in a dream without ever having seen us before in the real world leads me to believe that you have prophetic abilities. In fact, I know you have prophetic abilities. You're the Fateborn."

"There's that word again," Richard jabbed. "Except I wasn't seeing the future in my dream. I was seeing the past. Where was that city? Why did you destroy it? Why did you deprive me of my senses?"

Tregor pondered for a moment, drumming his fingers rhythmically against the table.

"I was under the impression that that event had been removed from your memory," he said, alarmed. "It appears Valerie is just as incapable as her sister. Come, we must begin the conversion immediately."

The members of the Council hesitantly stepped forward and surrounded the table. Tregor had neglected to introduce him to the remaining three – an old-looking man whose primary feature was a long, unkempt beard which caused him to look as close to the stereotypical image of a wizard as could be; a blonde woman with sky-blue eyes and a slender figure who looked about as far from the stereotypical image of a witch as could have been; and a handsome man with neatly combed red hair whose face appeared to have more surface area covered in freckles than clear skin. None of them talked, instead obediently awaiting Tregor's command.

"On three," Tregor asserted. "One, two—"

"Stop!" another voice called. The mages stood up straight to face the new figure who had appeared from seemingly nowhere, not even having opened a portal. Richard tilted his neck as far as the table would allow and laid his eyes upon a human-like creature with ruby eyes and stone-grey skin, and a head of unnaturally dark jet-black hair.

"You cannot do this, Tregor," the creature said. "You've gone too far this time. We had a pact."

Tregor sighed.

"This complicates things," he muttered to the other mages.

"Who the fuck are you?" Lynn asked. It appeared the handsome man and the blonde woman shared her sentiment.

"I am – or rather was – a member of the Council. Much like you. However, I... lost my faith in their morals. Ironic, I know."

"Tregor, who is this?" Lynn asked, redirecting her attention.

"Kalahar Kefrein-Lazalar," he coldly responded.

"You thought I forgot?" Kalahar asked. "I'm hurt. Deeply. I may be very old, but I do not share the pitifully weak biological capacities of humans."

"The Council needs the Fateborn, Kalahar," Tregor said. "We've already fallen dangerously close to extinction once before. We need his protection."

"My old friend, it seems you don't understand how this works," Kalahar cheerfully responded. "You need the Fateborn for the protection of your archaic order of seclusive magicians. I need the Fateborn for the protection of the human race. And possibly the elder races. In my eyes, I need him for a terribly nobler cause. Not only that, but you assured me I would receive him after the impact of my role in the Siege of Pestion. It has been many hundreds of years, but I'm here. And I want my reward."

Tregor cursed under his breath, feeling paralysed by the hostile glares of his companions.

"Come, then," he finally said. "The Fateborn is yours."

"Tregor—" the blonde woman tried to say, but she was cut off with a wave. Kalahar strode proudly towards Richard and held out his hand, which Tregor reluctantly shook.

"A pleasure doing business," he said.

"Of course," Tregor mused, before revealing a glass of viscous red liquid from his robe.

He tossed its contents over the creature, and Kalahar howled in excruciated pain, hunching over and collapsing to the ground. He continued to writhe as Tregor revealed a small, silver dagger with a curved blade and an ebony handle adorned with intricate carvings and symbols. He furiously drove it into the creature again and again, choosing different body parts with every strike.

Kalahar continued to whine helplessly, animalistically, and then unearthly as he was decorated with more and more stab wounds. Richard noticed that he didn't bleed and was surviving far longer than was natural. But after an elongated period of pained, distorted moaning, the room was silent, the creature on the floor unmoving.

"What a dignified way to go," Lynn commented. "Now are you going to tell us who and what they were?"

"Kalahar was, as he said, a member of the Council," Tregor said, looking away. "He was a vampire. Of a unique class. Now we are rid of him."

"No," a demonic voice gurgled. "You are not."

CHAPTER 33

"No!" Kaesta cried, far too late.

Elaeínn withdrew the blade, dripping with the deceased sailor's blood.

"What? It was the kindest thing. He was going to bleed out otherwise," she said emotionlessly, walking to the river to clean the blade.

"We could have saved him – you forget, we're mages!"

"Saved him, so he could attack us again? Find Jaelaar and have us all hanged? No, he needed to be killed."

"I've... I've never seen someone die," she mumbled, tears forming in the corners of her eyes. It was then that Elaeínn remembered that Kaesta was only a child.

"We'll bury him. In the pit," she stated, taking charge. Nobody objected, though the look of distress on Kaesta's face never passed while they collectively gathered forest materials with which to cover the sailor's body after Elaeínn had dragged his body into the pit.

As the last branch was tossed on the pile, Lysíen lit the contents of the pit with a spell.

"No! Put it out! Are you insane?" Elaeínn cried.

He was startled but did as he was instructed, and a faint trail of smoke left the charred upper layer of the pit as the fire was extinguished with another spell.

"I didn't think about that," he murmured.

"Hopefully they're too far away to notice that." She gestured to the thin smoke column. "But that's in the best-case scenario. They didn't leave long ago."

295

"Are we going to follow them?" Erría asked, brushing a loose strand of hair from her eyes.

"I see no other way to go," Elaeínn confirmed. "Kaesta, am I okay to keep hold of your sword?"

"I don't even know how to use it," the girl muttered solemnly. "Here, take the sheath as well."

She unwound it from her belt and handed it to Elaeínn.

"Keep an eye out for signs of civilised life," she advised. "If something can set up a trap like that, then it's a danger. And simultaneously our objective to find it."

She stepped onto the trail along which Jaelaar and the rest of the expedition crew had set off after trapping Elaeínn in the pit, but was almost immediately distracted by a rustling in the brush to her left.

"Wait," she said.

Kaesta cowered behind the other two mages while Elaeínn shifted the intertwined branches and messy foliage.

Feet fell lightly to the ground behind her and she drew her sword to meet the drawn bow of her attacker. He was dressed in black and his face was concealed.

"Behind you," the attacker said.

Keeping her sword pointed in the direction of her attacker, the usefulness of which she wasn't entirely certain, she tilted her head to look behind. There was a second drawn bow in the hands of a second black-clothed man.

"You bastards are the ones who took me and Kíra," Elaeínn hissed.

She looked back at the first attacker, who had now been joined by three more figures behind him, who quickly encircled and trapped her newfound allies.

"Move and we kill you," the archer stated. "All of you."

She allowed herself to be disarmed, as did her companions.

"Where's R, then? Are you going to take us to him?" Elaeínn asked as she was corralled towards her allies. The anonymous figures first bound her hands and then tied her to the others like slaves. They also never answered her questions.

Elaeínn, Kaesta, Erría and Lysíen were led along the same path taken previously by Jaelaar. They walked, in silence, listening only to the sounds of the jungle and the rustling of the assailants' weaponry, the rhythmic pattering of soft footsteps and arrhythmic huffing of heavy breathing.

They continued walking as the mountains loomed ever taller. At no point did they stop for a break, and they weren't allowed anything to eat or drink, despite their pleas. They simply had to keep walking.

"You must have got Jaelaar and the others, I take it? How else could we not have come across them by now?" Elaeínn panted, maintaining a sense of strength in spite of her growing fatigue. As could have been expected, they didn't answer.

The path along which they had been taken was well-worn. Nothing Elaeínn experienced ever explained to her why they had been on the continent or what their objective was.

Eventually, they began to slow down as the brush began to clear. They had reached the base of the mountain – and with it, a camp. Milling around the camp were High Elven men, women and even children, large numbers of which had golden hair and similar pale olive skin. These people noticed the masked figures, and they were not alarmed in the slightest. They glanced at them and then continued with their own objectives.

The masked figures also deemed it time to remove their masks and at last the captives were able to view the faces of their captors. They were about as average in that camp as could have been.

"What now? Are you going to string us up for entertainment in this wacky village you've got going on?" Elaeínn persisted.

"No," the lead captor finally provided her with a reply. "We're taking you to R."

A fire burned in the centre of the camp, over which roasted the carcasses of a few unrecognisable animals. More dead animals were being dragged in from one of the corners of the camp by people who evidently acted as the hunters of the group, armed with bows and arrows and dressed in green-brown camouflage, unlike the ominous black of Elaeínn's captors. When she thought about it, she didn't really understand it. *Perhaps they do wear black just to intimidate*, she thought.

They were taken into a tent made of a woven fabric held up by a framework of lashed-together branches of relatively equal length. It reminded her of when she met Tynak.

"Miss Tinaíd," he said, with a voice as soft as silk.

R appeared from behind a pair of curtains separating the tent into two sections. He dragged a seat across the hardened ground and gestured for Elaeínn to sit.

"Take the others away. You know where to leave them. Oh, and don't forget the jägar root."

R was almost unrecognisable. He wasn't adorned in a speck of black – instead, his tan-highlighted forest-green robes would have seen him fit perfectly into High Elven society. He, like seemingly everyone else in the camp, had the same pale olive skin and golden hair, a tuft of which fell untidily over his forehead and shadowed his left eye. The rest fell immaculately below his shoulders and Elaeínn couldn't spot a single curl.

"Welcome to Ríyael," he spoke warmly.

"Cut the shit," she interjected. "Where's Kíra?"

"Not a hair on your friend's head has been harmed... to a significant degree, anyways. Her consciousness has been... inconsistent... but I assure you, we've not resulted exclusively to torture in the same method that I tried on you. I deemed that impractical. It didn't amount to a lot of progress. Instead, we've settled on emotional torture. That has been far more effective. At least, with your friend. She holds a great many feelings for you that we were able to exploit with maximum efficiency."

"Fuck you!" she slammed her fists on the table and stood up.

"Sit down, or I'll kill you where you stand," he said calmly, not even flinching. "I have no need for you anymore – Miss Karíos has told us nearly everything we need to know. Really, you're only here because I thought it interesting to know the objectives of your expedition team."

"The expedition team which you haven't found?"

"Oh, we've found them. They'll not be obstructed in their journey. I was only interested in you."

298

"Who even are you? What the hell is this place?" she questioned exasperatedly, R's steely composure slowly whittling away at her confidence.

"I believe I was introducing you before you interrupted. This is the island of Ríyael. This entire land belongs to me. We don't have much, but we do have the support of external sources. External sources which you and your FTA jeopardise the existence of."

"Is that what this is about? That's the entire reason you kidnapped me?"

"That is correct. It is also why you will never leave this island."

The tent shook, as if a gale had suddenly swept across the area. The branches holding up the tent creaked under the pressure and Elaeínn realised an opportunity.

She grabbed the table in front of her and quickly flipped it up, throwing it at R. Then she fled the tent.

The rush of wind almost blew her off her feet. Tents around the camp were struggling to keep up with the sudden onrush of weather, which Elaeínn now realised was coming in bursts.

She looked up and was lost for words.

Soaring from the heights of the mountain was an enormous, majestic, winged reptile, the sun's rays brightening its matte white scales. It opened its mouth and roared, sending vibrations through the air and the ground. And then from its mouth spewed a stream of vibrant turquoise fire.

The dragon flew towards the camp, which was now in a state of panic. R had recovered from the assault but wasn't focused on Elaeínn, instead choosing to run and save himself.

As the creature moved closer to the ground, beating its wings to slow itself and in the process knocking over a few tents and other constructions, it set its gleaming turquoise reptilian eyes on Elaeínn, frozen in place.

The ground shook as it landed, lowering its head to scrutinise the lone elf.

You're the one, a voice in Elaeínn's head spoke. *You're coming with me.*

The dragon stepped towards Elaeínn, who cautiously stepped backwards towards the border of the camp, where R had reappeared alongside a number of armed enforcers.

Do not run. I am not going to harm you, but you're coming with me.

Elaeínn spotted movement on her left coming from within the jungle and she pivoted on the spot, drawing her sword. As she had expected, Jaelaar and the expedition team had noticed the dragon and had made their way to the camp, with the Prime Minister at the helm. He drew his sword, again gazing expectantly at the runes along its blade, and was again disappointed. But the dragon reacted wildly to the sight of the blade, letting out a roar into the sky and gazing icily at Jaelaar.

He has the Dragonsteel Blade, she said.

"That sword – it glowed gold when I used it. Do you know what it is?" Elaeínn asked, stepping slowly towards Jaelaar.

It is a weapon forged in dragonfire. It is almost as old as I am. And it connects to its wielder, but only if its wielder is unconnected to magic. That is why it reacted to you.

"Well I plan on getting it back," she seethed, running at the Prime Minister.

Their blades clashed as the Dragonsteel Blade sang melodically through the air.

Elaeínn was purely focused on her duel, intent on finally finishing what she should have done in the Common Square. The reaction on the faces of the rest of the crew was very mixed – nobody outwardly supported the FTA fighter, but there were a few who looked on, wincingly, while the sailors shouted words of encouragement.

"Miss Tinaíd!" the voice ever as smooth as silk called from the far corner of the camp.

Her attention faltered and Jaelaar disarmed her, sending her sword into the fire. He was about to deliver the finishing blow when a large white claw was placed between him and Elaeínn. His sword was worthless against the dragon's scales.

"If this doesn't stop right now, I will be ending your friend's life," R said, holding a blade to a bedraggled Kíra's throat. Elaeínn gasped at the sight of her, which was almost unrecognisable – from the torn clothes to the bruised patches all over her body to her eyes, which she seemed almost incapable of staying open.

"Let her go!" she screamed, unsure of where to run.

"No such thing will be happening. You – beast." He gestured to the dragon. "Make yourself scarce. We have matters which need to be sorted here."

The dragon snorted, puffs of smoke escaping her oversized nostrils. R was unfazed.

"Let me rephrase. I have sentries positioned ready to loose an arrow into your little minion's head. Whatever it is you want from her, you won't get it if you don't leave right now. You understand me?"

She narrowed her pupils and let out a ground-shaking roar. "Now! Mages!"

Jaelaar dropped his sword and extended his hands towards the dragon, as did the majority of the mages in the expedition crew. Some were apprehensive about the idea of challenging a creature of her size, and they were rewarded for it.

The dragon's roar of pride turned into one of pain as the magical force extending from the mages reached her, but they had greatly overestimated their power.

She quickly recovered from the initial shock and turned to face the mages, and at her feet, Jaelaar.

Elaeínn trusted R to stay true to his word about killing her, so she ran – the first arrow sailed past her head from the jungle to her right. The second she was able to narrowly avoid by suddenly stopping mid-run and allowing the arrow to fly in front of her eyes. The third struck the dragon's scales and clattered uselessly to the ground.

The dragon unleashed a stream of turquoise flame, incinerating the mages who had stood against her. Elaeínn debated running to retrieve the Dragonsteel Blade but didn't trust her luck to avoid any more arrows.

Jaelaar managed to escape the range of the fire and used the moment to quickly open a portal and make an escape. Where to, Elaeínn didn't know, as the portal had been anonymised.

The flames coming from the dragon's mouth ceased, but the jungle had been set alight and burned vigorously. All that remained of the mages who had chosen to follow Jaelaar's orders were ashes. And at last, R finally seemed to be experiencing symptoms of doubt.

I will not be lectured by you, the dragon spoke telepathically, though Elaeínn assumed she was directing her voice through everyone's heads this time. *Release the girl.*

"Elle?" Kíra mouthed, briefly stirring.

"I suppose I could," R said, smirking. "But that would be of no benefit to me. No benefit at all."

He dropped his sword and traced a portal with his one free hand, leaping through it with Kíra still in his clutches as the dragon's flames scorched the soil on which he had stood.

"Fuck!" Elaeínn swore, stumbling forwards.

The camp was deserted. The inhabitants had fled a long time ago, unnoticed in the excitement. R's henchmen were nowhere to be seen and she felt confident stepping into the open to retrieve the sword. The sword which glowed a vibrant gold as soon as she had grasped its hilt.

"Help me find Kíra, dragon," Elaeínn said. "And I will help you with whatever it is you need from me."

My name is Alazarioss. And I think I know where to start.

Alazarioss flattened herself to the ground and looked expectantly at Elaeínn, caught up in admiration of the weapon she had finally reobtained.

"You want me to get on?"

I know where R went. We must be swift, for I only know the geographical location. I cannot teleport us there, so we must fly.

"I thought his portal was hidden?"

Such is the power held by a creature created by magic. We must go, now.

She sheathed the weapon and climbed the dragon's enormous legs, finding a comfortable position between two of the spines lining her back.

"FTA girl! Don't leave us!"

In the excitement, Elaeínn had completely forgotten about her companions who had evidently been set free upon R's departure.

As Alazarioss was in the motion of raising her wings, ready to lift off, Elaeínn found herself under the close scrutiny of

302

Kaesta, Erría and Lysíen – each of them expressing different sentiments about the situation.

"Is that it then? You're just going to leave? Just like that? And we'll be forced to go back to Tyen'Ael as traitors while you fly around on your dragon?"

Lysíen led the other two towards the mages who hadn't been incinerated in the torrent of blue flame, the majority of which were still in a state of shock and hadn't decided on their next move.

"I'm sorry!" Elaeínn tried to reason. "A friend of mine is in danger and I have to save her."

"You used us," Lysíen growled. "You would never have left that pit if it weren't for us killing one of our own for you."

"I never used you! I absolutely appreciate everything you've done for me and I never undervalued you, any of you!"

"If we're so important to you, bring us with you. Bring us with you to find this friend of yours and perhaps we will be of some use. I'm sorry – help."

"Alazaríoss?" she asked quietly, speaking towards the dragon's ear, unsure whether there were actually any restrictions on the capacity of her hearing.

We will bring them with us.

"She says it's fine! Come on, let's go!"

Any remaining harsh feelings soon dissipated into the winds as they lifted into the air. Elaeínn felt a rush like never before as they soared over the boundless jungle, eventually leaving the island behind in pursuit of the West.

"Where are we going?" a notably jubilant Kaesta shouted, struggling to be heard over the wind as it whipped through their hair and their clothes.

"I don't know! I guess we'll find out when we get there!"

CHAPTER 34

FREE CITY OF DANNOS, SANTEROS

The spear sailed straight over Elton's head and clattered against the cobbles behind him. That was enough for all hell to break loose.

Elton retreated as fast as his old, unfit legs would allow him, while the Salyrian knights whipped the reins of their horses and raised their swords. They charged into the crowd and began hacking and slashing, betraying the stereotypical notion of Salyrian honour and elegance. The Syndicate henchmen finally relieved their urge to let fly the bolts of their crossbows. As predicted, the shields were useless in stopping them and many fell immediately while the swordsmen moved into position to attack at close quarters. Felix relieved his jerkin of three throwing knives and sprinted into the fray. Paul drew his sword and followed closely. Rosa stayed behind with Elton and drew her own sword.

This time, the Santerosi soldiers understood that they had to bring the Salyrian knights to their level in order to stand a chance. Elton watched in despair as a number of horses were impaled by a thrown spear, some by more than one. The knights knew the rehearsed moment to leap from the saddle and didn't leave themselves vulnerable for more than a moment. And once on the floor, they continued to fight, a veritable whirlwind of frenzied sword strikes among a sea of flimsy spears and shields.

At the other end of the skirmish, the Syndicate weren't holding up so strongly against the spearmen, who were using their extra range extremely effectively. The sword wielders simply couldn't get close enough to engage and relied on the crossbowmen, who also weren't able to attack as the Santerosi soldiers had figured out to crouch behind their shields and advance that way. The bolts were powerful enough to penetrate the shields and probably their armour, but every fired bolt meant precious seconds required to reload.

But the one thing the Santerosi didn't figure out was the city's layout. The battle had taken place in an area entirely encroached by tall, multi-layered buildings – the roofs of which started to bear more and more crossbow-armed Syndicate henchmen. That was when the tide of the battle turned in the Syndicate's favour.

Utterly defenceless, the Santerosi soldiers rapidly fell under the sudden onslaught from above and broke formation, allowing the swordsmen to move in and clean up, while the crossbowmen turned their focus to groups of soldiers not yet engaged in conflict, so as to avoid friendly fire.

Those who didn't fall were pushed back further. The density of the crowd steadily grew until the Santerosi were packed uncomfortably tightly. This made it harder for them to defend, and easier for their assailants to attack.

It was over. Someone in the mess of people raised a white flag, a motion audibly supported by his comrades. The Salyrian knights immediately stopped their assault and sheathed their swords, stepping back from their opponents. The Syndicate henchmen took a few moments longer to understand.

Elton stepped forward again, having to manoeuvre through a mess of mutilated bodies and pools of blood, flowing into the gaps between the cobbles.

"Have we come to an agreement, then?" he asked sadistically.

"We will leave Dannos at once. I cannot promise we won't return," one of the soldiers said.

"Very good. Drop your weapons, and then you may leave."

"Drop your weapons!" the soldier loudly reiterated. His call was echoed a few times by others while they produced a cacophony of metallic and wooden clattering.

Felix appeared, every physical aspect of himself dishevelled, a streak of stained blood decorating his face from his hairline to the bridge of his nose.

"Felix, tell the men to withdraw," Elton ordered. The young thief nodded and ran down an alley which he knew would lead to the right-hand crowd of henchmen.

Some of the Santerosi soldiers were still bristling with anger and fidgeted to grab their weapons, but the collective knowledge that it would only result in their deaths staved off their urges. They unhappily accepted the rough grabs from Syndicate henchmen as they were hauled off in the direction of the nearest city gates.

"I'm going to be honest, I expected you would turn on us when they attacked," Elton said to Hortensio upon the King's return to the Redhouse, having stayed out to root out as many of the remaining Santerosi soldiers from the city as possible.

"I understand the risk from the vampires," Hortensio said. "It wouldn't be right to kill you. Our very futures rely on you."

Elton retrieved a cigar from a pocket inside his gambeson and snatched a torch from a passing henchman to light it.

"I'm still blind about the entire thing," he explained, expertly blowing a smoke ring. They both waited and watched as it collided with the ceiling and dispersed. "I've never completely trusted Kal. He bullied me into listening to him, and there was nought I could do about it. He knows things, sure, but he tells us about some superstition and some history involving eclipses, warns us of an incoming disaster and then buggers off without a word? What even defines a vampire? Peasants will tell you it's their appetite for blood and their aversion to garlic and silver. He's not a bloodsucker, nor does he seem vulnerable to silver. And the nonsense about garlic is truly blather. Sure, he cut off his hand and it regenerated. Sure, he looks like a mutant freak of nature. But what if it's all a lie? I've never personally met a powerful mage, and Rosa can't even manage clothed teleportation without knackering herself. But what if our Kal is really just a powerful mage? What if he's playing us, destabilising us? We've spent loads of money on this prophesied war of his. Drained the coffers. We never considered the possibility the Kal isn't who he says he is. He could be a phony."

"I think you're being paranoid, old man," Hortensio said dismissively, snatching the cigar from Elton's mouth and deeply inhaling from it, much to the old thief's dismay.

"Healthy paranoia is always a good thing," he stated.

"Paranoia is never a good thing," Hortensio said back, attempting and failing to imitate the trick that Elton had done. Elton grabbed back the cigar and effortlessly pulled it off again.

"If I may intrude," Rosa intruded, standing between the two men, "there may be some truth to what you say about Kalahar playing us for fools. Thank you, Elton, for your faith in me as a mage, by the way."

Elton shrugged.

"The Lazerian sorceresses who I'm learning from, while not as adept as Kal, have shown me similar tricks to this biological regeneration you speak of. What did he do, exactly?"

"Chopped off his hand and vaporised it," Elton recalled.

"And it grew back?"

"Seemed like it."

"Did it grow back through a conscious effort? Did he draw his power from anywhere?"

"I don't know what he does, he just points and does things. I don't pay attention to the method in which he grows his hands. If I remember anything, it's that it had started growing back damned soon after he chopped it off."

"That wouldn't support my theory about him being a powerful mage, then. The masters in Lazeria are capable of regenerating body parts – one chopped off a finger and then completely regenerated it within half an hour, at the cost of a rat's life. It doesn't sound to me like Kal did anything of the sort. I say he's to be trusted."

"If he's to be trusted, then where the bloody hell is he?" Elton shouted, wildly gesturing to the air around him. He grabbed the attention of a few onlookers who stared bewilderedly before averting their eyes when Elton looked in their direction.

"He'll turn up," Hortensio said calmly. "Have either of you seen Jannis?"

Elton and Rosa shook their heads.

"In that case, I'll be off. I must speak with him," he said imperatively, before walking up the stairs towards the back end of the Redhouse.

Elton sighed and followed him. But then he turned around again and walked back towards the entrance.

"I don't know what to do, Rosa," he stated. "I've spent the past weeks boggling my head with this vampire business and now I just don't know what to do. There's nothing more I can do."

"You need a break," she suggested. "Go home, boss. Relax."

"How can I relax? I've never been able to relax! I was nearly killed today and it's only just reached me now. How many times a day do I sidestep death only to have to subsequently sidestep it again? I always feel as if I'm being watched, as if someone is constantly looking over my shoulder. I can't stand it and all I feel is stress! My head hasn't been clear ever since I met that bloody vampire! Curse him for it!"

"I'm going to take you home, and then I'm going to practice my magic on you. It really will help," she said softly. "Let's go."

They didn't make it out of the entrance before they were almost ploughed over by Sir Jannis and a troop of knights astride their sand-stained horses. Jannis leapt from the saddle and strode directly to Elton.

"Where is the King?" he asked desperately.

"He's in the back, upstairs somewhere. What's going on?"

"I need to speak with him."

"That's funny, because he needed to speak with you. What's the issue?"

"I cannot tell you. Only King Hortensio."

"You can tell me right now," Elton growled, "or you won't reach King Hortensio."

Jannis frantically looked around, his usual steely composure completely absent. Little did Elton know that it was all an act.

"Now!" Jannis shouted.

Elton instinctively drew his dagger and turned around, horrified, to watch his own henchman stab one another in the back. Some were slow to react and died, cards in hands. Other were quick, but soon overpowered by larger groups of traitors. Then the knights dismounted and drew their swords, advancing on the Syndicate leader.

"Jannis, you treacherous bastard, what the fuck is going on?" Elton shouted, backing towards the centre of the two groups.

"What is going on? It looks fairly clear to me. Your drones have betrayed you. In favour of a city in which they have more opportunities than to be at your beck and call. A city which King Hortensio has promised them in return for your head on a spike."

Jannis rushed towards him and swung his sword over his head, overly cocky. Elton, despite his age and weight, side-stepped the attack and jabbed with his dagger. It collided with the solid steel plating which covered the knight everywhere from the neck downwards.

"I'm afraid you'll have to do better than that," Jannis taunted, turning purposefully slowly. Rosa drew her sword and stood beside Elton, but they soon had another problem in the form of another knight rushing towards the pair, looking very intent on striking them down. Rosa had to abandon Elton in order to deflect the advance of the second knight, and Elton was left alone to face Sir Jannis.

"You're so fucking fat, it's truly repulsive," Jannis stated. "I don't know why anyone followed you in the first place."

"I'm fat because I'm bloody wealthy. And those who followed me wanted to be wealthy too. And many became wealthy. As was their reward for respecting honour above greed."

"Honour among thieves! There's never been such a thing and there never will. Even King Hortensio is merely using these fools as tools to depose you and then we'll dispose of them. Did you really think that you would get away with having the King under your whip? The moment we agreed to help you with the vampires, we'd been planning this. And there didn't seem a better opportunity than after helping put down a foreign attack."

Elton and Jannis kept their eyes on one another, stepping around in a circle, neither moving a step closer, neither moving a step further away. They simply bore their eyes into the other, sharing the same venomous glare.

"I can't wait to demolish this place. To melt down all the overly luxurious supplies you waste on imbeciles who run off

309

and sell them for a quick turnover. King Hortensio is smart, Elton, because he understands people. He understands that if you allow criminals to be in possession of wealth, they squander it. Through one way or another. And you enable it, you pretentious fool. You might well make a lot of money through your organised thievery, but how much of it is wasted on the boors who claim to be on your side, come in every day, claim their share and leave? Likely to the nearest brothel to shower some lice-ridden whore with it? Is this the kind of society you want to build?"

Jannis finally took two steps forward and slashed in a diagonal arc. Elton ducked that strike and the two which came after it in quick succession.

"Your time is up, old man. Give up now, and we might kill you quickly. But believe me, I would much rather do it another way."

Rosa's sword slid across the floor, passing Elton and sliding to a stop at Jannis's feet. She quickly stepped backwards to stand at Elton's side, quickly glancing at him and taking notice of their increasingly dire situation.

"Grab my hand!" Rosa screamed.

"Fucking stop her!" Jannis screamed with greater urgency, understanding what was happening as Elton sheathed his dagger with blinding speed and grasped Rosa's extended hand.

They teleported as the sword penetrated what would have been Elton's neck.

Rosa had teleported them somewhere Elton didn't recognise. It was cold – a shiver ran down his spine and an army of goosebumps appeared down his arms as he walked towards the clean, steel-framed glass window, crossing his arms in a feeble attempt to retain some warmth.

The window provided a beautiful view of rolling hills, lush, green forests, colourful flower meadows. He had never seen so much colour since leaving Salyria, and even then he didn't remember it being so vibrant.

He jumped when a jay with sparkling aquamarine feathers landed at the window and tilted its head to study the strange man with its small black eyes. It didn't appear alarmed in the slightest.

310

Rosa wasn't so dazzled by the sights. Instead, she was more focused on regaining her strength and had collapsed onto the floor, cradling her knees to her chest and drawing deep, long breaths.

"Haven't you got any better at this yet?" Elton asked, taking his attention from the outside world to examine the room in which they had landed.

"Yes! But it just so happens that… I haven't ever teleported more than… than myself! Your fat arse makes it… a lot more effort!"

"Alright, lay off. Where are we?"

"Lazeria," she said, increasing her breathing rate to make up for that which she had lost while speaking. "I've never been able to do it in one go."

"Well done," Elton mused, somewhat sarcastically. "Why?"

"I don't know if you noticed, Regi, but your son and Jannis—"

"Don't call him that," Elton growled, cutting her off. "He tried to have me killed. He's no son of mine."

"Oh, so you did catch the part about them trying to kill you. Not for the first time, I might add. And really, you threatened to kill him in the first place so I don't blame him for feeling spiteful about it."

"What are we supposed to do here?" Elton said, pawing through a collection of books written in some language he didn't recognise which happened to be splayed across an opulent wooden desk.

"You know what, boss, I didn't think about it. In the heat of the moment, our lives on the line, I teleported us to the first place outside of Dannos that came to mind. And I've been here plenty, so this happened to come to mind. When the time is right and when we're ready, we'll go back to Dannos. But at the moment, it's not ideal. So shut up and sit down and let me fucking breathe!"

They both stayed silent for a little while as Rosa wrestled her breathing back under control. She then stood up and walked lazily to the desk, where she sat down and began to tidy up some of the mess.

"We've still got our clothes," Elton remarked.

"Good spot," Rosa sneered. "It's almost as if I'm learning things."

"What happened to needing to open a portal?"

"Turns out that funnily enough, there are multiple methods of doing things."

Elton paced up and down the room, periodically gazing out of the window, admiring how the trees swayed rhythmically with the wind.

"What about Paul? Felix? We've left them behind!" Elton said, panicking again.

"No shit," Rosa responded, continually sarcastic. "Were they with us at the time of departure? No. How was I meant to teleport them?"

"They're going to be killed..."

"I didn't see them go back to the Redhouse. They're smart enough— well, Felix is smart enough, and Paul has... street smarts... they'll survive. And they can fend for themselves if they get captured."

A black cat with emerald-green eyes entered the room through a flap built into the door and strolled over to the desk, where it jumped up and found a comfortable spot in which to lie down and fall asleep.

"What's next? Are you going to have us ride back to Dannos on your broomstick?" Elton said.

Rosa stroked the cat and it purred softly, stretching out its front legs.

"This is Akha. It means 'night sky' in Archaeish. That's the language the sorcerers use."

The cat stood up, walked in a circle, and then settled down again, completely disregarding the sheets of paper it disrupted and sent drifting onto the floor.

"We need to do something, Rosa," Elton said with authority.

"I'm aware," she responded. "But I say we should maybe have some time to think before we do anything."

Elton had adapted to the temperature by now, so it was easily noticeable when it dropped once again. The goosebumps reappeared and he shivered more vigorously than before.

"So now you decide to reappear? Out of all the times you could have turned up, you choose now?" Elton shouted angrily, seemingly into thin air.

"What can I say? I live a busy life," Kalahar said, materialising from the thin air into which Elton had shouted.

"Kal, why the bloody hell didn't you turn up sooner? Are you aware of what's just happened?" Rosa said, finally siding with Elton.

"Something to do with being overthrown, your son turning on—"

"Don't call him that."

"I beg your pardon, but was it not you that revealed your fatherhood of the young King? If you didn't want to refer to him as your son, then why ever would you reveal it to him?"

"Don't bullshit me, vampire. You know exactly why I told him. Unfortunately, he's just as heartless as I."

"You get sharper by the day, Elton. You're right, I do know why you told him. A shame your plan fell apart."

"And I was genuinely trying to do what you told us to do. For once in my life, it was a motion driven not by greed but by desire to do the right thing. And I got backstabbed by that traitorous bastard and his knights in shining armour. I need to go back, Kal. I need to go back to Dannos."

"What a ludicrous proposal. I've already been – it would be futile to go back. Young Hortensio is currently in the midst of killing every last Syndicate man and woman that doesn't bow to his demands. I know you've only been here for a matter of minutes, but it's enough. You have no chance of winning back the Redhouse. It's lost."

"He can't have taken it that quickly. We can still go back. You can kill him, vampire. You can kill him and all his knights. We can be rid of him at last."

"I could," Kalahar said, crossing his arms and leaning against the stone wall. "But I'm not going to."

Elton angrily stomped up to the vampire, who didn't react in the slightest.

"Why the bloody hell not?" Elton seethed.

"Because it's not my place to," the vampire said matter-of-factly. "I've meddled in human affairs more than enough. It's your job to organise your own organisation."

"Boss, it will be fine," Rosa interjected. "Dannos isn't the only Syndicate stronghold. We have a number of locations across the continent, which I don't need to remind you of."

"Dannos is the heart of the Syndicate," Elton said. "And it happens to be where I control it from. Some organisations can work without a central place of control, but the Syndicate needs me."

"And it can have you. You'll just have to abandon Dannos and control it from elsewhere."

"And be subject to the rules and regulations of basal nations. I'd rather stuff a sandy sock down my throat."

"Would you stop bloody whining? You act as if it's the end of the world but in fact you have nothing to worry about. Perhaps if Hortensio attacked the rest of our many strongholds then we would have a problem. But you understand that none of what we do is legal anywhere and yet it continues to take place? You hold a lot of power, Regi, and not just in Dannos. That's probably why Hortensio attacked in the first place."

Elton eased himself into a seat, grunting and slowly running a hand through his thin, wiry hair. He looked out of the window once again, where the scenery continued to be the same rolling hills, swaying trees and colourful flower meadows.

"I miss this," he muttered. "It's so... fresh. It's so clear. Why do I choose to reside in that desert shithole?"

"Wealth and power," Kalahar provided, his tone implying it to be the obvious answer.

"Stay out of this," he barked, turning back around. "You can't possibly understand humans. You aren't one and never were one. You're an otherworldly beast – a monster. How could you possibly understand?"

"Because I possess intelligence far greater than yours, which allows me greater understanding of your trivialities. Anyone with a half-functioning brain can work out that wealth and power are the only two driving factors of human progression. Why else are wars fought? Why else does crime exist?"

"A bloody big head is what you've got. Vampire – in your infinite wisdom, tell me what to do. You set out to help us

314

fight the upcoming eclipse, now tell us what to do now that our head of operations has been compromised."

"The lady said you have more than one location?" he said, gesturing to Rosa.

"We do. There are men there prepared and well-informed about what's to come."

The vampire shrugged and looked between the two with an expression of ridicule across his pale face.

"I'm sorry, am I missing something here? Has Rosa not already suggested you just go to another of your locations? Why haven't you listened to her?"

"I think, Kal," Rosa began, "that Elton doesn't particularly fancy going to another of the Syndicate strongholds and is rather hoping that you'll just help him dispose of his unruly son."

The end of her sentence was met with a harsh glare, but she carried on.

"Hortensio isn't going to stop with Dannos – he's made it very clear that he intends to extend his reign across the continent and he's made it very clear that he is no fan of the Redwinter Syndicate. Until he's put down, our entire organisation is at risk. And the fact that he's already taken Dannos, apparently through bribery of our very own ranks, means that the other, weaker divisions of the Syndicate will be even easier to take over. And it's not a good look for Dannos to fall, because it makes us look weak. It's embarrassing enough that they managed to turn our own people against one another, and it highlighted the fragility of their loyalty. Dannos is the beginning of the end for the Redwinter Syndicate, Kalahar. Which is why Elton is so desperate for your assistance."

The vampire stroked his chin, now with a quizzical expression.

"I still don't see how this involves me."

"For the gods' sakes, stop being obstructive for once!" Elton said, rising from his seat. "I know that you know everything we're thinking, so stop being such a pain in the arse and just tell us what you're going to do. We haven't seen you in weeks, so for you to turn up as the city falls really doesn't seem like a coincidence. You need us for something, vampire. You sought me in the first place to deal with your vampire problem and

315

never properly explained why. And for you to reappear now, when we might not be able to carry out the required task? Well, that just won't do for your little plan, whatever it is. Because I don't know and frankly, I don't care to work it out. But please, I beg you to just speak the unhindered truth!"

"Don't you appreciate a touch of mystery in a relationship? Fine, I do need you. I have my reasons for wanting this event put down swiftly, which I'm not obligated to reveal. It should be more than enough for you humans that I've pledged myself to assist you. Hortensio sacking Dannos is... inconvenient. But it will still work out. You've planned exceptionally well and are more than ready. If I'm honest, you really needn't worry about retaking that wretched desert slum. You would gain nothing from it."

"This eclipse you talk about," Elton growled, "are you quite sure you know what you're talking about? Because I believe I'm correct in assuming that in fact the rest of the world won't see the moon pass in front of the sun. Only us and every other land close by. How will this vampire shit affect everyone?"

"Oh, my dear, uninformed Elton. It's nothing to do with the physical location of celestial bodies in reference to different locations on the planet. It's all about magic. More complicated than you need to worry your little head about. Just know that it's the truth."

The door to the room swung open and Kalahar vanished in an instant. An opulently dressed woman came in and handed Rosa a scroll, fiddling with her chestnut hair at the same time, attempting to fashion it into a bun at the back of her head.

"Penn har sakk?" she said, viciously scrutinising Elton with her hazel eyes.

"Har sakk Elton Redwinter, dol il yen fendazar heb," Rosa quickly explained.

"Hep tar, Elton Redwinter," the woman said kindly, any previous scrutiny wiped from existence. She extended her hand, which he hesitantly shook.

"Il srakk naz Archae," Rosa said when the woman looked as if she was going to continue speaking. "Elton, this is Master Ellegaard of Yaarda. She's one of the sorceresses here and also teaches at the Yaris University."

Master Ellegaard bowed and left the room, her fur cloak trailing behind her. Rosa stepped forward and closed the door.

"What's that she's given you?" Elton asked.

Rosa unfurled the scroll and her expectant expression gradually changed to one of dismay as she continued to read it. Elton spied a look, but it was written in Archaeish, as could have been expected.

"What does it say?" he finally asked as she finished, slowly rolling the scroll back up.

"She's been kicked out," Kalahar spoke for her, reappearing in exactly the same place from which he had originally disappeared. "She hasn't progressed fast enough for them to legitimise her continued study."

"What?" Elton said, growing angry for the umpteenth time that day. "We pay a veritable fortune for you to go here. How can they justify this? Do they not appreciate the gold?"

"It's bollocks!" Rosa exclaimed. "Absolute bollocks! I've progressed plenty! Sure, I don't pour my life into study and practice, but it's ridiculous to expect that. These bloody people are out of their minds."

"Is there anywhere else you can go? This... institution... seems rather remote. What about a proper university?"

"They would never accept me. I get enough abuse as it is and I barely see anyone other than the sorceresses, who themselves dole out a sizeable portion of the abuse. I'd be lynched within a day of visiting anywhere populated in this place."

"Perhaps I can teach you," Kalahar chimed in. "You seem to forget I'm proficient in magic, hell, I'm born of it. I could teach you far more than any of these charlatans. And far faster."

Elton and Rosa looked at each other and she carelessly dropped the scroll onto the desk.

"But if I am to teach you," Kalahar said, raising a finger, "then it is to be until the vampires are put down. And then I must leave. Permanently."

"Whatever, it's better than nothing. What are we going to do about Hortensio?" Rosa asked.

"Nothing," the vampire shrugged. "How about we go back to Dannos anyways?"

Before they could respond, he traced a circle in the air and pressed forward, creating a portal which displayed the sand-stone pillars at the entrance of the Dawn Bank, guarded by a pair of Salyrian knights.

"After you," Kalahar prompted, raising his arm towards the portal.

"What the bloody hell is going on? Do we even have a plan? One moment, you aren't bothered about Dannos, and now you want us to go back. What are you doing?"

"Going through this portal without you in a moment. Let's go!"

Elton's eyes darted between the expectant-looking vampire and Rosa, who was equally as hesitant as he was. But feeling the comfortable hilt of his dagger on his back gave him the confidence he needed to step through the portal.

CHAPTER 35

A dark, translucent sword sailed through the air as Kalahar rose swiftly to his feet. It looked as if it was going to impact Tregor but he materialised a dark, translucent blade of his own just in time to deflect the incoming blow. Not completely recovered from the assault, the vampire advanced with predetermined movements and materialised a second blade in his left hand, his damaged skull still regenerating itself. Tregor was fast – faster than any normal swordsman. But even he was unable to make any progress in fighting the supernatural creature.

"Olga!" he cried. "Help me hold him back! The rest of you, get the Fateborn to safety!"

The blonde woman materialised a sword of her own identical to those currently engaged with one another, if not slightly shorter. She leapt into battle and found a position behind Kalahar which forced him to constantly divert his focus between the two assailants.

Meanwhile, the other mages released Richard's binds. With a burst of adrenaline, he jumped from the table and landed cleanly on his feet. He drew his sword, backing away, keeping his eyes trained on the three mages who walked carefully towards him as he felt the room slowly reaching its end.

"Now, now, there's no need for this," Lynn asserted. "We're going to open a portal. You're going to go through it. Your options are clear, Fateborn. Go with us or go with the bloodsucking monster."

Richard said nothing and continued to pace backwards. He glanced over at the ongoing scuffle, which was still at a complete stalemate, though it looked as if Kalahar was only trying to deflect their strikes at this point instead of actively trying to defeat them. While the two armed mages expended their energy on constant movement, Kalahar remained planted on the spot, parrying every incoming blade with ease. He even looked to be enjoying himself.

"You need to come with us, Fateborn," the handsome red-haired man ordered gruffly. "We're your only chance of survival."

"I've done well enough for myself thus far," Richard retorted, brandishing his sword. "What I need is for you lot to open a portal to Mirados and let me go through that one."

"That's unfortunately not an option," the older-looking man replied. "Not now that you know what you're capable of."

"I might be capable, but as long as I never learn how to use my powers then I can cause no harm. Let me go back to the life I was living."

His legs gave way and he fell. One of the mages rushed forwards to secure him while another traced a circle in the air and opened a portal and the third concentrated the paralysis spell holding him down.

"Alright," a voice boomed. "I've had my fun. Time is up."

Richard watched as hundreds of dark tendrils exploded from the surface of the vampire. They shot through the air at unpredictable speed and pierced both Tregor and Olga multiple times, who were left hanging in the air, suspended on the constantly growing tendrils as they looped around and around to pierce again and again. After sufficient mutilation, the tendrils then flew towards the other mages.

They knew when they had been beaten. All three forgot about Richard and dived through the portal, closing it just as the tendrils reached their location. The vampire's cackles rang across the melancholy chamber as he retracted the tendrils and finally allowed the corpses of Tregor and Olga to succumb to gravity's pull.

Richard, still on the ground, crawled behind a row of seats. He tucked his sword to the side, unsure of whether it would be useful in any possible outcome to his situation.

The vampire hadn't taken notice of the bounty hunter just yet. Instead, he paced slowly around the corpses and the surrounding pond of blood, their faces and skin completely drained of colour.

"You embarrass yourself, Tregor," he scorned. "That devil's brew you threw over me is for killing malevolents. You tried to kill me with it. Damned fool."

The almost-certainly dead body of Tregor Lopan twitched a couple times but remained in the same position.

"You lied to us," he rasped. Richard couldn't believe it.

"Of course I did. It would have been terribly foolish of me to tell you my true weakness, no? I never trusted you, just as you never trusted me. You've always put yourself and your own priorities first, believing that mine couldn't possibly be valid as a creature of the undead. Even when your priorities and ideals are flawed. You really think the Council is capable of safeguarding this continent? A band of adept human magic-wielders? And, what is it, a single elf, one who didn't even feel the need to accompany you here today? You're hopeless. Perhaps if you opened your arms to embrace diversity then maybe – just maybe – you would stand a chance at survival. But do you know what would have guaranteed your survival? If you had trusted me. If you had valued me. Because like it or not, my abilities surpass yours by the largest of leaps and bounds."

Tregor coughed, but without moving. Meanwhile, Richard scanned the room for an exit and started inching towards a door on the far side of the room, away from both the vampire and the mages.

"The Council should have trusted me, Tregor. It has had its time, which, at last, draws to a close."

He reached his hand up and Tregor vanished. Nevertheless, the vampire released a dark tendril from each of his fingertips, angrily obliterating the wooden panels making up the floor beneath him.

"Fateborn!" he snarled.

Richard stopped in his tracks.

"We must go – we have much to discuss. And not much time."

Richard didn't respond and kept tiptoeing towards the door which felt like it kept moving further and further away.

"You have seen what I am capable of. Please, all I ask is that you join me willingly – I will not carry out the archaic, unforgiving procedure of conversion as they enjoy in the Council. I merely invite you to be my apprentice. The world needs you. And I'm the only one who can teach you in time."

Richard still carried on towards the exit, having left his sword behind to be as quiet as possible.

You are coming with me whether you do so by your own choice or not, the vampire said. The voice had not come from across the room and instead had been delivered by telepathy.

The mages are gone. I can ensure you never run in with them again. But you have to trust me.

Richard stopped. He peered through the gap between the two seats to his side and immediately ducked back down when he laid eyes upon the vampire, staring directly back at him.

A terrible time is upon us, Kalahar said. *You can protect those you care for, those you love. Only if you choose to. If you don't, you will watch the world burn and fall to darkness.*

Richard stood up.

"There's no one left I love," he said.

The vampire evaporated and reappeared at his side. Richard jumped back in fright.

"We both know that isn't true," Kalahar said, smirking.

"And how do you know anything?"

"Linelle."

It was like he'd been punched in the throat and the stomach simultaneously. It only hurt more when the vampire's form changed to become an image of Linelle, exactly as Richard remembered her. The way she always had her cedar hair in two braids – one either side of her head. Her soft blue eyes, much warmer and inviting than the snakelike, piercing green of Valerie. An innocent grin which he knew exactly how to expand.

"I can lead you to her," Kalahar spoke, his voice having changed to be that of Richard's former lover. "You can be reunited."

Richard averted his eyes and instead focused on the plainness of the floor beneath him.

322

"She doesn't want to be reunited. She abandoned me because she was done with me. I'm never getting her back."

"Sweet bounty hunter," Kalahar said in his regular, frightening voice, having changed back to his regular, frightening form. "I know a great many things. I know why Linelle left you. I know where she went. I know where she is now. I know what she thinks and I know what she's thinking of you."

Richard bore his eyes into the vampire's, looking for any sign of deceit. All he saw was an ambiguous red glow.

"How—"

"How are you meant to trust me?" the vampire finished, barely allowing him to start. "I just killed Olga Feragaard, who has sat on the Council for just over two hundred years. She was one of those in favour of the land's curse, which produces what you call the Corrupted. I also nearly killed Tregor Lopan, the head of the Council. I did not allow him to get away due to my own desires. Instead, a foolish mistake."

"But—"

"But I just want you for my own plans? In a way, you're correct. I want to teach you to harness your ability so you can protect the realms of men. The upcoming disaster will have no impact on my life. It will wreak havoc on yours."

Richard tried to argue back but the vampire gestured for him to be silent.

"If we must do this now, so be it. Sit down, it's a long explanation."

The vampire explained in detail about the creation of vampires and the history of total eclipses. He told Richard about the ancient Nightwatch and the Redwinter Syndicate across the sea who he had employed to complete the same task as the elves of long ago. He didn't miss a single detail about the abilities of both lesser and malevolent vampires. He didn't miss a single detail about the various ways to stop them, from the alchemical method to the magical method of creating an entirely new dimension to serve as a prison where they would stay until the end of time.

"Nobody has attempted such a feat since the elves of the Nightwatch," the vampire explained, "And even with the combined strength of their adept skills, they were forced to sacrifice the lives of many to create single, miniscule dimensions

323

the size of a peasant's kitchen, enough to hold a single vampire each. But you, Richard – you could create dimensions enough to hold every scourge this world has ever seen without breaking a sweat. You could be the sole saviour of this continent."

"If I'm apparently so powerful, why did you tell the thieves in Santeros to kill them manually? Why aren't you making me do all the work myself?"

Kalahar smirked. "The man in charge of the Redwinter Syndicate – Elton Redwinter – intrigued me. I immediately realised that beneath his cold, unforgiving exterior was a kind-hearted, gentle man. However, this interior was buried beneath years and years of the undesirable exterior for which everyone knew him. It was more or less lost. You're right – I could have tasked you with eliminating the vampire threat the world over. But there are people like Elton Redwinter who have a chance at redemption, and I'm pressing them towards it."

"Why don't I just cancel the solar eclipse?" Richard suggested. "Again – if I'm as all-powerful as I keep getting told, surely it's within my abilities to manipulate the sun and the moon?"

Kalahar shook his head.

"Magic is a fickle construct. It may be within your capacity to manipulate dimensions, but you would struggle to safely control powers greater than you or I. Humans, elves, dwarves, any sentient, intelligent creature that lives on this planet – we all squabble about who is superior to who. The elves believe themselves to be above everything and everyone – the dwarves believe the same. Humans disregard the elder races as subjects worthy of conversation or mention. But we are all the subjects of greater powers. Some believe the greater powers take the form of omnipotent gods. I believe this to be nonsense. However, there's absolutely no nonsense in the fact that there are greater powers in this world and beyond. To fiddle with the sun and the moon, constructions of the greater powers, would be a step towards total annihilation. It would be enormously risky. A bigger risk than even I would be willing to take."

324

Richard had to take a moment to process the constant bursts of information. He liked the idea of learning to use magic but didn't want that to be overly evident in his reaction.

"If the vampire threat is defeated," he queried, "would it be within my power to end the war?"

"You could end war the world over," Kalahar chuckled. "And yes, you would be able to dismantle the Empire. Though only through means which would have to be carried out by a normal person – liberating occupied land. As an unstoppable mage, though, you could simply overthrow the rulers of various lands and order hostile military forces to leave. Make no mistake, magic is a tool. There would be no way to magically end the war in an instant.

"Above all, though, I promise you one thing. I promise to show you to Linelle. But only if you agree to come with me."

The bounty hunter's eyes glazed over with a sparkling sheen of tears.

"I'll do it," he decided. "Where do we go?"

"I... have a place," the vampire said, smirking.

In an instant, they were no longer in the dingy, poorly lit operating theatre. Instead Richard stood up and walked over to rest his arms on a stone barrier to his right and gazed out to take in a view of snow-capped mountains forming a barrier against the raging sea. Occasionally a wyvern would dive from the peaks headfirst into the water and snatch a fish. He had never seen a live wyvern – now he had seen at least five. More came down from the dark clouds overhead and he delighted in watching them engage in what seemed to be a game of chase as two of the small, dragon-like creatures careered through the air.

"A storm is coming," Kalahar predicted. "The wyverns, as you call them, are making the most of their time below the clouds. The ones you see diving in to catch fish won't actually be eating them immediately but instead taking them to their nests, cradled way up in the rocks. Whole colonies of wyverns live together up there in seclusion. It's only when humans tread too closely to the mountains that there are conflicts. They're terribly intelligent creatures – the ones who manage to be killed by humans are usually very young or very old.

The healthiest wyverns are too fast, too strong, and too clever to fall into any trap."

Richard continued gazing at the view of both boundless mountains and ocean.

"It's beautiful," he remarked, inhaling the fresh scent of ocean breeze as it permeated the stone structure to which he had been teleported. The ocean breeze clashed with a colder mountain breeze which tousled his hair in a much more vigorous fashion and the overall experience was pleasantly refreshing.

"Welcome to Letham Deregor. Ancient vampire stronghold. Constructed here thousands of years ago, before even I existed. In honesty I have no idea how this building came to be, as it doesn't seem feasible that any lesser or malevolent vampire would be capable of creating such a structure or would choose to. It's a long way to travel for a lesser vampire, though I suppose they did have eternity to create it."

"Are you saying there are more vampires here?" Richard asked, frantically turning to face Kalahar.

"They will not touch you, be assured. Everyone in this stronghold is subject to my word as I hold complete power over them. And they are only lesser vampires – their powers are limited. Apart from being able to utilise the simplest of spells and change their face, there's not a whole lot they are capable of. They can't even shift into a different form. Well, most of them."

Richard turned back around to gaze over the view of the mountains and the ocean. He hadn't even taken in the fact that his newfound location was also home to an expansive pine forest. It was a nice reminder of home.

"Come, I must introduce you to some acquaintances. They will act as your teachers – alongside me, of course."

Richard hesitantly left the balcony and followed Kalahar, who moved intently through a pitch-black labyrinth of corridors and stairwells.

"Why's it so dark?" Richard asked.

"We can see in the dark, of course," Kalahar supplied. "No need for light."

They eventually reached a grand hall with a high roof supported by elegantly carved stone pillars, a long table dressed with a longer red tablecloth and a dramatically large stone throne inlaid with what looked to be thousands of gleaming gemstones. Silver braziers hung from the ceiling but they were not lit when they entered and Kalahar had to utter a command to provide the room with light.

"The braziers are mainly for decorative purposes," Kalahar explained. "As I mentioned, we can see in the dark. So they're somewhat redundant for any useful purpose."

"This looks like a dining hall," Richard remarked.

"Again, decorative," Kalahar said. "We don't need to eat. Some of the lesser vampires occasionally have a sip of blood. But we never use the long table for dining."

Kalahar strolled across the room and took a seat in the throne, picking up a flawlessly cut, grape-sized emerald from a ceramic bowl at his side and fiercely examining it in his fingers.

"A beautiful stone, yes?" he idly asked. "To think that these simply came from somewhere deep beneath the surface and were then perfected by a craftsman. I don't know what it is about them, but I'm terribly drawn to gemstones of any kind. I suppose that's my weakness. Ah, look, here's Faefion."

Richard directed his gaze to the door at the other end of the room where he saw a pale-skinned woman with elongated, pointed ears behind which flowed neatly brushed auburn hair. Apart from her strangely shaped ears, she looked no less human than he did.

"Faefion is an elf of Junia," Kalahar clarified. "You'll find many of the vampires here are elves due to the fact that it's far more difficult to survive as a vampire in elven civilisation. Humans are... ignorant. They don't notice the enhanced magical aura radiated by a vampire, even if they have never learned to cast a spell in their life. We're creatures born of magic, so it leaves its trace on us for the remainder of our existence."

"Who's this you've brought us, Kal?" the elven woman gleefully asked. "Been decades since I saw a human up close. Actually, that's a lie. There was a party of vampire hunters who found themselves dangerously close to the stronghold a couple of years ago. I was tasked with getting rid of them. As this

327

one is actually inside the stronghold, I assume you have a very good reason for this?"

"Faefion, this is Richard Ordowyn. The Fateborn."

The elven vampire's eyes lit up and she feverishly extended her hand. Richard uneasily met it with his own as she spoke far too quickly about how long she had been waiting for this moment.

"You're a human, so I'm going to assume your abilities are limited. Can you cast any spells?" she inquired. Richard brushed off the insult, assuming it was typical of an elf.

"None," he bluntly replied. "I can shoot a bow and arrow. I can spar with a sword. I can't do anything magical."

"Not to worry, for I will teach you fast and hard. You'll be capable of saving the world with plenty of time to spare once I'm through with you. Time really flies, doesn't it? To think that the next eclipse is in what, two weeks? That's quite a troubling thought. I suppose we'll have to do the rounds and bring people back here."

"How many... people live here?" Richard questioned.

"Our numbers dwindle every year as more and more vampires succumb to boredom. Two centuries ago, there were probably a hundred of us. Now I'd say it must be around seventeen."

"Big place for only seventeen of you."

"It's fantastic, isn't it? I myself was only born three hundred and five years ago, just in time to hear about Elgaer the Fair establishing a democracy in one of the western elven kingdoms. Can you imagine that? A system where the country's ruler is actually determined by the people living in it. I suppose elves are intelligent enough but I can't imagine such a system working in a human country."

"I would argue, but you're not wrong..." Richard mused.

"Yes, it really is quite a nice home to move into. There is the occasional maintenance needed in places, but that's a small trifle. Now, am I to take him away and start teaching him?"

"Patience, my dear, patience," Kalahar urged. "We must prove ourselves to be worthy of his attention. Prove that we are more reliable than the Council and lack their deep-rooted corruption. Richard – what would you say to a tour?"

328

The bounty hunter shrugged and nodded his head.

"We will begin with that then. You'll also be needing some-where to stay – not to worry, we have plenty of spare rooms available. Spacious ones, too – that's something you wouldn't find at the Retreat. They focus very much on the necessity of efficiency over comfort, which means the sleeping quarters are about as barebones as it gets. Terribly cramped. I assure you, this really is a better accommodation, even if we aren't, well, alive."

Kalahar stopped rambling and dragged Richard towards another unlit stairwell, leaving Faefion behind. A quick glance back at the throne where they had been standing just a mo-ment beforehand revealed that she had already disappeared.

Blind and confused, Richard had no choice but to allow himself to be guided through the never-ending labyrinth of corridors and stairwells. He thought to bring up the fact that he couldn't see anything but as he opened his mouth to speak the vampire muttered something unintelligible and suddenly he could see everything, and in stunning detail, too – the cracks in the ancient stone bricks, the plants and fungi weav-ing through the cracks, the insects living within the plants and fungi, the individual strands of silk stretching across entire corridors to form elaborate webs on which spiders slept. The heavy layer of dust on the floor which hadn't been disturbed until now. Evidence of rooms left to ruin, given the doors left swinging on their hinges, the contents of the rooms aban-doned, whether it be an old map inscribed with the date of 564 or scattered books and utensils which were even older. Richard would have expected the wooden pencils and paper books to have rotted in the vast length of time they had been left alone.

"At last, here we are," Kalahar announced. "I don't miss travelling by foot at all."

The vampire opened a thick wooden door with a rounded top and a dated steel ring-shaped doorhandle to produce a bedroom – indeed spacious and not lacking luxury. The bed was simpler than Valerie's in Limara, but the craftsmanship of the frame was exquisite, featuring carvings of numerous dif-ferent animals in what looked to be a battle at the end of the bed. The sheepskin spread wasn't quite what he was expecting

329

and the vampire sensed this, or perhaps simply read his mind, as with another word it transformed into an opulent thick fur duvet, stuffed to the brim with goose feathers.

"Only an illusion, but it may as well be real," the vampire explained.

There was another door on the other side of the room which opened up to a balcony in the shape of a semicircle with the same design of stone barrier as had been on the long stretch of balcony on which he had first arrived. It boasted the same breath-taking view of the mountains and ocean but from a higher vantage point. He looked down over the barrier and spotted a long, rectangular slanted stone roof protruding from the main structure and assumed that to be the balcony from which he had watched before. There was no roof over his new balcony and it was shrouded in shadow, the sun setting behind them. It was a shame that he hadn't been assigned a room on the north or south end of the building, as that would have allowed him to view the mountains and the ocean in one direction and the sunset in the other. Despite his inability to see the sunset, the ocean glowed red with its reflection.

"There was a saying where I came from," Richard said, watching the gentle waves lapping against the beach. "Red sky at morning, shepherds take warning. Red sky at night, shepherds delight."

"It shall be a pleasant day tomorrow, then," Kalahar confirmed.

They returned from the balcony where Richard quickly noted the other items of furniture bestowed on him: a grand wardrobe with more than enough space for his limited collection of clothes; a desk with an inkwell and quills which he would likely never use; a bookshelf untidily filled with old, dusty books; a weapon rack onto which he placed his bow, quiver, and sword; a small shelving unit devoid of contents; and a chandelier bedecked with candles of varying heights. The two windows were no longer providing enough light, so the vampire lit the candles with a command and saturated the room with unnaturally bright light. Kalahar seemed to notice Richard's distaste for the fake brightness and dampened the candles' flames to a more realistic degree.

"How am I going to remember how to get back here?" Richard asked.

"Good question. One moment," the vampire responded, vanishing. He reappeared shortly afterwards, hands full with oversized parchments which he splayed over the desk. Richard examined the parchments to find they contained an elaborate floorplan of the entire complex, with each parchment being a different floor, clearly marked in the top right corner.

"Of course, you'll also learn your way around naturally, I should hope. Taking the odd wander, getting lost, finding your way, all part of learning, really."

The vampire paused and observed Richard's intense study of the floorplans.

"Oh, you really fell for that one. Here you go."

The vampire waved a hand over the bounty hunter's head and he didn't need to study the floorplans anymore, having been granted the complete knowledge of every corridor, room, and stairwell in the stronghold.

"Why didn't you do that from the start? And why can't you just do that to teach me magic?"

"I jest on occasion. And it doesn't work that way. Come, let us find Faefion. She'll probably be in the atrium."

This time, Richard didn't have to blindly follow Kalahar, and instead proudly followed him through what used to be a maze. They quickly found their way to the atrium, an expansive hall overlooked by a number of platforms from floors above. As predicted, Faefion was in the middle of the room, kneeling in the centre of a chalk pentagram, a lit candle on each of the star's points. Richard gave the entire scene a wide berth and exchanged glances with the not-so-worried Kalahar, who happily intruded and caused the candles to extinguish upon entering the circle.

"Richard is ready to begin," Kalahar informed her.

"He is? How exciting. Did you show him much?"

Kalahar stretched his arm behind his back and looked down sheepishly.

"As a matter of fact, no, we didn't. I showed him where he'll be staying, though."

"For goodness's sake, Kal, you pretend you're faultless, but your memory could do with some rejigging. Never mind, we have a lot to get up to. Master Richard, please join me."

Faefion caused a sizeable piece of chalk to fly across the atrium and land in her palm before tracing another perfectly round circle and filling it with a five-pointed star. A shelf loosely screwed into one of the stone pillars supporting an overhead platform conveniently held a store of candles which she levitated carefully onto each of the points of the new star.

"Kneel within the pentagon at the centre with me," Faefion instructed. Richard did as he was asked after searching for Kalahar's approval. The older vampire then vanished from the room.

"We'll start with the basics. An orb of light. I would teach it to you in your tongue, but I've no experience like that. I'm afraid you'll have to learn to speak some Archaeish."

"Archaeish?"

"Derived from the word archaism. It wasn't always called as such, but the name has changed over time to fit its origins. It's the main language spoken by human mages and vampires. Now, let me teach you some essential words..."

CHAPTER 36

Cold, hungry, and tired, they were still flying. Having spent hours flying across the ocean, Alazarioss finally spoke.

We're almost there.

They had reached a new body of land, covered in boundless swathes of dark pine trees beyond the almost unnoticeably thin stretch of beach. At the speed they were flying, if they had blinked, they would have missed it.

The landscape was torn by stony hills on which nature fought to survive, tilted trees clinging onto cliffs for dear life. Contrasting that was a maze of ravines weaving through the earth, fallen trees forming natural bridges across.

Alazarioss seemed to know where she was going and unexpectedly dived almost perpendicularly to the ground. The passengers were caught somewhat off-guard and clung frantically, desperately to her spines.

The dragon brought them down to a particularly wide ravine, large sections of which were completely covered in foliage stretching across its full width. She didn't hesitate to crash through this foliage, her enormous weight providing no match for the helpless trees and vines.

In the depths of the ravine, an entirely unnatural structure emerged into view – constructed from dull wooden planks which almost blended into the ravine's plain grey façade, only interrupted by intermittent splashes of green from tenacious plant life.

The structure, although protruding from the walls of the ravine, clearly went further, with much of the structure only comprising bridges and platforms. Holes in the side of the gorge had been carved out and tunnelled deep, at the very ends of which they could see the faint, constant glow of light.

Alazarioss landed at the bottom of the ravine and allowed her passengers to dismount. The planks of the structure creaked with age and a close look proved them to have, in many places, worn away and in some places even rotten.

He is here, Alazarioss announced. *Among others.*

"What is this place?" Elaeínn asked, creeping towards the largest of the tunnels carved into the gorge's sides.

I couldn't tell you, the dragon answered. *But it causes me great pain even to be near it. The crystal concentration here is... great.*

"Alazarioss – before we go in, we need an explanation. We need to know what we are doing, why we are here, what your mission is. We can't go in this blindly and hope to come out alive, especially not if there are others inside."

My mission is to search for and recover all of the world's stolen magical crystals – pieces of the very Heart of magic through which all magic in this world flows. Though the pieces here, and the one R is in possession of, are corrupted. They were corrupted when they were stolen from the Heart and further corrupted when filled with the souls of people they had killed. And it means that when magic flows through them, the corruption leaks into the general flow of magic. And damages it – and in turn, me. I am ready to serve you, and act as your champion. I will stay at your side. But you must help me recover the crystals and restore the purity of magic.

"Now that was a short enough explanation," Elaeínn said, helping Kaesta across a particularly unstable part of the platform which Lysíen was eyeing up uncertainly. "You could have told us that at any point already."

I beg your forgiveness.

Elaeínn leapt across a patch of rotten planks lining the balcony between them and the tunnel and landed securely on the stone. Kaesta, Erría and Lysíen followed suit and they all turned to Alazarioss for guidance.

I don't know what else or who else you'll find in there. And I cannot help you from here. All I can say is this – be careful. Those in possession of the crystals wield great magical power – significantly more than any other living creature. They route magic through the crystals to embolden their own strength. Should there be multiple foes, it will

be a fight which you are unlikely to win – but you have the Drag-
onsteel Blade, which you will find to be of surprising magical
strength itself.

And you will be guided, even if not by my desires, but your own.
Good luck, Elaeínn. And to you...

"Kaesta."

"Erría."

"Lysíen. And it's nice to finally know your name, FTA girl."

They crept into the cavern, carefully surveying every
square centimetre of the unnaturally smooth walls. The tunnel narrowed as it continued further into the bowels of the
ground, to the point where they had to walk in single file to be
able to fit. The screeching of Elaeínn's sword reverberated
throughout the tunnel when she drew it in preparation for
whatever was to come, and any ideas of stealth were forgotten.

The golden glow of the sword's runes almost allowed them
to see their surroundings in detail as the light at the end of the
tunnel grew brighter – the beginnings of colour were appearing at their destination. A splash of dull red decorated the
floor, a mixture of desaturated book covers lined an old
wooden bookshelf. They entered the room and found their
source of light in the form of an orb hovering above an old table in the middle of the room.

They collectively glanced back from where they had come
and saw the distant but bright reassurance of Alazaríoss's icy
reptilian eyes. And then they moved in the direction of a faint
chattering in a room to their right.

Elaeínn burst through the doorway and was frozen in
place. Her sword fell from her clutches and stopped glowing
as a pompous R appeared from the shadows of the room, his
arm extended. He clenched his fist, and her arms and legs
were spread involuntarily to block the door and prevent the
others from entering.

"Elaeínn, did you think me so foolish? That I would allow
you to waltz in here on the back of your dragon and take back
Kíra? Preposterous. We knew you were coming; I knew it the
moment I saw that beastly creature take your side."

Swords were drawn from the room behind Elaeínn, and
her allies attempted to force her limbs out of the way, with no
success.

335

"For Raeris's sake, I don't understand! All I want is Kíra: you can continue with whatever little cult you're running on the island and I won't interfere. Just give me back my friend."

"Er takk il kveklatin," a scratchy, aged voice said from an adjoining room.

From the adjoining room appeared an old man, whose ears weren't pointed. His beard, like many dwarves, reached his waist, though he was tall, almost as tall as the room in which they stood. His lavish robes gave the initial impression that he was portly, but from the areas of his body which weren't covered in layer upon layer of fabric, his skin was seemingly moulded directly to his bones.

"Who's this? A human?" Elaeínn hissed.

"That's correct," R said. "He has been helping me get through to Miss Karíos. Humans, despite their biological flaws, are surprisingly ingenious."

"Il mak intrak an ihv, Ríyael," R's friend said. "Dakh il ihv hezen carn."

"Is that your name? Ríyael? So you named your little camp after yourself? Could you possibly get any more narcissistic?"

"You may have her for whatever you wish, Den. After I'm through with her."

"Penn har sakk?" a third voice, feminine, piped up from the adjoining room. The third voice presented herself as a pale-skinned, green-eyed woman with jet-black hair cascading over her shoulders. She was dressed to match the dark energy emanating from the top of her head, causing a result where she seemed to blend into the shadowy corners of the room.

"Lynn – allow me to introduce you to Elaeínn Tinaíd. Senior figure of the FTA in Tyen'Ael."

"Why are you here, girl?" the black-haired woman, evidently Lynn, asked, but only after uttering a spell allowing her to be understood in whatever language she had been speaking beforehand.

"I want to get my friend back," she seethed. "And my new dragon pal wants me to collect some magical crystals for her."

"Is that right? Is she on about the lirenium crystals?"

"You know, I don't know. She said they were part of some Heart of magic. All very vague. But they're hurting her, and apparently they're also corrupting magic."

336

Lynn reached into her tight-fitting robes and pulled out a tiny purple crystal, softly pulsating with a dim light. As she did, Alazarioss's roar shook the entire cliffside and dust fell from the ceiling.

"Let her go, Ríyael," Lynn demanded. "I would like to speak to her under more agreeable conditions."

"Not on your life," he countered. "I have needed her for quite some time, and I'm not about to just let her go free now. She was foolish enough to leave the protection of her dragon – now she is mine."

"This Council isn't about what you want, Rí. It's a collective endeavour – we protect magic. We safeguard it from misuse. Why are you even here if all that interests you are your personal needs?"

"The Council is nothing, you fool. Look around you – this place is more comparable to a dungeon than a thriving community for magicians. Hundreds of years ago, this place was bustling with the finest talent the world had to offer. Now it is a shell of its former self, with a few stuck-up mages, all of which are purely there for themselves. And for control."

"Where's this dragon, girl? I'd like to converse with her before I hand over anything of mine."

"Tregor will not approve of this, Lynn," Ríyael warned.

"The Council is nothing, you fool. Remember? Let her go."

"Fine friends you have, R," Elaeínn contributed.

"Let her go," Lynn reiterated.

"She will take all the power you have left. Is that really what you want?"

"I joined this Council to protect magic. I don't know how much of this corruption theory you or Tregor knew about, but I'd like to know more. Let her go."

"I cannot do that."

Lynn outstretched one of her arms and pulled as if there were a rope attached to Elaeínn. She fell from the doorway and her friends ran in, two of them with swords in hand. The mages were far quicker to react than they had expected, and the blades flew across the room, pulled by an invisible force. Lysíen and Erría were pinned against opposite walls while Kaesta kept to the doorway, worry plastered across her face.

337

"Can we please sort something out before my head explodes?" Elaeínn shouted. "Quite frankly, my life for the past few minutes has been an incomprehensible blur. Put down my friends, stop fighting, everyone, and let's speak like civilised people. In the excitement, I think I heard something about control, so you can show your love of control by first controlling yourselves!"

Ríyael hesitantly withdrew his outstretched hand while the other nonchalantly did the same.

"You"—she pointed at Lynn—"you want to meet the dragon? Come with me. Meanwhile, perhaps you can have a chat with my friends, R. Sort something out diplomatically."

"You're a bloody terrorist – don't you try to lecture me about diplomacy. You and your band of good-for-nothings thrive on destroying the thought of diplomacy."

"Desperate times call for desperate measures, and my desperate measures are diplomatic ones. If we're to fight, then let it happen in the future. But not now, not at this moment. Especially not when one of your own allies are against you.

"Come on, Kaesta. You can come with us."

Elaeínn retrieved her sword and hustled her way back to the mouth of the tunnel with Lynn and Kaesta, where Alazarioss eagerly awaited. Lynn was taken aback by her majesty in much the same way Elaeínn had been at first.

You, Alazarioss said through them both. *You have a crystal.*

"We call it lirenium," Lynn explained, producing the crystal once again. "I need you to tell me a bit more about it before I hand it over to you."

Did you take it yourself? Did you hack it from the Heart?

"I don't know what you're talking about, but no. It was a gift from the head of the Council, Tregor Lopan."

Every time you route power through that crystal, you cause pain to the world. To everything through which magic flows. And to yourself. Give me the crystal, and I will take it back to the Heart, where it belongs. It will be cleansed, and the corruption of magic will be reversed.

"Do you breathe fire, too? Like in the legends?"

She got her answer from an impressive display which seared the foliage dangling over the ravine.

"I'm convinced," Lynn said. "But the others won't be so easily. They're keen on never losing power. And these crystals are our power."

As they are your demise.

Lynn handed the crystal to Elaeínn, who placed it in her satchel and made sure to fasten the lid tightly shut.

"My father and sister are away right now, but I should be able to convince them. They're independent enough from the Council anyways, and my father holds a different kind of power to the others."

From the cave's shadows appeared the bearded wizard, clutching a walking stick and squinting with the onset of daylight.

"Magnificent," he mouthed. "Truly astonishing."

"Denzel," Lynn cut him off. "Give me your crystal. We're harming the very thing we protect by using them."

"And leave us vulnerable to the rat race? The common folk? I think not."

The power you wield now will crumble in the years to come. You have been steadily destroying magic's ties with you. One day, those ties will snap, and you will be left powerless.

"And on that day, I'll hang a rope between my neck and the sturdiest oak I can find. I will never listen to you and your mindless, idealistic rambling, Lynn. For you don't understand the world."

"Give me the crystal, Den, or I'll have to take it from you."

The bearded wizard, who Elaeínn now understood to be called Denzel, eased a hand into his oversized robes and held a similar purple crystal between his thumb and index finger.

Alazaríoss acted before either he or she could do anything, swiping the mage's hand with an oversized claw, knocking Denzel forcefully to the ground. The crystal fell from his grasp and rolled towards Elaeínn, who stopped it under her boot before it could roll off the edge and into the ravine.

"You, child. You give that back to me before I incinerate you in a torrent of flame."

Blue flame engulfed the sorcerer and he was reduced to ash in an instant.

"You didn't have to do that!" Kaesta cried, looking angrily at Alazaríoss. "We could have negotiated!"

"I'm sorry, Kaesta, but this is the reality of the world. Some people are disagreeable," Elaeínn tried to convince her, though she also felt immense guilt for Alazarioss's actions.

"Especially Denzel Kestrenad," Lynn added, understanding the situation at once. "I'm honestly quite glad someone got rid of him."

"No, Elaeínn," she retorted, with surprising confidence. "You're ruthless and I don't want to be a part of it. I'm going back to Sanaíd."

Before Elaeínn had a chance to argue, the girl had opened a portal, gone through, and closed it.

"R," Elaeínn exclaimed.

"You and the girl weren't particularly close, then?" Lynn asked, following her back into the tunnel.

"No, but I still owe a duty to protect the other two. And you – do you know where Kíra is?"

"I'll take you to her myself. Rí might need her for something selfish, but I've no personal allegiance to him, regardless of what Tregor might want."

They reached the room in which Ríyael had initially trapped her and neither he nor Lysíen nor Erría were there. But the floor was decorated with blood.

"That's not a good sign," Lynn calmly observed. "Come, I'll take you to your friend. She may need some... rehabilitation."

She briskly led Elaeínn through the underground complex and they arrived at a dimly lit chamber, in the middle of which a shadowed figure was tied at the waist to a wooden pole reaching between the arched ceiling and the floor.

"Kíra!"

She flew across the room and crashed into the wall. Winded, she coughed violently and attempted to stand up but was hit with another force which pinned her against the wall.

Ríyael's blade flashed in the darkness, reflecting the light of the orb positioned at the room's peak.

"Diplomacy. You know well that diplomacy doesn't work. Why did you think you could dictate the way this would go?"

He stepped towards her and swung his sword, but missed spectacularly, instead turning around involuntarily and striking the floor behind him.

"Lynn Varanus," he hissed. "You're making a mistake."

"I've been making mistakes for a while through my continued membership of this Council," she said through strained breaths. "I was quite frankly blind to not yet realise the deep corruption which has infected you all. I was wholly foolish."

Elaeínn ripped her sword from its sheath and the runes glowed intensely – stronger than they had done aboard the *Wavestrider*. She bounded from the wall and swept her sword in an arc towards Ríyael, who had just managed to break free of Lynn's magical grasp. Their swords met with a sonorous clang while Lynn drew a blade of her own.

"The Ritual Blade," Ríyael noted. "You know, it was me who gave that to Jaelaar, all those many years ago. I had no idea what it did, and yet now it finally does something. In your hands. Do you know how many days and weeks I spent examining that worthless piece of metal in the hopes that it would be of some value? That those pathetic etchings would mean something?"

"Funny, this is the second time I'm hearing this. If only you had chosen to befriend the person who knew the blade, then perhaps your curiosities would have been satisfied."

Their blades clashed a number of times more with minimal progress on either side. Lynn cried a spell and Ríyael was knocked off his feet, landing next to Kíra.

"Convenient," he said.

He brought his sword up with one hand to the delirious Kíra's throat and Elaeínn was frozen. Her breathing was deep and rapid as she surveyed her options, which turned out to be depressingly bleak.

"You know, you've driven me to the point where I really couldn't care to get any more information out of either you or her. One more step and she dies."

"What's the problem? You don't think you could kill me by yourself?"

"Oh, don't credit yourself too much. I have no lack of confidence when it comes to my ability to kill you. I'm more worried about Lynn. Although by her breathlessness I'm judging that... oh, you did. You gave away your crystal."

He drew his blade away from Kíra's throat.

"Fool."

341

A ball of flame formed in his free palm and whizzed towards Lynn, who caught it in her own hands like would be possible with any projectile. But the effort it took was noteworthy.

The cave shook with a roar, vibrating throughout the entire complex, loudly and forcefully. The fireball Lynn had grasped dissolved and Elaeínn took the tremor as an opportunity to advance and close the distance between her and Kíra, and Ríyael was forced backwards, again brandishing his sword in both hands.

"Come on, you coward," Elaeínn taunted. "If you're so allpowerful, fight me without using magic as a crutch. As our ancestors once did."

"Only a fool would discard their tools in order to be 'honourable'. And I'm no fool."

He blasted her back with a thrust of his arm and jumped towards her as she recovered, skidding across the floor. She brought her sword up in time to block a strike from over his head, which met her blade with such force that it was brought down to mere centimetres away from her eyes.

"And now, you die, Elaeínn Tinaíd."

Ríyael was dragged into the air and his eyes grew in surprise. His sword fell to the floor as Kíra, tattered and deathly pale, screamed in pain, her trembling arms outstretched towards the sorcerer.

Elaeínn drew her sword back and sent it straight through Ríyael's heart.

The runes lining her blade shifted in colour from a vibrant gold to an ominous purple as the sorcerer's blood flowed from his skewered body. Kíra collapsed with a last puff of breath, hitting the ground in synchronisation with Ríyael, who was now beyond the point where he was able to issue threats or impetuous remarks.

Elaeínn dropped her sword, the runes having ceased glowing. She rushed to Kíra and cradled her in her arms as she wheezed for breath.

"Hey, Elle," she coughed. "I love you."

"I love you too," Elaeínn choked.

But the eyes into which she stared had glazed over, and the arrhythmic rising and falling of her chest stilled.

342

Elaeínn was still for a while, twiddling her fingers through Kíra's hair. And then she screamed, thunderously, piercingly, in a way which felt to her as if it made the walls shake as they had when Alazarioss roared. Her sword, growing cold on the stone floor, glowed with such intense light that it almost illuminated the entire room. Lynn stared bewilderedly at the weapon, shielding her ears as Elaeínn's scream dwindled, replaced by soft sobs.

She fell onto Kíra's motionless body and rested her head on her chest. She traced the contours of her body with her fingers, longingly, desperately wishing her to come back.

"You!" she yelled, very suddenly. She stood up, wiping rivers of tears from her eyes. "Use your shitty magic! Bring her back? What fucking use are you if you can't even do that?"

Lynn said nothing, only stepping forward to caress her hair. Elaeínn immediately broke down into tears again, her hardy outward appearance shattered.

"Wherever it is people go, she'll be looking down on you for the rest of your life," Lynn attempted to comfort.

It was Elaeínn's turn not to respond, and she nestled her face into the sorceress's armpit, wishing time to stop.

"I'm going to collect every last one of those damn crystals," she announced a few minutes later. "If not to help Alazarioss, to spite this 'Council' or whatever the fuck it was. And then I'm going to raze this place to the ground. And then I'm going to go back to that island and kill every last one of R's lackeys. And after that? I'm going to go back to Sanaíd and storm the palace with every last member of the FTA. I'm going to put my sword through as many Nationals as I can. Whoever gave that... mistake the reason to take Kíra."

"I will talk to my father and my sister. I'll try to convince them. Meanwhile, you've still got two others to find – Kasimir, who was close to Olga, until she was killed recently. And of course, Tregor – head of the Council. Unfortunately, I couldn't tell you where either of them are. But I know of someone who might be able to help you locate them. Kalahar Kefrey-something or other – he was the one who killed Olga. We never harvested her crystal, so he may well still be in possession of it. And he also managed to teleport to us while we were in the midst of something. One caveat which may stand

343

in your way – Kalahar isn't human. He's a vampire, and I don't know enough about vampires to be able to warn you of any particular details. But he's dangerous, despite the eccentricity he portrays. At least, that's what I gathered from my brief encounter with him and the subsequent conversations with Tregor, who's known him a lot longer."

"And do you know how to get to this... Kalahar?" Elaeínn's voice still trembled, but it continually sturdied through the evolution of her rage.

"Tregor might be able to. I might be able to make this work."

She produced a small looking glass from her robes and uttered a spell. Her reflection faded from its surface as a strange shimmering effect distorted its visual appearance and a mist swirled around its edge.

"Lynn?" a masculine voice began.

"Tregor," Lynn responded as the image of a dark-skinned man who didn't look a day older than forty appeared on the mirror. "I need your help finding Kalahar."

"For what do you need contact with Kalahar?"

"Information," she lied. "I want to know more about him and why he took the Fateborn. And I want to try to take the Fateborn back."

"I'm a step ahead of you, Lynn. Now, how about instead of lying to me, you explain to me why both Denzel and Ríyael are dead?"

"I'd rather not," she quickly dismissed. "Goodbye, Tregor."

With a wave of her hand, she dispelled Tregor's presence and returned the image on the mirror to her dim reflection.

I know where he is, Alazaríoss suddenly said. It was evident Lynn had also heard it, judging by her expression.

Who? Elaeínn thought, in the hopes that Alazaríoss would be able to read her mind.

Tregor, she replied. *If we find Tregor, I can use him to find Kalahar.*

"Go, quickly," Lynn said authoritatively. "Tregor is exceedingly wise. He will quickly catch on if you wait. I will go now to my father and sister in an attempt to persuade them – I haven't the highest of hopes for my success, as our bonds aren't as close as they perhaps could be. But it's possible."

"I can't leave Kíra here – not like this. She deserves a proper burial."

"I wouldn't recommend a burial – not in Valoria. The land is cursed. She would be resurrected, and not in the way you would wish for."

"I can't just leave her here! I need to take her with me. I'm going to bring her back to Fenalia."

"I know you felt a great deal for this girl, but her time has passed. The most you can do for her now is give her an honourable send-off and fight in her name."

Elaeínn made her way over to Ríyael's lifeless body, his face still struck with shock, and dug around in his robes until she found his crystal, which she placed into her satchel with the other two. She then retrieved her sword and Kíra's body, which she carried over her shoulder, and stormed through the empty corridors of the Council's hideaway, for which she was yet to discover an actual name. She didn't care to discover the fates of Lysíen and Erría, assuming them to be dead. And for that, she felt sorry. But not enough to deter her from her new objectives.

"Let's go, Alazarioss," she said upon reaching the open air. "Let's find the rest of your crystals. And someone who can help me get Kíra back."

CHAPTER 37

FREE CITY OF DANNOS, SANTEROS

The change in temperature was a shock and he began to sweat immediately as he removed the dagger from its sheath and walked up the steps of the Dawn Bank, trailed by Rosa and Kalahar. It was then that Elton realised only he was armed. His pace faltered, but Kalahar raced up the steps to take the lead.

A translucent, cloudy black sword materialised in the vampire's right hand as he walked towards the guarding knights. They fell upon him together and were both dead in seconds.

"Why are we at the bank?" Elton wheezed, struggling towards the entrance where a number of civilians cowered behind tables and desks.

"I thought you would want your buddies to join you," he replied innocently, striding proudly past the contemptuous gazes of the terrified civilians.

Said buddies appeared shortly afterwards, rushing down the stairs of the bank.

"Fuckin' 'ell, boss, where've you been?" Paul exclaimed, wiping the sweat from his forehead.

"An unscheduled trip," he responded, nodding at Felix, who had silently acknowledged their appearance.

"Your psycho son has done what he came here to do, I dunno if you've noticed," Paul stated. Elton felt the urge to interject but didn't have the energy.

"Nice of you to appear at last, Kal," Felix derided. "We really could have used your help recently."

"Alas, you couldn't use me, and events played out as if you had never met me. What a tragedy," Kalahar responded. "Shall we get the supplies, then?"

346

"What supplies? What are we even doing back here, Kal? You haven't explained anything!" Elton shouted. Some of the bank's visitors lost their fear of the newcomers and slowly began to rise and walk out, to which they didn't object.

"Goodness me, it must be terribly tiresome to lack the ability to mind-read. Let me spell it out for you — we're going to go back to the Redhouse, get the crates of alchemy reagents, gather as much of the already-produced solution as possible, and take it all to a secondary location. One where we can safely produce as much as possible without worrying about being attacked or disrupted in any way."

"Oh, really? And how do you plan to do that? The place will be a fortress, and that's if Jannis hasn't already carried out his promise of demolishing it," Elton ridiculed.

"Your endless unintelligence astounds me," Kalahar drawled.

Once again, he traced a circle in the air and pressed forwards, this time opening a portal to the storage cellar in which the depleted ingredients and completed bottles of solution were being held.

"Before we go," Elton said, as the vampire gestured them towards the portal, "where do you plan to take us with the supplies? I'm not about to go jumping off to somewhere I don't know anything about."

The vampire hesitated.

"Letham Deregor," he said ominously. The words sent a chill down Elton's spine. "It's a stronghold in which you will be entirely safe. It's remote, beyond the reach of humans. We can prepare in peace, without the constant flow of interruptions."

"And if we refuse to go?" Elton said, stepping away from the portal.

"Then I cannot stop you. But you must know that it is the only way you will truly be safe. And when we finish producing the oil, we can return to Dannos. We can distribute it to those who remain loyal to you. We can fight the beasts as they rise."

Elton glanced uneasily at the portal and its shimmering edges. The cellar was deserted — there was a clear path to the supplies.

"Alright," he finally said. "I will go to your Letham Deregor. But only in the satisfied company of this lot." He gestured to Rosa, Paul and Felix standing idly behind him.

"Well?" Kalahar questioned. "Will you go with him?"

"Haven't got much else to do," Paul said, scratching his head.

"Will you teach me there?" Rosa asked.

"Naturally," Kalahar responded. "And you will make unbelievably fast progress. Trust me."

Rosa shrugged and looked at Felix, who was fiddling with one of his throwing knives.

"I don't trust it," Felix announced.

"You don't trust what, Felix?" Kalahar asked politely.

"Any of it. You, your inconceivable plan, your endless supply of knowledge which for all we know is completely false, just anything that comes out of your mouth. I don't trust any of it."

"Need I remind you that I have supplied you with the recipe to a solution which renders my brethren mortal?" Kalahar seethed. "I do not carry out such an action lightly. But I did it for you."

"And why is that, O generous vampire? Why would you be so selfless? And anyways, how can we be certain that the serum you gave us is in fact what you say it is and not made up?"

"Because I have demonstrated its wretched effects on myself. I cut off my own hand to allow you to produce it, and I will tell you now that we vampires do not often donate our body parts, even if they do regrow!"

"There's not enough evidence," Felix said dismissively. "I want to stay here, in Dannos. I want to go back to the Redhouse and take back what's ours. I want to kill Hortensio and send his knights packing. If you truly are on our side, Kal, you will come with me and help."

Elton, Rosa, and Paul looked expectantly at Kalahar, whose expression was unreadable. He simply sighed.

"I know that this is difficult for you, but I need you all to understand that I've meticulously planned this out. Felix – I bear no ill will towards you or the Redwinter Syndicate. In fact, I respect the incredible way in which you carry out regulated crime. It's not something I thought I would ever see among humans. I have been on this planet for far longer than any of you and I'll be around long after you've turned to dust and been whisked away in the desert breeze. I know what I'm talking about, and if you want to live and return to this city and take it back from the Salyrians, then you must apply patience. Letham Deregor is the safest place in the world and you will have more than enough time to prepare. Its doors will remain open to any of the Syndicate for as long as it stands. That is my pledge."

There was a pause while Felix considered it.

"I will go," Felix decided. "But only on the condition that you tell us what Letham Deregor is – in detail."

"Very well," Kalahar quickly concluded. "Letham Deregor is an ancient vampire stronghold. There are others there – lesser vampires who have foregone their desire for blood. They bow to me. The stronghold itself is located many thousands of miles from here, across the ocean to the West and nested in a coastal forest, shielded by Valoria's eastern mountain range, known as the World's End. It is, as I've said, far from human civilisation. And it is safe."

"You never mentioned that there would be others," Felix scolded. "Why didn't you mention that?"

"Because it is unimportant. The safety of Letham Deregor would remain the same whether there were other vampires there or not. In fact, if you want even more details, then here's one: there's already another human there. And they've been there for a couple weeks, now. He hails from a southern Valorian country, and so does not speak your language, but there are ways around language barriers that we can manipulate in our favour. Now, I have no more secrets and I plead that you come with me. For your own sakes."

Felix was still making up his mind when they heard shouts followed by heavy, metallic footsteps clanking up the stairs at speed.

"There they are!" the knights called, thundering towards them while drawing their swords. Kalahar made the executive decision to grab Felix and thrust him through the portal before jumping through himself. The others were quick to follow and Kalahar immediately sealed the portal once they had all passed through.

"I'll open another portal now – get the crates and push them through."

The vampire's arms extended, and he looked oddly comedic as his elongated limbs traced a new, larger portal the width of the room. He retracted his arms and helped the others with the crates, which he chose to levitate across the room, doing a fantastic job at making their exhausted grunting look pathetic.

The last crate was hauled through the portal and Kalahar made a show of telekinetically lifting every single stored bottle of solution, passing them through the portal, walking through himself, and neatly placing them down on the other side.

It was cold. In Lazeria, Elton thought it had been cold. It was enough there for goosebumps to colonise his skin. Letham Deregor was colder.

They had landed in a storage cellar much like that beneath the Redhouse, only greyer. Unlike the cellar beneath the Redhouse, this cellar was not beneath the building. It had a window – a large window, supported by intricately carved stone pillars resembling bars in a jail cell. Through the window blew the icy breeze which refrigerated the entire room. It was clear that Paul and Felix were equally affected – they were shivering together in a corner which must have been warmer than anywhere else, and they didn't look like they planned to move. Rosa, having studied at the Lazerian sorceresses' convent, dealt with it somewhat better.

"Goodness me, humans' weaknesses know no boundaries," Kalahar ranted. "Here, hold this."

He reached for an unlit wall sconce and handed it to Elton, whose quivering arm struggled to take it. A snap of his fingers and its tip burst into flame, providing a valuable source of warmth for the shivering desert dwellers and a source of light for the blackened corridors they could see leading away from the storage room.

"Come, I must show you around, you really mustn't miss anything!" the vampire said enthusiastically while Felix and Paul fought over who held their hands closest to the fire. Kalahar rolled his eyes and snapped his fingers again, causing the flame to briefly explode in size and nearly searing both of them. They shot the vampire a glare as icy as the perceived

350

temperature of the stone fortress and sauntered over to the doorway through which the vampire intended to take them, not removing their attention from the delightfully warm fire of the torch.

"Why's it so dark?" Felix asked, squinting in an attempt to see anything past the pathetic range of the torchlight.

"One of the first questions asked by the other human," Kalahar chuckled. "We vampires can see in the dark. Rosa, did you reach that stage?"

"Indeed I did," Rosa proudly said. "Es tar fla'kadarr."

Rosa's eyes began to glow a soft yellow, much like those of a cat's in the middle of the night.

"Impressive," Kalahar said. "The sorceresses taught you one of the least efficient night vision spells. What in the land were you paying for?"

"Hey, it works," she snapped. "Inefficient or not, I can see better than these bumbling fools."

"Es tar an'dak'revvar," the vampire uttered. The torch suddenly lost half of its use – the three men could now see every surface, nook, and crevice as if they were basking in the noon's sun on a cloudless summer day. And their eyes remained physically unchanged.

"Bloody show-off," Rosa grumbled.

Letham Deregor was a maze and they had no choice but to follow Kalahar's every movement, otherwise they would risk being lost forever. Everything looked exactly the same – the same stone brick structure, the same intricate carvings along the top sections of the walls, the same recurrent pillars holding up the higher parts of the roof. As a building, Elton thought its design was frankly outrageous and it ought to be demolished and rebuilt with some semblance of a reasonable layout. The vampire was evidently reading his thoughts and said that they had no need to demolish the building, for they knew how to navigate it. And that if Elton didn't know how to navigate it, that very much worked in their favour.

They arrived at a long corridor lined with round-topped wooden doors embedded into the wall. Kalahar missed the first one and showed them into the second, which turned out to be a bedroom.

"I thought vampires didn't sleep?" Paul said.

351

"We don't. But we plan for everything," Kalahar pompously responded. "One of those planned occurrences is the housing of a creature which requires sleep. And look where we've found ourselves."

"You make us sound like guinea pigs," Elton spat.

"What can I say? You're humans. I suppose it's a reasonable comparison. However, a guinea pig does not receive luxuriously furnished chambers when being kept for the purpose of an experiment. They're lucky to have dry hay. So stop complaining."

The bedroom was more than any of them had expected. Paul made a beeline for the exquisitely opulent duvet and made no effort at politeness when he dived into the bed's depths and made himself comfortable.

"I could fall right asleep just like this," he exclaimed. "Are you sayin' that you vamps don't even get pleasure outta this?"

"We do not, indeed, find pleasure in sleep. If we ever are to sleep, it will be within an enchanted coffin for the purpose of sleeping through troubled times or merely to provide the illusion of time passing faster than is true."

"Ahah! So you do sleep in coffins! Some of the superstitions are right!"

"Indeed, some of the superstitions are true. Because funnily enough, all superstitions are based on a truth. There is no such thing as original thought – everything has its roots. Superstitions have their roots based in truths of varying significance, and then through passing down of superstitions through generations, those truths are buried. Until they are so inconceivably deep within the earth that they are lost forever."

Paul looked at the vampire, dumbfounded. Kalahar sighed and looked at the other three.

"It appears he has claimed this room as his own. I shall provide the three of you with your own."

"Why did we skip the first room?" Elton asked.

"Is it not evident? Have I failed to mention the other human living here?"

"You know, Kal," Elton said, furrowing his brow. "You may be some super-intelligent, all-powerful vampire, but in your appearance I see a human. You have your roots, just like the truths you lectured us about. And your roots are human. So insult us all you like – you're only insulting your roots."

"Don't make me laugh," the vampire dismissed. "I'm different. I have no roots. And if I do, they're certainly not human. Now, acquaint yourselves with your new rooms and I will return in a quarter of an hour."

As they stood in the corridor, three of the bedroom doors simultaneously creaked open and Kalahar vanished. Rosa chose to take the furthest one, while the other two were indifferent about who had to sleep adjacent to Paul.

Elton closed the door behind him, having chosen the room adjacent to Rosa, and allowed himself to take in the room's facilities and furnishings. It was more than he had expected – for once, the vampire hadn't exaggerated. The bed was more than spacious enough for two whole people and exhibited craftsmanship worthy of a master carpenter's approval, carvings worthy of a master artist's. There was more than enough space in the wardrobe for his gambeson and underlying chainmail. A small set of shelves proved a convenient location to conceal his dagger. He walked over to the desk and took a look at the collection of unintelligible books splayed across it. The leather-bound covers were coated in a layer of dust. It had what looked like a single word written on it in gold text, but the writing looked more like pictures, rather than the letters to which he was accustomed. The yellowed pages of their interiors bore more of the intricately written picture-like letters, hundreds of them on every page. It looked like it must have been a lot of effort.

If the room was missing anything, it was a fireplace. No matter what Kalahar had said about being prepared for anything, he had forgotten the crucial need for warmth, or at least the different expectations of normal temperature. The cold intrigued Elton to find information appertaining to their location, which a door on the other side of the room conveniently allowed. He only stood on the balcony for a minute before retreating to the relative warmth of inside, the wind having thoroughly pilfered any remaining heat from his body. Before going back inside, however, he was astonished to discover a view of both snow-capped mountains and the ocean glowing with moonlight. Surrounding them was dense coniferous forest and the vampire certainly hadn't lied about the remoteness of the fortress. It was a serene scene, the silence only interrupted by the whistling of the wind.

He decided to take after Paul for the remaining minutes until Kalahar undoubtedly wrenched them away to look at something else. The bedsheets, although no higher quality than those at his home in Dannos, were indisputably more comfortable, almost magically so. It then occurred that they probably were. That thought then irked him enough to rise from the bed and sit instead at the desk, in the comparably less comfortable wooden seat.

Elton continued to sit there, pondering, until the door swung open by itself, stopping short of collision with the wall. He sighed and sauntered outside, where the expected vampire was waiting. Rosa and Felix joined them – Paul did not.

"We'd better check on him," Felix suggested.

Elton peered around the doorframe and looked instantly to the bed, where Paul had fallen sound asleep, snoring at a volume comparable to cannon fire.

"Let him sleep," Elton said, grabbing the door handle and pulling it closed. "It's deserved."

"He is the stupid one, anyways, so I don't suppose he'd be interested in the next bit. On our way!" the vampire cheerily replied.

Elton sighed and trudged behind the vampire as he strode off into the labyrinth of corridors they called a stronghold.

They arrived in what Kalahar called the atrium. At the centre of the open room was a pentagram etched onto the floor in chalk, each of its points occupied by an unlit candle.

"Now I'm seeing more of the satanic sides of vampirism," Elton mused.

"Satanic we are not, dear Elton – the pentagram is a terribly effective intensifier," Kalahar said. "Who knows why, but it holds magical significance, and many things can be done from within one. In fact, something is being done right now, although you cannot see it. Step into the centre of the pentagram, I insist."

Elton warily stepped into the centre of the unassuming chalk-drawn shape and nothing happened. He looked expectantly at the vampire who merely shrugged and gestured for him to walk back from the confines of the pentagram.

Kalahar snapped his fingers and the candles lit up. A person simultaneously appeared in the centre of the shape – she had almost white skin, paler than Kalahar's, and bright auburn hair, a trait unknown in North Santeros.

"Why the bloody hell did you do that? I was watching him!" the woman complained. She brushed her hair behind her ears and revealed them to end in points.

"What's he up to?" Kalahar inquired.

"Before I was rudely wrangled away, I was about to watch him take down a stag. It would have been an excellent display."

"Take down a stag? Surely that's rather simple?"

"You would think, but he's using a bow and arrow. No magic at all, in fact – no muffling, no distractions, no anything. He only does it when you leave."

"Typical. Elton, Rosa, Felix, meet Faefion. She is one of the few lesser vampires proficient in magic."

The elf-vampire smiled warmly and stood up. She stepped out of the pentagram, extinguishing the candles.

"I've been told a lot. Especially about you, Mr Redwinter."

"Should I be proud?" Elton asked disinterestedly.

"Well, when Kalahar obsesses over something, there's always ample reason for it. So yes, I would be proud."

"That's difficult, as Kal said that we would be coming here to prepare for the eclipse. He's yet to explain what is going to happen with that. It's incredible visiting this place, but frankly, I have things I need to do. Kalahar, when are we going to move on?"

"Some people really have misguided senses of urgency," Kalahar remarked. "Let your troubles go, Elton. You will achieve nothing through unrestrained stress and panic. Trust yourself to make the right decisions and end up with the optimal outcome. Because that will be what happens."

"That's it. I've had enough!" Elton roared. "I've put up with your drivel time and time again. Ever since that dreadful day I met you, you've done nothing but fuck up my life in every

355

way imaginable. I've lost my fortune, I've lost my business and I've managed to travel halfway across the bloody world to end up in some freezing castle with a load of bloodsuckers who advocate for the destruction of their adversaries. I'm trying to do the right thing, and make the right decisions, but you do nothing except stand in my way and elongate the entire process. If you brought us here to be safe while we prepare, then allow us to prepare in safety! I have no desire to hear your ramblings about the history of this building, the magical magnificence of a pentagram or how I should go about organising my thoughts!"

Faefion's cheerful expression dropped from her face and she looked wordlessly to Kalahar, who seemed to understand everything she hadn't said. Meanwhile, Felix and Rosa stepped away from the vampires and assumed a defensive stance behind Elton.

"It appears we are at an impasse," Kalahar remarked. "Unnecessarily so, I might add. Very well – I shall take you to the laboratory. You will be left in peace to work. In fact, you may take yourselves to the laboratory."

He waved his hand in their direction and granted them the complete knowledge of Letham Deregor's layout. It was even grander than he had first comprehended it to be, with a number of seemingly useless floors deep underground in addition to those which towered above the surface.

At last, Kalahar kept his promise. For the next few days, the only times they saw him was when he wordlessly brought them food and water and then promptly disappeared. He still taught Rosa, but in private, in a different part of the stronghold to where they prepared the oil. They never met the other human that allegedly lived there, even though he was supposed to be living in the same corridor as them.

There was a chill in the air. Elton slowly rose from his bed, rubbing his sleep-encrusted eyes. Rain thundered against the windows and balcony door. Elton walked to his window and thunder boomed overhead as he watched a bolt of lightning strike a tree in the distance.

"It's time," he said to himself.

CHAPTER 38

When Alazarioss claimed that they had found the origin of Tregor's communication, Elaeínn was sceptical – because all she could see were pine trees, snow-topped mountains, and the ocean.

The weather had taken a turn for the worse as Alazarioss had flown south. Cold rain sliced her face and had soaked her thoroughly to the bone. Her hair, normally kept relatively tidy, had been reduced to a wet, dishevelled mop. She was freezing, but she gritted her teeth and endured it.

Alazarioss had carried Kíra's dead body in her claws for the entire journey, despite questioning Elaeínn's motives at first. She wasn't quite sure what she would do yet, she just hoped she would find someone who would be of some use.

As they careened over a hill, Alazarioss undeterred by the wind's ferocity, something unnatural finally came into view. In the distance, situated near the oceanside, was a cubic stone structure.

We've just passed Tregor's position from which he spoke to Lynn, Alazarioss stated.

I'm hedging my bets on him having gone to whatever this place is ahead of us. Come on, let's land on the roof.

357

CHAPTER 39

LETHAM DEREGOR

Elton quickly dressed and retrieved his dagger from the drawer in which it had been stowed since they arrived, sliding it firmly into the sheath on his back.

"Hey, Paul, Rosa, Felix, get up!" he shouted, storming from the room. "We need to leave!"

Paul, Rosa, and Felix failed to appear. Instead, the first door creaked open and produced a pale man with loose, pine-bark hair, bow and quiver in hand. They locked eyes and he slung his quiver across his back, keeping the bow in hand.

"Are you—" Elton began, but the man stopped him.

"Hablar Arcaea," he whispered. Then he extended his hand. "Richard Ordowyn."

"Elton Redwinter," he responded. "Are you the other human Kal was on about?"

"If he rambled about another human living here at some point, then I would assume so. And he's talked about you – you're the leader of the Syndicate, is it? In Temerios?"

"Yes," Elton confirmed. "But the Syndicate is lost. I was betrayed, and I lost everything. I don't even know why I'm still here. I shouldn't care about whether some bloody vampires run rampant across a land I once called home. Bah, I'm being irrational. I've lost Dannos, is what I've lost. The Syndicate stretches beyond Dannos. I have more to fight for. Why are you here, Richard Ordowyn?"

"I'm apparently what they call the Fateborn. In short, I have magical powers that they don't. And they're teaching me how to use them. I've been tasked with eliminating the vampires on this continent."

358

"Is that it? What do you get out of it?"

Richard's eyes locked to the floor.

"Hope," he said. "At the moment, only hope. Hope that Kalahar knows what he's talking about. And, I guess, a place to live."

"Rise and shine, feeble mortals!" Kalahar said cheerily, striding into the corridor and clapping his hands.

"I think you'll find that I've already tried that," Elton scorned.

"Yes, but you haven't tried this," Kalahar said.

With a dramatic swing of his arm, the doors to each remaining room swung open and noisily crashed into the adjacent wall. Felix and Rosa could be heard cursing in harmony from within their rooms, while only snoring escaped from Paul. Rosa's door slammed shut again with exceptional force, sending tremors throughout the corridor.

Elton leaned into the room in which Paul could be seen fast asleep, one arm hanging over the side of the bed, a strand of saliva dangling from his open mouth.

"Paul!" he shouted.

"Ehh?" Paul gurgled, beginning to show signs of stirring.

"Get up, you lazy oaf! The time has come! We're going back to Temerios!"

"Fuckin' 'ell, I'm still not used to this time change," he complained.

"Get over it and get dressed and ready. If you're not used to the time change, that will suit you when we go back to our own continent."

"Richard, are you ready?" Kalahar asked the modestly dressed Fateborn.

"I believe I am," Richard confirmed. "When are you going to tell me where she is?"

"In due course, dear Richard. In due course. You must complete your task first."

A groggy Felix stumbled out of his room, completely dressed and making an effort to remain conscious. Rosa joined them a moment later, much livelier and more composed.

"Who's this?" Felix asked.

"Hablar Arcaea," the man uttered again, this time directing the spell at Felix. "Richard Ordowyn," he provided, offering his hand, which Felix shook. "I'm a bounty hunter."

"And, more importantly, the Fateborn," Kalahar reminded.

"I've got magical powers. Big ones," Richard unenthusiastically explained.

After enough fumbling around, everyone was ready. They were preparing to go to the storage room when a sound they thought was thunder split the sky. But thunder didn't strike fear into the heart. This sound did.

"What in the seven hells—" Kalahar muttered, striding straight through Elton's room without a second glance, heading straight for the balcony. He opened the door and allowed it to flail around in the wind and rain as he rushed through the doorway. He didn't look back, and his eyes remained fixated on whatever was outside. His feet remained firmly planted and had the wind not rustled his hair and clothes quite so vigorously, he would have passed for a statue.

"What the bloody hell is he looking at?" Elton asked, walking over to join him.

He understood why Kalahar was so shocked.

Soaring overhead like a physical manifestation of a bolt of lightning was a great winged lizard. It roared again and let loose a torrent of aquamarine flame. It dived down towards the lonely stone stronghold and it was then that Elton noticed it wasn't alone. Along the ridge of its back was a rider.

By now everyone had squeezed onto the tiny balcony and they were all equally as awestruck as the vampire, who had regained his composure and floated from the edge of the balcony to allow more space for the others.

"I imagine it will have to land on the roof. Come on, jump through here!" Kalahar called, briefly opening a portal at the balcony's edge. They routinely climbed over the balcony railing and into the portal, where the weather really made itself felt. Heavy drops of rain lashed their faces, wind permeated every unbound crevice across their bodies. They had to squint to be able to see at all.

The dragon unexpectedly swooped low and almost knocked them off their feet. It circled around and landed surprisingly gently against the stone roof, sending tremors of much weaker intensity than any of them had expected.

"Kal," Elton finally broke the silence. "That's a—"

"Vos'kanath," Kalahar mouthed. "A dragon."

Now that the dragon had landed, the group had a clearer view of its rider – an elf bearing no resemblance to Faefion other than her identically pointed ears. That being said, the elf-woman was taller than Elton, Rosa and Felix. They received an even clearer look when she jumped down from the dragon's back and walked confidently towards her eager observers.

"Kaen'a," she said, her expression indicating that she knew none of them could understand her.

Kalahar strolled towards the elf, who assumed a defensive stance and took a few steps back towards the dragon. But she did not turn away. The vampire slowly extended a hand in a display of truce, and she seemed to understand.

"Hablar Arcaea," he muttered. "Now we can understand one another."

"I am Elaeínn Tinaíd of Sanaíd," the elf promptly began. "This is Alazarioss."

"What the fuck is that thing?" Paul blurted, now experiencing a close-up view of the dragon.

"That thing," the elf-woman called Elaeínn spat, glaring at the bald thief, "is a dragon. She has the power to incinerate all of you in moments. It's in your best interests to maintain respect."

"Before we continue, may I insist that we continue our business where it is warm, dry and quiet?" Kalahar interjected. "It would be terribly tedious to have to listen to you all fight to be heard against the wind."

Elaeínn looked back at the dragon, whose expression remained unchanged. But the elf still apparently received some form of understanding.

"Take us inside, then," she agreed.

Kalahar nimbly traced a circular portal in the floor. Elaeínn looked distrustful, and rightfully so – the visible exit to the portal was completely dark. The vampire stepped through and they watched him through the shimmering circle as he gestured to the braziers, sconces, and chandeliers around the room, basking the central dining table in light. She then took charge of being the first to enter the portal.

"Take your seats, one and all," Kalahar said. "I could even rustle up something for you all to eat, should it be necessary. In fact, there are others that can do that for me. I wouldn't dare miss a meeting with an elf who appears from nowhere astride a dragon."

"Can someone please explain what's going on here, and why the physical manifestation of evil is lecturing me like my old teachers?" the elf interjected.

"I assure you, I'm not evil," Kalahar insisted between hushed words with a lesser vampire who had seemingly appeared from nowhere. "This is my natural appearance as a chaotic vampire. Most vampires bear my skin colour, but only malevolents share eyes similar to mine. However, should I ever care to, I can do this."

The vampire made a show of covering his eyes, and when he revealed them again, Elton audibly gasped. Not from horror, but from shock. Because they looked entirely normal. The bright, gemstone-like eyeballs had been replaced by white eyeballs with cinnamon irises and unsuspectingly normal-sized pupils. Meanwhile, the elf was only mildly shocked.

"Behold, the eyes of Rafio Benito," Kalahar said. Elton, Rosa, Paul, Felix, and Richard in particular couldn't tear their eyes away. "These were the eyes I wore for years before that man there—" he pointed to Elton, "—killed me. Of course, he didn't kill me, because nobody can. But it was convincing enough that I could no longer exist as Rafio Benito. And that series of events led us here. Now, that's enough of that."

His eyes swiftly reverted to their normal ruby-like appearance and he cast his attention to the new arrival.

"Elaeínn Tinaíd," he reiterated. "I am Kalahar Kefrein-Lazalar. Of no particular origin."

"Kalahar," Elaeínn started, "I came here in search of a Tregor, with the hopes of finding you through him. I need your help."

"Let's begin with introductions, first, hmm? It's like this: you are guests at the vampire stronghold of Letham Deregor,

362

overlooking the sea through a gap in the Valorian World's End Mountains. Those you see at this table are from different origins: Richard Ordowyn, the whiter fellow, was a bounty hunter from the southern Valorian nation of Mirados. He has since discovered that he is the Fateborn, and now he learns to harness his abilities here. The others you see are Elton, Paul, Felix, and Rosa. Elton is the fat one, Paul the bald one and Felix, by process of elimination, is the other one. Rosa is also training in magic at this stronghold, and I must say, she was wasting her time in Lazeria. They must not have been teaching her, because in only a few days she has progressed leaps and bounds.

"I'm rambling – they are all here for a reason. And you haven't hesitated to inform us that you are as well, Elaeínn Tinaíd. Tell us – why do you expect to find the person you seek with us? Why do you seek him?"

"The dragon, Alazarioss, has told us how magic is being corrupted by those who make use of lirenium crystals. We were told by Lynn Varanus to search for you."

"Lynn Varanus – loyal to the Council, last I remember. Are you aware that she was among those who tried to abduct Richard?"

"I was not, nor was I aware that anyone had ever tried to abduct Richard. But we visited the Council and it was in shambles. There were three at their little hideout – Denzel, Lynn and Ríyael, two of which are now dead, and Lynn played her part in that. Lynn now seeks out her family to help me in my cause, because she feels betrayed. We collected Denzel, Lynn and Ríyael's crystals. But we cannot stop until we collect them all, and that is why we were advised to come to you. Because Lynn says that you killed Olga Feragaard, who was also in possession of a lirenium crystal. And that you would be able to help us find the others."

The vampire eased himself into a seat beside Elton, who had eagerly listened to the entire conversation, genuinely interested in something the vampire had to say for once.

"I did kill Olga Feragaard. I did not, however, collect her lirenium crystal. It was of no use to me. So I left it with her corpse. If anyone is likely to have it, it will be Nendar Varanus.

363

Lynn's father. After all, it was a Sanskari institution where we left her body."

"Lynn said she was going to talk to him and her sister."

Elton noticed that at the mention of her sister, Richard crossed his arms and assumed a brooding expression across the table.

"If that is the case, then I would trust her to do her job. Lynn was very persuasive, in her own way. Now, you haven't come to me just to ask for Olga's crystal, have you?"

"I have not. I still require the crystals of Tregor and Kasimir. I request your assistance in locating them, for even Alazarioss has proved incapable of doing so. And then engaging with them, because Lynn has made it clear that they won't be quite as simple to deal with as the others. Alazarioss did manage to track Tregor – to here. But he was nowhere to be seen, and we found you instead."

"I would love to help you, my dear, I really would. And knowing that old Tregor Lopan is confident enough to approach Letham Deregor really does interest me. And perhaps, in due time, I can help you. But there are more pressing matters at hand, starting with today. Elton – I will leave it up to you to explain while I... I search for Hallen, who appears to have forgotten how to fetch f-food. Though I'm sure you can forgive h-him – none of us have ever n-needed to."

Kalahar vanished and Elaeínn blinked a few times to make sure she was believing what she was seeing.

"Did he just start stuttering? Whatever. Alright, Elae-however you pronounce your name. A month—"

"Elaeínn," the elf enunciated.

"Whatever. A while ago, I came home to find that obnoxious waste of space. He introduced himself rather violently as Kalahar Kefrein-Lazalar, a vampire. And he prophesied that come one month's time, we would be facing a total solar eclipse, which he claims only happen once every hundreds of years. And these solar eclipses, if Kalahar is to be believed, cast a curse on those born on the day of the eclipse. Babies born naturally become lesser vampires, which aren't what we're worried about. We're worried about malevolent vampires, the product of a slain pregnant mother. They are the violent ones – he says they're capable of razing not just towns, but cities.

And they will be rising today. For today marks one month since my first encounter with the beast."

"If you had told me this before I met Alazarioss, I wouldn't have believed you," the elf stated. "But in the past month, there have been a number of things I wouldn't have ever believed would happen. Now, what are we supposed to do?"

"Well, the organisation I run back in Temerios – a continent in the West – we've been preparing. We have vast reserves of a specially brewed oil which we're supposed to apply to silver blades. The oil renders the vampires vulnerable to silver, and the silver kills them. In truth, I have no idea about the other continents."

"I'm going to deal with the ones in Valoria," Richard provided. "I can do it with my magic."

"Okay, then, that leaves you, elf. What land do you hail from?"

"The continent of Fenalia," she answered. "If what you're saying is true, this could be bad. My homeland is about to be engulfed in war. We really don't need something else to make our lives more difficult."

"That dragon on the roof," Elton began. "Is it powerful? Could it not obliterate any vampires? I don't know whether it's a magical creature, but I would have thought dragonfire, if anything like it is in legend, would be hot enough to melt vampire."

Elaeínn didn't say anything, instead appearing to be focusing intently on the tablecloth. Elton refrained from asking her about it.

"Alazarioss says she can destroy them," she confirmed, finally drawing her eyes away from the tablecloth which Elton had concluded she wasn't the centre of her focus. "You say this is happening today?"

"That's correct. Though I believe it will only be visible in my part of Temerios."

"If vampires are going to rise today, then we need to move fast!" Elaeínn prompted. "Why aren't we going?"

"Because," Elton sighed, "Kalahar is bringing us food. And he would be most distraught if we were to leave before that."

"That's ridiculous, we need to go!" she snapped. "Kalahar can bring us all the food he wants, but I refuse to eat it while such a threat hangs over our heads! I'm going back to Tyen'Ael right now!"

She rose from her seat at the very moment a different vampire returned to the room with two silver platters covered with an assortment of different delicacies, from squares of delicately cut salmon to glacé cherries to a coarse, black substance which Elton thought looked more like ashes than food.

"Caviar?" Elaeínn asked. "Why do you have all this lying around?"

"Kalahar likes to be well-stocked, even when we don't need it," the vampire responded, with a hint of dissidence.

"Well, I would love to stay and indulge, but I'm going this instant. Unless any of you vampires have any experience in resurrection, I could do with that."

"It's not my place to stop you," the vampire stated.

"Everyone was acting so lazily about it; I didn't understand the urgency of the situation," she continued. "But now I do. Thank you for the hospitality, but I really must go."

She said nothing afterwards, only walking to the nearest window and jumping out. They heard the dragon roar and watched as it flew off into the distance.

CHAPTER 40

Berri stood atop the northern tower of the abandoned castle. When the dwarves had directed them to it, he had thought it resembled rubble, rather than a castle. But a swift restoration had brought it back to life, and it was flourishing.

A successful propaganda campaign meant that the courtyard below was full of new recruits, mainly from the South, where dwarves were a far more common sight than in the North – and on the flipside, authorities were far less common. Berri had made a point of speaking to each of them individually when they arrived at Fallía, the name he had designated to their new base. *Freedom.*

"Any luck with contacting Elaeínn?" Delíen asked, appearing from the stairwell. He had been promoted to the rank of general when construction began, and now Berri entrusted him with oversight of training the new recruits.

"None, but she can't use magic," Berri responded sharply. "And I've not been able to reach Kíra, either. Complete silence. Meanwhile, Jaelaar has returned to Sanaíd, without any ships and half his crew missing. And we've heard nothing from Caeran or Aegard since they told us about Elaeínn's visit."

"Elaeínn knew about this project," Delíen said. "You don't think—"

"No, I don't," Berri cut him off. "Elaeínn was one of our most passionate fighters. I see no way that that could possibly be the case."

"Have you tried directly contacting Caeran? He and Elle were close. He might not have thought to inform you."

"I have," Berri sighed. "And I received no response."

CHAPTER 41

LETHAM DEREGOR

The food went largely untouched.

"Don't you have any proper food?" Paul complained, carelessly grabbing some of the powder-like food the elf had called caviar and closely examining it in his hand. The vampire ignored him.

"I take it you'll soon follow her lead," the vampire suggested.

"Her lead?" Elton questioned. "Are you implying we should be doing the same? After all the deliberation your master caused? In fact, where is Kalahar?"

"I'm afraid I can't help you. Kalahar likes for his location to remain secret unless he has given explicit permission to share it."

"Fucking hell," Richard muttered.

"In that case," Elton pronounced, "I want to go back to Temerios. I want to supply all our locations and I want to be ready to fight. You can help me with that, vampire. Even if you're not Kalahar."

"Very well. And you, bounty hunter? What will you do?"

"Something I really wish I didn't have to," Richard drawled. "But I do."

"Very well. Elton, I will teleport you to Temerios now."

Elton didn't have a say in choosing the method or timeframe of transportation to the storage room. The vampire forcefully teleported him, Rosa, Paul, and Felix there.

"Devious little bastard. He's just left us on our own."

"I can open portals," Rosa said. "But I'll need your prior knowledge of the locations."

"Take whatever you want from my head. We need these distributed equally between our locations in Santhion, Veye-nia, Thorne and... not Dannos. That's remarkably few, now that I speak it aloud."

"There are plenty of other locations. We'll be working hard for the next few hours."

"In that case, we'd better not waste any more time."

Rosa extended a hand towards Elton's head and muttered a spell before opening a portal in the wall, leading to a dingy, unremarkable cellar. It would be the first of many portals and many dingy, unremarkable cellars.

And in under an hour, those cellars were adequately filled with enough oil to slay hordes upon hordes of rampaging vampires.

Elton stood at the peak of one of the towers of Fort Red-winter, a rundown, abandoned castle he had purchased a number of years ago from the Veyenian throne to become his base of operations in South Benetia. Until three years ago, it was operated under the management of a Dannosi man Elton had sent personally. He had since died of old age, and a South Benetian man had taken over the job and done a better job than Elton would have expected. The castle flourished, reno-vated to a point where it looked as if it had only just been built and lacking nothing in terms of wealth. The man who had taken over, Altio Verez, stood with Elton, and they watched together as the light of the day dimmed and shadows crawled over the surrounding grasslands and stretching highway.

"It's time," Elton stated.

"We're ready, Mr Redwinter," Altio said.

"I'd bloody hope so," Elton responded, slowly unsheathing his specially crafted silver dagger. "We've certainly got no op-portunities to falter."

CHAPTER 42

"Milord, there is someone here to see you."

"Who is it?"

"I-I don't know, milord. He never gave me his name. He just appeared."

"What?" Nendar said, averting his attention from his desk and subsequently spilling his tea over its side.

"Nendar!" the intruder called, turning the corner and pushing the servant out of the way. Nendar raised his eyebrows in surprise.

"Fateborn. I didn't expect to see you again. Surrendering yourself from the vampire?"

He shooed the servant from the room and she obeyed without hesitation, though looking somewhat flustered.

"I am still working with Kalahar and I'm not surrendering to anyone. I've come to ask for your help."

"My help?" Nendar ridiculed. "You, the Miradosi insurrectionist, want to ask for my help? I must say, that's rich."

"Leave politics out of this. This is about survival. Both the survival of Mirados and the Empire."

"What has Kalahar been filling your head with? False prophecies through which he intends to manipulate you into giving him power? He's a dangerous creature, Fateborn. You should distance yourself from him as soon and far as possible."

"Bold words coming from one who intended to 'convert' me. Kalahar has taught me how to wield the power I possess. You have done nothing but invade my home as a man and in-

371

vade my mind as a mage. But these are differences I am willing to set aside as I ask for your help. I need you to call a truce."

"Bounty hunter," Nendar spoke slowly. "I'm sure your intentions, whatever they may be, are noble. But you have been tricked. That vampire excels at telling half-truths, to give the impression of honesty. Whatever he has told you, it will be partially correct. But there's something more that he isn't telling you. And as I don't trust Kalahar, I'm afraid I cannot call a truce. Because I may be a sorcerer, but I will always be the Emperor of Sanskar. And I cannot risk looking weak."

"You can disagree all you like, but there's no denying that today will wreak havoc on the continent if you don't intervene. You're the most powerful man for thousands of miles and if the fighting continues, it's guaranteed to produce swathes of malevolent vampires. War is evil, and soldiers immoral dogs. You and I both know this – if the fighting doesn't stop, civilians will be caught up in it."

"So today is the day of the eclipse," Nendar concluded. "I see."

He rose from his chair, setting aside his empty mug and snapping his fingers. The flustered servant rushed back in with a towel and cleaned up the spillage before immediately rushing back out.

"You cannot trust Kalahar," Nendar quietly, but firmly, reasserted. He stood no further than a foot away. "If today is the day of the eclipse, then you are right, Richard. There will be terror and destruction. But there is something else that he hasn't told you about eclipses. Total solar eclipses."

Nendar backed away, but his eyes remained trained on the bounty hunter.

"Total solar eclipses do curse those born on the day to vampirism. And they do curse the wombs of slain pregnant women. By the end of the day, populations will have been slaughtered. But we will keep them under control, because I will help you. Myself, Valerie, and Lynn. But know this, Richard. When I still believed in the strength and unity of the Council, I wanted to track down the Fateborn to provide you to them. Then I began to lose faith, prioritising the Empire. I still wanted to track you down. Do you know why? Not just because of your immense capabilities, but because before Kalahar trained you, your mind was malleable. I could have turned you to our side with force. That is no longer a possibility."

"So what's there to worry—"

"However," Nendar interrupted. "Kalahar has omitted a handful of crucial details about his species when explaining to you. For example, that throughout the duration of the magical influence of a total eclipse, the power of every vampire across the world heightens. Dramatically. Including your Kalahar."

"How so?"

"I take it you have experimented with your powers. Tell me – what is the biggest achievement you've pulled off?"

"I created a dimension, like I've been constantly told I would be able to. I closed said dimension. It was little more than strenuous."

"As I expected. Kalahar is guiding you, but not towards your true potential. Oh, no, no, no. He's misleading you. There is plenty more you can achieve with the pent-up magical energy you hold within yourself. Plenty more than opening and closing dimensional gateways. But he would never tell you that. Nor teach you how to do anything that would jeopardise his plans."

"Are you suggesting he has some sort of grand plan? This all sounds very conspiratorial."

"It does. But you haven't outright denied it to be the case because you know that the vampire is a lying scamp. He purposefully appears irritating and indecisive to give the impression that he's harmless. But that couldn't be further from the truth."

"I would hardly say he pretends to be harmless," Richard defended, crossing his arms.

"Is that right? He's deceptive, Richard. He flashes his dark magic in your face every now and again to make you think he's a vicious creature of the undead, but he hides his true abilities. Conjuring a blade is far from his limit. What is his limit, you might ask? You. Controlling you."

"You said that my mind was malleable before he trained me. He has since trained me. Surely that contradicts your foreseeable claim about him wanting to control me?"

"He has lived on this planet for numerous years, Richard. He has mastered the art of patience. He has trained you in order to gain your trust. To make you believe his deception. And when the eclipse occurs and heightens his powers, his first move will be to seek you out and carry out the very conversion that Valerie and I attempted when she captured you."

Nendar stepped closer again and stared directly into the bounty hunter's indifferent eyes.

"Valerie, Lynn, and I will help you, bounty hunter. We will help you. Not Kalahar. And I suggest you apply a similar method of thinking. Save yourself, Fateborn. Do not allow yourself to become a plaything of the vampire."

Nendar clapped his hands and the sound echoed around the spacious chamber. Two rifts appeared, and from each stepped a different, though remarkably physically alike, daughter of Nendar Varanus.

Valerie gazed at Richard and he returned her look with an icy glare, which the other two Varanuses noticed and about which refrained from commenting.

"I'm afraid Valerie and I are going to have to hold onto our lirenium crystals for at least the remainder of today, Lynn," Nendar stated. "We've got a vampire uprising to quell."

CHAPTER 43

Upon entering, the snow left on his hunting jacket melted immediately in the comforting heat of the fire roaring in the hearth.

"Master Ordowyn! A pleasure to see you again!" the innkeeper beamed, setting down a tankard he had been in the process of scrubbing. "What brings you here again?"

"Board up the tavern," Richard gravely instructed. "Put out the fire. You can't let there be any sign of life."

"What's this about?" the innkeeper asked, his happiness faltering. "What's going on?"

"A catastrophe," Richard mumbled.

The door swung open to produce a detachment of Miradosi soldiers. The captain, recognisable by his golden rose badge, met eyes with Richard and crossed his arms.

"Master Ordowyn. It's been some time."

"It has. I apologise for not bringing you evidence of the bandits' elimination, but I killed them. There was then a series of unforeseen events which followed. I wasn't able to bring you his head as a result."

"It's my duty to investigate suspicious activity in these times. Where did you go after our meeting, bounty hunter?"

"My business is my own. I killed the bandits for free – you owe me my privacy."

"We owe you gratitude, Master Ordowyn. But nothing more. But there is someone else we owe further gratitude to. Our new suitors."

The soldiers drew their swords in unison, the screeching of steel drowning out the crackling of the fire in the hearth. The innkeeper didn't think twice before hiding under the bar.

"Traitors," Richard hissed, drawing his own sword.

"I suggest you turn yourself over without a fight, Master Ordowyn. That way we won't have to wade through blood to claim our share of the innkeeper's profits."

Richard twirled his sword around, holding it across his body.

"Not on your life, faithless dogs. You betrayed your king and your country. Your heads belong on pikes."

"Ha! And yours belongs in my sack to deliver to our generous new boss! 'Ave at it!"

The captain stepped and thrust his sword forward, which Richard effortlessly parried with inhuman speed. He ducked under the captain's heavily armoured arms and shoved him into his comrades, who quickly sidestepped and allowed him to crash into the tavern's wall, splintering the wood. The other soldiers advanced on the bounty hunter and, with varying degrees of skill, attempted to strike Richard with their swords. He evaded each swing and thrust before kicking one of them out of the way, piercing another's femoral artery and grabbing the third's sword arm and wrenching his weapon from his grasp. He threw the Sanskari blade aside and drove his own blood-soaked weapon directly into the soldier's heart.

The captain charged at Richard like a bull and he had to leave his sword embedded in the Miradosi soldier's chest as he sidestepped the captain's onrush. He picked up the sword he had discarded only a few moments ago in time to parry the captain's series of heavy strikes. Richard then used the momentum of the strikes against him and swung the sword aside. The captain couldn't hold onto it and it sailed through the air, its tip landing in one of the tavern's tables and remaining there. In one clean swing, Richard sliced open the captain's throat.

The last able soldier lost heart and tried to run, but he couldn't. Despite his every attempt to place one foot in front of the other, he was unable to move any part of his body and remained frozen in place.

"A traitor and a coward," Richard seethed, throwing the Sanskari blade aside again and retrieving his own sword from the chest of the slain soldier. The one whose artery he had pierced was on his way out.

"What have you done, wizard?" the soldier cried.

"Traitors don't deserve to run."

Richard swung his sword and the soldier's head fell to the ground. The bounty hunter stopped concentrating the spell and the headless body collapsed to the ground with a metallic clang.

"What have you done?" the innkeeper wailed. "It was a noble gesture when you removed the bandits for me, Master Ordowyn. But you've just slaughtered a detachment of soldiers – they'll burn this whole inn down by tomorrow if I don't clean this up!"

"They were no soldiers. They were Sanskari traitors. Faithless degenerates who gave up their honour for money."

"I don't care who paid them, they were soldiers bearing the Miradosi coat of arms! Now not only will the Sanskari run me out of business but also the Miradosi will have me hanged! Curse you, Richard Ordowyn!"

"Yeah," Richard mumbled. "Curse me."

He tore the golden rose badge from the slain captain's scarf and affixed it to his lapel before tentatively leaving the tavern, facing the ground. The cold air and snow felt even more penetrative than before he had walked in.

He walked into the stables where a month ago he had saddled his horse for the night and simply sat down, ignoring the chill as it progressed from nipping his cheeks to freezing his joints to chilling his bones.

377

CHAPTER 44

SANAÍD, TYEN'AEL

12 hours before

When the well-attired men arrived to speak with Caeran, he assumed nothing of it. When they entered his office without knocking, he thought them to be rude. But otherwise he thought nothing of it.

"Caeran Aebythys?" one of the men asked. They were both elegantly dressed in trench coats and trilbies.

"That would be me," Caeran responded enthusiastically. "How can I help you, gentlemen?"

When one of the men reached a hand into their trench coat, Caeran thought nothing of it.

"We come on behalf of the teachers' union," he said, producing a neatly printed piece of paper. "We're looking to recruit."

"I thought Jaelaar had banned the teachers' union," Caeran said, fetching a pitcher of water. "Are you thirsty?"

"A drink would be wonderful," the apparent spokesperson for the two replied.

"Normally I have something a bit stronger, but the head has recently cracked down on alcohol," he said, placing three glasses of water on the table and gesturing for the men to sit.

"Jaelaar has banned the teachers' union, yes," the spokesperson confirmed. "But there is nothing he can do to stop us if we unite all the teachers of Sanaíd. The schools will grind to a halt."

"He'll have us removed and replaced," Caeran said. "Striking won't work."

"That's what the union thought at first, too. But we decided it was worth the risk – either we go down fighting, or we slowly lose our position through the deprecation of our rights."

"You may have a point," Caeran said, taking a sip from his glass.

"Tell me, Mr Aebythys, who is in that portrait hanging above your desk?"

Caeran craned his neck to look at the desk behind him, and above it, a portrait of an older elven woman.

"That's just my late mother," Caeran said drily, turning back to face the men, whose expressions were disturbingly unchanging. "I keep her there so she doesn't take up space in my memory. Really, I ought to take her down. I'm not actually sure why I want her hanging above my desk, the old witch."

Caeran sipped his water again as the men tried to ask Caeran more questions about his office. But from the moment the water had passed his lips, something was wrong.

The room began to sway gently, and then the men's words became incomprehensible as external sound was dulled to a hum, replaced by an incessant ringing in his ears. He began to sweat as if on an excessively hot summer's day.

"I—I think something is wrong," he tried to say, but he couldn't hear his own words, and couldn't be sure that he'd said them. The men were unwavering and remained seated, their expressions grimly still. At least, he thought they were, as vision was becoming as blurred as his hearing.

"What... what have you done?"

"Goodbye, Mr Aebythys," the spokesman said, though Caeran couldn't hear it. The men opened an anonymised portal, though the anonymisation was really useless in Caeran's condition.

Caeran stumbled up and tried to reach his desk but came crashing to the floor. He crawled to his seat and fumbled for the drawer handle, but it was moving, and whenever he thought he had a firm grasp, it would simply slip away.

Darkness began to envelop his blurred vision and he began to cry to himself.

"No, no, no!"

He fought for a further twenty seconds before the darkness won the battle.

CHAPTER 45

SANAÍD, TYEN'AEL

"Where are we supposed to go? Berri never told us where the new HQ was going to be."

Elaeínn flew atop Alazarioss over the picturesque grassy meadows of Hamatnar, passing the occasional village as they headed north. She was growing sick of flight, having spent far too many hours away from the ground. And she was also worried about Kíra's body, acutely aware of the fact that it would soon begin to decay.

"I guess we can go to Sanaíd," she suggested. "Though I think a dragon might well be something they will notice. We'll have to land in the outskirts."

CHAPTER 46

"It's all gone, Your Highness! The lot of it!"

"What the fuck do you mean, it's all gone? We had someone guarding this bloody bunker around the clock!"

King Hortensio of Heathervale, first of his name, Kingslayer and Saviour of Salyria joined Sir Jannis in the cellar
where the anti-vampire blade oil had originally been stored.
He surveyed the empty room and swore profusely, using
some words Jannis hadn't heard before.

"Round up everyone tasked with guarding this room and
fucking hang them," Hortensio seethed.

"Your Highness, I suggest we do not act with such haste,"
Jannis cautiously suggested. "It's a ludicrous proposal that
thieves could get in here, past all the guards, and then go and
haul out containers filled with supplies. To go unnoticed
throughout the entire process? It's frankly impossible."

"They got paid off, you fool," he rasped, kicking a wall.
"They've come to this bloody wasteland and their minds have
been infected. They've all turned into greedy little bastards."

"Possible. Or something else is going on here. Your father
was—"

"Don't call him that," Hortensio growled. "He's no father of
mine."

"As you wish. Elton was in cahoots with witches. What if
they magically... transported themselves into the cellar?
There's also that Kalahar, the bloodsucking devil-spawn. They
shared perhaps the closest bond."

Hortensio kicked the wall again.

"We're fucked, Jannis," he announced. "We've got no means of defending ourselves. We're well and truly fucked."

"May I suggest an alternative course of action? One that ensures the continuity of our lives and those loyal to us?"

"Go on."

"Round up the knights. Let us leave this bloody desert once and for all. We're unlikely to run into vampires on the road back to Salyria. We just have to stay away from civilisation. And wait."

"And give up this city we fought to take over? Pah!"

"We either give up the city, which is worth shit in terms of political power play, I might add. Or we go back to Salyria, muster a stronger army, and go straight for Santhion."

Hortensio briefly contemplated it before nodding his head in agreement.

"We have to get out quickly. I have no idea how this is set to go down, but what I do know is that the sun is disappearing. Let's move."

They left the cellar and ushered the pair of guards with them, Hortensio having forgotten his order to have them killed. There were others in the Redhouse, those who had defected from Elton Redwinter's command and now worked to provide for the young King of Salyria. They took notice of the King's sudden activity but didn't act on it. A number of knights were stationed as sentries outside the repurposed Syndicate headquarters. They were also ordered from their stations.

Messenger boys were plucked from the streets and handed a single mark to find as many knights as they could and direct them to the City Guard headquarters. They were also given a document signed by the King himself to certify the boy's words.

Hortensio, Jannis and a small group of knights arrived at the City Guard to a throng of blindingly brightly armoured Salyrian knights. Apparently having already guessed the King's intentions, as many were on horseback and many more were busy attaching supplies to the horses and carrying as many as they could themselves.

"We're leaving," Hortensio said briefly, mounting his personal horse, a pearl-white mare named Heather.

383

Hortensio and his forces had left the city quicker than they had entered in the first place. Within the hour there was no trace of the conqueror or any trace of Salyria at all. The citizens of Dannos were left to wonder who assumed power, though they now had other, more significant problems about which to worry.

As the Salyrians travelled the long road home, they were exempt from the screams of those citizens as malevolent vampires rose and descended on the city.

The eclipse had concluded by the time Hortensio reached the border of Salyria. He had no idea about the scale of the damage in his country, but Syndicate forces had done an effective job at repelling the vampires. Not a single member of the Salyrian invasion force fell afoul, while he expected the Free City of Dannos would have been ravaged and fallen into anarchy.

Hortensio didn't hear what actually happened to Dannos for weeks, though he thought of many possibilities from upon his throne.

Jannis approached Hortensio from a side corridor leading to the royal chambers, where Jannis had been granted a room as the King's closest aide.

"He's ready for you, Your Highness."

"About bloody time!" the King exclaimed, physically leaping from his seat. "Let me see him."

"Please, follow me."

CHAPTER 47

Elton withdrew his oily dagger from the vampire's skull.

Storage of the slain undead had been an oversight and the castle residents had resorted to throwing every slain vampire into a shallow grave dug in the courtyard – a shallow grave which was far from full.

"Kal made this out to be a bigger deal than it turned out to be," Paul remarked, reapplying a fresh layer of oil to his sword.

"Don't assume anything yet. We've taken refuge in the countryside. The cities will be in a state of disarray if they're getting anywhere near a relative proportion of bloodsuckers as we are."

"Aye, bossman."

Elton, though he didn't say it, empathised with Paul's sentiment and left the front gate in search of Kalahar.

Instead, he encountered Altio, casually sipping from a bottle of wine in the warmth of the canteen.

"Your friend deceived you, Redwinter," Altio declared.

"Any sign of said friend?" he asked, ignoring Altio's suggestion.

"Probably pilfering the coffers."

"Only the jewels, I assure you."

Elton left the canteen and continued to search for Kalahar, eventually resulting to shouting his name. But to no avail.

"Kalahar!" Elton called. "Kalahar! Show yourself, you treacherous beast!"

He abruptly shouted in anger before storming away. The first person he found, evidently bored and spending more time twirling her blade than actively searching for a fight, was Rosa.

"Come on," Elton stated. "We're leaving."

"Leaving?" Rosa echoed. "Where, exactly?"

"Dannos. I'd like you to take us back to Dannos."

"But there's nothing left, Regi. We're on our own now."

"We can rebuild. We have the money; we have power in our other bases. We can divert resources back to Dannos. We can turn it into a utopia."

"But nobody there supports us. We'd probably be killed before we can attempt to restore any fraction of the Syndicate in Dannos."

"What if we tried something different?" Elton prompted. "What if we instead formed a government?"

"Am I to take that as a serious suggestion?"

"Think about it – we made it rich through organised crime. What difference is charging tax? If we changed our methods from stealing to stealing under the guise of government, then we could make away with even more – the richest bastards would finally stop giving us a wide berth, since they wouldn't be afraid of having their wealth stolen by cutthroats, as it would instead be stolen by the taxman like everywhere else. And we could even inspire confidence in people. People have faith in governments, in a king. Not an enterprise."

"You mean to become the next King of Dannos?"

"Yes. That's right."

"Well." Rosa sheathed her blade, oil splattering over her scabbard. "If it doesn't involve compromising our ideals, then I'm willing to try."

"Good," Elton grunted happily. "Good. Let's find Paul and Felix, and then let's get out of here."

CHAPTER 48

Some hours later, they landed at the border to the capital of Tyen'Ael. Elaeínn instructed the dragon to stay put and avoid detection, which she understood was easier said than done. It was Alazarioss who came up with the much cleverer idea of retreating elsewhere while she waited, assuring Elaeínn that they would be able to communicate through a mental link.

She raced into the city, where guards and soldiers were stationed at increasingly frequent intervals. It was becoming hard to cross the street without running into a detachment of army troops heading either into or out of Sanaíd. And even those in service of the Regal Guard seemed to be positioned on every corner.

She covered her face with a cowl and continued, with the intention of reaching one place: the School for Young Magicians. With Caeran's help, she could reach Berri, and perhaps even teleport to him.

An atmosphere of fear hung over the city, with guards and soldiers even outnumbering civilians in some of the poorer areas. Everyone she passed in the street without some form of face covering bore some expression of distrust. At least, that's how she interpreted it.

As she progressed towards the centre, the civilian density only increased. She passed through a square where a National politician was speaking from atop a platform, choosing to stay and listen.

"Generous rewards will be granted to any who inform on FTA sympathisers!" he called. "Any who choose to withhold information or even conceal a terrorist within their home will be punished with the full force of the law! This is Tyen'Ael, where order is our priority! We do not allow terrorists to attempt to disrupt our way of life!"

"Free Tyen'Ael!" a girl in the crowd shouted.

Nobody echoed her cry and the politician speaking from the platform nodded to two Regal Guards standing behind him. They converged on the girl, who attempted to escape, but she was cut off by a further two guards. She was then bound and led away, towards the palace.

Well, Berri has done some work, Elaeínn thought optimistically, moving on towards the school. *Nobody shouted her down, at least*.

She reached the front door of the school and was unpleasantly surprised to see two guards stationed outside. She didn't have much choice but to try to get inside.

"Please remove your mask," they ordered. She complied.

"Name?"

"Del— Laettía Karíos."

"State your business, Dellaettía Karíos."

"I'm a student," she lied.

"Likely story. Clear off."

"Alright, fine. I'm here to visit a friend. Caeran Aebythys – he's one of the teachers."

"I'm afraid you've come too late. Mr Aebythys was found dead last night."

"What? How?" she exclaimed in a state of shock.

"The initial proclamation was overdose. He was found in a pile of sweat, dilated pupils, all the rest. The autopsy is yet to be performed."

"Caeran didn't use any drugs! He can't have overdosed!"

"I'm afraid we know nothing more. Now, if you have no other business, I request you leave."

"He was murdered! There's no question about it!"

The guard placed a hand on the hilt of his sheathed sword.

"Please leave immediately."

"Hang on, I thought I recognised you," the other guard said, having been quiet until then. "That's the FTA girl who tried to kill Jaelaar. Delía Hatten!"

She bolted, the Regal Guards in hot pursuit. Their armour slowed them down, but they had the advantage of having backup everywhere.

She dashed down a narrow alley and climbed a ladder onto the roof of a block of flats, running and jumping from building to building. The guards' shouts were still clearly audible beneath her, and it sounded like they, too, were climbing onto the roof. She had to move fast.

Fuck, she thought, leaping a gap that must have been four metres across. *Now what do I do?*

She climbed down a progression of lowering buildings and reached the ground, wrapping her cowl back over her face and head. A group of civilians provided excellent cover and soon, she was nowhere to be seen.

Aegard, she thought. *He's my last chance.*

She also took notice of the fact that there didn't appear to be any panic to do with vampires. There also didn't appear to be any vampires. Given the severity of the situation Kalahar had implied, she had expected pandemonium. But all focus still remained on the tension between the FTA and the government.

A flyer was swept past her feet by the breeze, and she stopped to pick it up. It was an advertisement – an advertisement to join the FTA.

Join the fight against the dictatorship, she read. *Join the Free Tyen'Ael Army today. We await you at the largest mouth of the Darklight.*

Alazarioss! This is it!

Elaeínn raced back to the city's exit even faster than she had entered, eager to find Berri before anything else was destroyed.

389

CHAPTER 49

NORTHERN MIRADOSI TUNDRA

Twenty minutes later, the biological urge to survive forced him to his feet. Longingly gazing at the bare, dirty space where he had once left Rosie for the night, he opened a portal to the Miradosi garrison from which the soldiers had come. He hadn't ever been there but had extracted the knowledge from the last soldier's head before severing it.

"Oi! Wizard!" a guard shouted, weakly pointing a gloved finger at the approaching bounty hunter.

"This badge," Richard said, directing attention to his badge. "Does it mean anything to you?"

"That's the captain's badge!" the guard exclaimed. "He left a while ago to collect... levies. Have you seen him?"

"As a matter of fact, I have. I'll tell you where he is, but I need information."

Richard trudged up the mud-trodden path closer to the garrison's gate.

"Who's paying you?"

"Depends," the soldier growled. "Why are you asking?"

"Curiosity," Richard growled back.

"Well, stick your nose where it belongs, pedestrian. And scram, before I stick a spear through you."

Richard's arrow had entered the soldier's eye before he even had time to cry for help. Another guard stationed behind the gate watched the entire encounter and screamed in surprise as he watched his comrade fall. He turned around to call for help but fell as the second of Richard's twelve arrows flew through the gaps in the gate and pierced straight through the soldier's exposed neck.

Richard retrieved his first arrow and wiped it clean in the thin snow sheet covering the surrounding landscape, snow lightly continuing to fall. More soldiers appeared to assess the situation and saw Richard standing outside the gate, brandishing his bow and freshly cleaned arrow. He dramatically placed it against the bow and drew the bowstring slowly, giving the soldiers a chance to run. They chose to be arrogant, and a third soldier fell as a result. That was enough to make them realise a smarter course of action.

Richard waited. He listened intently to the calls of the remaining soldiers.

"We're safe in 'ere! He can't get through that gate!"

"Who is it?"

"It's just a man! He can't be that dangerous!"

"Yeah! Why don't we go out and take him ourselves?"

"He just killed Pat, Danny, and Pete without battin' an eye! That's why we ain't takin' 'im ourselves!"

"He can't get us all at once! Let's get 'im, boys! Praps the blackplates'll give us a reward!"

The soldiers finally came around the corner, armed with halberds, spears, swords and one with a longbow. They saw Richard, standing proudly, bow on his back.

The soldier armed with the longbow reached for the bucket of arrows they had brought to the gate and clumsily nocked one, taking more than one attempt. Once it was straight, he began to draw it back, evidently lacking the upper-body strength to pull the bowstring the full way back. Richard simultaneously unsheathed his sword. The soldiers looked at one another in a state of confusion as the bow-wielding soldier sought confirmation that he should release the bowstring.

One of the soldiers, a brute who towered above the others, gave the confirmation. And the arrow flew straight at Richard, too fast to avoid.

Richard didn't avoid it.

The arrow struck Richard's sword with a piercing clink as the fine steel arrowhead collided with the solid material of the blade. Its newfound trajectory made the arrow find its way to a final destination in the snow equidistant from Richard and the soldiers behind the gate.

"It's a fuckin' wizard! Run!" one exclaimed. They didn't stay to slander the wizard, valuing their lives over their prejudice.

Even Richard was still reeling from the experiment, having been unconfident that he would actually be able to parry a mid-flight projectile.

Richard kept his sword unsheathed and walked towards the gate. With a gesture, it slammed open. He walked inside.

The soldiers were still frantically scrambling around the courtyard, finding themselves the best weapons and armour in preparation for retaliation against the intruder. In their frenzy, they hadn't realised the intruder was already inside.

He approached a soldier half-dressed in a rusty iron breast-plate, a left pauldron, and a right greave. As he attached the right pauldron, Richard's blade lacerated his exposed left thigh, sending a stream of blood into the delicate, snow-dressed ground. The unsuspecting soldier squealed in pain and pivoted around, instinctually grasping his damaged leg and allowing his assailant the perfect opportunity to finish him off with a strike to the back of his neck.

The rest of the soldiers converged on him at once, but Richard sensed it to be from fear rather than bravery. The lone bounty hunter found himself at the centre of an on-slaught of steel. In a series of precise movements, he dodged the overhead blow of a halberd, deflected the swing of a sword from his right and grabbed an incoming spear from behind. Twisting the spear from the soldier's hands, he threw it with his weak arm into the chest of a fast-approaching axe-wielder, then rolled out of range of the second swing of the halberd. He sprang to his feet and faced the soldiers appearing out of what he assumed to be an armoury, armed to the teeth and ar-moured from head to toe. Meanwhile, the soldiers who hadn't been completely prepared backed away, allowing space be-tween them and the intruder.

"You speak Miradosi, wizard. Why are you killin' us?"

"Because you're faithless traitors and a stain on my honour if I don't."

Unsuspectingly, Richard took two leap-like steps towards the halberd-wielder and swung his sword in an arc. The sol-dier didn't have any more than a second to react before his head was removed from his shoulders. The others roared in

surprise and immediately ran at the bounty hunter, who realised his magically enhanced reactions and foresight weren't
enough to stop the nine remaining soldiers, and more kept
appearing from the armoury.

Nevertheless, he kept fighting. He had to move his sword
faster and faster, dodging more and more often. It was too
much. Their attacks came in one after another without any
break and Richard could do nothing but block, parry and
evade. He had to try something else. Something he wished he
didn't have to.

"El'kak favor!" he yelled.

Every single soldier and every single implement in their
hands froze in place. Their eyes could still move and he suffered under the panicked gazes of seventeen helpless soldiers.

"Fuckin' hell-spawned wizard! You cheat!" one of them
swore, discovering that their mouths were also still capable of
movement.

"And you betray the cause for money," Richard calmly retorted. "Which I deem far less honourable than cheating."

Richard sauntered to the gate, stopping to wipe his sword
in the snow. He sheathed it and turned back around to take
one last look at the frozen soldiers.

"Oi!" one of them called. "Are you just gonna leave us 'ere?"

He turned around, making sure to close the gate behind
him. And left them there.

CHAPTER 50

DARKLIGHT FOREST, TYEN'AEL

The northwest mouth of the Darklight, the safest passage through the international forest. Easily the most travelled, and the primary route through which wealth flowed between the dwarven and elven kingdoms.

Alazarioss landed in the meadow over the hill neighbouring the worn road and the start of the treeline. The advertisement had been vague, so now Elaeínn was forced to wait or search.

It turned out that she didn't need to wait at all – the moment she dismounted, she was faced with the distrustful faces of camouflaged elves, wearing animal skins and face paints to blend in with the forest. They were armed with bows and swords, all of which were aimed at Elaeínn and the dragon, who snorted with contempt.

"Lower your weapons, I'm a friend!" she called as the elves stepped into the meadow. "I am Elaeínn Tinaíd – I must speak to Berri immediately!"

They were unwavering, keeping their weapons raised. One of them took charge – he was wearing a unique identifier in the form of a badge sown onto his jerkin, bearing a dove on a yellow field.

"You claim to be Elaeínn Tinaíd. Prove it," he said, his eyes constantly flitting between her and the dragon, whose sheer size engulfed them all in shadow.

"What do you want me to do, hand you my birth certificate? Berri will recognise me – take me to him! I am your superior, damn it!"

394

"Fallía is a few kilometres down the road," he said. "The old Darklight Castle."

"Excellent – I'll meet you there," she quipped.

Alazarioss flattened herself to the ground and allowed Elaeínn to mount.

The reception upon their arrival at the castle was even more hostile than they had received at the border of the Darklight.

Alazarioss landed atop the vast stone walls which encircled the entire bustling settlement. The sentries were surprised, to say the least.

Troops rushed to the walls to defend against the sudden presumed attack and Elaeínn had a sword placed against her throat the moment she dismounted. Alazarioss lowered her head to stare down the soldier, but they held their ground.

"Get this away at this moment, for Raeris's sake – I'm Elaeínn Tinaíd! Has Berri not described me to any of you?"

From the fortifications of the keep, Berri finally appeared, sprinting along the walls, pushing his way through the throng of defenders, utterly in awe.

"Berri! We need to speak right now!"

"Elle, what in Raeris's name is that? And you lot, put your weapons down!" he rasped.

"She is Alazarioss. A dragon. She will not hurt anyone. However, I've been told that other creatures will, yet I don't see any of them anywhere."

"Elle, what are you on about?"

"Vampires, Berri – I've been across the world and seen a lot of things, one of which was an actual vampire, who warned me and others that vampires are to rise today. But I don't see any."

"Has nobody ever told you?" he asked quizzically, the drama of the situation diminishing almost entirely. "The elven and dwarven kingdoms have taskforces specifically trained for the case of eclipses. Vampires are not a threat to us. Not an immediate one, at the least."

"You've got to be fucking kidding me," she swore.

"Elle," Berri said softly. "Who is that?"

He raised his hand and pointed at Kíra's lifeless corpse still atop Alazarioss's back, her face covered with fabric. Elaeínn looked between her and Berri and felt the urge to break down again. But surrounded by comrades, she fought it.

"It's Kíra," she whispered. "I... I thought I might be able to... I don't know, save her. It sounds ridiculous. I've dragged her body halfway across the world just to finally accept that resurrection isn't possible."

Berri was silent. He walked along the rampart to the dragon, who was initially distrustful. But Elaeínn insisted that she allow him to take Kíra's body.

He held her and walked down the steps from the castle wall, entering the dark back streets of Fallía. Elaeínn followed and admired – in such a short time, Berri and the dwarves had thrown together a thriving community, fit with families and individuals alike. They stayed in brand-new houses, which were still under construction by teams of people throughout the old ruin. The sheer work ethic and the shared energy filled her with passion, with enthusiasm, with confidence that they really could be a force to be reckoned with, no longer having to reside in the shadows.

"This is the vision that Kíra fought for," Berri finally said as they approached the castle's central hub, a cobbled circle fed by five different streets with a stone platform in its centre. The keep loomed in the castle's elevated levels, but the sun still bathed the entire area in light.

"She would have been proud to see what we've achieved. She was one of the ones that allowed this to happen. She is one of the reasons we are here."

He stepped towards the stone platform and laid Kíra's body across it.

"We'll build a statue on this very spot. Fallía will grow and continue to support generations of those who believe in freedom, in justice, and they will walk past one of their founders every day. Even if she can't live forever, her memory will.

"You there – Allíya – inform the artists that they are to begin work on a stone sculpture of Kíra immediately – one to two scale. And no nudity or anything vulgar that artists tend to enjoy – she is to be remembered as a valiant hero. And she is to be carved as such."

A young woman, no more than fifty, nodded and dashed away.

"I hope that's enough," Berri said. "I wish I could do more. Not just for your sake, either – Kíra was an excellent fighter. Truly magnificent. It's an enormous shame that she can't be with us anymore to witness our ascension to power.

"Speaking of which – I have a plan which ideally involves you. Come with me, quickly."

The castle, which Elaeínn now understood was called Fallía, was enormous. At least, that was how it felt, and the keep had a large part to play in this impression. Fallía was situated on a hill, surrounded by a moat only partially filled with water, and cobbled roads led up around the hill to the keep at the top. It was a monumental construction, reminiscent of the scale of the Tyen'Aíde in Sanaíd. When they arrived, it was even palace-like, complete with a hall which could have easily been turned into a throne room. But that wasn't the FTA's belief, and as such, no throne was ever implemented.

"Del," Berri acknowledged in passing.

"Berri," he responded, tagging along with the duo. "And it's good to see you again, Elaeínn."

"And you, Del," she returned.

"Kíra?" he inquired, but he never received an answer. Only solemn hangings of heads.

"It's like this," Berri said, presenting them with what Elaeínn could only refer to as a war room. There were maps everywhere – on one wall, a map of Tyen'Ael. On another, all of Fenalia, both west and east. On the table in the centre of the room was a map of Tyen'Ael and Hamatnar, adorned with pins, markings, and figures. This was the one to which Berri drew their attention as he gesticulated enthusiastically at various locations on the map.

"The Hamatnarian Elites are on their way through the Darklight right now, by order of King Kagyan. They are going to help us with an assault on southern Tyen'Aeli cities, where support for the FTA is already high. We're turning this into a civil war – one which, with the help of the dwarves, we can win.

"Obviously, we can't win in head-on combat with the army. So we're going to infiltrate from the inside. We need to cut off supply lines, exploit the disloyalties of those who would rather control regions themselves. Unitary government will be the

Nationals' downfall, because there are no regional rulers which have a strong desire to maintain control of their land.

"Now, you're obviously too important to be sent on these missions – you're going with me, Del, and the Elites to the fortress at Evekar – the most significant military fortification on the entire southern border. If we can capture that with the help of the Elites, the dwarves will be able to move their armies in across the South."

"Berri," Elaeínn interrupted him. "I have a dragon now. She will quite happily raze Evekar and spare the lives of both our FTA and the dwarven soldiers."

"I don't doubt that," Berri said nonchalantly. "But I would quite like to capture Evekar, not raze it. It would be an excellent expansion to the might of our growing faction. Your dragon is welcome to join us in the assault, as long as she doesn't burn the place to the ground."

"In that case," Elaeínn began, "when are the Elites arriving? And how far away is Evekar?"

"Fortunately for us, it's very close – militarily speaking," he pointed to a red pin on the map, east of Fallía. "Half a day's march, which will be even quicker for the dwarves. Would the dragon be willing to take the three of us on her back?"

"I don't see her objecting too strongly," Elaeínn said.

"Very well, then," Berri concluded, rising from the war table. "Let us depart at once – the Elites should be arriving shortly."

They were interrupted on their way out of the keep by the woman that Berri had sent off to order the construction of Kíra's statue – only this time, she was in a state of alarm.

"Berri – the army is here! They're coming down the highway right now!"

"Are the defences prepared?" Berri replied calmly.

"Yes, but—"

"Has everyone been armed?"

"Yes, but Berri—"

"No, Allíya. We have no reason to worry. Fallía is impenetrable. No army can cross our moat, no army can scale our walls, no army can combat our dwarven defences. The Nationals have no reason to be prepared to siege a castle of this scale – they've no understanding of how to fight a war.

There's not been a war on this continent in more than two hundred years.

"Whatever they throw at us, we are prepared for it. Put the castle on high alert. Sound the bells. Everyone is to be ready to fight."

"Yes, sir," she acknowledged, running deeper into the keep.

"You're really that confident?" Elaeínn asked as they climbed the walls, returning to Alazarioss.

"They'll take one look at the dragon and scatter. And if they don't, then yes, I am still confident. We've not been preparing for nothing. If only you had been here to see the effort, Elle. It's really been quite motivational. The strongest sense of community I've felt in my entire life."

"We're heading east, Alazarioss," Elaeínn informed the dragon, who responded with a snort. "Make sure you fly over the approaching soldiers, though, just to scare them off. Or, you know, you could incinerate them."

They took off and flew towards the road. As had been reported, the army was on their way. But even Berri looked shocked when they realised the scale of the attacking force.

Jaelaar hadn't just sent a battalion to attack Fallía. He had sent a legion.

Thousands upon thousands of soldiers marched along the wide highway, stretching away into the distance. At the fore of the boundless troops were alternating arrays of footsoldiers and archers, interrupted periodically by trebuchets, ballistae, and cannons in equal proportion. The army's march grinded to a halt as Alazarioss flew overhead and cast them in shadow.

"Alazarioss," Elaeínn said softly. "Torch them."

"Wait!" Berri cried.

But it was too late.

Flame streamed from Alazarioss's mouth as she descended on the rows of soldiers. She left a trail of destruction, scorched earth, and death in her wake, melting the soldiers into piles of flesh and metal.

The army was quick to respond and soon the sky was dotted with cannonballs, boulders, and ballista bolts. The roar of the crowds below was drowned out by the explosions of cannons as they fed the sky with further projectiles and Alazarioss was forced to suddenly swerve away from the road to avoid the onslaught.

The dragon suddenly roared and jerked momentarily downwards before steadying herself again. Elaeínn turned her head to see a ballista bolt wedged in a chink in Alazaríoss's scales, which she had previously thought to be impervious to damage.

"Alazaríoss! Fly away!"

The dragon's pride won out over Elaeínn's instruction and she dived once more on the endless array of soldiers, specifically targeting the siege weapons, and reducing them to cinders.

A stray cannonball found its mark, striking the side of the dragon's face. She roared again in pain and careered towards a group of archers, their bows drawn in preparation. Elaeínn held tightly to Alazaríoss's spine, as did Berri and Delíen, as they prepared for impact.

She crashed to the ground, crushing a number of the soldiers in the process, but she managed to fight back and took off, groaning in such a way that sounded more like a guttural rumbling as she did so.

Another well-placed cannonball struck her side and a second ballista bolt lodged itself in her stomach.

She flapped her wings tenaciously and still avoided surrender as yet more projectiles flew over their heads. The cries of the army were growing more and more confident, turning into cheers with every spray of blood from the dragon's mortal scales.

"Alazaríoss, abandon this now! You won't survive!"

She roared for a third time and ascended higher into the sky, beyond the range of the projectiles, which fell pathetically back to the ground. Her normally graceful, majestic flight was now erratic, and even though they were out of range of the army's weaponry, Elaeínn feared they wouldn't make it far enough to remain that way.

"I don't think we're going to make it to Evekar in this condition," Berri echoed her thoughts.

"I agree. We should return to Fallía."

"That is an enormous force to send just to fight us," Berri stated. "It's a waste of resources. I know I inspire confidence in our fighters, that I tell them they can do anything, but I'm no fool. We're nothing against a legion of that size."

"Unless that force isn't intended to defeat us," Elaeínn suggested. "Alazaríoss! Go back to Fallía! You need to heal!"

The dragon flew in an arc to return to the direction of Fallía, forcing them to fly over the highway again, where they were subject to another volley of various projectiles, none of them finding their marks.

Alazaríoss landed atop the square roof of the keep and after her passengers had dismounted, she immediately focused on the two ballista bolts which were evidently a source of immense pain. She clenched them in her jaws and ripped them from between her scales, spraying a jet of blood over the stone and narrowly avoiding drenching Elaeínn, Berri and Delíen.

"I would stay, but we're under attack," Berri said. "Del, I need you to come with me. It looks like we won't be leaving for Evekar just yet."

Delíen glanced uneasily at the wounded dragon, who was producing a soft rumbling sound from her throat, before briskly walking away with Berri.

The bells were ringing across the castle and Elaeínn watched in awe as the ramparts filled with more and more troops, all completely armed with military-grade weapons, unlike the refuse they used to throw together with whatever was lying around, or whatever they could scrounge from local smiths. Even a few trebuchets were rolled into the streets, positioned in such a way that their payloads would be launched over the walls in the direction of the highway.

Alazaríoss was still producing a guttural rumbling and Elaeínn turned to inspect the damage. The bleeding was slowing, but she had already stained almost the entire roof's surface area red.

"I didn't think you'd be vulnerable to our weaponry," she commented.

Neither did I, she responded, managing to sound angry through her thoughts. *I will survive, but I must spend time to recover. You are on your own, Elaeínn.*

Alazaríoss beat her wings and rose into the sky, blood still pouring from her wounds. The height meant that it splashed against the surface of the roof with force and Elaeínn's face was decorated with a streak of hot dragon blood as Alazarioss soared into the southern distance, while she pleaded for her to stop. She didn't stop.

Elaeínn cursed and surveyed the castle, looking for Berri. She found him and Delíen at the top of the castle's highest tower and quickly raced away to join them.

"The dragon – we watched it fly away."

"She said she needs time to recover," Elaeínn grunted. "Let's not focus on her – we have an army at our hands."

"That's what we thought – but it appears we've acted too quickly. Look."

Berri offered his spyglass to her. Elaeínn used it to gain a close-up view of the marching army, who were now within range of Fallía's walls. But they didn't turn to attack; they didn't even turn to look. They marched straight towards the Darklight.

"It's an invasion force," Berri declared. "Hold back! Do not attack!"

The message spread along the walls and bows were lowered, swords were sheathed.

"This isn't good – the Elites are marching along that very path. If they encounter the Aeli army—"

"They're as good as dead."

402

CHAPTER 51

"Hold up," Tynak said. "Do you hear that?"

"Not more crawlers, I hope," one of the soldiers behind him said.

"Shut up and listen."

The entire Elite Division fell silent and listened as the synchronised marching of many boots grew steadily louder.

"Captain, I hate to be the one to tell ye, but that's coming from ahead."

"Speak to me like I'm stupid again and I'll throttle yer arse. Everyone, to the brush!"

The dwarves split in half, one half hiding amongst the foliage lining the western side of the forest path and one half in the eastern side. The marching from the north grew louder and Tynak rose from the trough into which he had dived to survey the oncoming soldiers.

He saw the approaching elves and cursed under his breath as they marched straight past the hiding places of the dwarves. Tynak watched uneasily as the swathes of foot soldiers, archers, and intermittent siege machines seemingly endlessly revolved past. He looked to his right, where his deputy was suggesting action. He firmly rejected any such idea.

One of the elves walking alongside a trebuchet, armoured much more elaborately than his comrades and wearing a plated helmet shaped almost like a crown, called loudly in High Elven for the troops to stop. The marching halted immediately in perfect harmony.

"Men! Our mages have provided us with the understanding that our enemies are among us! Those that Jaelaar himself ordered us to eliminate!"

"What's he on about?" Tynak's deputy whispered.

"I don't know," Tynak whispered back, not peeling his eyes from the crowned elf, who he assumed to be a commander of some degree.

"The Hamatnarian Elite Division hides in the very trees lining this road! Anyone who kills an Elite gets an aerrin from the royal treasury, by order of Jaelaar!"

"Run!" Tynak cried.

CHAPTER 52

Paul and Felix, once found, were both equally as enthusiastic about the idea of going back to Dannos. And so, they bode farewell to Altio and teleported back to the Redhouse.

They landed beneath a crippled pillar and a half-collapsed roof. Entry to the former Syndicate headquarters was blocked – not that it mattered at that moment.

The streets were paved with mayhem. Citizens fought one another for scraps and mutilated bodies lined the roadsides. Not only were people engaged in skirmishes with their neighbours, but also grey-skinned, red-eyed creatures of the undead. And the creatures of the undead were far quicker and far deadlier.

One of the vampires dashed towards the group of four, taking the appearance of a grey blur. Elton drew his dagger and placed it into what he imagined would be the vampire's torso, impaling it upon his weapon as it flew towards them. It cried animalistically before falling in true death.

"The effect is a lot stronger here," Felix commented, coating each of his silver daggers in a fresh layer of oil. "It's like the sun isn't there at all."

"These people are helpless," Elton observed. "Utterly helpless. We should have left some of the solution here."

"Suddenly gone soft, boss?" Paul asked, drawing his blade from the slain body of another malevolent vampire.

"No... of course not," he dismissed. "Come, let's make our way to the bank. We can wait out the time there. And realistically, I should still be the legal manager."

They fought their way through the streets, dealing with vampires and people alike. Some of the people Elton even recognised – they had worked for him before his departure.

"Mr Redwinter!" a young boy called, crouched behind a smashed wagon. "Mr Redwinter! Where are you going?"

Elton stopped and recognised the boy as his messenger. He was covered in blood and armed only with a dagger.

"The bank," Elton said. "Why?"

"I wouldn't, sir! It's full of those devil spawn! They're crazy! Obsessed with jewels, sir! Diamonds and rubies and emeralds and whatever else they keep in there, sir!

"What's happening, sir? Why is the sky dark in the middle of the day? Why are we under attack?"

"A series of unfortunate events," Elton said sombrely.

Elton looked at his crew and they decided without words not to go to the bank.

"The City Guard," Elton asserted, to no opposition.

They continued paving through the anarchy, at one point even being jumped by a group of raving bandits, their eyes red and their cognition slowed under the influence of drugs. They ended up being the least of their worries.

"How many fucking vampires are there here?" Felix cursed, retrieving his dagger from a malevolent's chest.

"The city has fallen. Any sense of decency disappeared with us and, as far as I can see, the Salyrians. Slimy bastards," Elton deduced. "I can imagine a lot of these fuckers came from your Pillared Paige's."

A flash of grey managed to escape Elton's peripheral vision and was with him in an instant, slashing his arm with a razor-sharp set of claws. Elton growled in pain, wildly swinging his dagger in a circle around his body and failing to strike the blindingly fast creature. It stopped and sized up the group with its ruby eyes but quickly descended on them again, this time being struck down by Paul's blade.

"The bunker," Elton suddenly remembered. "We can go to the bunker. In the Redhouse. There's no way we can fight them all off by ourselves."

"And the population will be slaughtered," Rosa said drily.

"The smart ones will lock their doors, board up their windows and batten the hatches!" Elton retorted. "Half of these fools probably aren't even aware of the situation, let alone trying to save themselves from it!"

"My knives are going dry," Felix supplemented. "If we're really going to be of any use, we need more oil."

"We need to go back to the Redhouse – if not to hide, then to fortify. We need to find people who are still loyal to us and we need to carry out the original plan, before Hortensio came along and forced us out. Rosa – I know you've been working yourself to death with magic, but we really need just one crate of oil. Could you manage that?"

"Practice makes perfect," she mused.

"Right," Elton concluded, turning back in the direction from which they had come. "Back we go."

Upon their return to the Redhouse, it was evident that he had been noticed by more people in the city than he had anticipated, as they were greeted with a welcome party.

"Regi, bossman," a young man with a scarred face and bedraggled blonde hair said. He, and the others, were wearing the emblem of the Redwinter Syndicate. "We've come to serve."

"Excellent," Elton acknowledged, impressed with the size of the group – there must have been thirty. "Excellent. You all have weapons?"

"The silver you gave us back before the Salyrians booted you out," he said. "And we kept some of the oil, before they locked it up."

"You'll be glad to hear it's not in the hands of the Salyrians anymore. How much do you have?"

"Not enough for long, boss. But we can defend the Redhouse from however many bloodsuckers want to try us."

"Good. You lot, stay out here and use the debris for shelter. Rosa is going to try and get us some more oil. Paul, Felix – you both stay as well."

"Alright, bossman."

Elton and Rosa climbed over the fallen pillars and the collapsed portions of roof and found that they weren't the first to enter the Redhouse since the installation of the barricade at its entrance. Several groups of people had already settled themselves throughout the abandoned headquarters, and all heads turned in the direction of the new arrivals as they entered the lobby.

"Smart," Elton remarked under the wary gazes of the squatters. "Now, do you think you could open a portal back to Veyenia?"

"Against my body's wishes, yes."

She grunted and traced a large, rectangular portal. Barely a dent had been made in the total supply of the solution that had been originally transported to Fort Redwinter, and Elton hauled four of the crates through to Dannos without encountering any opposition from the Veyenian castle.

"You lot!" Elton shouted, again grabbing the attention of the squatters. "Make yourselves useful and help us fight!"

He received varied responses ranging from colourful language to threats to silence, but a handful stepped up to volunteer.

"And what are they going to fight with, exactly?" Rosa observed, as the volunteers came forward, unarmed.

"We'll have to ask the lads out front where the rest of the silver swords went."

Defence of the Redhouse became their new task, and the building became the epicentre of the city as news spread of Elton's return and more and more people flocked to the crippled Syndicate headquarters in search of protection. And with them came weaponry.

Silver swords trickled in from the original recipients, many of which had remained in Dannos. Those who were adequately armed were placed on the front line, while those without suitable weapons were tasked with supplying the front line with a constant stream of solution. And they managed, despite the chaos, to establish an aura of hope.

The vampires appeared to be drawn in by the crowds, with the promise of fresh blood. The fighting continued seemingly endlessly, the absence of sunlight only serving to slow time. But even with the magical prowess of the undead creatures, the Syndicate managed to hold them off with miraculous resolve.

Elton withdrew from the front line, gifting his silver dagger to the messenger who had warned him against visiting the bank. He assumed his much more familiar role away from the fighting and closer to the management.

The original squatters within the Syndicate's lobby were now accompanied by crowds of refugees and the building was on the verge of full capacity. This led to some disagreements and fights, but these were quickly put down by the new Syndicate guards.

The Syndicate was winning. Their front line did not break, and although fighters were falling, there were always more to take their place. And even though the vampires had magic on their side, the fighters had pride. Resolve was unbroken, and the bodies piled high – far more grey than human.

CHAPTER 53

NORTHERN MIRADOSI TUNDRA

"They'll start appearing any minute now," Nendar announced, looking over the remains of a recent battle with dismay. Every last body had been removed, and the shed blood covered with a layer of snow. But there were still dropped weapons, shattered carts, abandoned pieces of armour, missed arrows and faint footprints.

"We're nowhere near a settlement. They come about as a result of death. Shouldn't we move on?" Richard queried.

They walked up the remainder of the battle-torn hill and observed a distant village of notable size – not big enough to be a town, but on the larger side of villages.

"I beg your pardon?" Nendar said. He ignored him.

"Lynn – are you going to be able to help us? You don't have a lirenium crystal."

"I can help plenty fine by myself, thank you very much," she retorted. "Crystal or not, I'm still a bloody strong mage."

"But extraordinarily limited without the crystal's aid, dear daughter," Nendar reminded her. "Don't be cocky. Never overstep your boundaries, or you might end up killing yourself."

"Don't you worry, father. I'm perfectly aware that I'm about as useful as a hole in the head. The least I can do is hold off any attackers while you put them away."

"Should we go to the village? We don't want to risk anything."

"Patience, Richard," Nendar advised. "There might not even be any vampires that arise from here. It may be a big village, but village communities are tight knit, unlike those of town folk. The only reason for bloodshed would be if— fuck."

Nendar extended a finger and directed their gazes to a group of shoddily equipped riders approaching the village along the road from the North.

"Bandits," Richard said.

"If we're to take them on, we cannot use magic. It must be with our weapons."

"Not a problem. Let's go."

The group ran at speed in the direction of the village, hoping to cut off the marauders before they reached the settlement's undefended boundaries. Richard looked back at Valerie, who to this point hadn't uttered a word. She met his gaze and he quickly flitted his eyes away and focused back on the approaching brigands.

One of them noticed the group and shouted something to the other riders, and they brought their horses to a stop. Richard reached the beaten path first and stood in their way, joined by Nendar, Lynn and finally Valerie.

The leading marauder, dressed in damaged steel plate armour and a helmet bearing the blue of Mirados, drew a sword from his sheath and pointed it at Richard.

"Just who in the fuck do you fink you are?" he asked. His comrades laughed hysterically, as if he had told a joke.

"Richard Ordowyn, bounty hunter," he calmly responded. "And you?"

"Sinner. You know why they call me that, Richard what's-'is-face? Because I don't give a flyin' fuck what any god tells me to do. Now get outta my way, I've got some peasants to rob."

He sheathed his sword and shook the reins of his horse. Richard took his bow from his back, nocked an arrow, and pulled back the bowstring, aiming for Sinner's head. All in under two seconds. The brigand brought his horse to an abrupt halt in surprise and the horse squealed in response.

"What the fuck are you doin'? 'Ave you got a death wish, you bloody halfwit?"

"Turn around, go home – or wherever you live – and refrain from pillaging today. I would really advise that you listen."

Sinner mockingly opened his mouth in shock before slapping his knees and laughing. His followers chortled in accordance.

"Get out of my way, dickhead," Sinner said.

And that ended up being the last thing he would ever say.

Sinner's horse, now riderless, charged forward in panic and Richard rolled out of the way. The other riders unsheathed their swords and incited their horses to rush at Richard, who quickly nocked an arrow and took out another marauder. Valerie revealed a wickedly sharp sabre from a sheath at her belt and ruthlessly sliced clean through the leg of one of the stampeding horses. It stumbled and threw its rider to the ground where Valerie finished him off with a stroke. The crippled horse provided an obstacle for the other horses and the first tripped over the obstacle, also throwing its rider to the ground. This time it was one of Lynn's daggers that finished him off. The other riders quickly directed their horses around their fallen comrades and converged on Nendar, who had drawn a blade of his own – a scimitar with a carved wooden handle and patterns forged into the steel of the blade. He deflected the first bandit's attack but was caught off guard by another who appeared abruptly after the first. This bandit managed to land a blow on Nendar, slicing open his black doublet and drawing blood. The old mage swore and reached his hand out to cast a spell, but stopped himself.

Richard found himself in a position off the road, away from the fray, and began taking out the bandits one by one. Each arrow he nocked found its mark, be it an arm, a leg, or a head. Some of the arrows he loosed killed their targets; some debilitated them enough to be killed by the vicious Varanus sisters. Nendar had stepped back from the fighting to look at his arm which was bleeding much more profusely than he had originally thought.

Richard loosed one last arrow and struck the last bandit in the chest. He fell from the saddle and landed on his back. Valerie swiftly finished him off by driving her sabre into his head.

412

As she withdrew her blood-stained blade, the mages realised they had garnered a somewhat significant crowd. Peasants from the village expressing varying degrees of approval
stood behind a ramshackle fence made of lashed-together
branches which acted as a border. One of the peasants, a decrepit old man, stepped over a collapsed area of the fence and
walked towards them.

"You've killed Sinner," he wheezed. "What are we going to
do?"

"We were under the impression he was a brigand," Richard
patronised.

"You don't understand, foolish cur! You've killed Sinner!"
he repeated. "You've doomed our village to destruction!"

"We've done the very opposite," Richard muttered under
his breath.

"It won't be long before his lackeys find out he's dead," the
old man continued, noisily rapping his walking cane against
the cold-hardened ground. "And if they discover he died in
our little village then they'll slaughter us all!"

"They won't find out unless you lot blab about it," Richard
asserted. "We need to burn the bodies anyways so that they
don't corrupt. That will remove evidence of his death."

"We will burn the bodies," the old man retorted. "We don't
want you anywhere near our village, curs. This is the problem
with bloody travellers – they always stick their noses into
other people's business. Begone with you, stick your noses
where they belong."

The old man looked back to the ever-growing crowd behind the village fence and waved for two burly young men to
join him. While the young men started to transport the bodies, first removing the armour and weapons, the old man
shooed away Richard and his companions and they walked in
the direction from which Sinner's troop had arrived.

"People have never appreciated heroes, Richard," Nendar
said, clutching his bloodied arm. "That's why I chose to be an
emperor."

"Are you going to be alright?" the bounty hunter asked.

"It's nothing to worry about. Let's just get to some cover so
I can heal it."

413

"I'm starting to think our best option will be to wait for the vampires to appear," Lynn suggested. "If the reception anywhere else will be akin to that, then there's no point in preventative methods. Only curative."

"You might be right," Richard agreed.

They found cover in the form of a small cluster of trees off to the side of the northern road leading away from the village. In half an hour, Nendar's arm had stopped bleeding and all the evidence that remained of his injury was the scar-like layer of new skin cells where he had been cut.

Richard felt a sensation in the pit of his stomach, which he could only describe as butterflies – but far worse. He hunched over and could now only describe the feeling as terrible starvation, which he had experienced during dry periods of his early career.

"What is it?" Nendar alarmedly asked, tearing his attention from a hushed conversation with his daughters.

"I have no idea," Richard responded. "But it's not good. It's not good at all."

A chorus of screams destroyed the serenity of the winter scene. Richard abandoned focus on the sinking feeling in his stomach and the four took off back in the direction of the village.

When the village came into view, it was nothing but death and destruction. A blurry, dark figure dashed at breakneck speed from peasant to peasant, killing each with seemingly a touch, sending a fountain of blood into the air each time.

"Split up. Don't waste any time," Richard ordered.

Richard and Nendar paired up and sprinted into the village. They both stretched their hands out and froze a red-eyed vampire in place as it was about to drive foot-long claws into a hopeless young peasant woman. She stared wide-eyed at the mages, paralysed with fear.

"Go! Run!" Richard shouted. She stayed as frozen as the vampire for a few moments but overcame her paralysis and ran.

"You have to start the spell, Fateborn! I may have a lirenium crystal, but I cannot match you. I can only assist you!" Nendar affirmed.

414

"Rez'kevar, dellessar, tan'barath galar!" Richard murmured, feeling Nendar channelling his own magical efforts into the spell.

A rift with a similar physical appearance to a portal appeared between them and the crazed beast, slowly growing from the size of a pea to that of a boulder. Inside the rift was nothing but blackness, utterly devoid of substance. They couldn't see the vampire on the other side of the rift, but they were still grasping desperately onto him with the restraining spell.

"Now pull him through," Richard calmly said.

Richard and Nendar clenched their fists and pulled backwards as if holding a length of rope. The vampire was pulled through the rift, yet they continued to restrain him. They watched as his emotionless ruby eyes, extraordinarily alike to Kalahar's, focused on Richard. They may have looked physically devoid of emotion, but the vampire still somehow exhibited unambiguous rage.

"Kezekevar closs," Richard said.

The window to the dimension Richard had just created closed in an instant, never to be reopened.

"Are there others?"

A cry of anger from Lynn provided them with an answer.

They dashed around a broken hut which looked as if it had been crashed through, past a chicken enclosure, around a well and came across the Varanus sisters, in very much the same position as Richard and Nendar had been a minute earlier, though with much less success. Richard immediately began to channel his energy into the process and the vampire they had wrangled watched as another empty rift ripped open the boundaries of their universe. Valerie and Lynn then worked together to force the vampire through the tear in worlds. Finally, Richard closed the rift and Lynn collapsed with exhaustion, desperately breathing in and out as if having sprinted a mile.

"You two should... try magic... without your crutch," she huffed. "It also turns out that... Val, despite her assurances... is incapable of creating a dimension... on her own. And I'm frankly incapable of helping... helping her. Splitting up won't be an option from now on."

"How's your stomach now, Fateborn?" Nendar chimed in.

"It's gone now. I guess that explains that," he said, surveying the damage. Mutilated bodies littered the frozen ground, the snow was more red than white and debris from the village's buildings were scattered around every path and clearing. The bounty hunter dreaded to think what it would look like in a city.

"And stop calling me Fateborn, if you would. My name is Richard, and I'd appreciate if you would call me as such."

Nendar wordlessly agreed and helped Lynn to her feet, having slowed her breathing.

"Witches," an old voice croaked from behind them. They turned around to face the old man who had previously ousted them from the village.

"Sorcerers and sorceresses," Nendar corrected.

"I don't care what the bloody hell you are. I told you to get out of our village. And now look what's happened!" he cried, gesticulating as frantically as his old body would allow for.

"Nothing good ever happens where a witch goes. You've cursed us, bloody curs. Now get out. Get out of our village."

"We just saved your bloody village, you pretentious old fool!" Richard snapped. "Those were vampires and we just spent a great deal of energy on banishing them from this world for eternity, as we lack the resources to kill them. You owe us your gratitude and more, for without us, this village would've been reduced to rubble."

The old man stubbornly planted his cane and clearly wasn't interested in anything any of them had to say.

"Get out, magicians. I'll be sending some boys to the garrison, and they'll have you hunted down and burned at the stake, like you should be. Now get out."

Richard turned to the others and silently acknowledged that it would be best to move on. They left the village and set off along the northern road once more.

"I wouldn't count on the garrison being able to help," Richard mused. "They're... short of staff."

"Is that where you went before meeting us?" Nendar asked.

"Yes. Know that your funds will no longer help in controlling that particular outpost."

416

Nendar stayed quiet, knowing that there was nothing he could say that would change the situation.

"What's our next move? Travelling on foot certainly isn't going to be of much use."

"We need to go to cities," Valerie supplied, speaking out loud for the first time. "It's no use defending little villages like this. If anything is certain to happen, it's that the vampires will arise in the countryside and converge on cities alongside those who already spawned in cities. We should go to Virilia."

"Why Virilia?" Richard countered. "The damage will be just as bad in Myana, and I hold the capital of Mirados to much higher importance than your Virilia. And as I am the only one of us capable of ridding these vampires from our world forever, I'm making the executive decision to go back to Myana."

Valerie scowled but said nothing, knowing that there was nothing she could say that would change the situation.

Richard traced a circle in the air and pressed forward, opening a window to the southern seaside Miradosi city of Myana. When looking through the portal, nothing looked amiss. That was different when they stepped through and materialised on the wet cobbles of the industrial harbour.

Bells rang loudly and constantly, their message transmitting across the city and beyond. Frothing waves indicative of an approaching storm crashed mercilessly against the array of ships in port and some even reached high enough to spill onto the walkway.

"They're here," Richard seethed, clutching his stomach. "We're not far from the hospital. We have to protect them first."

The bounty hunter set off at a sprint, bounding up a set of stairs which led to a wider portside road. The Sanskari mages followed at the same rapid pace, acknowledging the critical gazes of the passing civilians but incapable of doing anything about it.

The hospital came into sight as the population density steadily increased. Richard was brushing past more and more frantic pedestrians, all of which had a different response to being shoved out of the way. The Varanuses were much more careful in manoeuvring through the minefield of people.

A black shadow blazed past, escaping an alley between a bakery and a bookshop. It sliced the neck of an unfortunate passer-by but was frozen by Richard's magic before it could touch anyone else. Without Nendar's help, and under the fiercely contemptuous looks of disapproval from the sudden crowd, he repeated the process that he had already carried out twice that day. It was proving to be easier with every attempt and he had locked the vampire away within only a minute of having frozen it.

"Heresy! Black magic! Witchcraft!" a priest called from a podium, dressed in the blue robes of the Lanthanist Church. "Seize the wizard, for he must feel the wrath of the prophet Lanthanis for his crimes!"

The crowd roared in assent and stormed towards the bounty hunter. Richard looked at the Varanuses, eyes wide, as they stood at the edge of the crowd, expecting him to save himself one way or another.

"Zala'kivoss!" Richard cried. And just as he would have been the victim of a fatal crush, he leapt into the air, clearing the air over the attacking civilians and landing next to his allies.

"Chase the wizard! Waste no breath in bringing him to justice!" the priest called, unmoving from the podium. Although he didn't move, the crowd unquestioningly followed his orders.

Let's hope no more vampires appear near the hospital, Richard communicated to the others.

Where to now? Nendar asked.

The palace, Richard stated. *I must protect the King.*

"Saka los," Richard muttered. And the crowd stopped rampaging after him, in a sudden collective state of confusion. For the mages had disappeared.

"They'll soon disperse," Richard said. He was right – the civilians muttered to one another for a while, some angrily, some confusedly. But ultimately, they all heard the continuous ringing of the city bells and had their own places to be.

"Saka veil," Richard said, stripping the group of their invisibility. They stepped out from the alley in which they had previously taken shelter and Richard took lead in guiding them towards the palace, not yet visible through the lines of terraced houses towering above the cobbled streets. Valerie knowingly looked at Nendar behind Richard's back. He nodded.

They soon came across the aftermath of another vampire attack. It was evident it hadn't happened incredibly recently, as the bodies had been swept to the sides of the street and left out of the way. Some of the bodies weren't in one piece and assorted fractions of organs and limbs were placed in different piles of corpses.

"It's passed elsewhere," Richard declared. "I don't feel anything."

They continued at full pace towards the palace, now visible from the top of a set of ancient stairs leading from a circular intersection to the market district of the capital.

"Get inside, you fools! Are you deaf? We're under attack!" Richard shouted to the passing civilians. He had no time to listen to their responses.

They swept through the market district like the wind. It was clear that even with the ringing of the bells, merchants valued their merchandise and money over their lives and if they weren't vainly attempting to sell their wares, they were packing them up as quickly as possible in order to take them with them.

The market district fed into Regal Lane, the street housing the entrance to the King's palace. Lynn's remarkable physical fitness was beginning to fail and she slowed, unable to continue sprinting.

"Come on!" Richard called.

"I'm sorry, Richard. I can't keep bloody running," she panted. "Go on without me. I'll catch up."

Richard faltered, but only for a moment. He looked back at the sorceress and carried on with only Nendar and Valerie to the heavily guarded gate to the King's palace. He suddenly felt uneasy.

"State your business!" one of the guards barked, crossing his halberd with a symmetrically positioned second.

"Protecting the King. Have you heard the bells?"

"The Sanskari are attacking, yes. The King is safe."

"Not the Sanskari, you bumbling fool! Vampires! Do you see any soldiers?"

"I don't see any vampires, either," the second guard snorted. "Remove yourself from our presence, civilian, or we will be forced to do so ourselves."

Richard scowled and pressed his hands forwards. The guards flew sideways, collapsing into adjacent walls, while the gate swung open on both hinges. He rushed through with Nendar and Valerie close behind.

A well-kept stone staircase wound in both directions around a carved fountain spewing crystal-clear water from the mouth of a flopping carp. They flew up the stairs and came to the mouth of the palace, also guarded by two halberd-wielding guards. They could do nothing as the bounty hunter rushed past them and forced open the doors with a burst of strength. Pursuit proved to be pointless.

Richard swept past a passing courtier, wove through a nobleman and woman engaged in conversation on their way to the exit and almost crashed into a guard. By now, the message was clear among the protectors of the palace that there was an intruder, but there was still confusion as to who and where.

Richard made it to the throne room. The King of Mirados, Gerard, immediately broke free of his conversation with a brightly dressed man and his eyes widened at the sudden appearance of the bounty hunter and his companions.

"Bloody useless guards," he swore. "Seize them!"

"Please, Your Highness, give me a moment of your time. I am Richard Ordowyn, born and raised in this very city and I have always been loyal to you and Mirados. I don't mean to cause you alarm, but I needed to get to you."

King Gerard waved for the advancing guards to halt and cautiously nodded at the bounty hunter to continue.

"I've come a long way in the past month. I've done many things I never thought I would, or even thought possible. And now I come to you in this time of crisis. But not empty-handed. I bring you a gift – in the form of the Emperor of Sanskar."

Neither Nendar nor Valerie saw it coming and subsequently failed to react in time to Richard's next move. He twirled around 180 degrees and shouted a spell, freezing

Nendar in place. Valerie leapt forward in an outburst of fury, her sabre shrieking from its scabbard as she sailed through the air. Richard drew his sword just in time to deflect the incoming sorceress and they engaged in a duel.

"How does it feel the other way around, traitor?" Richard asked, blocking blow after relentless blow.

"You're making a mistake," she hissed, sidestepping and slashing again. "Tregor will have you flayed. Nendar will survive your treachery and then you will be hunted. And you will die, Richard. You will die, just like that bitch Linelle."

Richard faltered for one moment too long. Valerie clashed her sword against his and utilised the momentum of her swing to send her opponent's sword flying across the throne room. It landed on the floor behind the audience of guards, who appeared to be rather enjoying the spectacle.

"If you so much as open your mouth to breath, I'll kill you where you stand," Valerie threatened, the tip of her sabre to his chest. "Kneel."

He did as he said and slowly, carefully fell to his knees, staring downwards all the while.

"How does it feel?" she spat. "You don't get to hold power over me. You will never get to hold power over me."

She lowered her sword.

"Undo the spell."

"Over my dead body," Richard seethed, crossing his arms across his body.

"What are you doing now? Submitting?" she laughed confidently.

"And you," she snapped, turning to the King. "Don't move a muscle or I'll kill you in an instant."

Richard's dagger hissed and sliced cleanly through the sorceress's right wrist. She screamed in surprise and pain, looking in shock at the constant stream of blood where her hand had been attached a moment earlier. Valerie rendered defenceless, Richard stood up and kicked her to the ground, making no effort to avoid unnecessary brutality.

Richard knelt on Valerie's chest. She winced, but not from the pain of his knee buried in her bosom, but instead the glacial look which penetrated straight through her normally hardy exterior.

"What did you say about Linelle?" he whispered calmly, which was even more frightening than if he had shouted at her.

"I lied, Richard, Linelle isn't dead," she fumbled. "I-I just needed something to say to deal with you, to distract you. I—"

"How do you know about Linelle?" he continued quietly.

"I read your mind, you fool. I read it a great number of times while I travelled to Virilia with you. She was always there in the background, regardless of whether it was in the clutches of the Kal'sennar, almost being killed by a siren, or in bed with me. I note that the latter was when she appeared most prominently."

The bounty hunter fought hard to stifle a blush and ultimately failed, but maintained his composure.

"This has gone far enough!" King Gerard bellowed. "Master Ordowyn, you have provided quite the show, but I'm still deserving of an explanation."

"And I will give you one when I'm done with what I need to do!" Richard impertinently retorted. The King's face shifted to a deep shade of purple, but he chose not to argue back.

"You have been one evil bitch to me, Valerie," he hissed, throwing a great deal of emphasis onto her name, as if it were a curse. "And I'm not letting it go on any longer."

He raised his dagger and looked into her eyes.

But they weren't her eyes anymore.

The eyes into which Richard looked no longer sparkled like exquisitely cut emeralds. No longer did smoothly brushed anthracite locks adorn her shoulders, but instead slightly unkempt cedar hair cut just above the shoulders. Her eyes were blue like the sky on a clear winter day. Freckles appeared one-by-one at an exponential rate.

"You can't kill me," Linelle said, her voice sounding exactly as Richard remembered it – soft, comforting, and warm.

Valerie screamed and drew her right leg from under the emotionally disarmed bounty hunter and kicked him away with all her strength. Pain exploded in his chest and rippled through his body to the tips of his fingers and toes. She cried a spell and a translucent black sword materialised in her left hand and any duelling technique was forgotten. She attacked him with the ferocity of a wolf, the persistence of a hungry bear.

The King finally snapped and ordered his guards – who had until that point observed with great enthusiasm – to apprehend the rabid sorceress. She stood no chance as four suits of armour encircled her, halberds only inches away from killing at every angle. Richard dropped to the ground and rolled under the array of weaponry, reappearing behind the wall of steel.

"Master Ordowyn," King Gerard rasped. "It would be expected of me to order you burned at the stake. However, you've more or less just ended the war with your gift. So I'm willing to let you go this time. But not without telling me what to do with this witch."

Valerie's face was red with rage and she stared intently at the ponderous bounty hunter, sword still in hand.

Richard turned around to Nendar, still hopelessly incapable of moving so much as a finger. With a wave of his hand, Richard allowed the Emperor to speak.

"I must admit, Fateborn," he said, without even a trace of anger. "You outsmarted me. I didn't expect it in the slightest."

"Save your flattery for the headsman," Richard spat. "You see your daughter over there? Her life is in my hands. I wanted to ask you for your opinion. What should I do with the woman who lied to me, manipulated me, led me halfway across the continent, attempted to brainwash me to serve you and her, and then tried to kill me?"

"Is that a rhetorical question, Richard?"

"I'm glad you picked up on that."

Richard turned away from Nendar and sauntered over to his sword, picking it up with a flourish.

"Step away, please," he said to the guards. "I wish to finish this my way."

The guards looked to the King for approval. King Gerard, having long since realised that Richard didn't appreciate the basic concept of feudalism and respect, exasperatedly gestured for them to step aside.

Valerie's face grew increasingly pale as blood continued to stream from her wrist. Her eyes still reflected immense rage, but her face was no longer able to support it.

This time it was Richard who struck first. Quite simply thrusting his sword at the increasingly lifeless sorceress, she deflected the blow with ease. But not energy.

He stepped forward and slashed first from his left shoulder, then horizontally from the right. Once again, she deflected both blows, but did nothing more.

Richard extended his left arm and clenched his fist.

"Evectus," he whispered.

The translucent black sword evaporated from within Valerie's grasp and she stumbled forward, falling voluntarily to her knees and clutching her bleeding stump.

"You win, Richard," her voice trembled. "I hope you do well in crushing the Empire."

Richard nodded in affirmation.

"For certain."

In one clean swing, he ended the eighty-seven-year life of sorceress Valerie Varanus.

Richard stooped down and rummaged through the headless sorceress's robes, searching for one item.

"You treacherous bastard!" Nendar cried. "You've killed her – what bloody else do you want with her body? Are you that starved of a woman's touch that you'd go so far as necrophilia?"

He found what he was looking for. A rough-edged, amethyst-coloured crystal. He tucked it away in his satchel and stepped away from the corpse.

Without a word, he then tended to Nendar, who adopted his late daughter's fiery disposition at the bounty hunter's presence.

"You want my crystal, is that it? What the bloody hell do you want with the crystals, anyways?"

Richard found it in one of the pockets of the immobilised emperor and placed it with the other lirenium crystal. He then stepped away.

"He's still powerful, but greatly weakened without his crystal," he informed the King. "I must go now. The entire continent is threatened."

King Gerard, flustered, nodded in agreement and allowed Richard to exit the throne room. Richard left the palace under the critical gazes of the guards he had displaced on his way in.

424

I don't feel anything, he thought. *Kalahar must have overstated the urgency of this 'disaster'.*

I have to find her.

He searched the thoughts he had extracted from Valerie before killing her. Searching for any sign of Linelle, to know if she had lied once more. But she hadn't. It turned out that every single piece of knowledge about the bounty hunter's former lover had come from his own memory. He had to do this another way.

He opened a portal and returned to the border. Immediately his stomach dropped and he searched frantically around for the characteristic flash of grey as it moved beyond the limits of human speed.

CHAPTER 54

FALLÍA, TYEN'AEL

"We have to do something, Berri! The dwarven King won't be happy if we let his best troops get slaughtered!"

"There's nothing we can do," Berri curtly responded. "We fight for Fallía and without these walls, we are nothing. We cannot fight an army."

"We can disrupt, that's what we're built on! We don't need to take them on in direct combat, we just need to make their direct combat with the dwarves a lot more difficult!"

"The Elites number one hundred and twenty, Elle. Have you seen the size of the approaching army? There are thousands. No matter how skilled the Elites, they have no chance against thousands of elves."

"We can at least give them a chance to escape, then! It's the Darklight, the army won't be able to follow them. And the dwarves, being smaller than us, will quite easily be able to manoeuvre their way through the foliage."

"Where they'll then fall victim to crawlers or worse. I won't allow it – I'm not putting any FTA fighter on the line for a suicide mission."

"Stop with the pessimism for a moment, Berri! What if that was us? What if we were the ones being ambushed? Would you expect, or at least hope, for the help of the dwarves, even to escape? Because I would and they helped me get away from Ríyael so it would be damned impolite of me not to try to return the favour!"

"Ríyael?"

"It doesn't matter. I'm going to distract the army. If you want to come, be my guest."

"Elle, wait! You're making a mistake!"

Elaeínn rushed down the keep's steps and made her way to the outer wall. Rushing along the walls, she encouraged the statue-like defenders to join her. She received a few hesitant steps, but no more.

But if Berri were to order them to move, they would do it without hesitation.

Even those in the streets were unmovable from their preassigned tasks and duties, despite her urgency and her pleas.

Alazarioss, you could well have stayed here to heal...

She didn't know whether the dragon was listening or even could listen to her thoughts, so she just had to hope.

"You!" she interrupted a random person carrying a crate past the gatehouse, who nearly dropped it in surprise.

"Y-yes, Commander?"

"Why are you so bloody terrified? And it's not Commander, it's Elaeínn. Where is the armoury?"

"There's a section of the gatehouse with weapons, Comm— Elaeínn."

"Bombs? Do we have any of those?"

"A very limited stock – Mr Berri said we weren't to use them without his explicit permission—"

"I'm breaking the rules," Elaeínn said. "Go off with your crate, then."

The woman exasperatedly hustled away while Elaeínn ignored the objections of the guards as she searched the gatehouse for the weapon stock, and after finding it, the bomb supply. It was, as the woman had said, limited – two crates. She took one crate, all that she could carry, and chose strong words to prevent the guards from taking it back.

The people in charge of manning the gate and the drawbridge didn't hesitate to allow her to leave, and she couldn't tell if they were more scared of her or the inferred punishment they seemed to expect as a result of their actions.

A lightly worn path led from Fallía's moat to the highway – she followed this for most of the distance between the castle and the army before rerouting onto the neighbouring hills to gain a better vantage point.

The army was moving at an accelerated pace into the forest, their tight, organised formation having broken apart as troops swarmed around the slower-moving siege machines, though still restraining themselves to the boundaries of the road.

She set the crate down atop the hill and felt one of the bombs in her hand. It was roughly the size of her fist and surprisingly light, with a fuse leading from its top.

"Fuck," she swore, realising her mistake.

She heard sudden footsteps behind her and jumped, turning and drawing her sword impulsively from its scabbard. Her attacker stepped back and raised his arms in immediate surrender.

"You shouldn't scare me like that," she warned, returning her sword to her belt.

"Would you like some assistance with that?" Delíen offered.

"You're not staying behind to be Berri's lapdog?"

"Berri seems to have forgotten who we are. Your return is a breath of fresh air."

He snapped his fingers and the fuse lit, burning rapidly. Elaeínn launched it towards the crowd and recoiled at the deafening volume of the subsequent explosion.

The uproar following the explosion was perhaps even more deafening as the troops completely broke their formation among scattered limbs and shattered blades, searching vehemently for the origin of the explosion, while Elaeínn launched more and more bombs into the throng.

Some of the soldiers noticed the two crouched at the peak of the hill and called to the archers, who began to return projectiles of their own. These were easily avoidable from their position, but it was only a matter of moments before the infantry decided to advance.

Elaeínn was tapped on the shoulder and she swivelled around even faster than when Delíen had startled her – and to her surprise, it was a group of soldiers from Fallía, holding another crate of bombs.

"We're with you, Commander," they said confidently.

"It's Elaeínn," she corrected, ducking to avoid an arrow flying dangerously close to the peak of the hill. "And you can start by dealing with them." She gestured to the detachment of soldiers marching up the hill. "While we make our way towards the Darklight."

The FTA soldiers saluted and drew their swords but stayed on their side of the hill to cover Elaeínn, Delíen and a few of the other fighters as they rushed towards the forest, spontaneously stopping at points to throw bombs into the advancing army.

"We need to block the entrance," Elaeínn asserted as they reached the mouth of the Darklight path. "All of you – take a bomb and blast the daylight out of the trees surrounding the road. We need them falling."

The Tyen'Aeli army was flooding into the forest and didn't seem to be expecting the first of the FTA's bombs, which detonated directly in the middle of the path – causing significant damage to the soldiers unfortunate enough to be passing at that point but achieving little in the way of blocking the path. The next two bombs were significantly more successful – one landed directly at the base of a tree, obliterating it and sending the tree toppling over. It ended up blocking half of the path and crushing a group of Tyen'Aeli soldiers with no way of escaping. The second landed on the other side of the path and achieved the same for the other half of the path. The third, fourth and fifth bombs only exaggerated the destruction, displacing dirt from the road and creating a trench for the slain soldiers to fall into.

As had happened before, their position was noticed and arrows began to fly over their heads, an affront which was met by a constant depletion of their bomb supply.

As the deaths tallied up, the Aeli soldiers realising their easy access to the rest of their comrades had been barred, they began to turn to the hills in which Elaeínn and the FTA fighters resided. The fighters which had stayed back to fight off the initial advance had now joined them, and they were left with the option of fighting the bulk of the Tyen'Aeli army or fleeing.

Their decision was instant and unanimous, but the direction of their flight was a further decision which Elaeínn had to make for them. She turned towards the forest and ran, ushering the others to follow her as the jangling of armour and weapons grew noisier.

The Darklight's worn roads were in place for a reason. The foliage underfoot as Elaeínn transgressed the treeline acted as

429

an enemy in almost the same way as the one with swords. Vines, roots, and pitfalls made navigation treacherous, and the density of the canopy meant that light was thin, allowing the obstacles to hide in plain sight.

The soldiers followed them – slowly. They appeared to be having more trouble than the generally nimble FTA fighters in their clunky suits of armour, which allowed Elaeínn and her allies to escape, forging their way further into the depths of the forest.

"If anyone sees a web, we run the other way," she dictated, to no objection.

The interruption to the march of the army meant that until they caught up with the troops who had progressed past the entrance, they were now free to listen to the sounds of the forest – which were few and far between. The Darklight was often defined by its eerie silence and general lack of wildlife commonly seen in other woodlands. Apart from the trampling of foliage underfoot, all they heard was the whistling of the wind, the rustling of leaves and the occasional birdcall.

Until they caught up with the clashing of steel, the cries of pain and the roaring of destruction. It wasn't only coming from the neighbouring road, either – throughout the untameable wilderness, they began to spot dwarves engaged in battle with Tyen'Aeli soldiers, sometimes multiple at a time. And littered among the frequent skirmishes were the lacerated bodies of the fallen – encouragingly, far more elven than dwarven.

Those of the dwarves who weren't fighting were running – and they were being hunted down like prey.

"This is our chance to help!" Elaeínn called. "How many bombs do we have left?"

"A handful, Commander," one of the fighters said.

"I give up," Elaeínn muttered. "Right – use them to do what we did earlier. Trap them in – the ones on the road."

With their limited supply of explosives, they opted instead to plant the bombs at the bases of trees which they expected would make excellent barricades – and they did. The road was completely blocked with the felling of a hefty oak, with the added effect of sunlight finally breaching the canopy.

430

They then had another task at hand – passing through the fray to get to the other side of the army.

"I vouch for the option of running as fast and hard as we can," Elaeínn announced. "They're too caught up with fighting the dwarves, they might not even notice us. And even if they do, we're elves. They won't know we're their enemy. But... keep your sword arms at the ready. Let's go."

They bolted through the fighting, past clashes which they would rather have separated, stumbling over trenches and roots, one of them falling over and narrowly avoiding smashing their head against a rock. But Elaeínn had been right – the Tyen'Aeli soldiers paid them no attention.

To this point, she hadn't quite realised the scale of the force which had managed to pass the entrance to the forest before they were cut off. It felt like they just kept moving, and with every glance at the road, their hopes of saving the Elites diminished more and more.

A blazing orange head of hair caught her attention, standing out like a fire against the dingy backdrop of the Darklight. Tynak leapt from a log and sank his axe into a soldier's head, crippling their helmet in the process. He turned around and struck another soldier in the knee, throwing them off balance, before delivering the final blow to their neck.

"Tynak!" Elaeínn called, trying not to attract attention.

Tynak spotted them at once and rushed over.

"What in the blazes are ye doing here?" he asked exasperatedly.

"I made the executive decision to come and help you before you were destroyed."

"Quickly, get behind this mighty bloody oak, otherwise they'll attack yous.

"We were not told that the elven army was marching down this very path at this very moment, Elaeínn. Mr Berri has some explaining to do. I've lost and am losing many of me fighters."

"We blocked the entrance to the forest, so any more troops coming in will be doing so slowly, until they move the trunk, at least."

"They'll do that in no time. I told me men to run but honour and bloodlust got the better of them and now we've ended

431

up in this situation. I have a group of around twenty who obeyed me orders – it's not much, but we'll be able to carry out Berri's plan to attack Evekar. We'll just have to be mighty careful."

"Whatever – we'll discuss our next move once we escape the Darklight. Lead me to the others."

Tynak moved rapidly through the brush, his smaller size enabling much safer traversal with which the elves struggled to keep up. A few soldiers interrupted them along the way, but Tynak made swift work of them.

"This is it, ladies and gentlemen," Tynak announced, gesturing to a tightly packed group of dwarven soldiers, surrounded periodically by mutilated elven bodies. "We're leaving this damned forest. The elves might have got the upper hand this time, but that won't last, oh no. King Kagyan's armies will be on their way to crush the bastards within no more than a week, and it's our job to cripple them from the inside out. And though we are now few in number, we were given a job, and we will carry it out to the letter. Now let's get out of this blasted place."

With a rallying cry from Tynak, echoed ferociously by the remaining dwarves of the Elite Division, they tore their way back towards the entrance to the forest. Any Tyen'Aeli soldiers posed awkwardly around the forest acted only as roadblocks, posing no real threat.

The Tyen'Aeli army had managed to slightly shift the fallen tree by the time the dwarves arrived at the forest's entrance, and they were streaming around it in a much more orderly fashion than had preceded the FTA's disruption. This, unfortunately for them and the dwarves, meant that they were much more vulnerable.

"The dwarves! They're getting away!" one of the elves shouted, and all ideas of order immediately evaporated.

Dwarves were strong, nimble in enclosed areas and remarkably physically resilient. But they were not quick. And elves, with their height, were.

Alazarioss, this would really be a good time to show up! Elaeínn thought, as the FTA fighters and the dwarves backed up the hill, becoming quickly surrounded on every side by Tyen'Aeli soldiers.

432

They were trapped. At the top of the hill, Elaeínn surveyed her surroundings and found that the elves had outmanoeuvred them. They knew this and slowed their advance, drawing their swords and rearranging themselves to approach as a wall.

A roar reverberated through the air from behind the hill and the Tyen'Aeli army was caught off guard, faltering momentarily, and then entirely.

Berri stood at the centre of the onrushing army of FTA fighters, directing them forward with his sword. His hair swayed slightly in the breeze as he shouted rallying cries.

The two armies clashed with a wild ferocity, the pure strength of emotion on both sides engaged in its own battle. But as the FTA pushed up the hill, it was immediately clear where emotion was strongest.

The dwarves, clearly well trained for the scenario, sprang into action and began to cleave their way towards the FTA, splitting the soldier wall. The remaining soldiers fell upon them from the opposite side of the circle and hacked their way through the dwarves at an alarming pace.

Elaeínn had been in the middle of the dwarves for long enough – she drew her sword and lifted it above her head before forcing her way through the Elites and decorating the Tyen'Aeli army gold with splashes of crimson.

Within moments, the dwarven and FTA forces were joined and with their combined might, the Tyen'Aeli army began to fall. The dwarves, and particularly the FTA, were fuelled by passion, a passion which proved much more effective than the pay and the patriotism powering the National soldiers.

Elaeínn, after having sufficiently wetted her blade, made her way to Berri, who wasn't avoiding combat himself, made clear by the thick red liquid coating his sword.

"We need to get back to Fallía," Berri commanded before Elaeínn even had a chance to open her mouth. "That's our only chance not to be annihilated. It may look like we're winning now, but that will only last for a matter of minutes. Their army is far too large for us to defeat in open battle. We have to hope for a siege, or, in the best case, for them to pass us by entirely and continue into Hamatnar.

"And don't go protesting, either – I've made enough of a risk bringing them down from the castle as it is. You will stop this naïve crusade of yours and come to terms with authority. Society would collapse if we all did as we wanted, Elle. You need to set an example by following my command."

Elaeínn turned around to observe the progress of the battle – Berri was right. The impact of the FTA's initial charge had waned, the factor of surprise removed. Now, the generals of the Tyen'Aeli army were beginning to redirect all their troops from the forest to the hill and for every National soldier they felled, another five joined the fray. She watched in terror as progress first halted and then began to reverse.

"FTA! Retreat! To Fallía!" Berri cried. "Mages! Block their pursuit!"

Robed figures which, to this point, Elaeínn hadn't noticed, dramatically waved their arms in the air and began to chant spells. A white barrier of light split the front, rising into the air and acting as an artificial physical barrier between the two armies. The FTA and the dwarves turned and ran immediately as the National soldiers reacted unsurely – some lowered their swords, some prodded the barrier and some attacked it all out. Projectiles launched from the Tyen'Aeli siege weapons crashed against the barrier, the rocks shattering and the bolts snapping. But with every impact, the strain of the mages concentrating the spell grew visibly stronger, noticed by the soldiers of the National army. So they began to strike the barrier.

By this point, the FTA and dwarven forces had retreated a safe distance and looked as if they would make it to the castle. Berri, Elaeínn, Delíen and some other commanders Elaeínn didn't recognise had stayed behind to accompany the mages, whose resolves were rapidly deteriorating. The light of the barrier flickered, an occurrence which only spurred the Tyen'Aeli soldiers to hit harder and faster.

The barrier disappeared with a final bright flash and the remaining FTA fighters turned to run. The army charged, roaring with confidence and bristling with blades. Further projectiles flew over their heads, some landing dangerously close and burying themselves, sending a shower of dirt over the surrounding grass.

"I'll teleport us back, quickly!" Berri said to Elaeínn and Delíen. He stopped and traced a portal through which he promptly stepped. Elaeínn and Delíen did the same, and on the other side, Berri closed the portal just as a group of soldiers reached it.

The tip of a military-issue Tyen'Aeli sword clattered to the ground, sheared off by the closing of the portal.

Elaeínn picked up the hunk of metal, scrutinising it, particularly its weight.

"I think this might be one of Aegard's swords," she commented. "It's shit."

"Are you insinuating the smith has no proficiency in his trade?" Berri asked.

"Not at all," she retorted. "Quite the opposite."

They ascended to the ramparts and watched the battle develop. Their forces reached the drawbridge, which had been pre-emptively lowered to allow them access into the castle. But the Tyen'Aeli forces were dangerously close behind.

"You still think they'll just leave us be?"

"No," Berri curtly responded. "I think we'll be here for a while."

"You sacrificed the mages, Berri," Elaeínn said as the chains on the drawbridge creaked, barring the way across the moat.

"They sacrificed themselves to save us all."

The drawbridge slammed to a halt and the battle was left at a stalemate as the Tyen'Aeli troops reached the edge of the moat and were left with no option but to stare at the troops lining Fallía's walls. But then, minutes later, when the FTA's forces had reorganised themselves, the battle reignited when arrows were traded between those in the castle and those on the hills.

Arrows evolved into rocks, cannonballs, and ballista bolts. The FTA commanders fled to the keep, extremely aware that any extra moment spent on the walls only increased the likelihood of a stray projectile knocking them from said walls.

"These cannonballs are going to tear our walls to shreds," Berri paced up and down the war room. As if on cue, the sound of metal crunching through stone shook the room.

"Then what do you want to do, Berri? You said we have to defeat them in a siege."

"Well I've never commanded an army before! I've never controlled an entire castle! I have no experience as a military leader!" he shouted. "I am leading a community of freedom fighters against the military of an entire nation! We were never going to win! You know, Elle, when you turned up on that dragon, I genuinely thought we might have something. I thought hope might not be lost – that perhaps, with the might of a living mythical creature, we could turn the tide. But said dragon has since buggered off to Raeris-knows-bloody-where!"

A young, white-haired woman entered the room unexpectedly, seemingly innocently.

"What's the meaning of this interruption?" Berri stopped pacing and funnelled his anger into the question.

"We've come with a message, sire," she said.

CHAPTER 55

Elton worked tirelessly throughout the affair ushering refugees into the deeper caverns of the soulless Redhouse to make space for those who were supplying the fighters. It felt as if the entire population of Dannos was taking refuge in the headquarters of the crime boss – and perhaps they were, Elton thought. He had no idea as to the situation outside, and had no idea how many of the city's residents were left alive.

"Kalahar might have been a little bit right," Elton admitted to Paul and Felix, who themselves were fighting on the front line and had been for nearly the entire day between breaks.

"Well," Felix grunted, kicking a slain vampire aside. "I don't see the bastard."

Eventually, the assault began to slow. At last, the seemingly endless flow of enemies was beginning to dry up, and now there was time to breathe between each provocation.

The sandy cobbles of the Syndicate's front entrance, usually a pale beige, were now stained a deep crimson. There had been no time to remove the bodies effectively, so they had been used to crudely block the gaps between the crippled pillars and the ground. And they had been effective.

The sun, still shrouded in darkness, sank below the horizon as one of the defenders at the front of the Redhouse withdrew his blade from a vampire's skull. He kicked the grey body aside, where it came to rest next to his fallen friend, whose place he had taken.

The moment the moon entered the sky, it was like a switch had been flicked. A vampire rounded the corner and the de-

437

fenders pre-emptively readied themselves for its swift on-slaught – but the onslaught never arrived. Instead, the vam-pire flashed its ruby eyes and walked towards them, as casu-ally as a king would enter his throne room.

It stopped when the defenders extended their weapons and the vampire sized them up before extending an arm, mutter-ing a spell for several seconds. The defenders allowed it to happen, still stunned by the creature's docility.

Elton was rushed to the front as soon as the monster ap-proached, and he stood to witness as it uttered its first words in Santerosi.

"May I speak with Mr Redwinter?"

Elton apprehensively pushed his way through the rigid line of guards. The vampire spoke with an accent identical to Kala-har's.

"What the fuck are you?" Elton enunciated.

"I... I believe I'm a vampire, in your tongue," the beast said unsurely. "You believe me to be a... malevolent."

"That's because we've just spent all day slaughtering the likes of you while you do the same to us."

"Slaughtering... are these bodies... my brethren? But... I can't remember anything."

The vampire looked down at his hands. Elton did the same, expecting to see claws protruding from its fingertips, but that wasn't the case. However, his hands were coated in a thick, dried layer of blood.

"I... I have no recollection of any of this..."

A second vampire, this time female, approached the first in a similarly calm manner, again exhibiting no signs of aggres-sion.

"Ik'zash kavosh?" she asked, directed to the vampire.

"Erenash gal'kak."

"What the fuck are they saying, bossman?" one of the de-fenders asked concernedly.

"I don't know," Elton said. "But it's Archaeish."

"And what's that?"

"Language of the mages."

"Then how do they know it?"

"I don't know," Elton firmly reiterated.

The female vampire touched the first vampire's forehead and her ruby eyes glazed over momentarily as the spell took effect.

"We... we are not the enemies you think we are," she said, turning to face the increasingly impatient swordsmen. "We... we have been deceived. And you... you have also been deceived."

"Your kind just spent all day slaughtering entire populations and I'm to believe that you mean no harm now that you can speak?" Elton questioned. "I'm to believe that you suddenly understand some truth that I don't?"

"Kalahar... Kefrein-Lazalar... he betrayed you..."

As if summoned by his name, Kalahar materialised behind Elton and grabbed an oiled sword from one of the defenders. He then flew towards the two vampires and swiftly thrust the blade through them both in one fluid motion.

"Elton, you fool, you were supposed to kill them," the vampire said hastily, discarding the bodies from the blade. "Are you trying to get yourself killed?"

"They could speak to us, Kal. And they sounded just like you."

"A trick, a terribly devious trick, my friend. They had been animated for too long, had gained some control of their sentience. They tried to trick you with clever words and mind-reading."

Elton grabbed a blade of his own from another of the guards and approached Kalahar aggressively and determinedly.

Elton thrust the sword to the vampire's cloaked chest, and he recoiled violently upon contact with the oil.

"You think you're so invincible, Kalahar? You think that you can mislead us all into obeying your every command? Into carrying out your dirty work? Well, I've been foolish enough up to this point to believe it, but no more! I will not take any more orders from a creature who has fed us constant lies and taken everything from me that I believed in! You're no 'chaotic' vampire, you're a malevolent just like those you just slayed, and the many others we've killed today. That's why you disappeared, isn't it? You're bound by the curse in

439

very much the same way as the others are. And if you're a malevolent, then that means you must share the same vulnerabilities."

Elton thrust his sword forward but Kalahar was far quicker, leaping backwards, snarling.

"You foolish miscreant! My goals may well be different to yours, but you only survive because of me! Without me, your miserable city would have been razed to the ground. Everything you know destroyed. Humanity reduced to shreds. But because of me, humans have been able to continue existing for their miserably short existence. So what if I'm a malevolent? I've conquered my nature, I've conquered my vulnerabilities. I am the only one that deserves to continue existing, and I've made it my goal to ensure that remains the case. A goal which you imbecilic humans benefit quite directly from!"

"Leave," Elton growled. "Leave and never come back."

"Oh, Elton," Kalahar chortled. "You have no power over me."

Elton raised his sword.

"Is that so?"

"You have no idea the mistakes you've made, old man," Kalahar laughed maniacally. "Nobody gets the better of Kalahar Kefrein-Lazalar! I am eternal! A living deity! And if you think you can best me, Elton Redwinter, then you are sorely mistaken!"

"Get out of my city," Elton growled.

Tendrils shot from Kalahar's fingertips and Elton brought his sword in front of him defensively. The tendrils collided with the oiled weapon and immediately shrank away, Kalahar crying in monstrous pain.

"You've made a terrible, terrible mistake, Elton," Kalahar reiterated, furiously caressing his hand.

And then, as he had done so many times before, he vanished.

"Good fucking riddance," Elton said with assurance. "Now, let's get to work."

440

CHAPTER 56

Upon Richard's departure, King Gerard immediately ordered his guards to apprehend the seemingly defenceless Nendar Varanus. But they were unable to.

The Vanquisher smirked and quickly rose to his feet. He threw a lightning bolt at the first and second guards to approach him, killing them instantly. The remaining six raised their guards at once and stood more defensively as the sorcerer materialised a pair of short swords and grinned with excitement.

"Kill him! Kill the wizard!" Gerard cried in horror.

The guards tried to do as they had been told. And they began to fall.

Nendar pirouetted towards the first, who had chosen to approach without staying in line with his counterparts. With the sword in his right hand, he knocked the guard's halberd away to provide the necessary space for his left sword to strike the finishing blow, opening his neck with pinpoint accuracy and sending blood spurting from the thin gap between the guard's helmet and his breastplate.

Another stepped forward from behind Nendar and swung his halberd over his head. He dodged the oncoming attack without looking before twirling through the array of armoured assailants, deflecting and dodging their blows as he went.

Nendar moved closer and closer to the throne as the guards moved out of his way, fearing their chances in close quarters against the sorcerer. The King frustratedly shouted at

441

those employed to give their lives to protect his, but to no avail.

Nendar leapt over the last of the guards between him and King Gerard and held one of his blades to the King's throat. The guards pointed their halberds at the sorcerer but managed to show even less intent to attack than before.

"Oh, Richard," Nendar said aloud to himself. "As expected, you just couldn't account for every possibility. A terrible shame."

He raised his sword and plunged it into the King's heart. Finally, the guards found the will to move.

But it was too late. For the sorcerer had disappeared.

CHAPTER 57

The woman rapidly created a large portal the length of the room through which appeared a further three people – this time, much older and elegantly dressed. And over their hearts, they wore the badge of the Tyen'Aeli State Security Service.

The officers of the SSS drew their daggers and bounded towards the three FTA commanders, expertly disarming them before they even had a chance to draw their weapons and then pressing them to the floor.

"Berri Efraean," one of the officers said gruffly. "Elaeínn Tinaíd. Delíen Faellorn. You are all under arrest for high treason and sedition. There will be no trial – you are to be executed as the terrorists you are. And as of today, as it always has been, Fallía is under the jurisdiction of Prime Minister Jaelaar and the National Party."

"That's right. As it always has been."

Jaelaar stepped through the portal, a sword at his belt and an oversized badge on his breast.

"Hello, Elaeínn," Jaelaar said drily. "And Berri, the mastermind behind it all. I don't believe we've had the pleasure."

"How did you know, you bastard?" Berri asked, receiving a sharp slap to the face in retort.

"I have a better question. How did you, a group of worthless, disorganised miscreants, have any expectation that you could waltz over to the King of Hamatnar, take his money and found a state of your own?"

Jaelaar paced around the war room, admiring the maps.

"King Kagyan is dead," Jaelaar said nonchalantly, placing a red pin through Rockfell on the map of Tyen'Ael and Hamatnar. "But you didn't account for that, did you?"

He picked up some more pins from a container on the main table, all red.

"And your little teacher friend, Caeran," Jaelaar continued, placing a pin through Sanaíd. "He's dead, too. But you already knew that, didn't you, Elaeínn?"

Elaeínn scowled and struggled against the officer holding her to the ground, to no avail. Meanwhile, the muffled sounds of battle grew in volume. Shouts and roars, possibly from either side, became particularly audible.

"And the smith, what was his name? Aegard?" he said rhetorically, placing another pin adjacent to Caeran's. "The one who sold us shit swords? Yes, he was hanged publicly."

"How? How could you know?"

"Dear Elaeínn," Jaelaar chuckled. "You are foolish and naïve. And that is why the FTA had no chance.

"Mind you, those I've listed just now are only a fraction of the traitors we've had eliminated. But as far as I know, those are the ones you've visited most recently, hmm?

"And as for you, Mr Efraean. You thought we wouldn't hear about your subordination to the dwarves? That you were planning to attack Evekar with the Elites?"

"Beg my pardon for underestimating you, Prime Minister," Berri retorted. "I didn't think your men had it in them to dress up as dwarves."

Jaelaar chuckled.

"That's a good one, Berri. Could you imagine it? We'd have to chop their legs off and compress their torsos before we could possibly have a convincing short arse. Not to mention fattening them up. No, that's not what we did. Much more practical than that."

Jaelaar stepped over Elaeínn and reached for her side. He forcefully wrenched the Dragonsteel Blade from her waist and placed it on his own so that his swords lined up symmetrically.

"And now, this will return to its place above my hearth," he concluded. "Now, you've slipped from my fingers more than I'm willing to admit, hmm? Let's not allow that to happen again. Officers – kill them now."

The officers thrust their daggers towards the throats of their captives. Elaeínn rolled over and attempted to kick her captor from his feet, but only succeeded in hurting her shin. Still, she had avoided the first attempt to kill her, and the second one followed only moments later.

Berri had managed likewise and was now on his feet. He quickly uttered a spell and channelled a gale-force wind through the room. Jaelaar was blown against the wall, where he fought to move forward. Of the three SSS officers, two were blown from their feet, including the one against which Elaeínn had been struggling. It provided her with the opportunity to stand up, although Berri's gale was resulting in difficulty.

Delíen hadn't been so lucky and his dead body, throat slit, was battered against the wall, his blood spun around the air like a whirlpool. It spattered across Berri's maps, staining entire countries red.

"You bloody incompetent fools! I told you to kill them!" Jaelaar spat. He drew the Dragonsteel Blade and slowly approached Elaeínn, who had no choice but to step towards Berri.

Berri lowered his arms and the gale stopped. The officers wasted no time in bounding across the room, forcing Berri to raise his arms again, this time uttering a different spell.

A barrier appeared between them and the officers, very similar to the one which had been employed on the battlefield. The officers went straight to work concentrating their own magic in an attempt to break through.

"Beneath us, Elle," Berri grunted through gritted teeth. "A door. Open it."

She knelt down and opened the trapdoor, invisible against the wooden panels of the floor. A glance at Berri confirmed that she was to enter it.

A ladder led the long way down into a cold, foreboding chamber, crammed with old crates, barrels and ruined items of furniture, all connected with a network of cobwebs. She jumped as a rat scurried across her path, darting between two ancient sofas, each looking equally unsuitable for seating.

A crash from above signalled that Berri's barrier had broken and she picked up her pace, keen not to be captured

445

again, but also keen to discover whatever it was in the cellar that Berri wanted her to find. Even if it was just an escape route.

The staccato clattering of footsteps echoed throughout the silent walls as Berri and his pursuers made their way closer.

Berri, evidently knowing the layout of the cellar, was soon with her, while she had been unsure of which direction to take.

"Are you crazy? Why are you still here? Let's go! Follow me!"

The officers were close behind, as was signified by the heavy pattering of their feet as they thundered through the chamber, disregarding the obstacles and apparently outright removing them from their paths, which they could tell from the occasional clattering and splintering of wood. But then they reached a blank wall.

"This way," Berri whispered, opening a crate in the corner. The crate was empty, and it lacked a base. In its place was an entrance to yet another secret passage, one cloaked in complete darkness.

Elaeínn vaulted the crate and landed gracefully in the tunnel beneath, followed by Berri, who extended his legs to hold himself up while he placed the lid back onto the crate.

The musty air forced Elaeínn's nose to contort and the displaced dust triggered a sneeze, which she suppressed at the last moment. The lid of the crate was placed quietly back and Berri dropped, experiencing a similar reaction.

"And now," Berri whispered, wandering away, "we hope they don't find that soon. Follow me."

CHAPTER 58

The vampire caught him by surprise, dashing from a cluster of alders lining the side of the road onto which he had teleported. It reached out with dagger-like claws and nicked the bounty hunter in the side, ripping his jacket and drawing blood. Richard cried in pain and stretched out his arm, freezing the beast in place. He then repeated the ritual to banish it to a new dimension.

He had chosen a stretch of highway he knew was situated near a Miradosi encampment – different to the garrison near the Old Oak. This encampment housed at least a thousand soldiers in tents and was almost a functioning settlement – they even had a bounty board from which he had taken a series of contracts in the past. When he arrived, the bounty board was even more full of contracts, to the point that there was fierce competition for each to have a place on the board and it even looked like some had been ripped off and thrown into the snow.

Smoke belched from grand bonfires situated periodically throughout the camp, the stench of pine smoke clashing with that of the burning flesh of fallen soldiers. The camp had fallen into a state of chaos, with people urgently darting from tent to tent gathering various supplies, their expressions betraying intentions to desert. Though as swathes of soldiers flooded from the camp's borders in every direction, the captains and commanders didn't look particularly interested in stopping them – many were among the deserters.

Richard stepped into the fray and drew his sword as a precaution, knowing his bow and arrow would be no use when it

447

came to stopping the vampires. His blade, however feeble against their power, might offer the necessary delay between them appearing and him magically restricting their movement.

Immediately he was knocked aside by a boisterous trio of shivering infantry. Armed with pikes, dressed in rusted iron armour, the blue paint of Mirados long since having chipped away. Only mostly unnoticeable flecks of blue remained scattered across their breastplates.

He pressed his way through the throng, however unruly. Everybody was too preoccupied with the current upset to worry about hassling the bounty hunter.

The void in his stomach deepened and he felt the desire to keel over but fought through it and marched forwards. More soldiers ran past.

"Are you fuckin' mad, bounty hunter?" a soldier not quite as distracted as everyone else asked in passing. "There's somethin' rippin' through the camp! If you don't run, you die! Only Lanthanis knows what it is!"

"Lanthanis and me," Richard muttered, pressing on.

It was near. More soldiers ran past.

Richard raised his sword to clash with the vampire's elongated claws as it flew past, a clang resonating throughout the area and prompting those already fleeing to hurry their pace. The vampire continued forwards as Richard reached his arm out to freeze it, but he was too slow to save the life of an infantryman who was unlucky enough to run directly into range of the vampire's rage.

It was a standard procedure at that point. One he was becoming remarkably quick at carrying out.

"Come on, let's move!" a female voice called to his left, deeper into the camp's reaches as he finished sealing the gate between the vampire's dimension and his.

He picked up his pace in accordance with that of those fleeing the camp. But he continued inwards, the pit in his stomach still ever-present.

His worst fears were confirmed when he found the source of the female voice.

He broke into a sprint, disregarding his surroundings, focusing only on the woman situated at most fifty feet away, standing atop a broken cart, ushering others past her. Linelle wasn't a soldier, or at least she wasn't when he had last spent time with her.

She was indeed ushering others away, but not soldiers. Others dressed in expensive, light armour. Other bounty hunters. She herself was dressed in a man's tight-fitting umber breeches, loosely buttoned off-white linen shirt, and heavy fur cloak.

He collided with a charging soldier's pauldron and crashed to the ground, pain rippling through his jaw. He prodded it with a finger and pain ricocheted through his body, but it was still in one piece.

Painfully and with an orchestra of grunts, he forced himself to his feet just in time to step out of the path of a stampede. They passed, and he ran towards Linelle.

His stomach somersaulted.

"Lin!" he cried, clutching his abdomen. She looked around, unsure of the source of the sound. Then she saw him, and her eyes widened to the size of discs.

"Rich?" she whispered in disbelief.

More soldiers ran past. Richard forced his way through them.

"Lin!" he repeated.

He tripped over a loose stone and crashed into the stew of snow and mud, once again bashing his jaw. Paralytic pain exploded through his chin and face, enough to make him salivate and tear up.

She leapt from the cart and ran towards him as a nearby soldier screamed as something took his life.

"Rich! What are you doing here?" she exclaimed, reaching the bounty hunter and gently caressing his cheek with hands as soft as silk.

"It's not safe..." Richard mumbled, still dazed. "It's not safe, Lin... You need to get out of here."

"I'm helping others get out of here," she stated. "What are you doing here?"

"I came to kill them... the vampires..."

"Vampires? Rich, you're rambling. Vampires aren't real."

"That's what I thought. A lot has happened recently, Lin. A lot of things I wouldn't have expected. You need to get out of here, fast. It's not your place to defend these people – they know to flee themselves. Don't sacrifice yourself for them."

"It's absolutely my place," she retorted. "I'm a medic, Rich. You know that well. It's shit like this that you're saying now that drove us apart."

"You don't understand. I've spoken with vampires. This was planned. It's something to do with an eclipse on the other side of the world. People are going to die unless I step in and prevent it. I've learned to do magic, Lin. Not only can I do magic, but I'm much stronger, more powerful than any other mage. Something to do with fate – I'm what others call the 'Fateborn'... I can explain it all later. I came to find you. It's pure chance that I found you here, and I'm not letting you go again."

His stomach tied itself into knots and he keeled over through an attempt to get back to his feet.

"What is it? What's wrong?"

"It's near... it's so near... we have to run..."

"The vampire?"

"Please don't question it, I need you to trust me, just please trust me, before it attacks—"

He got to his feet with the aid of the medic. She gazed longingly at him and he savoured the way the sun reflected off her sky-blue eyes. The harmony and bliss provided by her presence. The remarkable softness of her hair, her skin, her breath.

His stomach twisted itself into knots, somersaulted and then unravelled again.

"Run, Lin, we have to run..."

She looked down at her stomach, where four spots of crimson had appeared on her shirt, growing at an exponential rate. She looked back once again at the bounty hunter, eyes ripe with fear and regret.

"I love you, Rich," she whispered.

The vampire withdrew its claws from the medic's back and she succumbed to gravity, slumping face-first into the snowy ground. Richard roared inhumanely and stretched both hands out with the intention of freezing the vampire. But instead, he tore it apart.

450

Only a moment ago, a black-haired, grey-skinned, ruby-eyed monstrosity stood before him. In a burst of anger, its stony skin was ripped from its skeleton and vaporised, its ruby eyes ripped from their sockets and burst. Nothing remained of the beast but its bones.

But Richard's anger was unending. Even after destroying the vampire, he continued producing noise unheard from humans, terrifying those feeble soldiers attempting to escape the camp. He clenched into a ball and slowly began to rise into the air, floating. An icy-blue veil encapsulated him in his entirety, mostly transparent and shimmering like the still surface of a lake. His eyes, normally green like oak leaves, were stripped of not just the green of his irises, but the black of his pupils and the white of his sclerae. All were replaced by the icy blue which constituted the magical veil in which he floated. His eyes glowed like torches, but much brighter, dazzlingly brighter.

"*Kalahar!*" he shouted, his hair flowing wildly, uncontrollably, as if in the midst of a storm.

A lightning bolt escaped his fingertips and penetrated the veil. It found one of the tents in the camp incinerated it immediately.

Richard floated higher into the sky. His thoughts were focused only on two things – Linelle's dead body on the ground below him and his strong desire to find Kalahar and... he didn't know what then. He just knew he wanted to find him.

Another lightning bolt caused a larger tent to catch fire. A group of soldiers shortly afterwards streamed out of it, collectively carrying the charred body of one of their comrades.

The shimmering of the veil became more and more energetic, seeming increasingly visually unstable. It began to regularly pulsate, not unlike an arrhythmically beating heart, while Richard's eyes glowed ever brighter.

Even the fleeing soldiers, still under threat, stopped to watch the event. There were chants of 'witchcraft!', 'sin!' and more. Nothing of value to their situation. And nothing which would have saved them.

Richard floated higher. The pulsating became more and more rapid.

And then the veil exploded.

Boundless magical energy rippled outwards, destroying everything in its path. The camp from which soldiers fled was reduced to rubble. Every living – and unliving – creature within a mile was instantly wiped from the face of the earth. But that was only the instant effect.

For the magical energy didn't stop. It continued outwards, expanding in the shape of a sphere, Richard at its centre. An unstoppable force swept through snow-dusted pine forests and left only scorched trunks and branches. Snow melted and evaporated while the dead ground underneath was singed and blackened. A doe perked its ears up upon hearing a soft rumbling. And then it too became a victim of the cataclysm. As did all other wildlife unfortunate enough to be close to the camp.

A pack of wolves surrounded a lone, crippled elk. They didn't manage to be the ones to kill it.

The magical outburst continued with unrelenting speed, engulfing anything and everything in its path.

Richard fell. And the magic disappeared, as if it had never existed. What didn't disappear was the destruction.

He landed on the hardened earth a few feet away from Linelle's intact corpse. Through immense effort and pain, he crawled to her and embraced her.

"I'll save you, Lin. I'll bring you back."

And he fainted.

CHAPTER 59

FALLÍA, TYEN'AEL

"Where does this lead?"

"It's a catacomb. A hidden one, where the late House of Eragor would entomb their deceased alongside expensive treasures. It was then discovered by the House of Aerría, who captured the castle from the original dwarven inhabitants. And then we discovered it almost untouched when we inherited the castle. It serves an excellent network to navigate almost anywhere in Fallía in complete secrecy. Dozens of generations of Eragors and Aerrías are entombed here – as such, a large crypt was needed."

After they had moved a substantial distance from the crypt's entrance, completely reliant on Berri's prior knowledge of its layout, Berri uttered a spell and generated an orb of light in his palm, which he cast above them. Now, when they walked, the light followed.

The new source of light unveiled an intricate mixture of dwarven and elven architecture – the many pillars supporting the roof between the graves of the dead alternated between the sharply cut, efficient design of the dwarves and the more elaborate, artistically carved preference of the elves. The actual graves themselves were where these designs had been woven together, evidently with elven efforts to remove the crypt's heritage.

It was a maze – designed as a grid of long, narrow passages, which really did stretch across the entirety of the castle's grounds. Despite their depth, the roar of battle penetrated even to the catacombs, shaking the walls and scattering dust from the ancient ceiling. But eventually, with Berri's navigational prowess, he led them to a set of stairs.

"This is the official entrance, so to say." He led her through the arched doorway and up the narrow stairs. "It's still not an obvious entrance, but they had to get the bodies respectfully in somehow."

The stairs led to a wooden door, opened with a round handle which looked to be more rust than handle. Berri opened the door and the crescendo in volume of battle peaked.

The door was located inside the Raerist church, which had been filled with weapons and supplies due to its proximity to the gatehouse. The Tyen'Aeli soldiers were yet to pass the moat, but the projectiles being traded over the walls were so dense that they cast shadows over areas where the sun should have been shining.

The gatehouse was, though still standing, looking worse for wear. The Tyen'Aeli cannons had crippled it, parts of its roof having collapsed and the drawbridge controls having been made inaccessible as a result of a cave-in along the wall. The mechanisms which would otherwise control the drawbridge had been left dangerously unguarded after cannonballs had disintegrated the surroundings.

"We're going to be left with the bloody ruins we started with at this rate," Berri cursed.

"If we don't confront them, you're right," Elaeínn declared.

"What do you suggest, then? That we drop the drawbridge and engage in open battle against six thousand troops? With our, what, one thousand? In what scenario could we possibly emerge victorious?"

"In what scenario do we emerge victorious where they destroy our defences and then march in to slaughter us? Come on, Berri! We need to fight!"

"No, what we need to do is capture Jaelaar, Raeris only knows where he is right now. I can assure you that him and his officers are probably already making a good start on infiltrating from the inside. Let's go – we're going to the keep."

The streets were still crowded with FTA fighters running to and fro, still in the process of arming one another and amassing supplies near the gatehouse, where the bulk of people had gathered, ready for the ever-increasing likelihood of the drawbridge collapsing.

"You lot—" Berri stopped a group of well-equipped fighters, numbering seven, "come with me and Elaeínn. We're on our way to capture Jaelaar. You seem to fancy yourselves good with the blade? That's why you've taken all the best supplies for yourselves?"

"We served as mercenaries before joining up, sire," one of them exclaimed. "We used to be known as the Ekkas."

"I should hope you're just as fearsome as the creature itself, then. Follow me."

They raced up the hill towards the keep. The Ekkas, which until their sudden recruitment into Berri's personal security had been raucously loud, were silent as they followed.

"Jaelaar, if he's still inside, is our target," Berri dictated upon their arrival at the keep. "I want him alive – but if there's any circumstance where our choices are dead or not having him at all, then kill him. And beware – he brought officers of the SSS with him. And we have traitors among us, too. So beware of them."

They breached the keep as if it had been taken, so those who were still inside were left baffled by the dramatic entrance. Then, they were told that the Prime Minister was inside and suddenly they understood.

"To the war room. That's where we left them," Berri ordered, drawing his blade and suggesting the others do the same. Elaeínn was forced to grab a sword from a bystander.

"How are you with magic?" Berri asked as they forced their way through the mess hall, which was mostly empty. Only the chef was still wandering around.

"Irría and Henna are the best, sire. The rest of us can do the basics, but if we're up against the SSS, you'll be wanting to speak to them."

"And which of you are Irría and Henna?"

"Us, sire," two identical women said in unison.

"Twins?"

"That's right, sire," the first man confirmed. "And the most effective ones you'll ever know."

"Excellent," Berri exclaimed, briskly exiting the mess hall and climbing the stairs towards the war room two at a time. "I shall be expecting you two to prevent his escape, in that case. Provided he hasn't escaped already."

They crashed through the door to what used to be the lord's quarters and saw the first evidence of Jaelaar's continued presence in the form of a familiar white-haired young woman.

She bolted at the sight of the hunting party and was pursued at top speed. Berri attempted to shout a few spells but was evidently too tired and incapable of concentrating while they ran.

The woman turned the corner into the private dining room and used a quick burst of magic to send the table flying into the entrance. It was large enough to block the entire door, wasting precious seconds.

Two of the Ekkas, brutishly muscular, stepped up to remove it from their path. It hit the ground with a thunderous bang and they didn't stay behind to clean up the ensuing debris.

"We're going to bloody lose her," Berri cursed, panting as they continued in the spy's perceived direction.

As they made their way towards the balcony, where a door had been left swinging on its hinges, their fortune worsened.

One of the Ekkas suddenly cried out in pain as one of the SSS officers materialised from the effect of an invisibility spell. He had been slashed in the throat and his blood clashed fiercely with the deep blue hue of the carpet.

The officer grabbed the Ekka's sword as he fell and threw his dagger with expert precision into Irría's eye. She collapsed atop her comrade's body.

Elaeínn screamed and attacked from behind, a blow which was parried and returned with blazing speed. But as Berri and the rest of the Ekkas joined in, even a swordsman skilled enough to be a member of the State Security Service had no chance.

It was one of the brutish Ekkas who struck the killing blow, driving his blade directly through the officer's heart, an action opposed ferociously by Berri. The leader of the FTA at once approached the brute and grabbed his bloodied sword hand with anger, before releasing it and resorting to words.

"We could have used him for information. There are two more like him lurking around here, and we're yet to find Jaelaar or our mole. Henna – perform a scan. Anyone under the effect of invisibility in a hundred metre radius."

"A-aye, sire," Henna trembled, looking detachedly at her mutilated sister.

"And do it bloody fast, we haven't got all day!"

Berri plundered the officer's body of its weapons and hidden armour plating, which, through being light enough to allow manoeuvrability, had caused his demise through lack of protection against piercing. Berri slipped the plating under his own clothes and idly adjusted it while Henna continued to mutter a spell.

"I've got something, sire," she said as Berri finally fitted the plating comfortably, turning expectantly to face her. "On the lower levels. Not invisible, but a very strong magical signature. And I'm not sure if I'm mistaken or what, but I don't think it's coming from a person. It's coming from an object."

"The Blade," Elaeínn said.

"Where on the lower levels?" Berri pressed.

"It's... It's in a large room. Lots of people about. It must be the lobby."

"Are people blind? They can't recognise the Prime Minister of bloody Tyen'Ael? For Raeris's sake, let's move!"

They returned down the many floors of the keep in the opposite direction to their initial travel, in very much a boisterous fashion, careening around corners and barrelling through corridors.

The lobby was full of people, mainly women and children seeking refuge from the fray taking place lower in the castle.

"Everybody down, right now!" Berri hollered.

His order was met with general anxiety, conveyed verbally and physically, but every last person in the lobby, including the receptionist, crouched to the ground.

"Where in the hells is he, Henna?" Berri asked gruffly.

"He's... he's... he's not here. But the source still is! Right next to you, sire!"

"Berri! Look out!"

The white-haired woman stood up, ripped the Dragonsteel Blade from her scabbard and lacerated Berri's throat.

CHAPTER 60

FALLÍA, TYEN'AEL

"This bridge is coming down!" Tynak yelled to the Elite Division. They were gathered outside the gatehouse, watching preparedly as more and more cannonballs devoured the castle walls.

A troop of FTA archers had assembled, arrows nocked, and Tynak's troops brought up the rear. The soldiers atop the ramparts still continued to trade arrows with archers outside the castle, but they slowly started to retreat down into the courtyard with the largest mass of soldiers.

A stray cannonball finally crashed sonorously against the exposed eastern side of the winch and the chain was released on one side, causing the drawbridge to drop one side, leaving it tilted.

This drop, despite still not allowing passage, meant that there was now a direct line of sight between the soldiers waiting outside the castle and those defending within. And it meant that there was now another location through which arrows could be exchanged.

The size of this location was rapidly expanded when another cannonball obliterated the winch's western side and sent the drawbridge clattering to the ground on the outer side of the moat.

"For King Kagyan!" Tynak shouted as the Tyen'Aeli soldiers entered the castle.

CHAPTER 61

FREE CITY OF DANNOS, SANTEROS

Elton was honorarily elected the acting leader of the shattered city and immediately set to mobilising the remaining workforce, all of which owed him a debt. In terms of vampires, they were still around, and they encountered a handful, all of which were just as docile as those that had been slain by Kalahar as the day drew to a close. Despite their lack of hostility, the general population were still yet to trust them, and many were killed on sight, further adding to the pile of bodies which was being redistributed into carts to be shipped into the agzar pits of the surrounding desert.

Elton slept restlessly. Falling asleep was the easy part, having been awake for more than twenty-four hours, but his sleep was fraught with lucid nightmares.

Kalahar visited him in these nightmares, first appearing in the form of Rafio Benito.

"I ran this bank for decades before you came along, Elton," he said with an unassuming South Benetian accent. "And then you made the mistake of transgressing me."

The surrounding scenery of the bank changed and he was thrown to the windswept forests surrounding Letham Deregor, the stronghold itself visible in the distance, casting a shadow over him as the sun set behind it.

"I have lived for thousands of years, unchallenged," a red-eyed deer said, appearing from behind a tree. The deer then transformed into a bear, retaining its red eyes. "You are but a feeble human. A feeble human whose thoughts are weak, malleable. Controllable."

459

Snow began to fall and Elton looked at the grey sky. When he looked down, the ground had been coated in white.

"I am omnipresent," Richard Ordowyn, his eyes replaced with rubies, said ominously. On his back he carried a large bag, with which he was evidently struggling. "Even the supernatural cannot best me. I control everyone. And everything."

The trees disintegrated and the snow hardened, moulding into the form of a dragon's scales, a dragon to which Elton clung desperately for his life as they soared across the ocean.

"Even dragons, Elton," the dragon spoke, turning its head mid-flight to reveal its blood-red eyes. "Even the oldest, the wisest of dragons are nothing against me."

Elton returned to his study in his house in Dannos and was approached, dazed, by Rosa. Rosa drew her sword.

"Even the wills of your allies are mine," she said, her eyes flashing red.

Her blade hissed through the air and Elton lurched awake, grabbing impulsively for the dagger he kept under the bed. He grabbed it tightly and felt its handle before calming down and releasing his grip.

It was nearly dawn, the moon nearing the horizon. He took a few deep breaths before dressing and undoing the door's many locks.

A chill went down his spine and he was reminded of the first time he had returned to the house to find Kalahar. But he had no reason to worry, as the air remained comfortably warm.

"Mr Regi, sir," he was greeted at the front door by the messenger boy, who was holding the sheathed silver dagger. "I've come to give this back to you, sir."

"That won't be necessary," Elton waved him away. "It was a gift."

"O-oh! Thank you, sir!"

The boy departed and Elton made the short journey under cover of darkness to the Redhouse. It was a journey he wouldn't normally make without an escort, but the streets were startlingly bare.

He arrived as the sun crept above the horizon and Dannos was met with its first rays of sunlight since the day before the eclipse.

"Greetings, bossman," the sentries guarding the Redhouse said as he approached. Elton noticed the debris from the crumbled roof had been removed overnight, and builders were actively working on a repair – an action which he hadn't personally authorised.

"The lady paid for it, boss," one of the guards allayed his evident concerns. "Out of her own pocket, I heard."

"Right," Elton said, distracted. "Carry on."

The lobby of the Redhouse was mostly clear, but a number of people still milled and waited around, and not the type with which Elton was familiar. Most notable was a group of well-dressed people bearing no obvious sign of affiliation with the Redwinter Syndicate – they were the first that Elton approached.

"Who are you, exactly?"

"We used to work at the City Guard, sir," one explained. "But then it collapsed. We heard you planned to establish a government sir, and we've come in search of employment."

"Right," Elton said, unsure. "Stay right there."

He found Rosa upstairs, having fallen asleep at a table. He shook her awake, initially receiving a violent response, but she then settled.

"I'm going to do it, Rosa," Elton declared. "I'm going to take official control of this city. But not as king – I've had enough of kings. I shall be… Count Redwinter of Dannos."

"If you think I'm calling you that, you're off your rocker," Rosa mused.

The following weeks were spent revolutionising Dannos's traditional political structure to which the residents had become attuned. Elton's first act as count was the writing of a constitution, which outlined the most basic, fundamental laws and rights of the Free City.

The constitution was followed by the merging of the Redwinter Bank with the Dawn Bank, to create a brand new Dannosi Bank under the control of the new government. And the City Guard was reformed to serve the new House Redwinter with supple funding and recruitment.

"Count Redwinter, sir, I come bearing news from the West," the messenger boy said, approaching Elton in the renovated lobby of the Redhouse, now the centralised building in

461

which the government of Dannos took place. What had been a messy arrangement of open rooms serving no specific purpose had been reorganised into a series of offices, with the largest room, Elton's court, resembling a throne room, though the chair in which Elton resided was far from grandeur.

"Just a rumour, at this point, sir," the boy explained. "But some of the Salyrian traders have said that King Hortensio has a new court mage – a man, from Lazeria."

"And I'm sure he doesn't lift a finger to our court mage," Elton said confidently, glancing at Rosa, who stood, engaged in conversation with two courtiers, in the corner of the court.

"I wouldn't be so confident, sir," the messenger boy replied. "They say he's wicked – that he's a thousand years old, and that he's been doing magic all that time!"

"Poppycock, boy," Elton dismissed. "You shouldn't listen to the wittering of mindless travellers. They're all bored, tired old men – any old tale is enough to frenzy their minds."

Elton fished a one-mark coin from his pocket and tossed it to the boy, who thanked him profusely. Elton had abandoned his worn gambeson and replaced it with a similarly coloured tunic and a grey cloak, though he couldn't give up his chainmail.

He rose from his seat and sauntered up the stairs and into one of the now restricted areas of the Redhouse, entering a door labelled *Intelligence*.

Elton's arrival to the conference room prompted those inside, the officers of the Dannosi Intelligence Service, to turn and salute, an action which they insisted on despite his protests.

"The news about Hortensio's court mage isn't a secret anymore, it would seem," Elton said. "It's the travellers' new favourite rumour. Ant – have you got anything else for me?"

"I do, Count," Ant, the appointed deputy head of the DIS, replied. "Two things, actually. Remaining on the topic of Salyria, we've had a report from Fez that Jannis has assumed the role of general. They've also begun a conscription program, and, as such, they now have a much larger army than when they attacked Dannos the first time round."

"But they don't appear to be attacking us."

"Not yet, no," Ant confirmed, running a hand through his thick, centrally parted, wavy umber hair. "But Fez also reports that Hortensio plans to attack Santhion before advancing north. Dannos was written on the agenda."

"Wonderful. What's the second thing?"

"We've unveiled a hidden cell of Syndicate defectors – the ones who betrayed you when the Santerosi army appeared."

"And?"

"We're awaiting your order before we act, Count."

Elton contemplated his options, but not for very long.

"Round them up and exile them," he decided.

"As you wish, Count."

Elton continued through the conference room into a door labelled *Director's Office*.

"Felix? Have we had any news about the vampires?"

"We have, bossman." Felix turned from the window. "The cluster of malevolents we've been following have been murdered, just like the last. We found their bodies in the sewers. Just like the last."

"Bloody Kal," Elton cursed.

He walked over to the window and stood next to Felix, observing the activity of the pedestrians outside.

"It's different, isn't it," he remarked. "Peaceful."

"For you, perhaps," Felix said. "But I've got the grittier jobs."

"I saw him in my dreams again. He's tormenting me."

"The same dream as every night?"

"The same dream as every night. I don't understand his motives, Felix. I don't know why he doesn't just kill me. It would be trivially easy for him."

"He's a sadistic freak of nature. I can imagine he gets pleasure from the slowness of it."

"So nobody's seen him yet?"

"It's difficult when all the malevolents look the bloody same. But no, nobody's seen Kalahar yet. Of course, we haven't accounted for the idea that he might just have taken another form."

"Rosa says that he has to be close to Dannos to be able to influence my dreams in the way that he does. Or in Dannos. He's here, Felix, we just need to find him."

"We're working on it."

Elton left the office and returned to the court, which had been engulfed in commotion.

"What the hell is going on?" Elton asked Rosa, who had taken refuge at the door to the bowels of the Redhouse, avoiding the shouting and swinging of swords.

"A group of malevolents came in seeking protection, claiming they were being hunted. Then a group of self-proclaimed vampire hunters stormed inside after them and started slaying them. The vampires, naturally, fought back."

Elton watched as oil-soaked silver blades sliced through the vampiric visitors, leaving a messy array of grey bodies on the floor. The vampires, in the time since the eclipse, were beginning to understand their abilities and as such were capable of fighting back, which meant that accompanying the many bodies of the undead were also the lacerated corpses of the vampire hunters.

There was no point in intervening and the last vampire was slain. Elton stepped towards the guards, who had taken the collective decision of inaction while the fighting was taking place.

"Arrest them. All of them. And seize their weapons, too," Elton curtly ordered to a pair of guards, who nodded to his counterparts around the room.

The guards surrounded the vampire hunters in moments, confiscating their silver swords, chains, and aspen stakes. The arrest didn't occur without resistance, and the guards were forced to call for reinforcement.

"We're ridding the city of undead filth! Why are you gettin' rid of us?" one of the hunters shouted.

"Yeah! We're finishin' off the job you didn't bother with, Regi!"

"Regi's gone, you idiots! Now all we have is a fat lump of a man who thinks himself the new king! He's abandoned us and he's abandoned the Syndicate!"

The guards started shackling the crowd of around twenty men, which was struggling fiercely and continuing to shout their disapproval of Elton's change of ideology. But eventually they were all escorted out of the Redhouse.

"Why aren't we killing the rest of the vampires, bossman?" one of the senior guards asked uneasily upon his return to the court. "They killed half the city. Bodies are rotting in buildings all over the place. Businesses are going bankrupt all over because there aren't enough people to do the work."

"The vampires were deceived and so were we," Elton responded. "They serve no threat to us in their current state. We can track them and make sure it stays that way. And if we need to strike, then we can do so with ease."

And we need them to catch Kalahar, he thought.

"But what if they turn? What if they suddenly realise how dangerous they can be?"

"It's not going to happen. Now, get to work sending these weapons to the armoury. The stakes can go to the alchemy lab."

"Yes, Count."

"Bastards made a right mess," Rosa remarked, approaching Elton.

"They did, rather," Elton said, scathingly sweeping his eyes across the blood-and-oil-stained carpet.

"I thought you might want to know that I might have a lead on Kalahar."

"What? Tell me now!" Elton pivoted on the spot to face her.

"Let's go upstairs."

Rosa led Elton to her office, which had been outfitted to serve her purposes as the court mage. A number of magical trinkets and commodities were strewn around the room and a demonic-looking pentagram had been etched onto the ground in chalk, candles placed on each point of the star.

"I thought you were practicing magic, not worship of the devil. And why's it so cold in here?" Elton said.

"By-product of a spell I've been practicing. Draws energy from the air. Like in endothermic chemical reactions.

"This is how Faefion taught me at Letham Deregor. And it works extremely effectively. I spent this morning trying to track Kalahar based purely off his magical signature, which I obtained while I was learning. It's a coincidence, really, that we ended up needing it, because I tried to get it just for practice. And I can tell you, as we suspected, that he's still here, in

465

Dannos. And, perhaps more alarmingly, within the Redhouse."

"You mean to say he's walking around us as an imposer."

"That's my theory. If I were you, I would lock down right now and interrogate everyone. With the oil and silver."

"I'll get to it." Elton stood up and rushed from the room.

"Excellent," Rosa said, mulling over the contents of the room, alone. "Excellent," she repeated, her voice mutating.

Rosa's eyes flashed briefly red as she cast a spell to begin warming the room.

"Excellent."

CHAPTER 62

FALLÍA, TYEN'AEL

Elaeínn spiralled towards Berri's assailant and sliced her head off before she even knew what was happening. The head flew over the now terrified population residing in the lobby, splattering warm blood across an unfortunate row of older women and landing at the feet of an unassuming young boy. To that point, he had been curled in a ball in the corner. He turned his head to the source of the sudden noise and screamed.

As Berri feebly clutched at his throat, the door to the lobby slammed open as the two remaining State Security officers entered the room, already chanting a spell and drawing their hands behind them. Henna was quick to react and generated a shield just as the torrent of flame began to stream from their palms. But Henna stood in the middle of the room, and the shield sliced the lobby in half.

The Ekka was already evidently strained as the shield pulsated under the constant power of the magical flame, which crawled up the barrier's surface and incinerated everything and everyone trapped inside.

"Everyone out, quickly!" Elaeínn shouted.

Elaeínn leaned down and took the Dragonsteel Blade from the dead spy's warm clutches, discarding the steel she had just decorated with red. The blade glowed bright gold upon immediate contact.

The people who had cowered in terror now flocked towards the other exit in a state of panic. The pulsating of the shield increased in frequency and its bright green colour began to dim between flashes.

467

Elaeínn was the second-to-last to leave the lobby and she watched as Henna's magical barrier shattered and the flame engulfed the lobby, succeeding in incinerating the rest of the building's foundations. The flames exploded through the doorway, which Elaeínn narrowly avoided.

She peered into the incinerated remains of the lobby and saw both SSS officers marching towards her, tailed by Jaelaar. She stood defiantly in the doorway, sword drawn.

One of the officers struck quickly, thrusting his sword towards her torso. She parried the blow, guiding his sword upwards before attempting to bring her weapon back down and attempting her own offence. The officer blocked every one of her blows effortlessly.

Elaeínn knew that she shouldn't be able to defeat a trained officer of the State Security Service in a duel. She shouldn't have been able to last longer than seconds. Yet she and the officer continued to trade blows back and forth, back and forth.

The second officer pressed forward and joined the first, a development which made offence infeasible. That was, until she was joined by the two brutish Ekkas, and they were the upper hand that she needed.

The first of the officers fell after a coordinated attack in which the Ekkas used their strength to expose the officer's chest, allowing Elaeínn the opportunity to send her sword through it, piercing the lacklustre armour plating with minimal effort. As she retracted her sword, the second nicked her arm with the tip of his sword, tearing the fabric of her robe and leaving a deep gash running to her shoulder. She responded with a quick thrust of her sword and an angry cry, slashing the officer in the leg. He grunted and extended a desperate hand, attempting to utter a spell. Another lightning-quick movement and the hand was sent sailing through the sky.

The Ekkas disarmed the officer and felled him, leaving Jaelaar alone standing in the charred interior of the lobby.

Elaeínn rushed towards him as he sheathed his sword and held the tip of her sword to his neck.

"Take my weapon, Elaeínn. Go on."

"Gladly. You two – take his weapon."

468

The remaining Ekkas entered the lobby from outside and the brutish pair came forward and retrieved Jaelaar's weapon.

"As far as I'm aware, then," Jaelaar began, "Delíen and Berri have been killed. That would leave you in command?"

"I... I guess it does," Elaeínn realised. "What's your point?"

"That means you have the ultimate say on my fate, does it not?"

"I suppose. But first, one of you get some hevula shackles. There will be some in the dungeon downstairs."

One of the Ekkas disappeared and came back minutes later carrying a pair of rusted shackles, strands of hevula – a magical inhibitor – woven through them. Jaelaar extended his hands willingly as they were snapped on.

"What are you planning?" Elaeínn furrowed her brow sceptically as they led him to the ramparts.

"Nothing," he said nonchalantly, looking down at the shackles. "I've lost, haven't I?"

"That's what I hope."

As they ascended to the heights of the castle, Elaeínn looked down into Fallía's streets and felt a sudden weight upon her shoulders.

Houses burned as Tyen'Aeli soldiers moved through the castle like raiders. The FTA fighters were unrelenting in their resistance, but nothing could overwhelm the sheer size of the attacking force. Nothing except capture of their leader.

"You"—Elaeínn pointed at one of the brutish Ekkas—"hold him over the wall and call for the fighting to stop."

The Ekka gleefully grabbed Jaelaar by the scruff of his neck, to which the Prime Minister responded only with a grunt. He held him over the wall, facing the Tyen'Aeli soldiers stationed outside the castle walls.

The action was met with the sounding of the Tyen'Aeli war horn. The soldiers within the walls immediately stopped their assault and the fighting drew to a standstill.

A heavily armoured soldier on the Tyen'Aeli side, presumably a captain, stepped onto the drawbridge, clutching his sword and looking up at the helpless Prime Minister.

"What is it you demand?" the captain cried.

"Withdraw from Fallía!" Elaeínn yelled in response. "Tell your troops to withdraw and we will spare Jaelaar's life!"

"We don't negotiate with terrorists!"

Elaeínn drew her sword and placed it against the Prime Minister's throat.

"We are not terrorists!" she declared. "Withdraw your army from Fallía and be on your way! And never come back!"

The captain paced slowly back towards a group of other decorated soldiers and proceeded to have a quiet discussion, the tension between the opposing sides heating up. The occasional clash of steel resonated through the still air, but order was generally kept under control.

The captain returned to the drawbridge, Jaelaar looking less and less comfortable as time progressed.

"We agree to your terms. Free the Prime Minister."

"The soldiers leave the castle first."

The captain refrained from offering an immediate response.

"Elaeínn," Jaelaar choked. "Watch—"

"Quiet," she snapped. "You're not getting away with any silver-tongued bullshit."

Elaeínn only heard its whistling milliseconds before it made impact.

She gasped, curling over and dropping her sword on the rampart's stones. She placed a hand gingerly to her torso, where the arrow had pierced.

"Fucking treacherous bastards," she hissed through bloody coughs.

The battle, having temporarily resumed, immediately halted again as Elaeínn stood up, grabbed her sword and decapitated Jaelaar.

And then it resumed once more.

CHAPTER 63

FALLÍA, TYEN'AEL

Tynak stood shocked as the Prime Minister's head was re-moved from his shoulders. But there was no time for such shock, because the Tyen'Aeli army had already restarted their fervent hacking and slashing, and they had made significant progress. Progress which, as the battle waged on and his com-rades fell, he felt less and less confident about reversing.

He raised his axe and charged into the fray, accompanied by the fighters of the FTA and only a handful of the original one hundred twenty Elites with which he had set off.

CHAPTER 64

MYANA, MIRADOS

Nendar Varanus found Lynn approaching the palace and stopped her. He traced a portal to the palace in Virilia before she had a chance to ask any questions and thrust her through it with force.

"What the hell are you doing?" Lynn seethed.

"Getting you to safety," Nendar curtly responded. "Come, let's go to the balcony. We can watch the situation unfold."

"Where's Val?"

"Val is no longer with us. Slain by the Fateborn's blade."

"What? He can't have betrayed us. Not when he was the one who sought us out!"

"That's exactly what happened."

"And how exactly did you get out of there alive?"

"Magic."

They reached the balcony with the onset of golden hour and watched as crowds gathered outside the formidable palace gates in search of safety. Nendar ordered the gates to remain shut and he watched as the people were slain in droves.

Smoke belched from areas placed sporadically throughout the city as chaos and desperation engulfed those still alive. Nendar sipped a glass of Virilian Red while Lynn tried to convince him to hand over his lirenium crystal.

"We'll recover," Nendar said nonchalantly, ignoring her requests. "All death brings prosperity. The armies are stationed away from here. We'll not suffer from this."

The moon rose and the wails continued through the night, as did the crowd's persistence to make its way into the palace.

They came in waves, with each wave being turned away and put down by the subsequent wave of vampires.

And then, without warning, the deaths and the cries and the wails stopped. Nendar had stayed awake the entire night, encouraging Lynn to do the same.

Nendar left the palace through the main gates and observed the bloodbath. The sandstones leading up the hill to the palace had been painted crimson and were yet to dry. Vampires remained, though they did not attack as he had watched throughout the previous hours. Instead, they were calm – even passive.

"Eklash Kalahar?" Nendar approached one, who turned their head in alarm.

"Kalahar ix grev'az."

"Ki'tak. Lakk ehl pir'ake?"

"Til'gash li'sakk ols."

"Vos danakh."

Lynn treaded lightly on the blood-washed ground, careful to ensure her robe stayed clean.

"I cannot hand over my crystal, Lynn," he declared. "We have a new job to do."

"And that is?"

"We find Tregor. And we kill Kalahar once and for all."

End of book one